THE NIGHT STALKER

After ten years in London, working for a City law firm, Clare Donoghue moved back to her home town in Somerset to undertake an MA in creative writing at Bath Spa University. *Never Look Back* was her first novel and in 2011 she was longlisted for the CWA Debut Dagger.

You can say hello to Clare on Twitter @claredonoghue, or Facebook: www.facebook.com/claredonoghueauthor

Also by Clare Donoghue

Never Look Back
No Place to Die
Trust No One

CLARE DONOGHUE

THE NIGHT STALKER

WITHDRAWN

PAN BOOKS

First published 2017 by Pan Books
an imprint of Pan Macmillan
20 New Wharf Road, London N1 9RR
Associated companies throughout the world
www.panmacmillan.com

ISBN 978-1-4472-8474-1

1 3 5 7 9 8 6 4 2

A CIP catalogue record for this book is available from the British Library.

Typeset in Minion by Palimpsest Book Production Ltd, Falkirk, Stirlingshire
Printed and bound by CPI Group (UK) Ltd, Croydon, CR0 4YY

For Chris
My brother, my first reader and the best plot
trouble-shooter ever!
I couldn't have done it without you x

PROLOGUE

July

He watched as she threw back her head and laughed, her mouth so wide he could see flecks of food stuck in her teeth. She was drunk again, regaling the locals with one of her wild stories. His jaw tightened with each lie and exaggeration. His mother had warned him not to get involved with her, but he hadn't listened. He shook his head, despairing at his own idiocy.

'Drink up, gentlemen,' the landlord shouted. There was a chorus of disapproving murmurs. 'Have you not got homes to go to?'

'One for the road?' a voice called out from the crowd, the plea supported by a surge of movement towards the bar.

As he watched the stampede he pulled at the back of his neck, trying to tug away the tension that had bound his muscles into knots. He had only agreed to come for one drink. He had to be up at five, whereas she would laze in bed until mid-morning. What did she do all day? He had no idea. The kids were feral. The house was a mess. His dinner was always late, but not always edible. He ground his teeth as her cackle invaded his thoughts.

He could still remember the first time he saw her. She had been in the pub with her father, her cheeks pink from the fire, a half of cider in her hand, her tits on display. And that had been it. Within a week she was sneaking over to his place at night. He would haul her in through his bedroom window and then tip her out of it again in the morning after they were done. She wasn't forever, but she passed the time – or so he told himself. He sniffed and took a slug of his pint, coughing as it fizzed at the back of his throat.

When she had told him she was pregnant, he had hoped it was a joke. His father thought he should marry her, that it was his responsibility. What did it matter that he didn't love her, that he didn't want a baby? How would he even support them? He didn't earn enough to support himself, let alone a kid. Lucky for him, his mother agreed, and managed to persuade his would-be father-in-law that his only daughter was better off alone, but telling him that as the baby's grandmother she would stump up the cash to pay for the poor little bastard.

'Hey, watch it,' he said as his pint was almost jostled out of his hand by the crush of more people pushing past him, desperate for one more drink. He stepped back from the bar, lifting his pint above his head. The space he left was filled in an instant and the calls for service resumed.

He moved closer to the door and leaned against the wall, glad to be away from the crowd. 'It was fifteen hands at least,' she was saying, throwing her chubby arms up in the air. He knew the story well. She claimed to have been approached by an enormous stag up near the Seven Sisters. 'He looked up, sniffed the air and then just walked right up to me.'

'Must have smelled something he liked, Janey,' one of the locals drawled. He knew without looking that there would be an accompanying leer and fumbling hand along with the remark. Annie would never have let herself be pawed at by another man. He let out a long and heavy sigh. He wasn't good enough for Annie – then or now. From the day she agreed to marry him, their relationship was doomed to fail. She was clean and pure, like the spring at Lady's Fountain. He was young, stupid and led by his dick. She had forgiven him his affair with Jane, but it hadn't been enough to save them, not least because his mother had never approved of the relationship in the first place and so Annie had left, their engagement a distant memory.

'You tell me,' Jane said, offering her flushed bosom. 'Go on, have a sniff.'

The man buried his head in the pillows of flesh. 'Honey and heather,' he said with a satisfied groan.

'Give me strength,' he muttered, turning his back on the sordid show. He had seen it all before.

'You're a lucky man,' the man said, stumbling towards him. 'Oh yeah? How's that?'

'Your missus. She's one of a kind.'

'I couldn't agree more,' he said with a shake of his head. So why had he gone back to her?

He knew why. Without Annie he had felt empty, and Jane and her tits had been only too eager to fill the void – despite the fact that she had given birth to another man's child not four months before. The rumour was, his brother was the father. He supposed he should have been angry, but in truth he pitied Will for getting caught in the same trap.

'Better get 'em in, fella,' Alfie said. 'Pat's still serving and it's your round.'

'Fine. Fine,' he said, bracing himself for the slap on the back he knew was coming.

'Good man,' Alfie said, hitting him with such force it drove the air out of his lungs. 'Get me two.'

'Fine,' he said, shuffling his way back to the bar whilst digging around in his pockets. He was broke. But then he was always broke, and the reason was standing at the other end of the bar cackling like a fishwife. Her tits were now so far out of her top, she might as well let the group of slobbering men suckle straight from the teats. She was surrounded by half the men in the pub, locals and strangers alike. Why did he agree to bring her here? Why did he give her money? He gestured to Pat, who nodded and began serving half a dozen pints, passing them to their recipients with the words, 'Make it quick.' No one ever listened. He took his pint without enthusiasm, and handed over the last of his cash.

'Your missus is on form tonight,' Pat said.

'When isn't she?'

'Trouble?'

'No more than usual,' he said.

'That's marriage, my friend,' Pat said with a shrug. 'Drink up. Some of us actually *want* to get home.'

'Thanks,' he said, retreating to his place by the door, tipping his head back and downing half his pint in one gulp. He could feel his heart beating in his chest. She had used his loneliness to trap him. His eyes moved from the ring on her fourth finger to her swollen belly. He had escaped his paternal responsibilities once. Twice was too much to ask. He pushed through the crowd of leering men and took Jane by the arm. He squeezed her pudgy flesh harder than he needed to, but it felt good, so he increased the pressure.

'Ow,' she yelped. 'What are you playing at?'

'Time to go,' he said.

She pulled back and looked at him with a scowl. 'Andy just got a round in,' she said. 'I'm not leaving a pint of cider.'

He opened his mouth to argue, but knew it was a waste of time. She was a belligerent drunk. 'Drink up, then,' he said, feeling himself shrink as he skulked away.

'Guess we know who wears the trousers in that house,' someone jeered.

He wheeled round, his fists clenched, ready to pound whoever had insulted him; but no one was even looking in his direction. No one was challenging him. No one was interested in him. They were all looking at Jane. Her tits were holding court, a stain spreading across her top where her milk was leaking. Her growing belly was swollen and misshapen as she adjusted her weight from one foot to the other. Just looking at her made him want to gag. He turned away and took another gulp of his pint.

'I'm done.' Jane appeared at his side, swaying. 'You still nursing that pint?' she said, gesturing to his drink.

'Let's go,' he said, dumping his glass on the edge of a table and taking her arm, again squeezing just that bit harder than necessary.

'What a waste,' she said, snatching his glass and downing

the rest of the contents. 'Come on, handsome.' She stumbled towards the door, dragging him with her.

As soon as they were outside she let out an enormous belch. 'Urgh, I've been holding that in all night,' she said, giggling. Her breasts jiggled. He felt his body respond. Damn those tits. 'What's the matter with you?' She swiped at his arm.

'Nothing,' he said, crossing the road onto the dirt path that led back to the cottage in Bincombe. It was past eleven, but the heat of the day still hung in the air. It was suffocating.

'You've been a miserable bastard all night,' she said from behind him. 'You were the one who wanted to go out.'

'We both know that's not true,' he said, tramping ahead, his feet sinking into the moss at the side of the well-worn trail. The twisted trees surrounded them, their branches gnarled and stunted by the wind and rain, their bark pale and peeling. He had always hated this stretch of woodland. His father had left him up here once, insisting he find his way home alone. He couldn't have been more than five or six, but his father said if he didn't learn the land, how could he ever hope to work it?

'What did you say?' she shouted from behind him.

'Nothing,' he said, kicking at a clump of dry leaves, disturbing a cloud of mushroom spores.

'You really are pathetic.'

He could hear the sneer in her voice. He felt his fists clench at his sides. They would be home in ten minutes, she would pass out on one of the kids' beds, and he would have made it through another day.

'What kind of man are you? You're no kind of father and

you're certainly no kind of husband. Tell me,' she yelled, 'what kind of man are you?'

He slowed to a stop and bowed his head, taking a deep breath in through his nose, dragging in the hot air. The smell of the undergrowth filled his nostrils. He could almost hear the ground breathing, each breath warm and moist. He tipped his head back and looked up at the stars through the strangled boughs of the trees.

'What kind of woman are you?' he said, turning to face her, his voice low and rumbling like a storm rolling over the hills.

'Me?' she asked, pointing at herself and laughing. 'I'm a bloody saint.' She squared up to him, her saliva hitting his cheeks. 'I'd have to be a bloody saint to put up with you and your family. How many others are there? How many other women have you and your idiot brother used and left?'

'Only you,' he said. 'I only ever left you. I only ever wanted to leave you.'

'So leave,' she spat. 'Who's stopping you? You think I want you in the house . . . in my house?'

'It's not your house,' he said. He felt the sensation of someone walking their fingers up his spine. He shivered.

'Not what the judge will say,' she said with a grin. Her teeth flashed white in the moonlight. He didn't trust himself to speak. 'You are pathetic,' she said, pushing past him. 'I can't look at you. You make me sick. You are *not* a man. And I *need* a man.'

He spun around, his fist connecting with the back of her head before he knew he was going to hit her. She grunted and stumbled, but soon righted herself. She turned and charged him, her distended belly swinging. He dodged and watched her stumble and fall to her knees. His heel connected with something solid. He looked down. It was a length of wood, a discarded fence post covered in leaves and mulch. Before he could think about it he was bending down and picking it up, weighing it up in his two hands. It was heavy. Heavy enough. Her back was to him. She was swearing under her breath as she tried to stand. In one smooth motion he lifted the post and brought it crashing down on the back of her head. There was a satisfying crunch as she fell forward again, this time landing face down at the edge of the trail. He waited for her to speak. He dropped the post and stepped back.

'What kind of man am I?' he asked. He put the toe of his boot under her left hip and rolled her over. He could see the blood pooling in the leaves and long grass around her head. He bent down, leaned over her stomach and put his ear to her mouth. Her breath gurgled in her throat. He sat back on his heels and patted down his trouser and jacket pockets until he found what he was looking for. He took out the knife, unfolded it and, holding her hair with his other hand, tipped back her head and ran the blade across her throat. He was surprised how much pressure was needed. When he reached her right ear he removed the blade from her neck, wiped it clean on the shoulder of her dress, folded it and put it back in his pocket.

He was about to stand when he remembered something. With a sniff he reached into her top, found the money wedged between her breasts, took it out and put it in his pocket, together with the knife.

The walk home was quiet. The air seemed to have cleared.

The Night Stalker

He let himself into his cottage and climbed the stairs to his bedroom. He pushed her pillows off the bed with the back of his hand and repositioned his own into the middle as he kicked off his shoes. He shrugged out of his jacket and trousers and climbed under the covers. As he lay back, he closed his eyes and rested his hands on his chest.

He would sleep well tonight. And he did.

July

DI Bill Townsend looked down and blew out a breath. A bead of sweat trickled down the side of his face, irritating his three-day stubble. The sudden heatwave might be welcomed by the majority of the Country, but it was doing him no favours as the body of the woman in front of him raced towards decomposition – taking her secrets with her.

'We'll give you a second,' the CSI team leader said, ushering his team away so that Bill could observe the body in situ without interruption.

He took a step forward, taking care to remain on the network of raised platforms. They were there to protect any and all forensic evidence, though given the amount of walkers and wildlife in the area, Bill doubted they were preserving much of use. 'How's it going?' he asked the crouched figure in front of him.

Somerset's local pathologist was bent at the knees, hunched over the head and neck of the woman. Flies buzzed around Bill's head. He waved them away. The place was more akin to a tropical jungle than ancient oak woodland on a hillside in Somerset. The swarm left him and returned to its meal. Bile pooled beneath his tongue, and he looked away to compose himself.

His breakfast was not sitting well. The grease from the fry-up his wife had cooked earlier lined his mouth, refusing to clear when he swallowed. He took a deep breath and tipped his head back, swaying on his feet as he looked up at the trees. The branches were so intertwined and thick with leaves that the sun only penetrated in occasional shafts of light, burning into the ground.

'Much deeper and they'd have taken her head off,' Basil Reed said with a sigh. 'Both arteries were severed.' He cleared his throat and looked around him. Bill followed his eyes, taking in the darkened soil, blood-soaked leaves and plastic yellow markers that littered the scene.

'Anything else you can tell me . . . other injuries? Sexual assault? Anything you can tell me about her attacker?'

Reed straightened his legs and stood up. 'Blunt force trauma . . . back upper right,' he said, gesturing the position of the injury on his own head. 'Heavy, flat object.' He sniffed. 'Throat cut from the front – left to right.' He pointed to the woman's torn clothes and the skirt hoisted up on one side, almost to the waist. 'This and this,' he said, 'implies a sexual element to the attack, but I won't be able to confirm that until after the post-mortem.' He sighed. 'I'd guess the attacker was male, right-handed – physically strong – above average height . . .' He drifted into silence.

'And that?' Bill asked, gesturing to the smudges on the woman's torso.

'Carbon-based residue,' Reed said. 'Charcoal, by the looks of it.'

Bill nodded without understanding. 'And when can we expect the post-mortem to be carried out?'

'*We* can expect the post-mortem when *we* have time.'

Bill swallowed hard, his frustration fighting its way to the surface. 'I'm briefing my team later today,' he said, 'and no doubt the superintendent, not to mention the press, will want an update by close of business at the latest.'

'*Your* team.' Reed turned away. 'Didn't take you long,' he said under his breath.

What was this guy's problem? If anyone should be pissed off, it was Bill. He was the one who had been told to drop everything and get down here from Bristol. He was the one who had just cancelled his holiday to Italy. And he was the one who had been thrown head first into a violent murder inquiry with the sole instruction, 'get this solved quickly and quietly'. There was fat chance of that once the press got hold of the details of the attack. He measured his tone. 'It wasn't appropriate for DI Waters to continue with this investigation, given the circumstances.'

'She's pregnant, not made of glass,' Reed said.

'DI Waters' pregnancy aside, this was Atkinson's decision,' Bill said, hoping a mention of the superintendent would be enough to assuage Reed's misplaced irritation.

'Should have been hers,' Reed said, turning and skulking away from the body without so much as a backward glance.

Townsend opened his mouth to call after him, but decided not to bother. He rocked his head from one side to the other, easing his tired muscles. As his eyes came back level he stumbled forward, losing his balance for a moment. He reached out to a nearby tree and steadied himself. He looked down at the body, his eyes tracking from the wound at the woman's throat to the smudges of black on her torso, to the swell of her pregnant belly, to the blood still soaking into the ground.

'Seven months,' a voice said behind him. Bill turned to see a young detective he recognized from DI Waters' team. 'She was seven months pregnant – if that's what you were wondering. Her third kid . . . or would have been.'

'Tragic,' he said without inflection, remembering the detective's name as he spoke. It was Abbott.

'Her whole life was tragic,' Abbott said.

'You knew her?' Bill asked, frowning.

'Who didn't?' was all Abbott said.

CHAPTER ONE

7th December – Monday

Aaron rolled onto his side, wrapping his arm around Megan's waist. When she didn't stir he pulled her into him and buried his face in her hair, inhaling the scent of her shampoo. She breathed out a quiet snore. He smiled. Wasn't it the guy's prerogative to fall asleep after? He removed his left arm from under her neck and shuffled backwards until he was able to tip himself out of bed without making a sound. He covered her with the duvet before tiptoeing out of the room, snatching his boxers from the floor as he pulled the door closed. He wasn't sure why he was bothering to be quiet. An earthquake wouldn't wake her once she was out.

He padded down the stairs and into the kitchen, turning on the light. The rest of the flat was in darkness. It had been light when he had chased her up the stairs. He had never been a fan of winter, but working shifts seemed to make things even harder, and with Christmas only two weeks away there would soon be the shift-swapping bunfight to deal with as well. He took four pieces of bread out of the breadbin and put them into the toaster. Megan had asked him to spend

Christmas with her. He had never spent Christmas with a girlfriend before. He had never been asked, much to his relief. He took a plate down from the cupboard, a knife from the drawer and the peanut butter, lemon curd and butter from the fridge. Megan thought his version of peanut butter and jelly was repulsive. The toast popped. He slathered all four slices with butter, then peanut butter, then just a thin layer of lemon curd. He used the back of his hand to push an anticipatory bit of dribble back into his mouth. The first bite was always the best. First you tasted the lemon curd, bitter and sweet, then the cloying, stick-to-the-roof-of-your-mouth wonder that was peanut butter. All finished off with the salty, satisfying hit you could only get from real butter. According to his health-conscious girlfriend, he deserved to be the size of a house. He couldn't help it. He had always been slim. It was a genetic thing.

He walked through to the lounge, carrying his toast. He was about to turn on the main light, but then looked at the tree in the corner. It was covered in everything shiny – baubles, tinsel and four lots of fairy lights – all thanks to Megan. With his toe he flicked on the plug and the lounge was filled with a soft, colour-changing glow. He sat down on the sofa with a thump, folded a piece of toast in half and jammed as much of it into his mouth as he could manage, butter dripping onto his chin as he smiled. She had stayed over every night for the past two weeks. She had transformed his flat. She had transformed his life.

In previous relationships, if a girl stayed over, Aaron got nervous. He was nervous now, but for very different reasons. For the first time he wasn't trying to figure out how to end things, how to extricate himself without setting off a bitch-bomb. Instead he was terrified that he was going to wake up one morning and it was all going to be over – that she would leave him. He was in a constant state of agitation accompanied by bouts of nausea, personifying the term 'lovesick'. He had never felt so elated and shit-scared at the same time.

Given his day job as a PC in Lewisham's murder squad – soon to be DC, if he passed his promotion exam – he should be made of stronger stuff. But when it came to Megan he was way out of his depth. A day in the company of killers was a piece of piss by comparison. He put his plate on the table, licked his fingers and picked up the remote. Megan had a nine o'clock lecture and he was on an early, but he wasn't ready to sleep yet. He glanced at the clock. It was only half ten. He could catch up on a couple of *Top Gear* episodes. Megan wasn't interested in cars, or men talking about cars. His phone started to ring. He looked around the room, trying to locate the sound, when Megan's phone joined the chorus. The two ringtones clashed. His was a generic ring, but Megan's was some song by Rihanna. He groaned and pushed himself up from the sofa. He spotted the blue glow of Megan's phone under the coffee table. He bent down and grabbed it, glancing at the screen as his thumb moved to silence the call. He stopped.

It was DI Mike Lockyer – lead DI for Lewisham's murder squad.

Megan's father.

Aaron's boss.

CHAPTER TWO

7th December – Monday

Pippa reached into her handbag and rooted around for her phone. Her car pulled to the left. She yanked the wheel back to the right, but not before her wing mirror disappeared into the hedgerow. There was a scraping sound and a thud. Her mirror snapped back into place as it emerged from the dense tangle of bare bramble and hawthorn. 'Shit.'

Tonight's scrape was one of many. The lanes over the Quantocks were narrow and the locals drove at alarming speeds, day and night. As if on cue, a pair of blinding headlights bore down on her from the brow of the hill. She braked and swerved, her mirror and the left side of her car taking a further battering in the process. The oncoming car zipped past, flashed its lights and was gone.

'You're welcome,' she muttered as she flicked on her full beam. And people thought London drivers were bad. She upended her bag and emptied the contents onto the passenger seat, hurling items into the footwell; her wallet, tampons, her lanyard for work, her Kindle. No phone.

As she drove through Crowcombe village she dropped

down into third gear and accelerated up the hill, the hedge-rows coming in to meet her. The trees on either side were so dense that she only caught glimpses of the night sky above her. It was like driving into a black hole. She turned on her windscreen wipers as the first drops of rain fell. The drops turned into a deluge, sending her wipers into overdrive. She pulled her scarf tighter around her neck and dropped down into second gear as she heard the sound of a much more powerful engine approaching. She glanced in her rear-view mirror as the headlights of the other vehicle rounded the bend at the bottom of the hill and sped up to meet her.

'Hang on,' she said, tucking herself as far into the left bank as she dared. She shook her head at the sound of yet more scraping. This part of the road was wide enough for two cars – only just – but instead of overtaking, the car slowed and pulled in behind her. She had to squint to look in her mirror, they were that close.

'You've got your full beams on,' she shouted, flashing her own lights. She could just make out two silhouettes, the driver and passenger. They were right up her arse and seemed to be edging closer. She saw a turn up ahead, indicated and slowed to let them pass, but they stayed glued to her bumper. Her skin prickled as beads of sweat formed in her hairline. She stopped indicating and continued up the hill, her companions in tow. She shook off her feeling of unease and put her foot down. There was another turn-off a bit further on. If they wouldn't pass her, she would get out of their way and double back. She wasn't in any hurry.

Damp air seemed to seep in through the windows, making her shiver. She turned up the heat, her eyes darting to the seat next to her as she continued searching for her phone. 'Come on,' she said as the rain hammered down. 'Back off a bit, mate.' It sounded more like a plea than she had intended.

Pippa's car looked as if it was glowing from the inside out. The breath she was holding rushed out when she saw the headlights coming down the hill towards her. 'Thank you,' she said, turning her eyes up to the heavens. The oncoming car flashed its lights and pulled off to the side of the road, its wheels mounting the verge to let Pippa pass. As she slowed she saw the smiling faces of an old man in the driving seat and next to him, she assumed, his wife. They both raised their hands in greeting. She held up her hand and smiled back as she pulled alongside and inched past them. 'Thank you,' she mouthed as she accelerated away and up the hill, leaving her tailgater far behind.

She reached for her emergency pack of cigarettes. Her hands were shaking a little, and not just from her encounter. This stretch of road always gave her the heebie-jeebies. It was her sister's fault. Cassie used to tell stories on their way home from primary school, stories that frightened Pippa witless. She could still hear her voice, quiet and low as she whispered in Pippa's ear: *Shervage Wood is haunted.*

Pippa lit her cigarette and wound her window down just enough to flick her ash and let the smoke out without letting the rain in. *There used to be dragons all over the Quantocks, but Gurt Wurm was the biggest. He lived in Shervage Wood. People who saw him said he was as big around as three oak trees tied together.* Pippa smiled at the memory at the same time as her body gave an involuntary shudder. *In the spring-*

time he would gobble up all the sheep, horses . . . and children if he could catch them. They say you can still hear the children's screams on stormy nights.

A gust of wind buffeted the car, making Pippa grip the steering wheel. *One day the farmers decided they'd had enough and so they sent a woodcutter to fell some trees they said were rotten, but they never told him about Gurt Wurm. When the man sits down on a log to eat his lunch he suddenly realizes he isn't sitting on a log at all. Gurt Wurm swishes his tail out from under the woodcutter, turns his head and opens his mouth wide, ready to eat him whole. But the woodcutter is too quick. He grabs his axe and cuts Gurt Wurm clean in half. They say his blood took days to soak into the ground, and that's why the mud is red round these parts.*

Pippa had had nightmares for years because of Cassie and her tall tales. She took a drag of her cigarette, and glanced in the rear-view mirror. No sign of the other car. They must have turned off for Triscombe. Drink drivers using the back roads, no doubt. She blew the smoke out the window. What she wouldn't give to be back in London. She missed her flat. She missed her friends.

Pippa had been out of work for four months when her aunt Claudette called to say she had got her a job at Fyne Court, a National Trust place on the top of the Quantocks. She hadn't been keen. Why would she be? She didn't want to move back to Somerset. But when Claudette, who was friends with the catering manager, said they had refurbished their courtyard tearoom and were now serving lunches so needed a head chef, Pippa had relented. A head chef position

was a big deal, although in reality she was making sandwiches and heating up soup.

She flicked the remainder of the cigarette out the window,
watching the explosion of red sparks in her rear-view mirror
as it hit the road behind her. It wouldn't be much longer. All
she needed to do was save enough money to cover her
London rent for the next few months, and then she could go
home. She had managed to pick up some extra shifts at the
Farmer's Arms in Combe Florey as well, so with any luck she
would be out of here soon.

'What the—' She swerved as something darted in front of
her headlights. She slammed on her brakes, the car veering
to the other side of the road. Her tyres lost traction for a few
seconds as she skidded, but then she felt them bite and the
car juddered to a stop just before the cattle grid that led to
the open part of the Quantocks – the part they called the
Common.

Her heart was racing. She held her breath as she looked
around. Her mind filled with visions of dragons, men with
axes and blood. She could hear the wind as it ripped through
the trees. There was the sound of a branch cracking. She
turned, screamed and jumped sideways in her seat, banging
her elbow on the door. 'Christ,' she said as the small doe
bounded past the car and disappeared into the hedgerow on
the other side of the road. She blew out a breath as she
brought her shoulders down from around her ears. She
looked at the clock on the dashboard. If she turned around
right now and headed for the M5, she could be back in
London by three thirty. Tears pricked in her eyes as she

remembered she was working in the morning. There was no escape – not for tonight, anyway.

She put the car into gear and pulled away, her bones juddering as she crossed the cattle grid. The woodland retreated behind her as the road cut across open grassland pockmarked by rabbit warrens and badger sets. The few remaining trees were stunted and bent from the wind.

She heard the growl of another car before she saw it; she looked in her rear-view mirror, and tensed. The lights behind her flickered as the car passed over the cattle grid and accelerated up behind her. She could feel panic trying to surface, but as she looked back again, her shoulders relaxed a little. There was only one silhouette. There was only one person in the car. It was a different car. She sighed, her breathing returning to normal as she navigated the twisting road, glad now to have someone with her. She heard her phone beep, and looked for the illuminated screen. It was buried beneath a pile of tissues. She reached over, picked it up and unlocked the screen, trying to see who the message was from, but the car was bumping all over the place. Instead she grazed the phone icon with the side of her thumb, hit speed dial one and put it on speaker. The phone rang twice, but then clicked off as her call went to answerphone. An automated voice filled the car.

'Oh, come on, answer your bloody . . .' Before she could finish speaking, her car jolted forward. 'What the fuck?'

She looked over her shoulder. She could just make out the silhouette of the driver. They were holding up their hand, palm flat in apology. She shook her head.

'Try leaving more than an inch next time, mate,' she said,

raising her hand in response just as a huddle of sheep appeared out of the darkness in front of her. They were lying down, encroaching on the road. She pulled to the right and passed them without slowing down.

'Anything else?' she said. 'What with deer, dickheads and now sheep, I'm about done for the night.' She felt the road begin to slope downwards. Fifteen minutes and she would be home. She rounded the corner just as a shunt from behind forced her to swerve to the left. 'Jesus,' she said, grabbing the steering wheel. Her eyes darted to her rear-view mirror. She could see the silhouette of the driver, but this time there was no hand – there was no apology.

Without thinking, she started to accelerate. She had almost managed to convince herself she was wrong, that no one was capable of the things she had read about – names and fantasies she couldn't fathom – but he was here. Who else could it be? Who else would want to hurt her? She could see the second cattle grid up ahead. She didn't look back. She kept her eyes on the road.

The next impact threw Pippa forward with such force her chest collided with the steering wheel, winding her, before her head snapped back, only stopped by the headrest. She heard the cattle grid pass beneath the car. She couldn't see anything. She was surrounded by a blinding white light. She could taste blood. Her hand reached up, as if in slow motion, her fingers feeling for her mouth. Her tongue felt like a torn rag. There was another bang and she was thrown to the side, her head hitting the window. She heard a crack. Someone was coughing. She could hear a gurgling, retching sound. She felt drunk – as if she was lying on her bed in her flat after a heavy night, the room spinning around her. Another sound invaded her thoughts. A scream buried within a deep growl.

She could see the tree coming towards her, its trunk wide and thick like Gurt Wurm's stomach. Her face rushed forward to meet it as if in an embrace. Everything went dark. Pippa relaxed. She would chase up on those job applications tomorrow. Something would come through, she was sure of it. She loved cooking. It was her passion. She hoped one day to own her own restaurant. She remembered her sister lining up two chairs against the kitchen work surface: one for her, one for her brother. They each had a go at stirring, but Pippa always had the longest turn. They would each tip the mixture into their own little cupcake liners. Cassie would hold open the oven door and slide in the tray. 'Careful, it's hot,' she would say. Pippa could smell the oven now – the sweet burning of the sugar as it melted – the heat warming her face. She heard the crackle of the paper cases rustling against the heat.

She let the heat envelop her as the flames licked ever closer.

CHAPTER THREE

10th December – Thursday

Jane cupped her hands over her eyes, relishing the darkness before pulling her legs up and hugging them to her. She took a deep breath then sighed, stretching out on her back like a starfish, her hands and feet exploring the cold spots on her bedsheet. The king-size dwarfed her, but it was worth every penny. If there was a heaven, she reckoned it was this: cold sheets, a warm duvet and a lie-in on a winter's morning.

Her slow start was in part due to having the morning off work, but also because she had been forbidden to go downstairs. The novelty of time off had not been lost on her eight-year-old son. He had tiptoed into her bedroom at just gone four thirty this morning to announce in a loud stage whisper that he was going to make her breakfast, and judging by the racket coming from downstairs, preparations were in full swing. She was itching to get down there and see what he was up to, but he had made it very clear that her help would neither be appreciated nor tolerated. She looked at her watch. It was almost seven. He had been down there for an hour. He had promised not to use the hob without asking, but she knew that when it came to surprises her son believed all promises were rendered null and void. She threw her legs out over the side of the bed, sat up and stretched her arms up over her head. The creaks and pops of her spine gave her a pleasant shiver. She sniffed the air. There was only the faint smell of burning toast.

Despite her best efforts Peter was adamant that they would be spending the day together, just the two of them. He had their activities planned out hour by hour. Jane had tried to tell him that just because she had time off didn't mean he got time off from school, but he had refused to listen. She rubbed her face, pushed her fringe out of her eyes and pulled her hair back into a stubby ponytail. It was her unenviable job to eat whatever he had prepared and then shatter his illusions. Neither would be pretty. At least she had *Friends*. She had discovered the magical properties of the American sitcom last month during her parents' move.

She pushed herself up off the bed and walked over to the door, opening it just a crack. One false move and she would be in trouble. She held her breath and listened. She had to cover her mouth to keep from laughing. He was listening to the *Today* programme on Radio Four. She closed the door without a sound and started to get dressed, ignoring the rain hammering on the windows. There were days when she wished her son didn't have autism for both their sakes, but how many mothers could say their eight-year-old loved a topical debate? Yes, being autistic made Peter different, challenging at times; but life was never dull. She pulled on her favourite pair of slouch jeans and then sat on the edge of the bed to put on her socks. They had dinosaurs on them.

Another one of Peter's obsessions. She walked over to her curtains and opened them, using the silk ties her mother had bought her to hold them back. She ran her fingers over the fabric.

When her mother had announced, back in the summer, that she and Jane's father were leaving London and moving to Clevedon in the South West, she had assumed it was one of Celia Bennett's bizarre forms of mental torture. How could they move? Her mother worshipped Peter, and what would she do without Jane to berate? And John Bennett was a Londoner through and through. Jane's father's knowledge of the Thames and south-east London was encyclopaedic. Before his strokes he had spent every Saturday in central London, discovering new sites or visiting his favourite haunts like the South Bank book fair. He could spend hours sifting through all the second-hand books, or just sitting in a cafe where he liked to 'absorb the hubbub by osmosis', as he put it. What was he going to do with himself in a sleepy seaside town?

Their relocation was meant to be all about rest and relaxation for her father, who was still recovering from a series of strokes. If the constant bickering about what 'downsizing' really meant and the packing up of the house were anything to go by, her father was a lot stronger than he looked. Jane had bought Peter a label maker to 'engage him with the process' – she had read that somewhere. He had approached his task with gusto, although he was somewhat selective. Jane knew, for example, that one box, labelled 'dishwasher stuff' had contained two packets of dishwasher tablets, dishwasher salt, rinse aid, the instruction manual for the dishwasher they weren't taking with them, and six tea towels. That was it. He refused to allow anything else in the box, because nothing else fitted the category description.

Jane had discovered the wonder of *Friends* when she was sealing up yet another box containing fewer than twenty items. She had turned on the television to distract Peter, and gone to make a calming cuppa for her arguing parents. By the time she returned to the lounge her son had been lying on his stomach in front of the telly, his chin resting in his hands, his feet swinging, his face transfixed. He was watching a *Friends* marathon. When Jane had asked if he wanted any lunch, he had given her his 'I'm very busy' scowl. An hour later he had been in the same position. She had ordered the series box set off Amazon, and since then had doled out the episodes as treats. He was on the second series already.

Mind you, if she was honest, Peter had coped with her parents' move better than she had. She had been fully prepared for a nightmare transition. After all, her mother was Peter's primary carer when Jane was at work; and let's face it, when wasn't Jane at work? But like the little miracle he was, Peter had adjusted, and they had managed.

Jane turned and looked at the picture on her bedside table of Peter and her folks on Clevedon Pier. They were all smiling, waving at her behind the camera. She puffed out a breath. Even she had to admit there was something about the place, and as much as she hated to admit it, they were happy. She wished she could say the same.

The timing of their move could not have been worse. She had been in the middle of a stressful murder case involving children – not to mention that she was also dealing with Andy, Peter's father, who had chosen to re-enter his son's life after eight years. The fact that he had been absent for the previous seven birthdays was just 'one of those things', according to Andy.

She leaned her elbows on the windowsill and rested her forehead on the window, the glass cool against her skin. She had spent the past few months trying to extricate herself from the problem, but Andy was persistent. Now lawyers were involved. She closed her eyes.

'Mum.'

Jane turned to find Peter standing in her bedroom doorway. His walnut-coloured hair was sticking up at odd angles. He was much fairer than her. Her hair was almost black. She smiled. He was puce, holding a spatula that was dripping an unknown substance on the carpet, and he was wearing a pinafore that one of her colleagues from the squad had given her as last year's Secret Santa. It depicted a woman in bra, knickers, suspenders and fishnet tights.

'You look like you've been having fun,' she said.

'Breakfast will be ready in four and a half minutes,' he said, his expression serious.

'Four and a half minutes,' she said, looking at her watch. 'Right.' She gestured to her outfit. 'Will I do?'

'I don't like your jeans,' he said, leaving the room and pulling the door behind him. As the door clicked into place she heard him say, 'But I like the socks.'

She had to restrain herself from running out the door, scooping him up and kissing him to bits. He wasn't averse to physical affection, but it needed to be invited nowadays. She looked down at her jeans. Of course he didn't like them. They were a slouch fit, a.k.a. messy. He had gone to the effort of making her breakfast – the least she could do was dress the part. She went to her wardrobe and had a look through her clothes. There were at least a dozen 'work' outfits. She swiped the hangers to the left so only her casual clothes remained: a denim skirt she never wore, three summer dresses on the same hanger, and three pairs of black trousers that she wore to funerals and job interviews. She slipped on a pair over her dinosaur socks and changed her hoodie for a Christmas jumper with a picture of a reindeer on the front. Her phone beeped. She unplugged it from the charger and unlocked the screen. It was an email. She clicked into it, closing her eyes and taking a deep breath, preparing herself for yet another threatening epistle from Andy or one of his shit-bag lawyers. She opened her eyes. It was from Aaron, one of the squad's PC's. She had talked to him about his move up to Detective Constable last week and told him to get his paperwork sorted. She opened the email and started reading.

DS Bennett,

I need to take a leave of absence starting immediately. I am unable to come into the office this morning. I have cc'd in HR.

I will phone to explain.

Thank you for your help.

PC Aaron Jones

Jane read through the message again. 'Thank you for your help.' She had a pretty good idea what that meant. Lockyer was Aaron's direct superior, not her. If he should be emailing anyone, it should be him; but then, everyone knew Aaron had spent the past few months avoiding Lockyer, and vice versa. Jane was lucky enough to have been there when Lockyer met the boyfriend of his nineteen-year-old daughter for the first time. Megan Lockyer had decided the perfect occasion for her father to learn about her relationship with Aaron was at the wedding of Lockyer's ex-wife. As an event, it was right up there with the birth of Jane's son – long and painful.

Her phone started ringing. She looked at the screen, half expecting it to be Aaron. It wasn't.

'Hey,' she said.

'Where are you?' Lockyer asked, sounding irritated.

She rolled her eyes. 'I've got the morning off . . . remember?'

There was a sniff at the other end of the line. 'Oh yeah, that's right. You're interviewing for a nanny,' he said.

'A childminder, yes,' she said. She could tell by his voice that he hadn't forgotten. 'What's up?'

'Nothing much,' he said. She could hear him tapping away at his computer.

'Peter's made breakfast.'

'Of course, you go,' he said.

'OK,' she said, about to hang up, but then she remembered Aaron's email. 'Before you go, I just got an email from Aaron.'

'And?'

'He's asked for a leave of absence,' she said, deciding to help Aaron out by one, telling Lockyer for him and two, withholding the fact that he hadn't *asked* at all, he had just *taken* the leave.

'Why?'

'I'm getting further details on that,' she said.

She could almost hear the cogs of his brains turning. 'Fine. Let me know when you know.'

'OK,' she said, stretching out the vowels. 'So, I'll see you at the briefing this afternoon. I could do with going over the Mitchell interview before that, if you've got time?'

'I've got a meeting with Roger at midday so it depends how long that takes.'

'That's fine,' she said, making a note in her phone. 'I'll be in by one.'

'Not that I know what the meeting's about,' he said.

'What do you mean?' she asked. Lockyer's relationship with Roger Westwood was weather-dependent these days. Roger's promotion to superintendent had put more pressure on him, and so in turn, more pressure on Lockyer. Neither seemed happy about the situation.

'He wouldn't tell me. He just asked me a load of questions about my caseload, your caseload . . .'

'He asked about me?'

'Your name came up, yes,' Lockyer said.

'Maybe it's just a general catch-up,' she said.

'I missed my last occupational health . . . appointment,' he said, his voice flat.

So that was why he had called. In these modern days of policing the Met not only offered counselling, but sometimes insisted on it. The practice was meant to be a good thing, a sign of progress. However, Jane knew Lockyer didn't see it that way. 'Why did you miss it?'

'I was busy,' he said. 'It was just a . . . check-up or whatever. I don't see the problem.'

'You don't know there *is* a problem, Mike,' she said. He didn't speak. Of course, that was part of his problem: he didn't communicate.

She could hear Peter coming up the stairs. Her four and a half minutes must have been up a while ago. 'Listen, I've got to . . .' The door opened and Peter appeared. His face was still puce but Jane could tell it was from anger, not the exertion of cooking. She covered the phone with her palm. 'Sorry honey, I'm coming now.'

'It's cold,' he said as if she hadn't spoken.

'Oh, I don't mind. I bet it's gonna be delicious,' she said. 'I can't wait. I'll be down in literally two seconds.'

'That's stupid. No one can get anywhere in two seconds,' he said, leaving the room and slamming the door.

She put the phone back to her ear. 'Look, I've got to . . .'

'IT IS COLD!' Peter shouted. She heard him stomping down the stairs.

'Trouble?' Lockyer asked.

'I missed breakfast,' she said with a sigh. 'Sorry, Mike, I've got to . . .'

'COLD, COLD, COLD!'

'That doesn't sound too g . . .'

'COLD, COLD, COLD!'

'I'll see you later,' she said. 'I've got to go and put *Friends* on.'

'What—?'

Jane ended the call before he could finish speaking. This was going to be a two-episode tantrum. Maybe even three. She would deal with her son first, her boss second.

CHAPTER FOUR

10th December – Thursday

DI Mike Lockyer folded back the paper, taking care to keep his fingers clear of the ketchup, and took a large bite of the bacon roll. Fat and melted butter ran out the side of his mouth and dripped onto his desk. He opened his mouth for the second bite before he had swallowed the first and sat back, putting his feet up on the edge of his bin. Despite maintenance raising his desk, he still felt too big for his hobbit hole of an office. Traditional desks were not made for long legs. He arched his back, enjoying the stretch as he took another gigantic bite of his lunch, murmuring to himself with delight.

He had discovered the Lewisham delicacy last week when he spotted Franks, one of his DCs, eating one at his desk. Lockyer had never frequented the kebab shop opposite the station on Lewisham High Street, and for good reason. Suspicious smells emanated from the extractor grill, the pungent odours drifting into his office through his open window day and night, no matter the season. The kebab spit looked as if it hadn't been cleaned in years, if ever; the floor, walls and ceiling the same. Even the sad Christmas tree on the counter was covered in a layer of grime, which was disturbing considering it was only a week into December – unless it was still there from last year.

However, once he had sampled one of their bacon butties, he didn't care. 'Dirty but delicious,' he said, just as his phone started to ring.

His pleasure evaporated when he looked at the number on the screen. It was Roger – again. He put down the remains of his lunch and pushed speakerphone with his little finger, the only digit not covered in grease. 'Sir,' he said, swallowing a mouthful of food.

'You ready?' Roger asked.

Lockyer looked at the digital clock on his computer screen. It was ten to twelve. 'Can be,' he said. 'Do you want me to come to you?'

'I'm in incident room three,' Roger said. 'Give me ten minutes, then come on up.'

'Fine,' Lockyer said, hanging up and picking up his bacon roll just as his phone rang again. It was reception. He pushed speakerphone. 'Yes,' he said, holding his temper.

'Sir, I've got a DI William Townsend on the phone for you,' Dixie said.

'Can you take a number?' he said, wiping his fingers and mopping up the droplets of fat that were on his desk. He looked at the remains of his lunch. 'I'm due in a meeting.'

'Sure thing,' Dixie said, ending the call.

He reached for the butty just as his phone rang again. 'Oh, come on.' It was Roger again. 'Yes, boss,' he said.

'I'm free now,' Roger said. 'Incident room three.'

'Great,' Lockyer said without enthusiasm.

'I've not got long, so if you could come now.'

'Yes, sir,' he said, hanging up, pushing back his chair and throwing the rest of his lunch in the bin. His mobile beeped as he was leaving his office. He walked back in, picked it up off his desk and unlocked the screen. It was a text from Megan. His daughter would soon be twenty and yet he was struggling to let go, which was ironic considering it had taken him most of her nineteen years to let her, or anyone else, in.

Hi Dad, I can't make it to Uncle Bobby's later and I won't be able to stay tonight. Something's come up. I'll call you over the weekend. Hugs. M xxx

His finger hovered over the call icon. His office line started ringing again. He leaned over his desk. Roger. 'Jesus – keep your hair on,' he said, leaving the phone to ring and pocketing his mobile.

Incident room three was on the next floor up, so he walked across the open-plan office towards the lifts and stair-well. He hadn't managed a run this morning, so he would take the stairs. One flight couldn't be considered a workout but it was better than nothing.

He pulled open the heavy fire door and took the stairs three at a time. He was still unsure what he was going to say to his boss. He could lie. He could say he was in a meeting that ran over or was called out at the last minute. He pushed his fingers through his thatch of tangled curls. He opened the door to the third floor, nodding to a group of officers waiting for the lift. Or he could just tell the truth. He hadn't gone to the occupational health meeting because he didn't want to talk about *her* any more. At the start it had helped, but now all it did was tear open the wound. Sandra, his 'therapist', who spoke through her nose and used sentences like 'you have to forgive yourself', said that being able to remember was part of the healing process. He disagreed. He wanted to forget her, to forget what could have been, and more than anything, to forget his part in her death.

'Mike, there you are.' He turned to see Roger striding towards him.

'Can we?' Roger said, gesturing back towards the incident room. Lockyer followed him across the office without speaking. He tried to read Roger's face as he held open the glass door and ushered him in, tapping the back of a chair. 'Have a seat, Mike.'

'Look, if this is about my appointment with occupational health . . .' Lockyer said before he could stop himself.

Roger looked at him, frowned and took a seat on the other side of the conference table. His stomach pushed against the glass table. 'Not sure I'm with you,' he said, ruffling his dark mop of hair (courtesy of Just for Men, no doubt). 'But listen, I've got to make this quick. I've got another meeting in a few minutes.'

Lockyer stalled for a moment but then said, 'Go ahead.'

'So . . .' Roger said, 'I need a favour. A job's come in I need you to handle.'

Lockyer felt his shoulders relax. As long as he wasn't about to be sent off to the funny farm, Roger could have anything he wanted. 'What's up?'

Roger pursed his lips and cleared his throat. 'Well, I got

a call yesterday about an RTC. Possible hit and run. The victim's car left the road, collided with a tree and caught fire.'

Lockyer sucked air through his teeth. 'Nasty.'

'Indeed,' Roger said, steepling his fingers.

'Well, my team's open. So where am I going?'

'Somerset.'

Lockyer stopped midway through getting his pen out of his jacket. He looked over at Roger. 'Somerset? As in Somerset, Somerset?'

'Yes,' Roger said. 'The victim was only in the South West temporarily. She was a London resident. She's got a flat over in Bromley. Anyway, given the severity of the incident, the superintendent in charge of CID down in Bridgwater felt it was important to have the Met involved from the outset.'

'Sounds fair,' Lockyer said with a shrug. 'Will it be a joint investigation?' He started jotting down some notes on his pad. The rain was pounding on the glass outside, punctuating his words. 'Are they sending someone here? Am I sending one of the team there? What's the plan? How do they want to work it? Oh, and what's the superintendent called?' He looked up when there was no response to his last question – or any of the others.

Roger sniffed and cleared his throat. He opened his mouth and interlocked his fingers. 'It's not quite that . . . straightforward.'

'Why not?' he asked. 'What's the problem?' Silence greeted his question. 'You're gonna have to help me out here, sir.'

Roger pulled at his collar. 'It's complicated – delicate. It will require discretion.'

'I think I can handle it,' Lockyer said, although he doubted anyone would put diplomacy at the top of his CV.

Roger sighed and dropped his shoulders. 'You didn't hear this from me, OK?'

'OK.' Lockyer's curiosity was piqued.

'I got the call first thing yesterday morning from the superintendent – Terry Atkinson. He told me the basics and the London connection and asked if I could send a senior officer down to assist with the investigation, which, as you said, sounds fair,' Roger said. 'However, when I asked all the questions you just did . . . whether it'd be a joint inquiry, et cetera . . . he seemed unsure. He said he would reassess as the case developed, but for now he just wants you.'

'Me?'

'Well,' Roger said, 'he asked for an experienced senior DI, so I figured . . .'

'You figured you'd send in your best,' Lockyer said with a grin.

Roger raised an eyebrow. 'That remains to be seen.' He pulled his thumb and forefinger down the sides of his mouth. 'Anyway, as it stands it's a hit and run. However, there is a question over premeditation, and therefore what kind of charge they'd be looking to go with as and when they have a suspect.'

'I'm sensing a *but*?'

'The *but* is where it starts to get complicated,' Roger said. 'When I pushed Atkinson on exactly what kind of support he was after, he reluctantly admitted that he wasn't confident about the DI currently assigned to the case.'

'Why?'

'He didn't go into detail.'

'You didn't ask?'

'Of course I asked,' Roger said, sitting forward in his chair. 'Believe it or not, Mike, this isn't my first day on the force.'

'So what did he say?'

'Atkinson just said the DI was a recent transfer from Bristol and that he had struggled with his last case, so he felt it only prudent to put proper support in place ASAP.'

'Come on, Rog, what else? I can see by your face there's more to this than babysitting some green DI.'

'I got another call this morning,' Roger said.

'From who?'

'I can't say.'

'Someone high up, then?' Lockyer said.

Roger shrugged. 'Let's just say it was someone I trained with who has done better than me, career-wise.'

'OK. Do you know *why* they're involving themselves with us lowly folk?'

'Not really, no.'

'What do they want?'

'They want whoever I send – namely you – to take over the investigation,' Roger said, opening his hands. 'According to . . . my contact, the DI in charge is bordering on incompetent.'

'So why don't they get shot of them?'

'I don't know,' Roger said, shaking his head. 'It seems that information is above my pay grade . . . and yours. All I *do* know is that you will be lead DI in all but name. However, as far as Atkinson and this DI are concerned, you are just going there to assist. And as far as you are concerned, there was no second phone call.'

Lockyer blew out a breath. 'Bloody hell. Why all the secrecy?'

Roger opened his hands. 'Who knows? But if I had to guess, and given who my contact is, I'd say they want some kind of control over the case but don't want to be accused of . . .'

'Undue influence, abuse of power?' Lockyer said.

'Yes and yes,' Roger said.

Lockyer scratched the back of his head. 'How on earth am I going to lead without telling the DI I'm leading?' Roger looked at him, but didn't speak. 'Oh, I see. I'm going to have to figure that one out myself, is that right?'

'That's why it's a favour,' was all Roger said.

'You're telling me,' Lockyer said. 'Am I right in assuming I can't take the team with me?'

'You can take one.'

'Fine. I'll take Jane.'

Roger was shaking his head. 'DS Bennett will be needed here. She'll be picking up the slack on your cases.'

'Not a chance, sir,' Lockyer said. 'If I have to go down there and lead without *appearing* to lead, *and* run someone else's team without *actually* being able to tell them what to do, then I want Jane with me.' He could see Roger was about to argue. 'You want your best,' he said. 'Well, I want mine.'

Roger rolled his eyes and dragged his hands down his face. The new job was taking its toll. Lockyer would swear the poor guy was ageing before his eyes. 'Fine.' Roger pushed back his chair and stood up. 'I really don't have time to argue with you, but Lockyer, I want all cases covered and handed over *before* you leave for Somerset.'

'No problem,' he said, knowing it was a lie; but he had no intention of walking into the unknown without backup, and the only person he trusted was Jane. He followed Roger out of the incident room. He would call in some old favours. He would sort his and Jane's cases – one way or the other. He walked across the office, Roger at his side. Neither of them spoke. Lockyer was beginning to wish the meeting had been about his missed therapy session. He pushed the button for the lift. 'When are they expecting me?'

'As soon as you can get down there. Today, if possible. I've emailed the file over to you.'

'This just keeps getting better,' Lockyer said.

'Look,' Roger said. 'I know this is a big ask. Under any other circumstances I'd have said no. But I got the distinct impression that my career was on the line.'

'Don't you mean *our* careers?' Lockyer said as the doors opened.

Lockyer let the phone ring, but there was no answer. He left another message. 'Megs, I got your text. Can you give me a call back? I'm leaving town on a job but wanted to speak to you before I . . . well, just call me, OK?' He hung up as his office line started to ring. He picked up. 'Yes.'

'Hey, Mike, it's me again.' He looked at the call log on the phone. It was Dixie on reception. 'I've got DI William Townsend on the phone for you again,' she said.

'Shit,' he said. 'Sorry, totally went out of my head. Put him through.'

'Don't worry about it. My brain still thinks it's Monday,' Dixie said. 'I'll put him through now, hon.' Lockyer winced at the 'hon'. When had that started? He wasn't aware he and Dixie were that close.

'Hello?' a voice said.

'DI . . . Townsend,' Lockyer said, managing to drag the guy's name out of his addled brain. 'Sorry not to get back to you.'

'Not a problem,' Townsend said. 'I just wanted to get things sorted . . . manpower-wise so I know who's doing what, where.'

'Sorry, I'm not sure I—'

'DI Lockyer?'

'Yes,' he said.

'I'm Bill Townsend from Avon and Somerset constabulary.'

The penny dropped. 'Of course . . . sorry, Bill,' Lockyer said. Roger had never told him the DI's name. He hadn't asked. 'It's been a busy morning.'

'Here too,' Townsend said. 'I hope you don't mind me calling? In my experience collaborative investigations can be a minefield of problems and miscommunications so I wanted to speak to you and get things straight before you meet the team either later today or tomorrow, depending on your schedule.'

'Good thinking,' Lockyer said, trying to sound casual. His meeting with Roger had been less than ten minutes ago. He hadn't had a chance to check the details of the case on the computer yet. All he knew was that it was an RTC. He realized he didn't even know the name of the victim. 'I'm hoping to get down to you today. What do you need from me in the meantime?'

'I think it'd be better to speak in person, if you don't mind?' Townsend said.

'Sure, sure. Well, why don't you give me your mobile number and I'll call you when I know my timings and we can meet . . . get on the same page or whatever before I . . . before you introduce me to the team . . .'

But Townsend didn't give him his mobile number. There was no need.

Lockyer ended the call and punched in Roger's extension.

'Yes,' Roger said, answering on the first ring.

'I need to see you.'

'I can't, I'm due in with the Chief . . .'

'I don't give a shit who you're due in with, Rog. I need to see you now. I need to know exactly what your *friend* told you about this DI.'

'Why? What's happened?'

'He's here.'

'What do you mean he's here?'

'I mean, he's downstairs.'

CHAPTER FIVE

10th December – Thursday

Jane pulled into the station car park, found a space and reversed into it, turned off the engine and rested her head on the steering wheel. On a scale of one to ten, one being amazing and ten being Armageddon, today had so far been a twenty-seven.

She had paid for her tardiness to the breakfast table, and then some. Peter had thrown the mother of all shit-fits. The kitchen floor had ended up coated in cold scrambled eggs and the walls smeared with a combination of baked beans and buttered toast. There was no way she could reward his behaviour with a *Friends* episode, so she had ended up bundling him into the car kicking and screaming and taking him straight to school. The only small mercy was that as soon as he saw his teaching aide, he had forgotten all about breakfast and their fight. Mrs Roberts had been treated to a beaming smile and a detailed briefing about the feeding habits of the Velociraptor. When Jane left, he had turned and waved goodbye as if the entire morning had been wiped from his memory. She wished she had the ability to do the same.

She took her handbag off the passenger seat, ignoring her pale reflection in the rear-view mirror, and climbed out of the car. An afternoon in the office would be a welcome distraction at this point.

As she walked across the car park she pulled her coat tighter while searching in her handbag for her lanyard. It was bloody freezing and forecast to get a lot colder, but at least the rain had stopped. Her hands closed around the frigid piece of plastic and she pulled it out and put it around her neck. She realized she was muttering to herself. A morning off was meant to be more relaxing. She had only just finished cleaning the kitchen when the first of her childminder interviewees had arrived. She paused for a second before punching in the code and letting herself in by the back entrance of the station. They changed the codes on a fortnightly basis. For the first few days after a change it was commonplace to see officers milling about around the entrance, waiting for someone with a better memory to let them into the building. The door slammed shut behind her.

The highlight of the childminding bunch had to be Karen, the twenty-two-year-old. What a peach she was. Her first comment had been that Jane was small for a copper and then, with a straight face, she had asked whether Peter's autism was anything like Dustin Hoffman's in *Rain Man*.

Jane shook her head, deciding whether to take the stairs or be lazy and call for the lift. She didn't expect people to fully understand Peter's condition, but given everyone was meant to be on the spectrum these days, she was surprised to still find so much ignorance surrounding the subject. She unwound her scarf as she dragged herself up the stairs.

'Hey.'

She looked up. 'Penny, hi,' Jane said. 'You off to lunch?'

Penny walked down a few steps to meet her, a broad grin on her face. 'No,' she said. 'I'm going to meet my mum. We're off wedding-dress shopping.'

'You've set a date already?' Jane asked.

'Not yet, but it'll be towards the end of next year, so there's no time to waste,' Penny said, hopping from foot to foot. 'I want to look at favours, invitations. Max said we might even get a wedding planner. He's happy to pay for it.'

'Could this guy *get* any more perfect?' Jane asked, hoping she didn't sound bitter.

Penny shook her head, a wistful expression settling on her features. 'I just feel so lucky,' she said. 'I still can't believe it.'

'It's no more than you deserve, Pen,' Jane said as she began to climb the stairs again. She felt like she needed to get away. If she had to listen to any more of Penny's unbridled joy, she thought she might snap and say something she regretted. It wasn't Penny's fault Jane's taste in men was crap. It wasn't her fault that Peter's father was a pathological liar who seemed to be making it his mission in life to destroy everything Jane had built for herself and her son.

'Anything I need to know before you go?'

'Chris and Franks took statements from Simons and Rivers this morning,' Penny said. 'Both guys knew Bashir, but of course both are keeping schtum.'

'Of course,' Jane said. Gang-related deaths were a common occurrence – the team's bread and butter. The murders themselves might be different, but the interview process was always the same. No one saw anything, no one knew anything and no one was going to talk to the police, no matter what you threatened them with. 'When does this borough ever talk?'

Penny shrugged and looked at her watch. 'I've got to go,' she said.

'Go,' Jane said. 'Have a good time.' Penny seemed to float away. Jane turned and pulled herself up the last remaining stairs before yanking open the door to the murder squad's offices. The buzz of conversation and ringing phones made her head ache.

Lockyer was striding towards her. If his stubble was anything to go by, he was on day three of his personal maintenance embargo. How he made dishevelled look good she would never know. If she didn't wash her hair every day and plaster her face with BB cream, she wasn't fit to be seen in public. 'Jane, good, you're here,' he said.

'Only just,' she said as the heavy fire door hit her on the back, knocking her off balance.

'Good, great,' he said. 'I've got a few things I need to go over with you.' He had turned away and was heading for his office. He looked at her over his shoulder. 'My office?' he said, gesturing with his head for her to follow.

'Can I . . . ?' she asked, holding up her bag and her scarf.

'No need, this won't take long. Sasha,' Lockyer called across the office. 'I'm just sitting down with DS Bennett for five minutes. Can you go down to Bella's and tell a DI Townsend that we'll be with him in ten minutes, and apologize again for the delay.'

'What does he look like?' Sasha asked, pushing back from her desk and reaching for her jacket on the back of her chair.

Lockyer shrugged. 'I don't know,' he said. 'Just look for the out-of-place copper, and that'll be him.' He turned. 'Come on, Jane.'

She resisted the urge to roll her eyes, and followed on behind him.

Lockyer waited for Jane to take a seat before he closed the door, walked round his desk and sat down, positioning and repositioning his legs until they weren't pushing against the underside of the table. 'Cold out?' he asked. Her skin was the colour of weak tea, or gnat's piss, as he called it. The expression 'ridden hard and put away wet' sprang to mind. Without answering, she shrugged out of her coat, the smell of the freezing afternoon coming off her in waves accompanied by, if he wasn't mistaken, a sense of doom. He took a breath, but then decided it was best to plough on in the hope the warmth of his office might thaw her rigid expression.

'Roger has just assigned me to a new case.'

'Right,' she said without inflection.

'It's an RTC down in Somerset. It's been listed as suspicious.'

'Somerset?'

'Yes,' he said. 'Looks like a hit and run . . . possible premeditation.' She nodded, but didn't speak. 'How's your caseload?'

Jane looked up at the ceiling and let out a long sigh. Lockyer resisted the urge to do the same. He didn't have time for this. 'I'm finishing up three,' she said. 'Ayoade, Trenton and Assaf, and we're on second-round interviews for the Bashir hit.'

'Anyone talking?'

'What do you think?' she asked, with a lot more attitude than he was used to or happy with.

'OK,' he said, ignoring her tone. 'I've got four – Highdale, Davis, Woodland and Smith – and two active, Merrett and Morris; but both are close to wrapping up, given I am getting nowhere. All pretty straightforward. I will be able to remotely close off the four but I'll need to hand over Merrett and Morris.' He stopped to let her say something – anything – but she just stared at her hands. It was like talking to a zombie.

Lockyer looked at his watch, then back at Jane. DI what's-his-name was waiting for them down at Bella's, and he had just spent the past ten minutes with Roger trying to cram as much of the Pippa Jones case into his head as he could. He needed to get going. He dragged a hand over his chin, his stubble rough against his palm. 'OK, what's happened?' Given the past few months, it could be any number of things. Her father had been ill. Her parents had moved. She was struggling with Peter's childcare and on top of all that she was having a nightmare with her insane ex-boyfriend.

'I had a call from my solicitor this morning.'

'Andy?' he asked. She nodded. So it was door number four – the crazy ex. Lockyer could see she was trying not to cry. He reached into his pocket, took out his handkerchief and handed it to her. She held it under her eyes.

'He's claiming . . . he's trying to say that Peter's autism is somehow my fault.'

'Eh?' Lockyer said before he could stop himself.

'He's saying I drank and smoked weed when I was pregnant and that's why Peter is the way he is – starved of oxygen in the womb – a polluted environment, or something. That's actually what he said, that I had carried Peter in a *polluted environment.*' A solitary tear spilt over her eyelid and ran down her face, leaving a pale line in her make-up. She shook her head. 'I've got to supply hair, blood and urine for a drug screen.'

'Jesus,' he said, getting up and walking round his desk, sitting down on the edge of it facing her. He ignored the heads turning in the open-plan office beyond his glass door. He missed rooms, real rooms with walls and doors, but it seemed 'modern' meant glass – lots of glass. 'Jane, that is the most ridiculous thing I have ever heard.'

'Maybe, but . . .' she said, not looking at him, 'but what if he's . . . what if he's right?'

'Is this really why you're upset?' Lockyer was incredulous. 'You believe what that shit-for-brains has said?' She shrugged. 'Jane,' he said, reaching forward and tipping up her chin so she was looking at him. Her fringe was stuck to her forehead in dark triangles, her skin pale beneath. 'Did you smoke weed when you were pregnant with Peter?' She shook her head. 'Have you ever smoked weed?' She shook her head again. 'Did you drink when you were pregnant with Peter?'

'Maybe once, at a friend's wedding,' she said.

'So how could anything he said possibly be true?'

'I know, but what if . . . what if it's *because* of me . . . something I did . . . something I passed on?'

'What the . . . ?' He stood up and started pacing. He thought of his brother Bobby, and of their mother. He would love nothing better than to blame his brother's condition on their useless mother. She deserved to take some responsibility. 'I don't know much,' he said, 'but I'm pretty sure that's not how it works . . . and I know you know a lot more than me.'

'I know, it's just . . .'

'You cannot let him get to you like this, Jane,' he said. 'I told you. These custody hearings take an age. He's saying anything he can to discredit you. The very fact that he's stooped this low this soon into the process shows just how desperate he is. He's clutching at straws.' He could see his words were having little effect. 'What did your solicitor say?'

'She said not to worry. She said she only told me because as my representative, she is legally bound to pass on all information.'

'Well, there you are then,' he said, going back to his chair and sitting down.

'She thinks Andy will get visitation.' She looked at him. 'I can't, Mike. I can't let that bastard . . .' She trailed off and buried her face in his handkerchief.

'Come on,' he said. He was no good at this. Asking what was wrong was a new skill he was learning to master. Knowing what to do with the emotional outpouring that tended to follow – he was clueless. 'Take a breath.' He took a breath himself and waited for Jane's shoulders to relax. 'Look, we've talked about this. You knew he'd get visitation, but you said yourself he'll never turn up. As soon as this is over he'll disappear into the ether again.' He tapped his desk until she looked up at him. 'He's only doing this to get to you. He *wants* to drive you crazy. That's all this is.'

'Peter won't cope . . . he won't understand . . .'

'He's not going to see Peter, Jane,' he said. 'This has never been about Peter. His only motivation is you.' He felt his cheeks heating before he even spoke. 'You . . . rejected him and he's making you pay for it.' He saw her redden as well. They both knew she hadn't rejected him straight away, but now was not the time to split hairs.

She took a deep breath, tipped her head back and shook her shoulders. 'I'm sorry. You don't have time for this . . .'

'And neither do you,' he said, pushing back his chair and standing up, gesturing for her to do the same. 'You're coming with me.'

'To Somerset?' she said, picking up her coat, her face crumpled in confusion.

'Yes,' he said.

'I can't,' she said stammering. 'I've got Peter . . .'

'When does he break up? Next week?'

'Yes, but . . .'

'They never do anything last week of term, and I bet he'd love to see his grandparents this close to Christmas. Clevedon's in Somerset, right?' He knew it was. He had Googled it when he got back from seeing Roger.

'Well, yes, but . . .'

He could see she was softening to the idea. 'And . . .' he said, stretching out the word, 'it'll give you a well-deserved break from your idiot ex.' He could see that was the clincher.

She raised her eyebrows. 'True.'

'Exactly,' he said, ushering her towards the door and giving her a gentle shove out into the office. 'You can thank me later.'

CHAPTER SIX

10th December – Thursday

She stood at the counter in Bella's Cafe, looking out at Lewisham High Street. The Christmas lights had been turned on and, as if by magic, it had started to snow. That should make the drive down to Somerset interesting, and there was no putting it off. Lockyer had made it clear when they left the office that they were travelling down tonight, come hell or high water – she assumed snow fell somewhere in those categories. He had gone on about not wanting to waste the 'golden hour'. He hadn't seemed amused when she had pointed out that the golden hour had been and gone two days earlier. 'Not for us, Jane,' he had said. 'This guy Townsend's had his golden hour – now it's my turn.' She knew better than to argue with him when his mind was set. She glanced over her shoulder at him and the DI from Somerset. They were sat in a booth at the back of the cafe. Lockyer had wedged himself into the red leather bench like a marionette, hinged at the waist, his legs bent and awkward beneath the table. If he had chosen their position for privacy, his discomfort was wasted. They were the only ones in here.

Townsend sat opposite and upright, his hands resting on the table. If Jane had to guess, she would say he was in his mid to late fifties; grey hair, grey skin and grey clothes. Everything about him looked washed out apart from his striking blue eyes. He had the look of a tired Phillip Schofield. 'Sorry, can I have full-fat milk please?' she asked, spotting the waitress picking up a carton of skimmed.

'Of course,' the waitress said, giving her a wide smile.

'Can you make mine decaf,' Lockyer called from across the cafe.

She turned back to the counter to tell the waitress about Lockyer's amended order when the girl held up a manicured hand and said, 'No worries, I heard him.' She discarded one of the coffees and began preparing a fresh one. She gave Jane a knowing smile as if to say, 'Men, who'd have 'em?' Jane knew Lockyer came in here often. She also knew that *he* got table service. Not that she was bothered. The barista in Costa had asked for her phone number last month.

'I'll have a double espresso in mine,' she said, annoyed by her own peevish tone.

'I'm with you,' the waitress said in a conspiratorial whisper as she added the extra shot to Jane's mug. 'I wouldn't get past breakfast without my coffee. Here you go.'

'Thank you,' she said, managing a half-smile as she picked up the first two mugs. She took them over to the table and set them down in front of Lockyer and Townsend before heading back for her own drink. When she returned she pulled over a chair and sat down at the end of the table. Both men stopped and looked at her. 'So, where have we got to?' she asked.

Lockyer took a slurp of his coffee. 'Shit, that's hot,' he said. 'Not far. We were waiting for you.'

'Well, we'd better get a move on if you want to get down to Somerset tonight. It's snowing.'

Lockyer craned his neck to see around her. 'Is it settling?'

'Starting to.'

'OK, Bill,' Lockyer said. 'Let's get on with it. What can you tell us?' Jane took her notepad out of her handbag and searched for a pen. Lockyer did the same before looking at her. She passed him her pen, and searched for another.

'Right,' Townsend said when they were ready, pens poised. 'Female Victim. Pippa Jones. Caucasian. 5' 8". 63 kilos. Twenty-five years of age. She had been staying with an aunt – Claudette Barker, fifty-three, divorced – in Nether Stowey, about ten miles outside Bridgwater. Pippa was working as a chef in a restaurant at Fyne Court, a National Trust property up on the Quantock Hills. She also had a part-time job at the Farmer's Arms pub in a place called Combe Florey.' He paused, allowing her and Lockyer to finish making their notes. Jane nodded when she was done. 'Although she was born and brought up in Somerset the family moved to London when she was twelve – hence our desire to have the Met involved. Pippa had a flat-share in Bromley. Her previous employer was an Ashley Tanker. He owns an Italian restaurant on the Old Kent Road. The car she was driving was registered to her. It was—'

'Sorry,' Jane said. 'How are you spelling that Nether what-was-it?'

'Nether Stowey,' Townsend said. 'It's got a population of about a thousand.' He spelled out the name for her before taking a sip of his coffee. 'Where was I?' He rested his fore-finger under his nose and hooked his thumb under his chin as if holding his face steady. It made him look studious. He didn't wear glasses, but Jane thought he would suit them.

'The car,' Lockyer offered.

'That's right,' Townsend said. 'It was a 2004 Ford Focus, silver. Petrol 1.8 litre engine.'

'And she was the registered owner?' Lockyer asked.

'Yes,' Townsend said. 'As to the circumstances – member of the public discovered the wreckage at approximately 5.30 a.m. on Tuesday morning . . . that would have been the eighth. She left work at the pub just after half ten on the Monday night, the seventh, so we're assuming the incident happened on her way home. It's unlikely we'll get a time of death on this one.' He turned his mug around in his hands before picking it up and taking a sip. His hand shook, some of his coffee slopping out onto the table.

'Heavy night?' Lockyer asked.

Townsend raised his eyebrows and smiled. 'Something like that,' he said, taking another drink. This time his hand remained still. 'Her car left the road and crashed head-on into a tree. The front of the car took the brunt of the impact. An engine fire resulted in the right-hand side of the vehicle being damaged.' His voice had dropped to a whisper.

'And the victim?' she asked.

Townsend's expression was solemn. 'The victim was still belted in as far as we can tell.'

'Jesus,' Lockyer said, whistling through his teeth. 'Nasty way to go.'

'We're assuming she was dead long before the fire took hold,' he said.

'Has there been an official ID?' Lockyer asked.

Townsend pursed his lips. 'Yes and no,' he said. 'The contents of Pippa's handbag were found on the passenger seat and in the footwell of the vehicle. Some items were undamaged . . . her passport being one of them.'

'She carried her passport on her?'

'Evidently,' he said. 'Her parents want to see her, but . . .'

'Surely they won't allow them to see the body?' Jane said.

Townsend opened his hands and shrugged. 'They will be strongly advised not to, given the circumstances, but if they are certain they want to then I won't stop them. It can be hugely detrimental to family members if they are denied access. It does happen, but not often, and it's certainly not recommended.'

Jane looked at Lockyer. She couldn't imagine anything worse. She had seen her fair share of burn victims over the years, and it was an assault on the senses. The body charred, almost unrecognizable. The smell, a combination of burnt and cooked meat, coupled with something so sour it made Jane's mouth fill with bile. And then there was the taste. The first time she had witnessed a burn victim's post-mortem it had taken her half the day to get the stench off her clothes, but the taste had stayed with her for several days. A sort of charcoal tang at the back of her throat that seemed to burn her nasal passages each time she breathed. And that was her viewing a *stranger*. What would it be like for this girl's parents? To lose their daughter, and then see her like that? Jane's back stiffened.

'OK, let's move this along,' Lockyer said. Townsend looked at him. 'Sorry, go ahead, Bill. What else have you got?'

'The crash investigation team are still working on it, but their initial report states that the victim's vehicle appears to have been hit from behind at least twice, and from the back right-hand side once.'

'Trace evidence?' Lockyer asked.

Townsend nodded. 'Some,' he said. 'We've got good paint residue samples from the other vehicle. They've gone off for analysis. Fingers crossed we can get the manufacturer if not the model of the vehicle. We've also got various skid marks and tyre impressions on the road and on the surrounding grassland. We can't be sure which, if any, relate to the vehicle we're looking for, but it'll be good to have them in the file for comparison as and when we make an arrest.'

'What about the fire?' Lockyer asked.

'They're assuming the damage to the engine caused the fire and it then spread to the rest of the vehicle, though the left-hand side remained relatively undamaged.'

'And the victim?'

'As I said, she was still wearing her seatbelt and appears, according to the pathologist, to have died from a combination of head injuries and smoke inhalation. The body has been taken to Flax Bourton mortuary, where the post-mortem will be carried out by Dr Basil Reed.'

'It hasn't been done yet?' Jane asked, sounding more judgemental than she intended.

'No,' Townsend said. 'The body was only recovered forty-eight hours ago . . .'

'Sorry, Bill,' Lockyer said. 'Jane and I have been spoilt.

We've got a mortuary suite on site here and a resident pathologist who also happens to be a friend, so . . .'

'That's quite all right,' Townsend said. 'I assure you Basil has put this one at the top of his schedule. However, we only have three full-time pathologists and one part-time, and they cover everything from Basingstoke to Land's End and from Bristol right down to the Isle of Wight.'

Lockyer sniffed and pulled down the corners of his mouth. 'What time were your guys on scene?' he asked.

'The report came in at five thirty and we were on scene by ten past six.'

'And forensics?'

'The same,' Townsend said. 'We're all based at the new Bridgwater hub at Express Park. It's fifteen-odd miles from the crash site. The body was removed by eleven . . . the car by mid-afternoon.'

'That was a bit quick,' Lockyer said.

Townsend took a second to respond. 'I didn't have much choice,' he said. 'The scene was ghoulish to say the very least.' His eyes seemed to glaze over for a moment, but then his face cleared and he said, 'I had the press and locals trying to gain access. I even had people asking if they could walk through the crime scene, shouting legislation at me about rights of way for ramblers. I wasn't prepared to risk anyone getting in there and taking a picture of the victim in situ.'

'How did you get her out without damaging . . . without compromising any trace evidence?' Jane asked.

'I got the fire service to remove the driver's seat with her still in it,' he said. 'The whole lot's gone up to Flax Bourton.'

'Wow,' Jane said.

'What's been reported?' Lockyer asked, turning the page on his notepad. Jane could count on one hand the times she had witnessed him taking notes. He had never worked that way – not in the seven years she had known him – but today, he had made more notes than she had. A lot more. Townsend was here to get them up to speed, but the detail Lockyer was going into made it feel more like a handover than a catch-up.

'Not much so far,' Townsend said. 'A tweet went out on the day saying there had been a fatality involving a single vehicle and I've given a brief statement to the local press, but I haven't released the name of the victim yet; although I'm sure, given the close-knit community down there, that every-one already knows.'

Lockyer nodded, and pushed his mug towards Jane. 'That's good,' he said. 'The lack of information released will make a big difference when we appeal for witnesses.' He looked at Townsend's mug and pushed it towards her, too. 'I assume you were planning on launching an appeal?'

'In due course,' Townsend said.

'Right.' Lockyer tapped his pen on the page. 'Can you get the same again, Jane, please?' he asked. 'And one for yourself, if you like. I doubt we'll be stopping on the way down. May as well get your caffeine fix now.'

'Sure,' she said, getting to her feet without argument. Whatever was going on with her boss and his new efficient work ethic, she didn't care. She was just grateful to be included – to be going to Somerset. She had already put a call in to the head at Peter's school, who, to her surprise, had been fine about Peter missing the last week and a bit of term. There was no doubt a reason behind Mrs Hatley's quick acquiescence, but Jane wasn't about to go looking for trouble. Peter aside, the main reason she was happy to be here was that she hadn't thought about Andy once since she sat down. 'Another, DI Townsend?'

'Please,' he said, 'call me Bill.'

'Fine, Bill. Same again?'

'Can I have tea instead?' he asked, smacking his lips together. 'I'm parched.'

'Sure, builder's or something fancy?' she asked.

'I'll have Earl Grey, if they've got it?' he said.

'Of course.' Jane walked over to the counter. She hoped he hadn't take offence at her 'fancy' reference. She should have known he liked fancy tea by the way he spoke. He had the Somerset accent – or Zummerset, as it was pronounced down south – but he sounded as if he had been to a private school. His vowels were rounded, his consonants sharp and clear. She could hear Lockyer's phone ringing. 'Can we have the same again, please?' she said, handing the used mugs to the waitress, 'but substitute the Americano with an Earl Grey.'

'A pot?'

'Make them to go, Jane,' Lockyer called over.

She looked at the waitress. 'Did you get that?'

'Sure,' the girl said, turning and busying herself with their order.

Jane sifted through her wallet and put a tenner on the counter. She looked at her watch, and then outside at the snow. The sooner they finished up here, the sooner she could get herself sorted. They needed to be back to meet the DI and two DS's due to arrive from the north London branch, who had been drafted in to ensure Lockyer's cases and her own were dealt with. She was impressed he had managed to get them on board at such short notice. He could move mountains when he was motivated. Though what had got him so fired up, she wasn't sure.

She looked at her watch again, trying to figure out the timings in her head. She needed to get home, pack for her and Peter. He would be waiting for her with her neighbour. Cathy had been a godsend in the past month. Jane chewed at the edge of her lip, watching the traffic creep past Bella's. On a good day it would take an hour to get out to the M4, but she doubted they would be that lucky today. The snow and rush hour would have been enough to slow them down, but it was late-night shopping as well. There was no way they were getting to Somerset much before nine, at a guess. She pushed her tongue into the space between her upper lip and her front teeth. There was a lot to do. Both her and Lockyer's teams needed to be briefed and the handovers completed before they left the office. They would need to see Roger as well, to confirm plans for their transfer to Somerset. She drummed her fingers on the counter. She felt the familiar buzz as her brain kicked into a higher gear. She loved the beginning of a case. It was all about the planning, and if anyone loved a plan, it was Jane. The inquiry into Pippa Jones's death was like untouched snow on Christmas morning. They were yet to take a wrong step.

'Jane.'

She turned as Lockyer approached.

'I just got off the phone with Aaron.'

'OK,' she said, wary of his expression.

'He's taken the leave of absence because of a death in the family.'

'Right,' she said. 'That makes sense. When? Who? Was it expected?' She was racking her brains. Was it Aaron who had the terminally ill mother?

'It's his sister,' Lockyer said. 'His twin, in fact.'

'God. I didn't know he was a twin,' she said. 'What happened?'

'She died earlier in the week. A hit and run . . . in Somerset.'

'Hang on, you're not saying . . . ?'

'Yep. Pippa Jones is – was – Aaron's twin sister.'

CHAPTER SEVEN

11th December – Friday

Aaron continued to stroke the back of his mother's hand, her skin soft beneath his palm. The fingers on his other hand had gone numb from her vice-like grip. At least it matched the rest of him. He felt as if he had just been pulled from an icy lake.

His father was on the other side of the room, sitting in a high-backed rocking chair. He was dressed in black, his hands clasped in his lap, his dog-collar prominent at his neck. His expression remained blank as an ancient-looking cat wound itself around his legs unacknowledged. Aaron cleared his throat, restraining a peculiar urge to laugh. He felt like a player in a farce; the vicar, the wife, the twin, the aunt, the girlfriend, the cat and the dead sister. He imagined the audience's guffaws of laughter as the cast rushed in and out of the lounge, each one tripping over the cat, each one saying in a stage whisper, *Whatever you do, don't mention the dead daughter . . . sister . . . niece. [Cat howls. Kitchen door swings on its hinges.] Who's dead?* someone would ask. *The aunt's sister's daughter's sister's sister,* another would say. *You mean the vicar's daughter's son's sister's sister, surely?* Without warning he barked out a laugh, his chest heaving as if he might be sick. His mother squeezed his hand tighter. She didn't speak. She didn't need to. They were part of the same black comedy, rushing headlong into a parallel universe. When they had left London, all bundled into Megan's car, every passing mile had moved them further from the reality they all knew – a reality they could never return to. Not ever.

'I'll pop the kettle on, shall I?' his aunt asked, making a break for the kitchen. If she wasn't making tea, she was 'just popping to the shops', no doubt desperate to escape the cloying fug that had descended over her house. Her hair was dragged back in a severe bun, she wasn't wearing any make-up and her clothes were hanging off her thin frame. If anyone looked like a grieving parent, it was her. The two sisters were near identical, though his mother was the rounder sibling. However, in contrast to Claudette's washed-out state, Aaron's mother – the vicar's wife – was camera-ready. Her hair resembled a brown motorcycle helmet and her pinched, fox-like features had been plastered with a putty-coloured foundation, topped off by two pink swathes of blusher. The combination of perfume and hairspray had formed a noxious fog around them. Cinderella and one of the Ugly Sisters, Aaron thought as another bubble of laughter started to rise up in his throat. He had to get a grip.

'I'll help her,' Megan said, getting to her feet and heading off towards the kitchen, 'and I'm gonna make you a sandwich. You need to eat,' she said, stroking his cheek as she passed. 'Mrs Jones . . . Reverend Jones. Can I get you something?'

Aaron looked at his mother. Her eyes were glazed over. His father had picked up a newspaper and was staring at it although his eyes weren't moving. 'You should eat,' he said to his mother. 'Both of you need to eat.'

'I tell you what,' Megan said, her voice so soft it was almost soporific. 'I'll sort out a selection of stuff and you can pick and choose. OK?'

Aaron managed to smile and nod as she left the room, his gaze settling on the fire spluttering and dying in the grate. It wasn't his place to revive it. This wasn't his home any more. He was just a kid when they moved. He and Pippa had been born in the kitchen – much to his mother's dismay. They had both taken their first steps in this room. Pippa had been first – she did everything first. Cassie said she just stood up one day after church and walked from the sofa to the rocking chair his father was sitting in, as if she had been doing it every day of her young life. Without thinking, Aaron reached up and fingered the depression in his skin just above his left eyebrow. It had taken another three months before he even attempted walking. According to Cassie he had taken one faltering step before toppling head first into the hearth. *Head wounds bleed like hell,* his sister would say, *and I should know. I had to clean it up.*

He closed his eyes and took a deep breath in through his nose. The smell was so familiar; warm, dry and earthy, the thick cottage walls absorbing every scent during the day only to release them again in the evening. It was as if the house breathed with them. He wondered if it could sense pain – if it soaked up emotions as well.

'Sugar?' Claudette called from the kitchen.

'No,' he said for the hundredth time. 'Mum has a sweetener and Dad has his black, no sugar.' He heard the clatter of plates and cutlery and the banging of cupboard doors; Megan's voice an accompanying murmur. No doubt she was trying to 'talk' to his aunt. Megs believed it was important to share your feelings. He snorted. Claudette would be squirming. She didn't like to admit she had feelings, let alone talk about them. His mother and father were the same.

'She called me,' he said, without realizing he was going to speak.

His father nodded, his eyes opening and closing like a child's baby doll. 'It's well documented that twins have a sixth sense when it comes to communicating with one another,' he said in a robotic voice.

'No, Dad,' he said, shaking his head. 'Pip called me.'

His father's head bobbed in sync with Aaron's words, a knowing expression on his face. 'I'm sure it feels like that, son,' he said, tilting his head on one side. 'Why don't you try and relax?'

'Fuck relaxing,' he said, shaking himself free of his mother's grip.

'We don't need that kind of talk, son,' his father said without expression. 'It's lazy language.'

Aaron ground his teeth. He felt cheated. There was a time when he and his sisters were younger that a well-timed *'fuck'* would have their father chasing them around the dining table with a wooden spoon. Each sibling would try and trip the other up to ensure they weren't the ones who were caught and spanked. 'Fuck, fuck, fuck,' he shouted, desperate for a reaction; something, anything to break the spell he was under. 'What's the fucking difference?'

'Aaron,' his father said. 'You're upsetting your mother.'

'Her daughter's dead, Dad,' he said, getting to his feet. 'She should be fucking upset.' His body was trembling. He tasted bile in his mouth as he watched his father close his eyes and clasp his hands together in prayer. 'It's a bit fucking late for praying, Dad.'

'Aaron, that's enough.'

He turned on his heel at the sound of Cassie's voice, her warm Somerset accent mingling with an Australian drawl. His heart seemed to rise up in his chest, stopping his breath as his sister walked towards him, her arms outstretched. He couldn't move, his sadness overwhelming him, occupying every part of him, every cell fat and swollen with grief. She pulled him into a tight hug. His mother never hugged him the way Cassie did. His mother didn't like physical contact. It wasn't that their mother didn't love them – she did – she always had. It was just unfortunate that their childhood, his and Pip's, had coincided with their father being given his own parish to look after. *You have to understand, your father's parishioners are his children too. We can't be selfish,* she had said more times than Aaron could count. Cassie was the one who had played with him and Pippa. She had fed them, cared for them when they were sick, told them stories.

'She called,' he said, as a tear escaped and rolled down his cheek.

'What do you mean?' Cassie said, pushing him back and holding him at arm's length. 'When?'

'Monday.'

'You spoke to her?'

'I didn't answer,' he said. 'I was going to call her back. I *would* have called her back. Maybe if I had, I could have . . . I could have . . .'

'This is not your fault, Aaron,' Megan said, appearing at his side. He didn't know how long she had been there. 'It's no one's fault.'

He looked at her, then back at his sister. 'I think you'll find it's *someone's* fault,' Cassie said, her eyes hard.

'The police aren't sure what happened yet, Cass,' Claudette said, walking into the lounge carrying a tray laden with cups and an assortment of sandwiches cut into triangles.

'Why the hell not?' Cassie said. 'They've had, what . . . three, four days?'

'You have to let them do their job,' Claudette said. 'They know what they're doing.'

'You would say that,' Cassie said, pacing like a caged animal.

Aaron saw his aunt flinch. 'We're all upset, Cass,' Claudette said. 'Being angry about it won't bring her back.'

'We need to pray for patience and understanding,' his father said, getting to his feet and giving Cassie a cursory hug.

'I'm not really known for my patience, Dad. Or praying, come to that,' she said with a ghost of a smile.

'Me neither,' Aaron said, following his sister's lead. 'I'm more of a swift justice kinda guy.'

'It doesn't matter,' his mother said. Everyone turned to look at her. 'It doesn't matter what happened,' she said again. 'It doesn't matter who did this . . . or why. Nothing the police do – no prayers – no words will bring her back. Nothing will bring my daughter back.'

CHAPTER EIGHT

11th December – Friday

'I'm gonna grab a real coffee,' Lockyer said, striding away from Jane and the vending machine he had been eyeing for the past ten minutes.

'What about the briefing?' She broke into a jog to keep pace with him.

'I wasn't planning on collecting the beans and grinding the coffee myself,' he said over his shoulder. 'I'm sure a station as fancy as this can rustle up a takeaway cup.'

She followed in his wake, his mood coming off him in waves. At least he was talking to her. That was an improvement on yesterday, and who could blame him? Anyone who had witnessed the awkward display when Lockyer met Celia Bennett could feel nothing but pity for the guy. A group of uniformed officers passed them, kit bags thrown over their shoulders. All but one nodded a greeting in their direction. The one who didn't was sporting an elf hat. She guessed, given his sullen expression, that he was not wearing it by choice.

Jane should have expected it, been prepared, but her mind had been elsewhere. Of course her mother had insisted they all stay at the new house in Clevedon. When she told Lockyer he had assumed she was joking. And why wouldn't he? It was insane, but then, that was Celia Bennett all over. Jane had tried to explain to Lockyer that she had said no – she had said no in every way possible for forty minutes – but her mother had refused to listen. *What were you thinking, that you would drop Peter off each morning and pick him up at whatever time you finish work?* And, *The Met has so much money it's happy to waste hundreds . . . maybe thousands of pounds on hotel accommodation when you both have a place to stay right here?* Then the finale: *Would your boss prefer to stay in a hotel than here?* The answer to her rhetorical question was, of course, yes.

Lockyer had refused to speak to her, let alone share a car with her, so he had ended up catching a lift to Somerset with Townsend. She had tried to reason with her mother again on the journey down, to explain that whilst she was happy staying with Peter, it was inappropriate for Lockyer; but her pleas had fallen on deaf ears. *I've already made up the spare room. I popped to Cribbs Causeway this afternoon and got new bed-linen and towels and I'm just back from the supermarket. I've got enough food to feed you both for a week at least.* When Jane had pulled into the car park for the Bridgwater Police Centre at the Express Park trading estate she could see by Lockyer's expression that he was waiting for her to confirm that she had sorted it, that he wouldn't be subjected to her family. What could she do? Her mother's final words had been, *If DI Lockyer has a problem staying here, then you tell him to have the courtesy to call me and say so himself.* Not even Lockyer had the balls for that conversation.

It had been past ten by the time they arrived in Clevedon. The first ten minutes had been excruciating. Her father was monosyllabic, whereas her mother was like a cat on acid. The icing on the cake was Peter, who had hurled himself to the floor and barked like a seal pup as the stress of his new surroundings and companion took its toll. In the end, Jane had no choice but to manhandle him to his room and leave Lockyer and her folks to get acquainted on their own. Lockyer was yet to comment on her parents, either because he was being polite, which she doubted, or because he was still processing what had no doubt been a military-style interrogation from her mother.

'Jesus. Are we even going the right way?' he said, stopping dead, Jane ploughing into the back of him. 'We've walked past it once, I know. Which floor was it on?' She opened her mouth to speak, but he beat her to it. 'Am I going the right way for the canteen?' he said, blocking the path of a young detective Jane recognized from earlier. They had met some of Townsend's team – 'met' in the loosest sense of the word. Lockyer had badgered her out of the house by six thirty, keen to get started, but they had been twiddling their thumbs for the last thirty minutes while Townsend got everything together for a team briefing and to 'introduce' the newcomers. This guy was one of the officers who had looked up and grunted an acknowledgement when they were shown up to the CID offices.

'It's on the first floor on the other side of the concourse,' the officer said, pointing up and to the left.

The place was huge. From the outside it looked like a London skyscraper, all concrete, glass and metal, except this behemoth was lying on its side. Inside was no less impressive. It was split over three floors. The ground floor had reception, the custody suite and holding cells, the response teams, the kit room – which in itself was enormous, with multi-coloured lockers as far as the eye could see – and general office space. But it wasn't until they got past reception that the scale of the place could really be appreciated. The open-plan offices on the second and third floors that housed CID, armed response, traffic and all the other departments were divided by two full-height atriums, boasting cedarwood benches and an array of snack machines at ground level. The walkways and stairways at the end of each floor looked like they had come from an international airport. Jane didn't like to think how much it had cost. 'Thanks,' she said. 'It's . . .'

'Abbott,' he said with a scowl. Lockyer ushered Jane towards the stairs, oblivious to the animosity radiating off the junior detective. She wasn't surprised. Unlike Lockyer, she was hyper-aware that the two of them must look like the self-important Met swanning in on a local investigation – the implication being that country cops weren't up to snuff.

'Concourse,' Lockyer muttered under his breath as he started up the stairs. 'Could this place get any further up its own arse? Give me the rabbit warren of Lewisham any day of the week.'

'There you are,' a voice above them said. Jane looked up. Townsend was standing at the top of the stairway. 'Where are you two headed?'

'They were *trying* to find the canteen,' Abbott called up. The lack of 'sir' was noticeable.

'Lost, eh?' Townsend said with a smile. He beckoned

them to join him. 'I still get disorientated and I've been here for six months. I was with CID up in Bristol at Ken Steele House before, and this place couldn't be more different. What do you need?'

'We were just getting a coffee,' Lockyer said, 'while we waited for the briefing to start.' Jane knew he didn't like to be kept waiting, but this morning's hiatus seemed to be getting under his skin more than normal.

'Not to worry,' Townsend said. 'We're all set. Abbott?' He turned and caught the detective just as he turned away. 'Do you think you could rustle up a couple of coffees for our guests, please?'

Abbott looked like he would rather poke pencils up his nose. 'How do you take it?' he asked, looking from Jane to Lockyer.

'White, no sugar,' Jane offered with an apologetic smile.

'Same,' Lockyer said. He wasn't even looking at Abbott.

Townsend herded them along the walkway towards the CID offices. 'Here we are,' he said, opening the door to a large conference room. It was surrounded by floor-to-ceiling glass, with accents of black and lime green on panels hanging from the ceiling and a large oval table in the centre. 'The team are on their way.' Jane heard Lockyer sigh.

'Did you have to relocate?' she asked.

'No,' Townsend said, gesturing to two seats at the head of the table. 'Please,' he said, pulling out Jane's chair for her. She sat down, unaccustomed to such gallantry. 'I live in Clifton. It's a forty-minute commute down the M5, but I don't mind. It's twice the distance, but getting through Bristol in morning rush hour took me about the same time – and it was a lot more stressful.' He walked to the other side of the table and sat down. 'As I was telling Mike last night on the way down, I enjoyed Bristol CID; it was certainly varied. But on balance I'd say there's even more variety here – town and rural policing. It's been challenging at times, but . . .' There was a metallic clang as the glass doors opened.

'You ready for us, boss?'

Jane swivelled in her chair to see a stout-looking woman with short greying hair.

'Yes, Nicola. Tell them to come in,' Townsend said.

'What's on the agenda?' Lockyer asked, looking at his watch, then the door, then back at Townsend.

'I'll be allocating today's jobs . . .'

'Such as?' Lockyer asked. He had his pad out again.

'Well, there's the post-mortem. I'll need to arrange for you to be taken out to the crash site. We've got a lot of data to collate – reports to follow up on from the crash investigation team . . . the exhibits team.' Townsend wrinkled his nose. 'I was planning on having a proper chat with Jones's family as a starting point, and beyond that, work associates to establish a timeline, and then people local to the area – dependent on how things progress.'

'*As a starting point*,' Lockyer said to Jane out of the side of his mouth. 'He's had three days already.'

'What about CCTV coverage . . . to track her journey?' Jane asked, sitting forward.

'I've already assigned a couple of officers to speak to traffic to see what they can come up with,' Townsend said in an indulgent tone.

'Surely with traffic cameras you can follow her, if not for the entire journey, then for part of it?' Lockyer said.

'This isn't London, Mike,' Townsend said. 'The majority of the roads Pippa Jones would have used are B roads, if that. Most are no more than single-track lanes.'

'What about her digital footprint?' Lockyer asked, shaking his head. 'Have you seized her computer, phone, et cetera, for further examination?'

'We've got her phone, as it was in the vehicle with her, but it's damaged,' Townsend said. 'The forensic tech guys are yet to tell me if they can get anything off it. As for her computer, et cetera, I haven't asked the family for anything else at this stage.'

'Because?' Lockyer asked, stretching out the word. If Townsend was thrown off by the terrier-like interrogation, he didn't show it.

'It's early days, Mike,' he said. 'Pippa's death has been listed as suspicious but we can't say more than that at this stage. I don't want to jump the gun.'

'You told us yourself she was run off the road, Bill,' Lockyer said, his expression incredulous.

'Another vehicle was involved, yes,' Townsend said, 'but as I said before, we could well be looking at a drink driving incident . . . it was icy that night, which might explain the multiple collisions.' Jane bit her lip. Lockyer had told her that he and Townsend hadn't discussed the case on the way down in the car. What else hadn't he told her? It wouldn't be the first time he had withheld information. A familiar feeling of distrust settled in her stomach. 'Finding the other vehicle is my top priority as of right now.'

'I agree that we can't know at this stage whether the incident was premeditated,' Lockyer said with a frown, 'but surely we need to get into this girl's life to find out who she knew, what was happening . . . any problems she might have had?'

'If the driver of the other vehicle doesn't hand themselves in or we are unable to find them from the evidence collected so far, then of course I will certainly be *getting into* Pippa's life, but at this stage I feel moderation is the way to go.' It was clear from Townsend's tone that he was running out of patience. 'I'm sure once we have a clearer timeline we'll be in a much better position to consider what we're looking at here.'

'We're looking at murder,' Lockyer said.

'*I* am looking at manslaughter,' Townsend said, 'and until I have evidence to the contrary that is the line I am going to take. This is a close-knit community. We have a family coming to terms with the loss of their daughter . . . sister, colleague. Rushing in there talking about *murder* is unlikely to win you many friends, Mike.'

'I'm not here to make friends,' Lockyer said.

CHAPTER NINE

11th December – Friday

Lockyer watched as Townsend's team filed into the conference room. It was about bloody time. The morning was progressing at a snail's pace. Townsend and his team, not to mention the case, needed a serious kick up the arse – and it was Lockyer's job to ensure that happened, whether he liked it or not. Whatever the reason, he couldn't help but think the guy was dragging his heels. The investigation was three days old, and what had Townsend done? Well, he *had* come up to London in order to brief Lockyer, in person, on the case. Although yesterday's revelation had somewhat overshadowed his efforts. If Townsend had done even a basic check on the Met DI he had driven all that way to meet, he would have no doubt seen that Lockyer had a PC Aaron Jones working on his team, and that the victim just so happened to have a twin brother of the same name.

Lockyer pinched the bridge of his nose, ignoring Jane's searching look. He hadn't had a chance to tell her about his meeting with Roger – about the array of phone calls bouncing back and forth about Townsend's competence. And no wonder. She had put him in an impossible situation. He had witnessed Celia Bennett in action, albeit while earwigging conversations between Jane and her mother over the years. Call it cowardice, but he wasn't about to reject the woman's hospitality by phone, let alone in person. So now, on top of everything else, he was being forced to take part in an episode of *Keeping Up Appearances.*

'Sir,' a female officer in her thirties said as she passed him. She was shaped just like a pear. Her torso was almost funhouse long, giving way to an enormous arse and the shortest legs he had ever seen.

'Detective,' he said with a nod. She was the only one of Townsend's team that had so much as acknowledged him – or Jane, for that matter, in spite of the obsequious smile plastered on her face.

'Is that everyone?' Townsend asked, closing the door and walking to stand behind him and Jane. There was a murmur of yeses. When Lockyer ran a meeting, his team arrived on time, and each and every one of them would address him as 'sir' when they entered the room and throughout the meeting. Maybe Townsend was more relaxed – which would be fine, but that wasn't the vibe Lockyer was getting. He wouldn't go as far as to say Townsend's team were hostile, but they couldn't be described as welcoming or respectful. It made him wonder if his first impression of the guy was off base somehow. The higher-ups didn't like him. His team didn't appear to like him either. There had to be a reason.

'Thank you all for coming,' Townsend said, addressing the room. 'We'll get on to this morning's briefing in a moment, but first I'd like to formally introduce you to DI

Mike Lockyer and DS Jane Bennett from the Metropolitan Police.' There were a few murmurs, though whether they were positive or negative, Lockyer couldn't tell. 'They are going to be working with us to establish the events leading up to and including the death of Miss Pippa Jones on the evening of the seventh of December.'

'Not a lot to establish,' a lanky-looking officer on the opposite side of the table said. It was the same guy Lockyer and Jane had spoken to just now about the canteen. 'Some arsehole ran her off the road.'

'That, detective, is a matter of opinion,' Townsend said. 'As I've said before, whilst tragic, I am inclined to think this may come to nothing more than . . .' He seemed to be struggling to find the words. 'A . . . a non-malicious hit and run, most likely involving alcohol. In which case, we will say thank you and goodbye to our Met colleagues, who I'm sure have better things to do than chase down a drunk driver.' It was the first time Lockyer had heard real fire in Townsend's voice. He couldn't agree with his statement, but he respected his level of passion at least.

'Why the Met?' one of the female officers asked.

Lockyer looked at the grey-haired detective who had spoken. Her expression was unreadable.

'Well, Nicola,' Townsend said. 'As the victim in this case was primarily London-based, Superintendent Atkinson felt it prudent to have the Met's input from the outset.' He cleared his throat. 'There will no doubt be instances where we will need to see or speak to family members or associates of the victim, and in all likelihood they too will be based in London. That's where DI Lockyer and DS Bennett come in.'

He paused for a moment. 'So we are very grateful to them for taking time out of their busy caseloads to come and give us a hand on this one.' Again there were murmurs from the assembled team.

'So,' Townsend said, stretching out the word. 'Quick introductions. On my right –' he gestured to the grey-haired officer – 'this is DC Nicola Chandler. Continuing on round to the right, we've got DS Nathan Foster, DC Daniel Pimbley and DS Ben Abbott. Then we've got DS Clare Dunlop, DC Daniel Clark . . . or the other Daniel, as we call him.' He laughed. None of the team joined him, not even 'the other' Daniel. 'And this is PC Charles Farley and, last but not least, PC Emma Crossley.' Lockyer nodded to each one in turn, Crossley with the big bottom last. She nodded, but none of the others did. He bristled, but managed to keep his mouth shut.

'Who's running the case?' the long streak of piss asked.

'Sorry, what was your name again, detective?' Lockyer asked before he could stop himself.

'Detective Sergeant Abbott,' he said, folding his arms.

Lockyer had to use all his self-control to stay in his seat. 'Sir or boss will be fine,' he said. Abbott shrugged but didn't speak. 'Jane,' he said, turning to face her. 'How would you like to be addressed while you're here?' He gave her a warning look. She knew what he wanted her to say. She always knew what he wanted her to say.

'DS Bennett is fine,' she said, although he could see that she was saying it under duress. She would no doubt have said they could all call her Jane. That might work in a day or two, but right now Lockyer felt like they needed to put on a united front. He didn't need a 'sir' or 'boss' to blow smoke up his arse, but Abbott struck him as the kind of copper who would take the piss if you gave him the proverbial inch.

'Good, good,' Townsend said in an apologetic tone. Lockyer was unsure if he was apologizing *to* him or *for* him.

He pushed his seat back and stood up beside Townsend. 'Fantastic. Now we all know who's who and what's what, I suggest we get started. As DI Townsend rightly said, DS Bennett and I are busy people, so don't dick us around and we'll return the favour. OK?' He looked at Abbott, holding his eye until he looked away. Lockyer might not be able to *say* he was in charge, but he wanted these guys in no doubt who was calling the shots. He couldn't say yet whether Townsend was incompetent, but there was no doubt the guy was weak. He and his team were about to get a crash course in investigations *à la* Lockyer. By the looks he was getting around the room, it was going to be a baptism of fire for them – and him.

CHAPTER TEN

'Yeah, I had prawns last night,' Steph said, trying to make her voice sound croaky. 'They must have been off. I've been up all night.'

'Oh dear,' Connie said without sympathy.

Who could blame her? This was the third day that Steph had called in sick, and it was her third excuse. She realized now she should have come up with a better lie on the first day: a virus, the flu. That way she could have been off for several days, maybe even a week without causing an issue. 'I feel awful,' she said.

'You're not having a lot of luck, are you, Steph? You get bitten by a dog, have an allergic reaction to the tetanus jab and now you've gone and *given yourself* food poisoning.'

'I know,' she said. 'It's just not been my week.'

There was a pause at the other end of the line. 'Well, you see, that's the thing, Steph,' Connie said. 'It doesn't seem to be your week a lot.'

'I . . .'

'You've been with us for, what, two months? And how

many times have you called in sick or turned up late? To be honest with you, I've lost count.' It was true. Steph had hated the job at first, sweeping up hair and making cups of tea. It was so boring. She couldn't have cared less if she was fired then, but she didn't feel like that any more. This was a way out. This was her chance to be independent, to be a grown-up. She was eighteen. She was driving and yet she still felt like a little girl, living with her parents, having to ask permission to go out, to do anything. 'I'm beginning to wonder,' Connie said, 'if you really want this job, Stephanie. Many girls your age would jump at the chance to train *and* be paid at the same time.'

'I *do* want this job,' Steph said, realizing too late that she had forgotten to sound sick.

'Then you need to seriously consider whether or not you want to come in today.'

'But I really don't think I—'

Her boss didn't let her finish. 'Don't decide now, Steph,' she said. 'Your shift doesn't start until two, so there's plenty of time for you to have a think and, with any luck, be well enough to come in.'

'OK,' she said. What else could she say?

'And you need to understand, Steph, that if you do decide that you are too ill to come in to work again today, then you and I are going to be having a serious chat when you get back. I hope you understand me. No one can help it if they are sick, I know that, but there's sick and then there's sick. Do you hear what I'm saying?' The words dried up in Steph's throat. She felt so stupid; so weak. 'I am giving you a chance here, Steph. You come in for your shift this afternoon and that will be the end of it, OK? This conversation never took place . . . all's forgotten, OK?'

'OK,' she said in a whisper. 'I'll be in this afternoon.'

'That's good, Steph, that's really good to hear,' Connie said. 'Now, until then, you rest up and take it easy and then this afternoon we'll all get back to work.'

'Yes.'

'Great,' Connie said. 'We'll see you in a few hours.' The line went dead before Steph could respond. Who called in sick because of a dog bite? Of course Connie didn't believe her, but then no one ever did – even when she told the truth.

Her father had noticed the damage to her car, but when she told him what happened he had waved away her 'story' with a dismissive hand, taking two beers out of the fridge. *You're getting a bit old for stories, Stephanie,* he had said. *How many times have I told you? Driving is a privilege, not a right.* He had been furious, banging his fist on the kitchen table, making the cutlery jump. *Who's going to pay for the damage? Muggins here, I suppose.* She had made the mistake of saying it wasn't the only damage on the car, given that it wasn't brand new when he bought it for her. The rest of the conversation had been loud and one-sided. Steph had started to cry, then and now as she relived the argument. She dropped her phone and lay back down on her bed, pressing her face into the duvet, letting the fabric soak up her tears. Why wouldn't they listen? Couldn't they see how frightened she was?

It had all started two weeks ago. She had been out on a bender with Connor and Ash, who convinced her to drive them home even though she was way over the limit. They had all been drinking in the Hood Arms over in Kilve. The boys lived in Dunster, the complete opposite direction to Cannington, but she had never been very good at saying no. Connor and Ash kept goading her to go faster. *Don't be such a girl,* they had shouted. She had almost lost it when she rounded a corner and another car was racing towards her in the middle of the road. She had flicked off her full beam only to find she was driving way too fast now she couldn't see as far. Connor had screamed when she swerved. Ash had laughed until she thought he would cough up a lung. When they finally got to Dunster, Steph had gone to Ash's flat first. It was a dingy room he rented over a pub. She didn't go in, and breathed a sigh of relief when Connor climbed out of the car after Ash and said he was going to stay there, that they were going to keep on drinking. She made a weak excuse and left, never more grateful to be alone in the car. She knew if Connor had wanted her to take him home he would have expected a detour to the field next to his parents' place. It had happened before, more times than she cared to remember; sticky fumbles in the back of her clapped-out Ford Fiesta followed by some pushing, some grunting, and then it would all be over. He would slap her on the arse as she pulled up her knickers, then climb out of the back seat, wipe himself on his jeans and be gone, climbing over the back fence and letting himself in the back door with a key he had stolen out of his mother's bag. His parents didn't know he drank. His parents didn't know much. She wriggled herself under the duvet, and breathed in the smell of fabric softener.

'Do you want breakfast?' she heard her mother call from downstairs.

She took a deep breath. She felt sick at the thought of it, but she couldn't avoid the day any longer. 'OK,' she shouted back. 'I'm just getting in the shower now.' She threw back the duvet, swung her legs out over the edge of the bed and sat up. She didn't need to open her curtains to know it was raining. She could smell it, soaking into the thatch of her parents' cottage, dampening the walls. A spread of something fungal was growing up her wall behind her bookshelf.

'Don't use all the hot water,' her mother called from the bottom of the stairs. 'Your father will be back from his shift soon.'

'It's a combi-boiler, Mum,' she said, padding down the hallway in her socks. 'It can't run out of hot water.'

'It takes longer to heat if you have a long shower,' her mother said.

'Fine,' Steph said. 'It doesn't,' she continued under her breath, 'but since when does anyone listen to me?' She shut the door to the bathroom, pulled the curtain around the bath and turned on the shower. She picked up her toothbrush and toothpaste, climbed in and stepped into the flow of warm water. As soon as she closed her eyes it all came back to her in fleeting images, flashing before her eyes like a strobe light.

She had just passed Washford when she noticed the car behind her. It was close on her bumper, so close she couldn't see the driver. Her first thought was that it might be the police. She knew if they stopped her she would lose her licence.

She opened her eyes and grabbed her toothbrush and toothpaste, squeezed a glob onto the brush and started to clean her teeth.

The lights had been blinding, a combination of cold white and blue light. She had been convinced they were flashing at her. Maybe they had been. She still didn't know. Her skin flushed hot at the memory. She had been desperate to stop, to pull in somewhere to let the car pass, but she hadn't had the nerve; not least because she was about to drive her least favourite stretch of the A39. By day it was a beautiful route with views of the Bristol Channel and, on a clear day, Wales. The hills on the other side of the car rolled out into the distance, covered in gorse and heather and wild ponies munching on any grass they could find. But at night it changed. It became a pale slash on the landscape, the sea black and ominous, the hills remote and barren. Almost every ghost story she had been told as a child involved the Quantocks.

The one she remembered – the one her friends still told – was about the young couple who had driven up past Pines Cafe to make out. They had been getting down to it when the boyfriend heard a sound coming from the woods – a baby crying. He got out of the car and walked into the forest, walking further and further, desperate to find the child. It wasn't long before his girlfriend couldn't see him at all. He was swallowed up by the darkness and she was left alone. She waited and waited. Minutes turned into hours, her only company the sound of the woods, branches creaking, scraping the roof of the car. She opened her window and called out again and again, but she was too frightened to get out of the car. When the police found her the next day they told her to get out of the car, to come with them but not to look back. But she did. She did look back and saw her boyfriend, strung up by his feet over the car, his throat cut, his fingernails scraping the roof as the wind moved the tree he was hanging from.

Steph shivered and turned up the heat on the shower. It was just a story, but that and her fear of losing her licence had been enough to make her keep driving. She spat out a mouthful of toothpaste, and ran her toothbrush under the shower.

'Your father's home,' her mother said from outside the bathroom door.

'I'm almost done,' she said.

'He'll want to jump straight in the shower,' her mother said, 'best leave it running.'

'Fine,' she said, grabbing the soap and washing herself.

When she was done she pulled back the curtain and climbed out, grabbing her towel off the radiator. She patted herself dry before getting back into her pyjamas. As she opened the door she could hear her father telling her mother all about his shift and what an arsehole his boss was. 'Shower's running, Dad,' she called.

'Thanks, honey,' he said. 'I'll be right up.' She ran across the landing to her room. It sounded like he was in a good mood. Maybe if she asked, he might agree to take her to work. The thought quickened her pulse. She would give anything not have to drive home tonight.

It was as she passed Frog Lane that she had felt the impact from behind her. There had been a low thud as the two bumpers connected. She was jolted in her seat, and the shock made her throw up in her mouth – just a little. She had gripped the steering wheel with two hands. At first she had tried to convince herself that it was an accident, but when a second thud threw her forward in her seat, her seatbelt cutting into her stomach, she knew she was wrong. Without thinking she had begun to accelerate. She passed Kilve in a blur, desperate to put distance between herself and the car behind, but even more so to get off the hills. She didn't want to die up here, alone in the dark.

There was a soft tapping at her door.

'Honey,' her father said. 'You decent?'

'Just a second,' she said, grabbing an oversized jumper and pulling it on over her head.

The door to her bedroom opened. 'You OK?' her father asked. She nodded, swallowing back tears. 'I'm sorry about yesterday.' She didn't speak. 'If you say you were ill, of course I believe you. I'd had a long shift, I was knackered. These nights are killing me, you know that.' She nodded again. 'I remember what it was like to be your age,' he said, 'to have more important things on your mind than work, but seriously, honey –' he took a step towards her – 'I'm only thinking of you. If you can keep this job, work up through the ranks and get some qualifications, it's going to mean everything. You'll be able to do what you want . . . that's about the only perk there is to being an adult. The rest is responsibility and regret.' His face clouded over. She recognized the expression. She knew her parents' marriage had been over the day she was born.

'Are you working tonight, Dad?' she asked.

'I've got a late afternoon shift, yes,' he said, turning to leave, 'so I'd better get showered and get some kip. I've got to be out of here again in a few hours.'

'Would I be able to . . . would you mind giving me a lift to work?'

'Can do,' he said. 'Why?' He frowned. 'What's wrong with your car? What's happened now?'

She shook her head. 'Nothing, it's just—'

He held up his hand. 'Don't, Steph,' he said, 'just don't.'

Why wouldn't he listen? She felt the tears wanting to come. 'I . . . I just thought it'd save on petrol, if we're both going that way,' she said, swallowing the lump in her throat.

He looked at her, paused for a second and then shrugged. 'Fine,' he said. 'Only thing is I don't finish 'til half ten. How will you get home? You finish at six, don't you?'

'Not today,' she lied. 'They want me to stay behind to help set up for tomorrow. There's a load of people coming in to get their hair done for a Christmas party.'

'OK,' he said, looking at his watch, 'but be ready to go by one.' He turned away and left the room.

She closed the door after him, and went and sat on the edge of her bed. Her eyes pricked with tears. She felt overwhelmed with relief. She wouldn't have to drive home in the dark. She wouldn't have to risk it happening again. Once had frightened her. Once should have been enough, but it hadn't happened just once. It had happened again on Tuesday last week. They hadn't hit her this time, but they had ridden her bumper for over two miles. She didn't know it was the same car, and yet she did. She lay back on her bed, rolled onto her side and brought her legs up into the foetal position, rocking herself back and forth. When it had happened again on Thursday she had been left in no doubt. Someone wanted to frighten her; maybe even hurt her. She took a deep breath.

At least she would be OK tonight. She would be safe with her father.

CHAPTER ELEVEN

11th December – Friday

Lockyer leaned back against the stainless-steel countertop. The bench ran almost the full length of the room. It was interspersed with sinks, hoses, drawers of utensils and three sets of weighing scales suspended above. There were four permanent mortuary tables, each with their own sink, overhead light and white plastic rollers along the edges of the table to assist with the loading and unloading of the trays that carried the bodies to be examined. Above and behind Lockyer was the viewing room. Panels of glass on a forty-five-degree angle looked down on him. It was an impressive set-up.

'You OK there?'

He looked to his left as Dr Basil Reed, the senior pathologist for the county, walked into the room. 'Yes,' Lockyer said. 'Are you OK with me here?'

Basil nodded, pulling a plastic apron from a dispensing roll by the door. 'Sure,' he said, putting it over his head and tying it in a knot at his back. 'You might want to get a bit closer once we get down to it, but for now that's perfect.' He picked up some gloves off the end of the bench, passed Lockyer, and joined his colleague at the far left-hand table.

Nigel, Basil's assistant, had wheeled Pippa's body in from the fridge room ten minutes ago. He had transferred her onto the post-mortem table, head at the top end, nearest the sink resting on a block, her body covered with a piece of plastic sheeting. It did nothing to mask the smell. Lockyer had only witnessed half a dozen post-mortems on burn victims. He would have been happy not to add to that number. The smell was hard to describe. It came in waves. There was a smell like frying steak, overlaid with burning pork fat. The odour was by no means pleasant, as the dominant smell was sulphur. It burnt his eyes and stung his nostrils. He was about to take a deep breath, but thought better of it.

'Not much like London, I'd imagine,' Basil said over his shoulder.

Lockyer thought he sounded apologetic, as if the facility were somehow lesser than its London counterpart. 'It's bigger,' he said.

'They have their own on-site mortuary in Lewisham,' Townsend said over the speaker system. He had chosen to stay in the viewing room.

'Ah,' Basil said. 'I'm sure that must expedite things for you.'

'It can do,' Lockyer said, 'but our place is nothing like this. This is purpose-built, I take it?'

'Yes,' Townsend said, answering for the doctor. 'It opened in March 2009.'

'Two point three million,' Basil said in a hushed voice,

looking at Lockyer over his shoulder and raising his eyebrows. 'We've got the two rooms, one general and this one, forensic.'

'Impressive,' Lockyer said, and he meant it. When Townsend had pulled off the motorway and started driving further and further into the countryside, Lockyer had expected to find something out of date and old-fashioned. The building itself was nothing to look at: a modern single-storey block, with rows of opaque windows and a high pitched roof. There was nothing to indicate what went on inside. It was tucked away behind the main coroner's court, which was anything but plain; more like some gothic National Trust place, with lead lattice windows and gabled half-dormers.

'It replaced all the hospital mortuaries in the area,' Townsend continued. 'It's state of the art.'

Lockyer looked up over his shoulder. 'I don't doubt it,' he said. Townsend was standing above him to his right. It might have been the glass, but he looked pale. 'You don't have to stay and observe, Bill. I can manage.'

'No, no, I'm—'

'There's no point us both being here,' Lockyer said, cutting him off. 'I'm guessing . . .' He turned back to Basil. 'I'm guessing this will take a couple of hours.'

'About that,' Basil said.

'In which case,' Lockyer said, 'you may as well head back to the station.'

'How will you get back?' Townsend asked. He had already started to move towards the door.

'I'll get Jane to pick me up on her way back to Clevedon. We can't be far away . . .'

'Twenty minutes,' Nigel said, holding up his gloved hand and rocking it from side to side. 'Give or take.'

'Perfect,' Lockyer said. 'I thought as much.' He turned again to look up at Townsend. 'You go, Bill,' he said. 'There's nothing else scheduled for today.' *More's the pity*, he wanted to add but didn't. 'We won't have the accident report back until Monday; most of the interviews are scheduled for after the weekend. If there's anything significant here, I'll call you. I'll be in tomorrow, even if Jane isn't. I know she's seeing Jones's employer over at Fyne Court. One of your lot is taking her up there – not sure what time. I've got a meeting with the paint specialists booked in for the afternoon.' He registered Townsend's surprise. 'I don't know a lot about it, so wanted to familiarize myself with the process . . . especially if the paint transfer from the other car is going to be significant when it comes to finding the other driver.'

Townsend appeared to hesitate, but only for a moment. 'Fine,' he said. 'I'll go.'

'Great,' Lockyer said, turning away. He didn't want to see Townsend's face as he left. There was no doubt he needed a push, but still, railroading the guy didn't feel good.

The sun had been shining when they left Express Park. Townsend had started out like a hyperactive tour guide, pointing out the Somerset sites as they travelled up the M5. However, by the time they reached Weston-super-Mare the weather had changed and they were driving through sleet and snow. The London weather had made its way down to them, it seemed. The downpour had mirrored the mood in the car. The longer they were alone, the longer it was they weren't talking about the briefing, or the conversation beforehand when Lockyer had all but told Townsend he wasn't running the investigation right.

He half listened to Basil and Nigel talking in hushed voices as they continued the external examination of Pippa's body – her remains. She didn't have a body any more. The fire had seen to that. Lockyer moved towards the table and clasped his hands behind his back. He wanted to take notes, but Basil had said he would give him a copy of the post-mortem tape, so anything he wanted to highlight, he should just speak up and it would be recorded. In Lewisham Dr Dave Simpson didn't like anyone to speak when he was working, but then, Lockyer guessed every pathologist had their own approach.

'You ready for the internal examination?' Nigel asked.

'Yes,' Basil said, walking to the back of the room and collecting a stainless-steel tray covered in equipment: scalpels, forceps, scissors, rib shears and an instrument called a skull key. Lockyer licked his lips wishing he had said yes when he was offered a glass of water. He had always found the examination of the skull and brain the hardest to stomach. He couldn't stand seeing a person's face folded back on itself. If he timed it right, he could excuse himself at the opportune moment and miss that part of the procedure.

'Anything on the external worth noting?' he asked.

'Nothing unexpected,' Basil said, looking at him over the rim of his glasses. It reminded Lockyer of Dave: he did the same, now he wore glasses. 'The victim has first-degree burns covering about . . . I'd say seventy-five per cent of her body. Would you agree, Nigel?'

'I'd say less,' Nigel said, his mouth turning down at the corner. 'Sixty, sixty-five maybe?'

Basil took a step back and looked at the remains again. 'Fair enough,' he said. 'Let's meet in the middle and call it seventy, shall we?'

'Sure,' Nigel said. 'I'll go with that.'

'There's a significant amount of bruising and evidence of trauma,' Basil continued. 'You can see here –' he gestured for Lockyer to join them at the table – 'you can see where the seatbelt has cut into the sternum here.' He indicated a livid mark at the top of Pippa's left breast. 'You can also see, despite the burns, that she has a head contusion on the front right of her temple.'

'Her head hit the driver's-side window,' Lockyer said, remembering the crash scene photographs of the car he had been through this morning.

'That would do it, yes,' Basil said. 'The charring is quite severe around her face, so it's difficult to see, but Nigel noticed she has a broken nose.' He looked up at Lockyer as if waiting for him to explain the injury.

'The air bag didn't deploy, so no doubt she made contact with the steering wheel before . . .' Lockyer said.

'It melted?'

'Yes.'

'Yes, I remember,' Basil said. 'I was on site during the recovery. I had to insist they remove the entire seat with the body still attached. There was no way she could come out without it – we would have lost half the evidence . . . not to mention her.' Lockyer frowned. Hadn't Townsend told him that *he* was the one who decided Pippa's body and the driver's seat had to be removed in their entirety?

'DI Townsend was present?' he asked.

'Of course,' Basil said. 'Although he left before the fire team cut her out.' Lockyer wasn't sure that meshed with what Townsend had said either.

'She has three tattoos that I've been able to identify,' Nigel said. 'There may be more, but . . .' He gestured to Pippa's charred remains. 'Anyway, we've got one on her outside left ankle. It's an infinity sign. A cross on her left shoulder blade . . .'

'The father's a vicar,' Lockyer said.

'That doesn't always follow, detective,' Basil said. 'Do you have children?'

'Yes, a daughter,' he said with a slow nod. He had texted Megan the second he found out Pippa was Aaron's sister. He knew where she would be, and he was right. When he managed to get her on the phone she told him she had driven Aaron and his parents down to Somerset. Worse than that, she was now staying with them in the family home. It was too close for Lockyer's comfort. It was all too close. As Jane had pointed out in the car this morning, if Megan and Aaron were married, Pippa would have been Megan's sister-in-law. He shook his head. Did Jane think these titbits were helpful? Didn't she get it? He didn't want his daughter anywhere near any of this mess. He looked down at Pippa's blackened body and sighed. But yet again Megan was in the thick of it, dismissing his concerns like he was the one with the problem.

'Does your daughter want to be a police officer?'

'I doubt it,' Lockyer said with a snort. 'She hates my job.'

Basil held up his hands. 'As is often the way, detective. Children rarely follow the paths we have chosen. Anyway, what's the third tattoo, Nigel?'

'It's a silhouette of an eagle or some other bird of prey,' Nigel said, pointing. 'It's on her torso just under her left breast.' Lockyer craned his neck to see the tattoo of the bird. It was in flight, its head directed away from Pippa's body. He bent forward to get a closer look. The ink was buried deep in Pippa's soot-covered skin. 'That's it. No other identifying marks.'

'Right,' Basil said, resting his hand on the tray of instruments. 'Then let's get started on the internal examination, shall we?'

Lockyer checked his phone. He had a text. It was from Megan:

Hi Dad, how's it going? Fancy a coffee over the weekend? You say where. Happy to come to you. I spoke to Jane – hear you're staying with her folks ;-) Aaron told me you guys are coming Monday for a chat with the family. I'll make myself scarce. Don't want you worrying. Spoke to uni. My tutor's forwarding my coursework by email so no probs with end of term. Love you xx p.s. don't be angry with me. Aaron needs me.

Lockyer rolled his eyes and groaned. He took issue with several things, speaking to Jane being one. Since when were they buddies? Missing uni was another. And the final nail in the coffin – Aaron *needed* her. He shook his head.

'Are you with us, detective?' Basil asked.

'Sorry,' he said, pocketing his phone.

'If you need to make a call, please feel free to leave the room,' Basil said, his eyebrows halfway up his forehead.

'No, no,' Lockyer said. 'I apologize. It was a message from my daughter. I wouldn't normally check it during . . . this.' He gestured around him. 'But . . .'

'But you're her father and you can't help yourself?' Basil said, smiling.

Lockyer blew out a frustrated breath. 'That's about the size of it, yes,' he said. 'You got kids?'

'Seven,' Basil said.

'Christ, seven?' Lockyer's mouth fell open. 'How did you . . . ? How do you . . . ? I only have the one and I'm lost.'

'You get better at it as you go along,' Basil said, turning back to the mortuary table, unclipping the folded-back skin and muscle that was exposing Pippa's chest cavity. 'By number four my wife and I had discovered the secret.'

'I'm all ears,' Lockyer said, folding his arms.

'Control is an illusion,' Basil said. 'Your children are their own person from the day they arrive in the world, detective. They are pre-programmed to go their own way. To deny them that, to hold them back, to bend them to your will is to deny them life. Parents mistake responsibility for control. Those early years when they rely on you for everything makes the parent believe they are in charge, but it isn't true. We are merely caretakers. After that, all you can do is watch and worry.'

'Sorry,' Lockyer said, frowning. 'What's the secret again?'

Basil laughed. 'Learning to enjoy your life *in spite* of all the worry.' When he smiled the lines around his eyes multiplied and deepened. This guy had been around the proverbial block many, many more times than Lockyer had, or ever would. 'Be grateful for the times they *do* listen,' he said, 'and have faith that they will do the right thing when they don't.'

'Not easy for a man in my profession,' Lockyer said.

Basil shrugged. 'That's life, I'm afraid. And talking of life . . .' He had opened up the bottom half of Pippa's body, revealing her lower bowel and reproductive organs. The organs on the right-hand side appeared dry, split open in places, no doubt due to the heat of the fire. 'See here,' he said, pointing to the other side.

'What am I looking at?' Lockyer asked, peering at the mess of tissue, fat and muscle.

'This here,' Basil said, hooking his finger beneath a pale section of tissue. 'This is part of the victim's fallopian tube. This here is scarring. She had a tubal pregnancy at some stage.'

'And that is?' Lockyer asked. His knowledge of anatomy was limited at best.

'It's where a fertilized egg implants outside the womb; in this case it implanted in the fallopian tube. Otherwise known as ectopic pregnancy.' Basil motioned for Nigel to take over. 'Try and remove as much as you can intact, Nigel,' he said. 'It'll be difficult with the damage, but do your best.' Nigel stepped forward and picked up a scalpel.

'Would she have been hospitalized?' Lockyer asked. From the file he recalled the parents saying there was no boyfriend on the scene. 'Can you tell me when it happened?'

'Not necessarily, no,' Basil said. 'Some ectopic pregnancies resolve on their own. The foetus dies and is reabsorbed back into the woman's body all but for the scarring you see here.'

'And when?'

'I can't say, I'm afraid,' he said.

'I'm having trouble here,' Nigel said. 'I can't get the left-hand side out intact. It's like dealing with two different bodies.'

'Hang on,' Basil said, 'let me have a look.'

Lockyer watched with a mixture of fascination and disgust as Basil moved the blackened tissue, cutting every so often with his scalpel, his incisions quick and precise. Within a few minutes he had removed Pippa's uterus, fallopian tubes and what Lockyer assumed were her ovaries. The two sides couldn't have been more different. On the left side the tissue was pink, surrounded by sinew and yellowish fat. On the right everything was blackened and shrivelled. There was no resemblance between the two sides. 'The damage is unreal,' he said to no one in particular.

'Yes,' Basil said with a sigh. 'I'm afraid the kind of heat she would have been exposed to simply devastates the body, the tissues.' He used his wrist to push his glasses back up his nose where they had slipped down. 'Her parents can be thankful she didn't suffer for long, though I doubt that will be much comfort right now.'

Lockyer nodded. 'Sure. She was killed pretty much on impact, right?'

'That would have been the kindest thing,' Basil said, 'but no. I'm afraid there's evidence she was at least conscious when the fire took hold.'

'What evidence?' Lockyer asked.

Basil frowned, but stood back and picked up Pippa's left arm. 'You can see here,' he said, 'that the tissue has been all but removed from her palm and fingers where she tried to open the door.'

Lockyer felt his stomach drop. 'I'm sorry, can you explain that to me? I was under the impression she died from the head injury coupled with smoke inhalation from the engine fire. I assumed that would be pretty immediate.' He could taste bile in his mouth as the smell of Pippa's burnt flesh hit the back of his throat.

'I'm afraid not,' Basil said. 'Remnants of skin and fat were found on the driver's-side door, where we're supposing the victim tried to free herself.' He turned his body to the right, reaching both arms across himself as he mimed trying to open a door with his hands positioned side by side. 'This would have been after the fire had made its way into the main body of the vehicle. Her skin would have bonded to the door leather, hence the damage you see here,' he said, gesturing to what remained of Pippa's hand. 'DI Townsend and I discussed all of this at the scene. It was the reason I asked for her body to be removed with the seat to prevent further damage.'

Lockyer shook his head. Either he was going mad, or Townsend had said Pippa had died *before* the fire took hold. 'I'm surprised DI Townsend didn't mention it.'

'So am I,' Lockyer said.

CHAPTER TWELVE

11th December – Friday

Jane wound her scarf around her neck several times as she climbed out of her car. She should have brought gloves; the temperature had dropped on the way up here. As if to prove it, there was a fine dusting of snow covering the car park and the grassy banks surrounding it. In contrast the woodland floor appeared dry, a thick blanket of pine needles protected from the elements by the evergreens towering above her.

She shivered, slammed her door, locked it and headed for the path. She spotted a map of the area, but before she could get to it she slipped. She managed to right herself at the last second before looking down at her feet to identify what had made her stumble. There was a clear impression of her heel and subsequent slip in the wet mud that was lurking beneath the snow. She looked back at her car. She had parked on an incline, her front wheels nestled in the edge of a grass bank. Was she going to be able to get out of there? 'Great,' she said to herself, looking up at the sky. The clouds were low and threatening above the trees, the light fading. It would be dark within the hour. She had better tell the ranger guy she was meeting that they would have to be quick.

The offices for the Area of Outstanding Natural Beauty were tucked away beside the main entrance to Fyne Court, the sprawling National Trust property where Pippa had been working. Jane had already been up to the main house when she missed the turning to the AONB offices. She and DC Pimbley were booked in to see the catering manager, Derek Cooper, tomorrow morning. As she crunched along the shale path, she wondered how they would get up here if it snowed overnight. She had spent the majority of her journey over from Express Park on the A39, but once off that it was all single-track lanes. When she came across another car she had to stop, waiting for the obligatory standoff while each driver decided who was going to give way – or who had the talent to reverse. Lucky for her, everyone she met was in a 4x4. They just drove up onto the bank or into a hedge to let her pass. She would raise a hand in thanks and get a beaming smile and cheerful nod in return. They were a courteous bunch.

At one point she was sure she was going round in circles as she drove around, over, up and down the hills, never finding the actual hill Fyne Court was on. Her circuitous journey hadn't been helped by her out-of-date satnav. In the end she had stopped by a disused telephone box and asked a woman out walking two golden retrievers. Jane had listened to the detailed instructions; left, then left, then right, then left, then another two lefts and she would be there. She had made it to her destination, although the number of lefts and rights bore no resemblance to the ones described.

She reached out and steadied herself against a massive pine

tree, its trunk well over six feet around. The evergreens provided the only colour in the canopy above her. Their deciduous cousins reached out bare branches like fingers, clinging on for safety until their leaves returned. There had been places on the drive over where the trees and brambles were so intertwined above her that no light penetrated. More than once she had driven into shade so dark she put her foot down, longing to come out the other side. She wasn't skittish by nature, but her mother had been telling Peter all about the Quantock legends over breakfast – the ghost dog being one of them. Jane had only been half listening, but something must have stuck in her mind. The sound of a breaking twig made her turn too fast.

'Detective Bennett?'

Jane lost her footing and went down. 'Bloody hell,' she said, lifting her hands up, snow, mud and water now dripping off them. Her arse was very wet and very cold. A large hand entered her field of vision.

'Sorry. Didn't mean to frighten you.' She pulled on the proffered hand and managed to get to her feet, aided by another strong hand at her waist. She planted her feet and looked up, then up again. Where she would have expected to find his head she found she was still looking at his chest. 'I'm Barney,' he said.

'Wow,' she said, as her heels were sucked into the mud with a squelching sound. His hand was warm, dry and – like the man attached to it – huge. She had always been petite, so feeling small wasn't new to her, but she had never, not since she was a child, felt this small. Her hand disappeared in his – it was like a dinner plate. He reminded her of the Jaws character in the James Bond movies, except he had, she could see, beautiful teeth and an open, smiling face. Now that she thought about it, he was more like the BFG from the Roald Dahl story.

'I know,' he said. 'I'm tall.'

'No, no . . . I mean, well, yes.'

'Don't worry,' he said. 'I tend to have that effect on folks first time they meet me.'

She looked him up and down. 'What are you, six five?' She was used to being dwarfed by Lockyer, but this was ridiculous.

'Six seven,' Barney said, running his hand over his chin, which was covered in an impressive beard the colour of dark chocolate. He was wearing walking boots, dark green combat trousers, a matching collared T-shirt and a fleece, again the same colour, that said 'AONB Ranger' underneath a silhouette of a bird of prey. She had seen the same image on signposts on her drive over.

'I'm Detective Sergeant Jane Bennett,' she said, extending her hand. He looked down at it and back at her before she remembered the mud. 'Sorry.'

'This way,' he said. 'You can get cleaned up before we head over to the crash site.'

'Thank you.'

She followed behind him, taking care to step where he stepped. 'When did it snow?' she asked.

He glanced over his shoulder as he spoke. 'This morning,' he said, 'but it'll be off and on all day, I reckon.'

'We're forecast more later, I heard.'

'Normal forecasts don't really hold true up here,' he said. 'We've got our own microclimate. More so the higher you go. It can be ten degrees colder up here than down in Taunton.'

'I was just thinking it must be a nightmare to get up there when it really snows.'

'My 4x4 will get me most places,' he said. 'Although some winters I've had to park down at the bottom of Buncombe Hill and walk up.'

'I'd be calling in sick,' she said.

They approached a stone building and he walked to the right, into an open courtyard. 'Here we are,' he said, rounding the corner. 'This is the main site office. The admin and management lot work out of here.'

'And the rangers?'

'There's three of us,' he said, punching in a code before opening the door and gesturing for her to go first. 'The other two are part-time.'

'Are they here?'

'No,' he said, shaking his head. 'They're on radio, but I haven't heard from them for a bit.' He gestured to a small radio attached to his belt.

Jane looked around. The office was like any other. She could have been in a Portakabin instead of a converted barn. There were eight desks as far as she could tell, two sets of four facing each other, with the traditional felt-covered partitions. Each was littered with notes, maps and bits of paper pinned to every last bit of available space. Over by the door there was a fridge and a tiny kitchen area comprising sink, kettle and toaster. She gestured towards the sink. 'May I?' He nodded.

She rinsed her hands, drying them on a tea towel hanging on a broom handle. There was a large map of the area above the fridge. She peered at the roads and place names, trying to get her bearings.

'We're here,' Barney said, coming up behind her. He was able to reach out and point to where they were on the map without so much as brushing her shoulder with his arm.

'And the crash site?'

'Here,' he said, pointing to an area of green off to the right.

'And the road?' All she could see were pale lines, no names.

'Here.'

'What's the road called?'

'It doesn't have an official name,' Barney said, 'but people call it the Common Road 'cos it runs right through the Common.'

'Makes sense,' she said.

'Do you want a cuppa before we head out?' he asked, walking towards the kettle.

'I'm fine,' she said. He looked disappointed. Who could blame him? It was freezing. 'It'll be dark soon and my car isn't the best on mud . . . let alone snow,' she said by way of an explanation.

'OK. Let's get going.' He grabbed a coat off the back of one of the chairs and handed it to her. 'Think you might need this.' She hesitated, but decided now wasn't the time to be fussy. The odour as she pushed her arms into the sleeves settled inside her nostrils. It was a combination of horse manure and something else she couldn't place. 'Won't take us more than ten, fifteen minutes to get there.' He pushed open the door, picked up what looked like a horse blanket and ushered her out before him. 'Turn left,' he said. 'Keep going. My truck's round there.'

She picked her way over the snow-covered cobbles until

112

she rounded the corner of the barn and saw his truck. It was a large, half-covered 4x4 with 'Quantock Hills, Area of Outstanding Natural Beauty' stencilled down the side and a white outline of a bird of prey. 'They're everywhere,' she said, pointing to the bird.

'You'd see more in the spring,' he said, 'but yes, there are a fair few.'

'No, I meant the image,' she said. 'I noticed it on a few of the signposts.'

'Sure, right,' he said. 'It's a buzzard.' He walked around and got into the truck. Jane pulled open her door and held on to a handle to haul herself up and into the cab. 'Sorry about the smell,' he said, laying the blanket he had been carrying on her seat. She couldn't decide if it was for her benefit, or so she didn't sit her wet and muddy arse on the seat. 'Billy, one of the other rangers has had his dog in here . . . massive thing it is. He's meant to ride in the back but he never does.'

'Billy or the dog?' Jane said, looking around. Grey hairs and mud covered the seat, the footwell, the dashboard and the windscreen. There didn't appear to be a surface untouched. At least that answered one question: Barney had brought the blanket for her.

'Should be both,' he said with a chuckle. 'You ready?' He turned the key to start the engine. It took a few seconds, but then growled into life. She nodded as she decided where to rest her feet. 'Let's get going.'

As he pulled away Jane fastened her seatbelt and wedged one foot against the door and the other at the base of the gear stick so she could steady herself. However, as soon as he started over the uneven terrain she was sliding from side to side and back and forth in the seat. 'So is this part of the national park?' she asked as he swung the truck to the right and they headed off away from Fyne Court. There were pine trees to her right, hedgerow and rolling fields to her left. Barney changed gear and took a right. Jane frowned. Was this the way she had come? She couldn't tell. All the lanes looked the same: narrow, single-track, high beech hedges either side, bare trees and the occasional glimpse of the fields and farmland beyond when they passed a gateway or reached the rise of a hill.

'AONBs are different,' he said. 'They're not national parks. They were formed after the national parks . . . they didn't make the grade.'

'Why not?'

'Not remote enough. Not big enough,' he said with a shrug. He was almost reclined in his seat, with only one hand on the wheel. He filled the space, but he appeared a lot more relaxed than she was.

'How big is it?'

'Ninety-nine square kilometres,' he said. Jane tried to convert to miles in her head but couldn't remember the formula. 'Or thirty-nine square miles,' he added, as if noticing her confusion.

'Seems pretty big to me . . . and remote,' she said. It was beginning to feel more remote by the minute. Other than the occasional telephone pole, there was little to no sign of habitation until he turned again and they were on a proper road. Jane relaxed her shoulders down an inch. To her right was bare woodland on a steep incline, dead leaves mulched on the ground dusted with snow. 'Is this lower-lying?' she asked.

'Slightly,' he said.

'I felt like I went up and down a lot on the way here,' she said.

'The gradient changes a fair bit,' he said. 'Now we're gonna be coming at the crash site from the opposite direction. Pip would have come up through Crowcombe, up the hill and over the top, dropping down to where she crashed.'

'Can you take me back that way?'

'Sure,' he said. 'It'll take a bit longer, but that's no bother.'

'Thank you,' she said, wishing she hadn't asked. Longer meant darker, and darker meant the nervous knot in her stomach getting tighter. Her mind kept drifting back to one of the tall tales her mother had told Peter this morning, about animals going missing. The farmer would count his livestock at dinner time, but by breakfast one or more would be gone, just scraps of wool or hair left behind – the animals never to be seen again. She cleared her throat. 'So, I guess you must know the roads round here better than most.'

'No more than the locals,' he said, flicking the air vent nearest her open. 'For your hands,' he said, nodding at her frigid fingers in her lap.

'Thanks.' She held her hands up, grateful for the warmth.

'Most folk round here know their way around.'

'But you can go off-road?' she said, pointing to the four-wheel-drive gear stick.

'You'll be hard-pushed to find people who don't have four-wheel drive round this way,' he said, 'but me and the other rangers are the only ones *allowed* to go off-road, yes.'

'But other people do?' She took her notepad out of her jacket pocket, getting another whiff of the coat as she did so.

She uncapped her pen. Maybe if she got her mind into work mode she might be able to ignore the little voice in her head.

'If they want to . . . or need to, yes,' he said. 'We get people up here at the weekends or late at night on quads, motorbikes and all sorts.'

'No one stops them?'

'Who's here to see?' he said. She felt her shoulders creep up again. 'No one's here at night. My place is over in Doddington so I can get up here pretty quick, but who's to know they're up here? It isn't 'til the next day that we see the damage.'

'Damage?'

'It's young'uns mainly,' he said. 'They come up here to drink, smoke, take drugs . . . who knows?' He shook his head. 'They'd have to be on something, the stuff they get up to.'

'Like?'

'You name it,' he said, his mouth pulled to one side. 'They'll nick anything that isn't nailed down, and if they can't nick it, then they tag it.'

'Graffiti?'

'Everywhere,' he said with a sigh. 'They've even done the animals once or twice. One time I came up here and there were a couple of sheep gamboling about with luminous green tags on their backs.'

'They spray-painted sheep?'

'Sure,' he said with a shrug. 'Give 'em half a chance and they'll tag anything.' He looked around, as if checking they were alone in the truck. 'And you wouldn't believe the stuff they leave up here,' he said, his voice quiet. 'A simple roll in the hay isn't enough for these kids, I'm telling you.' Jane was intrigued and repulsed in equal measure. 'But the worst of it

116

is the tracks they leave . . . tearing up the ground. Wouldn't matter so much, but under the top layer of earth it's peat, and it can't recover the same. Graffiti I can get rid of, but once the peat gets damaged, that's it . . . takes years to recover. But like I said – there's no one here to stop 'em.'

'So what do you actually *do*, then?' she asked. She saw him flinch. 'I mean, what's your job description? What does a ranger do?' She could see that she had offended him.

'Anything and everything,' he said, turning off the main road and back onto another narrow lane, the hedges coming in to meet them. Jane tensed, and held on to the side of the truck. 'We keep an eye on the livestock . . . sheep, horses, et cetera. Talk to the farmers and deal with any issues they might have. We'll get called out if a tree comes down over a roadway. I've got a chainsaw in the back,' he said, gesturing over his shoulder.

'Reassuring,' she said with a nervous chuckle.

He turned to look at her, taking his eyes off the road. 'You're quite safe with me,' he said.

'I hope so,' she said. 'Chainsaw or no chainsaw, I'm not sure I could do much about it if you decided to do anything.' She laughed again, but it felt forced. Her shoulders were now up around her ears.

He shrugged and turned back to the road. 'Anyway,' he said. 'I do a bit of everything, big jobs, little jobs, whatever.'

'And who do you report to?' She was trying to make notes, but so far she had only written down random words that meant nothing on their own.

'No one,' he said. 'I mean, I've got a boss and everything, but I rarely see him.'

'So who tells you what to do?'

'No one,' he said. 'I sort myself out.'

'How does anyone know what you're doing? Or whether you're working your hours?'

'They don't,' he said, looking at her.

She shielded her page as she wrote 'free reign' next to the word 'ranger' and several question marks. There appeared to be a lot of trust involved in the job. As long as you had someone trustworthy, it was the perfect job for them and the boss. But what if they weren't?

'Here we are,' he said, pulling the truck off the road and half into a ditch.

There was no crime scene tape, no officer waiting for them. It was just her, Barney, a whole lot of countryside and very little light. There was a cluster of signs on the left-hand side of the road: two warning triangles, one with a deer on it and the other letting drivers know about the upcoming cattle grid. Beneath them was an old-fashioned white sign outlined in black that read 'Quantock Common' beneath the now familiar bird of prey silhouette. Below that sign was another that read 'Quantock Hills, Area of Outstanding Natural Beauty'. Beyond the plethora of signage was the cattle grid. A hedge and, she assumed, fields to her left, and woodland to her right. There was a wooden five-bar gate to the right of the cattle grid. Jane couldn't see where Pippa's car had left the road. 'Where . . . ?'

'You'll need to get out,' Barney said. He opened his door and climbed down into the leaf-filled ditch. 'This was cordoned off, but someone's been up and nicked the tape – a souvenir, I s'pect.'

She opened her door and jumped down to the road, hit

by the sudden rush of cold air. As she followed Barney up the hill, he pointed to his right. She had to step around him, given he was a wall of a man, and then she could see what he was showing her. On their side of the cattle grid, off to the right, there were clear scorch marks on the road surface. It looked as if someone had had a barbecue and then, once it was cleared away, all that was left were the marks where the fire had burnt through onto the ground. She noticed the skid marks leading up to the edge of the road, leading up to the tree. It was an oak. If she hugged it, her arms would cover maybe a third of its girth. The base of the trunk looked shredded; bits of bark ripped off and discarded, revealing the naked wood blackened by the fire. Scars cut into it from the bonnet and bumper as it made impact. She could even see where pieces of the windscreen had embedded in the bark, just above the main area that was damaged.

'You should have seen the car,' Barney said.

'I saw photographs.'

'You should have seen the car,' he said again.

She looked up at him. His cheeks were pale against his beard. Maybe she wasn't the only one to be a little freaked out. The reasons might be different, but the feeling was the same. 'How soon after did you arrive on scene?' she asked.

'I got the call right after they called the Bridgwater guys,' he said. 'I came up hoping to . . . hoping I might be able to help, to help her, but then . .' He held his chin, stroking his beard. 'But when I got here I realized it was over. It had been over for a good while.'

'Was the fire completely out?'

He nodded. 'Yes,' he said. 'We'd had rain, sleet . . . not

dissimilar to the weather now. The fire was out, but the car was still . . . smouldering.'

She touched his arm, pulling her hand back quicker than she intended when he flinched away from her. 'I've been to my fair share of accidents, Barney,' she said. 'It takes a while to get over.'

'I guess,' he said, 'but this wasn't an accident, was it?'

Jane stopped. She couldn't discuss the case with him. She was here to get information, not give it. 'It's too soon to—'

'Don't bother,' he said, waving her words away. 'You can't talk about it, it's fine. I know enough.'

She wanted to ask what he meant by that, but decided it could wait. 'I'm going to have a look around,' she said, walking up the road away from him. She was grateful when he didn't follow.

Her breath billowed out in front of her. She looked back at the tree, the scorch marks and the tyre tracks on the road where Pippa had skidded, trying to stop her car's progress towards the giant oak. It wasn't hard to imagine what it must be like up here at night. The waning light was already giving everything a different, more sinister feel. She shivered. The shadows lengthened in the woods to her right, making it hard to distinguish where the trees ended and the forest floor began. She heard a rustling in the leaves somewhere off to her right and stopped, her spine rigid. There was no way she would come up here on her own.

She looked at the snow touching everything around her. A fresh blanket of snow should make the land look pure and clean, but here it was different. The bed of leaves broke through, creating dark cracks and furrows. On the other side of the road, farmland stretched away to what she guessed must be the Bristol Channel. The water looked black from up here. She could see a road cutting through the countryside, the lights of the vehicles blinking in the distance. It was a good few miles away. She took a deep breath and closed her eyes for a second, noticing the smell of the earth, a combination of moisture, peat and foliage. She turned and looked further up the road, away from the crash site. There was a bend to the right, a signpost and a gateway.

'That's Walford's Gibbet,' Barney said.

'Jesus,' she said, almost losing control of her bladder. 'You've got to stop doing that.'

'Sorry.'

'For a big guy you don't make a lot of noise, do you?' His mouth turned down at the edges. His eyes were dark, darker than his hair.

'Let me show you,' he said, ignoring her comment and walking up the hill, gesturing for her to follow. She couldn't help but keep her distance. She knew she was being pathetic, but the darker it got, the more vulnerable she was beginning to feel. She was in the middle of nowhere with a six-foot-seven, beardy-weirdy ranger. At least, she hoped he was a ranger. She had never even checked. He could be anyone. He could have told her anything. She rolled her eyes at her own hysteria.

'This is Walford's Gibbet,' Barney said, pointing to a wooden marker post. The name was carved in capital letters running the length of the pole. The letters had been painted a snooker-ball green.

'What is it?' she asked, forcing herself to take a step towards him.

'This is where they hanged him.'

As he spoke, a branch cracked behind her. She whirled around, her pulse quickening. She felt sick. Barney just looked at her as she took a deep breath, waiting for her heart to steady.

'Hung who?'

'John Walford. He murdered his missus, back in 1789. He was hanged, and then they put his body in a gibbet . . . a metal cage,' he said, 'and left him here for a year as a warning to others.'

'Some warning,' she said, looking around her. 'Why did he kill his wife?'

'She drank too much, spent his money and kept getting pregnant,' he said with a shrug.

'Blimey,' she said. 'He wasn't a very tolerant husband, then.'

'No,' he said, 'I suppose not. He left her body near here . . . over that way, in Dead Woman's Ditch.'

'They called it that? Seriously?'

'It was called that before he killed her.'

'Odd,' she said, frowning. 'So *why's* it called Dead Woman's Ditch, then?' she asked, resisting the shiver that was hovering at the base of her neck.

He shrugged. 'No one knows. They think it . . . hang on, let me show you.' He started off back down the hill. 'It's about time we got back, anyway,' he said. 'I don't know about you, but I'm bloody freezing.'

If Barney was cold, then Jane must have gone hypothermic and not realized it. She jogged after him, grateful to climb back into the relative warmth of his truck, grateful they were leaving. It was almost dark now.

'I'll show you Pip's trip in reverse, so to speak,' he said. 'And I can show you the ditch at the same time.'

'Great,' she said, thinking that 'great' was the wrong word on both counts. In this light they weren't going to see much anyway. She should send Peter up here – bit of tinsel and a few strings of fairy lights, and he would have this place sorted. What she wouldn't give for a bit of illumination and Christmas cheer.

Barney started up the truck and pulled over the cattle grid. Jane glanced back at the crash site. So little evidence from something so horrendous. They passed Walford's Gibbet and rounded the bend. 'What's this wood here?' she asked.

'That's Shervage,' he said.

Almost as he spoke, the wood seemed to retreat behind them and they were on open heathland, the snow taking on the appearance of icing sugar dusting the landscape. It was like something out of *Wuthering Heights*: undulating grassland interspersed with pockets of earth where animals had burrowed. There were sheep grazing, although from what Jane could see they had bugger all to eat. There was the occasional tree, stunted and wizened, blown into submission by the crosswinds that must buffet this place. The road cut right through the centre, with an occasional pull-in for drivers to pass each other. She saw a brown smear in the distance.

'That's the main car park up here on the Common,' he said, pointing to what she was looking at.

'A real thoroughfare,' she said. They had been up here for about thirty minutes and she had not seen another soul; not a car, not a walker, no one. All she had for company was Barney and the sheep.

He pulled the truck off to one side as they approached more woodland to their left. The trees here were twisted and short; their trunks white like silver birches, and peeling. 'Locals call that the Petrified Forest,' he said.

'I can see why,' she said. 'Is anywhere around here called something normal? Something not out of a horror film?'

'There's Great Bear, Will's Neck and Frog Combe,' he said. 'They're not so bad.'

'That depends on the bear, and what they were doing to Will's neck,' she said, forcing herself to smile. If Barney had noticed her disquiet, he had the good grace not to say anything.

'Pip would have come up from that way,' he said, pointing at the road disappearing back down into woodland. 'This here is Dead Woman's Ditch.' He was out of the car again and heading for another copse of trees before Jane could protest. 'It runs from here over to where we were just now.'

As she climbed down, a different shiver worked its way from her toes all the way up to behind her ears. 'Let's make this quick.'

'Sure,' he said. 'There it is.'

Something occurred to her as she walked over to join him.

'Barney,' she said.

'Yeah.'

'You keep referring to Pippa as Pip,' she said. 'Did you know her?' She didn't know why she hadn't picked up on it straight away. It made sense. They worked right next to each other. She pursed her lips, annoyed with herself. She had been so busy jumping at shadows, she had missed something staring her in the face. Fear, it seemed, was not conducive to good investigative work.

'I went to the same primary school as her and her brother.'

'You know Aaron?' she asked, surprised by the sudden overlap in her worlds. Of course. If he knew Pippa, it followed he might know Aaron. For some reason, it made her feel better. Aaron was someone she trusted – someone she would feel safe with.

'Used to,' he said, shoving his hands in his pockets. 'I didn't know it was Pip until I got up here.'

'She worked over at Fyne Court,' Jane said, a question in her voice.

'Yeah, I know.'

'How well did you know her?' she asked, her head cocked on one side. There was something in Barney's expression that said this was more than a passing acquaintance.

He pulled at his beard and sniffed. 'I hadn't seen her since school,' he said, 'but when she started working at the Farmer's over in Combe Florey I recognized her, you know? We had a few drinks, went out a few times.' He looked down at his feet.

'You dated?' she asked, unable to keep the incredulity from her voice.

He shook his head, frowning. 'No, no, nothing like that. We went out . . . like, a group of us. Her and I talked once, maybe twice, but that was it.'

She looked at him. He held her eye. She couldn't decide if he was being defiant because he was telling the truth, or because he was fighting a lie. 'Why did you stay?'

'What do you mean?'

'When you realized it was Pippa, why did you stay?'

He opened his hands and shrugged. 'The guy in charge asked me to help,' he said. 'It was a circus up here. I might not have *known* Pip, not properly, but I didn't think it was right . . . folk seeing her how she was.'

'Who asked you? Townsend?'

'Yeah,' he said. He hooked his thumb at the copse of trees over to their right. 'You'd better take a look if you want, before it gets too dark.' He turned away.

Jane followed, but kept her distance. She had more questions, but they weren't for Barney. They were for Townsend. What on earth was he playing at, allowing someone who knew the victim access to the crime scene?

Barney had stopped. 'This is it.'

She turned on the spot. Dead Woman's Ditch was a lot less dramatic than the name suggested. Between two lines of bent and twisted trees there was a leaf-filled gully, banks of earth, shrubs and moss climbing up on either side. 'This is it?'

'Yeah. This is the start of it. It runs for about a mile back down over there, through Shervage.'

'It's seriously just a ditch?'

'Sorry to disappoint you, but yes,' he said. 'It dates back to the Iron Age . . . some fortification or other dividing up the lands around here.'

'Right,' she said, already planning her call to Lockyer. Dead Woman's Ditch might be a let-down, but she was pretty sure he would want to know about Townsend's crime scene management.

'Just thought you'd want to see it,' Barney said.

'Thanks,' she said, 'I appreciate you taking the time to show me.'

'It wasn't here he dumped the body,' he said.

'No?' she said, clapping her hands together. She had lost interest. It was time to go.

'No,' he said. 'It was over at the other end, more in the woods, near where we were just now, as it happens.'

She nodded. 'Sure, sure.'

'They were walking back from the pub when he did it,' he said.

'Really,' she said without inflection.

'I just thought . . . well, there's been talk that, you know . . . well, I'm sure it's just talk but with the other murder . . . well, it's got the locals in a bit of a state.'

'This guy Walford killed his wife back in, what, the seventeen hundreds?' she said, walking back to the truck. 'I think there's enough distance between that and this incident to alleviate any concern.' She smiled.

He didn't.

'It's not just Walford that's got them . . . unsettled,' he said. 'What with Walford, Pippa and the other girl . . . well, it all feels a bit close for comfort.'

'What *other* girl?' she asked, looking up at him.

CHAPTER THIRTEEN

12th December – Saturday

'Can you slow down?' Jane said, trying to keep up with Lockyer, who was tramping through the undergrowth at a speed her legs couldn't match. 'Is it much further?' She tripped on a tree root hidden in the snow, swearing under her breath. The forest floor was buried in a good inch or so, making walking without incident a challenge.

'Quit moaning. It's just up here.'

'You've been saying that for the last half hour,' she muttered under her breath, taking care to walk in his footsteps, which gave her a good excuse not to look too far ahead. Shervage Wood was no more appealing this morning than it had been last night, and Lockyer wasn't helping. He had spent the drive down from Clevedon rambling on about John Walford and other local legends, each tale creating a fresh knot in Jane's stomach. Before Peter, she had loved being scared: films, books, ghost tours, rollercoasters – anything to get the blood going. Not any more, it seemed. She had thought her tastes had just changed with motherhood and age, but her reaction to Quantock folklore was putting paid to that idea.

Mind you, if she was agitated, then Lockyer was a man possessed. He had all but dragged her out of her parents' house this morning, without breakfast. She had managed a gulp of coffee, but that was all. Her stomach rumbled. 'Do you actually know where you're going?'

He gave her a withering look over his shoulder, as if she had just questioned his manhood. 'I spoke to Ranger Boy Barney this morning and he gave me the coordinates.' He waved the map at her. 'I figured I'd better have a back-up plan, given your sense of direction is about as bad as your satnav's.'

As much as she wanted to refute his insult, she couldn't deny that her navigation skills were questionable. No one could expect her to know her arse from her elbow out here. Barney had used a different route. They had entered the woods just up from where Pippa's car had left the road. It had been a five-minute walk, if that. And it had been semi-dark. This morning's route-march had taken an hour so far. Lockyer had insisted on seeing the crash site, walking the road route to Dead Woman's Ditch, passing Walford's Gibbet and then coming back through Shervage Wood to where Chloe Evans's body had been found. The 'other girl'. That's what Barney had called her, as if dead girls were just par for the course around here. Jane couldn't imagine ending her life somewhere so remote, and yet two girls *had* died out here and within six months of each other. The trees were denser than she remembered. She turned and looked around her. She could neither see nor hear the road. Without Lockyer she might never find her way out.

'Ooh arr, what d'ye see?' Lockyer whispered.

Jane coughed as she choked on her own breath. He was

behind her, bent forward, his mouth inches from her ear. 'Are you trying to give me a heart attack?' she said, stumbling away from him, her legs like jelly. She was breathing hard. 'And just so you know, you sound more like a pirate than a southerner.'

He smiled. 'Keep your hair on,' he said. 'We're here.' He gestured to a clearing to the right of where they were standing. 'This is Wayland's Pool.'

With her blood still hammering in her ears, Jane forced her legs into motion and followed Lockyer to where he was pointing. 'Wayland's what? I'm not seeing a pool.' The clearing was ringed with oak trees, their trunks so close in places they were almost touching. It was as if they were jostling for space, their snow-laden branches leaning in, trying to get a better look.

'Well . . .' Lockyer said, lowering his voice and creeping towards her, his eyes shifting from left to right and a smile twitching at the edge of his lips. 'From what Barney was telling me there be many a legend up in these 'ere parts about dragons and ditches, but I'll be telling the story of Wayland the Smithy. They named the pool after him, though it's long gone now.'

She resisted the urge to smile.

''Tis rumoured Odin's master blacksmith used this 'ere pool to cool the shoes as he made 'em for Odin's hunting party.' Lockyer contorted his face. Jane hung her head and laughed. He really was something else.

'On stormy nights you can 'ear his 'ammer as he pounds the horseshoe on his anvil, and even see the sparks on a clear night.' He widened his eyes. 'When 'e's done 'e plunges the hot shoe into the pool with a hiss . . .' He leaned in and hissed in

Jane's face. 'Then Odin, 'e be ready for his hunt. The wild 'orses round these parts know better than to come into Shervage Wood, lest they become Odin's prey.'

She wiped her face with her gloved hand. 'Thanks for that,' she said, rolling her eyes. 'The accent was better that time . . . apart from the spitting.'

'Well,' he said, still in character. 'The legends don't sound right if you don't tell 'em in the local tongue.'

'Mm-hmm,' she said, turning to survey the space in front of them. There was a clear depression in the centre of the snow-covered ground. Jane looked around her. The spot was no more informative in the daylight than it had been last night in the semi-dark. Before Barney's revelation about Chloe Evans, Jane had been more than ready to get back to the truck and get the hell out of there. Instead she had insisted he bring her here. She tried to get her bearings, to see things as she had done last night. 'Where was she? Off to the left?'

Lockyer nodded.

'Those poor kids,' she said with a shiver.

'It's always the same,' he said, coming to stand next to her. 'You never want to be a kid or a dog-walker. If there's a half-naked body to be found, they're the poor sods who'll find it every time.'

She sighed, letting her shoulders relax for the first time this morning. 'OK, so we're here,' she said. 'What now?'

'We talk to Townsend,' he said, turning and walking back the way they had come.

'And we couldn't have done that in the first place? We had to come all the way out here because . . . ?' she said, stretching out the word as she turned, picking her way through the snow, leaves and mulch beneath her feet. Her toes felt like icicles in her boots.

Lockyer stopped and turned, Jane ploughing right into him. If he had worn glasses, she thought, he would have been looking over them. 'We're out here because,' he said, taking her by the shoulders and almost lifting her back onto her feet, 'I wanted to get a feel for the place. I want to know *more* going into any conversation about this case, not less.'

'But what have you learned?' she asked, using the back of her hand to wipe the end of her nose. 'I told you everything Barney told me. Chloe Evans was found back in July. As you've just proved, there's nothing to see.' He didn't appear to be listening. 'Forgive me, but I just don't see the point of being out here in the freezing cold . . . *particularly when I was out here last night*,' she added under her breath. A rustling sound off to her left made her pulse jump, her breath catching in her throat. She shook her head. She had hoped daylight would put paid to her hysteria, but it seemed her subconscious had other ideas.

Lockyer pulled the map of hiking trails out of his pocket and flattened it against his palm. 'Back in London I know the area, the people,' he said, as if that should answer her question. 'When a job comes in – a murder with an unknown assailant, say – what's the first thing we do?' She didn't answer. This was a lecture, not a Q and A. 'We look at the method and location.' He looked back down at the map. 'More often than not, we have a good idea who we're looking for, suspect-wise, just from that information.'

'I suppose that's true,' she said, though she felt far from convinced.

'I don't have that here.' He tapped the map, turned and walked away to the left. 'Hence the legwork,' he added, slapping his open palm on his thigh.

'I'd already done the legwork,' she muttered.

'Look,' he said. 'You might not understand this, but I'm coming in blind, and that's a problem. For me, that's a major problem. If you hadn't been out here with Ranger Boy yesterday, I'd be none the wiser.' He looked at her over his shoulder, a look of contempt on his face. 'I can't run an inquiry that way. He should have told me. It's as simple as that.'

She wasn't surprised by Lockyer's vernacular. It was always 'I' when he was angry – when he felt slighted in some way.

'What else don't I know?' he asked. She knew better than to answer his rhetorical questions. 'Is it an oversight? Is he withholding?' He seemed to weigh the two questions in his hands, his back still to her.

'Who, Townsend?' she asked, clueless as to the origin of his sudden irritation. He shrugged but didn't answer, his strides lengthening until she was almost trotting to keep up. 'I honestly don't see the issue here. From what Barney told me, despite the location, there's very little to compare the two deaths. Chloe Evans was killed back in the summer, so most likely before Townsend's time anyway.' Lockyer harrumphed, but didn't argue with her. She had no idea why he was being so pig-headed.

'And what about all this crap about John Walford and the locals?'

'What about it?' she asked, slipping and sliding on the mud and snow as she tried to keep pace with him.

'When was I going to hear about that?' He veered off to the right.

Jane followed, though she couldn't see how zig-zagging like this was going to get them back to the car. 'Walford killed his wife in the seventeen hundreds, Mike. Where's the relevance?' She raised her voice, to be heard over the creak and sway of the branches above them. They were walking into the wind. It whistled around her face and neck, chilling her skin.

'She was left in Dead Woman's Ditch,' he said, stopping again and turning to face her. 'Chloe Evans's body was left by Wayland's Pool, which just so happens to be on the same ordnance line, and Pippa Jones was found, what . . . four hundred yards on from that?' He raised his eyebrows. 'From what your friend Barney told me, the locals are a superstitious lot. According to him they're shitting themselves . . . won't come up here at night.'

'Is that why you were banging on about the legends before?' she asked, trying to make sense of his motives, not to mention his mood. He wasn't just frustrated. He was angry.

'Jesus, I don't give two shits about the legends,' he said, throwing his hands out at the woods around them. 'But what I *do* care about . . . what *does* matter is that the locals *do* and it is *exactly* the kind of information a DI in charge of a murder inquiry *has* to know.'

'I don't mean to be indelicate,' she said, choosing her words, 'but you *aren't* the DI in charge, Townsend is. Who's to say what he does and doesn't know? If he knows about the Evans case, I'm sure he's considered and dismissed it.' His mouth straightened into a line as she spoke. 'And as for the locals – again, I'm sure he knows and I'm sure he'd have told you . . . us, given half a chance. We only arrived on Thursday night, for pity's sake.' She blew out a long breath. His frustration was catching. She had been fine five minutes ago – cold, but fine. She closed her eyes, and took a deep breath in through her nose before opening them again. 'This isn't your first joint inquiry, Mike,' she said, keeping her voice level. 'You can't know everything right off the bat.'

He pushed his tongue between his teeth and upper lip, sniffed, turned and walked away. 'This is an important case for me, Jane,' he said, throwing the words over his shoulder, some taken by the wind. 'I *won't* have people saying I did a half-arsed job.'

'What people? Atkinson?' she asked, feeling like she was stumbling around both literally and metaphorically.

'No.'

'Then who?' She saw his shoulders stiffen. 'Roger?' He didn't answer. 'Someone else?' He didn't speak, but he had stopped walking again. She blew out a breath, a cloud of white billowing in front of her face. She could kick herself. 'I *knew* something was up.'

'What do you mean?' he asked without looking at her, the map snapping in the wind at his side.

She wrinkled her nose. 'Well . . . and I mean no disrespect by this . . .'

'But?'

'But you have been more . . . assiduous than normal.'

'Meaning?'

'Come on, Mike,' she said, toeing a hole in the snow. 'You've never been one for taking notes and getting bogged down in the admin side of things. You gave Townsend the third degree yesterday. I was waiting for you to ask him his wife's bra size.' Lockyer huffed out a laugh or a sigh, she wasn't sure. 'And you've been like a dog with two dicks since I told you about the Evans girl, so what's the deal? What's going on?'

He looked up at the snow-covered trees above their heads. 'OK,' he said, 'but this is just between us.'

'Of course,' she said, forgetting her cold face and freezing feet.

'Roger wasn't meant to tell me . . . though how that would've worked, God only knows, but anyway . . . he wasn't meant to tell me, and I would *definitely* be in the shit if he knew I'd told you, so keep schtum.' She nodded. 'You know Atkinson called Rog asking for Met assistance.'

'Yes,' she said. 'Because Pippa Jones lived in London.'

Lockyer tipped his head to the side. 'That was the official line, yes, but Atkinson told Roger he wanted support for Townsend because he'd struggled with his last case.' He looked at her, his gaze heavy with hidden meaning.

'Right?' she said, feeling none the wiser.

'It was a murder case. Townsend was brought down from Bristol when the DI in charge had to go off on medical leave or something,' he said. 'He mentioned it in the car on the way down, and . . .'

'And you think it was the Chloe Evans murder?' she asked as the penny dropped.

'I'd say it's a fair assumption, yes,' he said.

She frowned. 'So we're here to hold Townsend's hand.' Her thoughts were jumping like a needle on a scratched record. 'That still doesn't explain why you're so antsy.' He grimaced. 'Seriously, what is it?'

'Fine,' he said. 'Roger had two phone calls. One from Atkinson and one from someone else, someone . . . higher up.'

'Who?'

'He wouldn't tell me,' he said.

Jane folded her arms, shoving her hands under her armpits. If she was searching for warmth, she failed to find it. 'Interesting.'

He shrugged. 'Anyway, the higher-up . . . whoever they are, told Roger that Townsend was incompetent and I was to essentially come down here and take over the case but that I couldn't let on to Townsend or Atkinson.'

'That's ridiculous,' she said, shaking her head. 'How on earth are you meant to accomplish that? And . . . since when is Townsend incompetent? Is that instead of or in addition to his issues with his last case?' Her mind was racing. She was having a job keeping up with her own thoughts as they skittered across her mind like pebbles on a pond. 'From what I've seen he seems capable, notwithstanding your obvious issues with how he's run the Jones case to date . . .' She was about to go on when something occurred to her. 'But, having said that . . .' She saw Lockyer's mouth twitch. 'If he *was* the DI on the Evans case . . .'

'Exactly,' Lockyer said. He looked relieved. 'If the Evans case was his, then he *should* be cross-referencing it with the Jones case on location alone.'

'Like I said, maybe he already has and he dismissed it,' she said.

'Then it would be on file. *We* would know about it.' Jane couldn't help noticing Lockyer's conversion from 'I' to 'we'. She felt a little rush of warm satisfaction. 'Which means he hasn't cross-referenced them – because either it hasn't even occurred to him, or it has, but he doesn't think two young women dying six months apart in suspicious circumstances on the same hill range merits further investigation.'

'Or three, if you count Walford's wife,' she said, as the pieces slid into place. 'Goes some way to explaining the incompetence accusation.'

'Exactly,' he said again, stamping his feet and puffing out a breath. 'Come on, let's get out of here. It's fecking freezing.' He turned and started walking again.

'Why don't they just get shot of Townsend, if they're that concerned about his abilities?'

'I have no idea,' he said. 'We have to go up and around to the right to get back to the car, I think.' He stepped off what must have been an animal track they had been following, and headed deeper into the woods. His uncertainty didn't fill her with confidence, but now wasn't the time to question his map-reading skills.

'Maybe it's not Townsend that's the issue, as such? Maybe it's the case?' she said, sniffing, her mind manipulating the new information like playdough, her icy toes forgotten.

'I thought the same,' he said, pausing and looking off to his left. 'Although what's so special about the Jones girl, I have no idea. As you said, other than proximity there's nothing similar about the deaths.'

'Could be a PR issue,' she said, following him as he went off-piste. The snow was deeper here, the boughs above them thinner. 'Tourism must be a massive part of the economy down this way. One murder's bad, but two? Could be someone's trying to avoid a media storm in their little rural teacup?'

'That occurred to me as well,' he said. 'That's why we need to look at the Evans file – find out what the press had to say at the time.' They had started to climb, the incline hidden in the snow, although Jane could feel it in her ankles and thighs. 'Townsend aside, I'm surprised it took even this long to find out about it. You'd think the gruesome murder of a heavily pregnant, single mother of two would have made a bigger splash.'

'Chloe Evans was pregnant?'

'Yes, seven months,' he said, shaking his head. 'Did Barney not say?'

'No,' she said. 'He didn't.'

CHAPTER FOURTEEN

12th December – Saturday

Lockyer pinched the bridge of his nose with his thumb and forefinger. His head was thumping, his temples seeming to pulse with each heartbeat. He leaned his head back and rocked it from side to side, easing the tension in his neck. The pain had started during his and Jane's excursion into Shervage Wood this morning. He hadn't realized until they got back to the car just how cold it was. His extremities were yet to thaw.

He took a slurp of his tepid coffee and looked at his watch. He was waiting to speak to John Mills, the landlord of the Farmer's Arms and Pippa Jones's boss. The guy had been at the door of the pub to greet him when he arrived, but then excused himself for 'a moment'. The moment had stretched into ten minutes. Lockyer had been debating whether to go in search of the wayward publican for most of that time but had decided to stay put. He had positioned himself as close to the log burner as possible, and now that it was kicking out some real heat he was reluctant to move. Every time he took a breath his nostrils were filled with a heady smell of beer, charcoal, smoke and cooking fat. It was a proper old pub with real draft ales with great names like Will's Neck, Hound Dog and Tangle Foot. Lockyer would have no trouble drinking his way along the pumps. It used to be a challenge to find good beers in London. Not now. Not now the trend of unusual beers and bushy beards had come into fashion. But it wasn't the same. A place like this, a real pub, was as old as the brewers themselves and there wasn't a copper bar or any Feng Shui-ed furniture in sight.

He looked at his watch again, and then his phone. No new messages. No reply. Where was Townsend? He had emailed the guy before he and Jane left Shervage this morning. He opened his own message to read it again:

Bill, on my way into office now eta 30 mins. DS Bennett is meeting with Fyne Court catering manager Derek Cooper in an hour. She's got Abbott and Pimbley with her. Spoken to Joneses. Bennett has meeting with them at three – I'll meet her there. Be good to catch up with you. I've got paint guys due in at midday. Seeing Mills, Farmer's Arms landlord, at two thirty. Wanted to talk to you about a case. Chloe Evans. Summer of this year – body found in Shervage Wood. If you can get your hands on the file before I get in, that'd be great. I'm on my mobile, Mike

That was almost five hours ago. He shook his head. Granted it was the weekend and Townsend had said he *might* not be in but Lockyer had assumed he was joking. What kind of DI stayed home when he had a five-day-old murder inquiry on his desk?

He had spent half the drive back to Express Park devising inventive ways to take charge without making it obvious, but it was clear now he needn't have bothered. Townsend didn't seem to care if he was sidelined – his team, even less so. Why was anyone's guess, on both counts.

Lockyer leaned back and looked out the pub's old leaded windows at the snow-covered beer garden and woods beyond. The trees were close together, their branches intertwined, their trunks slim, the bark peeling and flaking off. They looked a damn sight healthier than some of their deformed and stunted cousins up on the hills. Jane had pointed out the 'petrified forest' that grew in line with Dead Woman's Ditch. No wonder the locals were agitated, with places like that on their doorstep. He uncrossed and re-crossed his legs to warm the other foot. The A-frame tables had a good inch of snow on them, the table-tops resembling the marshmallow-covered biscuits he had loved as a kid – the fallen leaves sticking up through the snow like the desiccated coconut sprinkled on top. His stomach rumbled in response to the memory. He had a sudden desire for all his old favourites: Garibaldis, fig rolls and the milk biscuits with the cow and calf on them. His stomach grumbled again. No breakfast and half a sandwich at lunch hadn't done him any favours. He had been about to bite into his second tuna and mayo when the front desk had buzzed him to say the paint specialists were waiting for him in reception. He had dumped his sandwich and headed down to meet them, his hunger a dim second to mining their expertise.

His phone beeped, vibrating across the smooth oak table. It was a text from Jane:

Cooper interview done. Not much to go on. Jones quiet, kept herself to herself. Somewhat agitated previous week but no indication why. No close associations.

Apparently she'd pissed off some of the other staff; thought the job was beneath her – so Cooper says. I've been up and down the motorway to Clevedon twice so far! Another story. Don't ask. Arrived at the Joneses' early. I've managed to pick up another chuckle brother. Neither's said much. Feel like a leper at a picnic. J.

He smiled as he typed out a reply.

Despite his frustration with Townsend, it felt good to have Jane 'in the know' when it came to his orders from above. If anyone could help him with his clandestine agenda, it was her. It had been her idea to call the Joneses and set up this afternoon's meeting-cum-interview. Townsend had booked it in for Monday, to give the family time to grieve, he said, but as Jane had pointed out, Pippa's parents would be keener than anyone that the investigation be dealt with in an expeditious manner. Aaron too, given he was a copper and knew how these things should run. Lockyer pushed the pad of his thumb into his right temple, his fingers tangling in the tight curls at his temple. He kept forgetting the connection with Aaron – or he suspected his subconscious was at work, compartmentalizing so he could focus on the case itself without thinking about his daughter and her *connection*. He had tried to get hold of her to let her know he would be seeing the Joneses today and not Monday, but so far she was as unreachable as Townsend. He pushed harder into his temple, feeling a not unpleasant crunch.

He had let Jane speak to Pimbley, Abbott and a few others on Townsend's team, enlisting their help before she made the call to the Joneses. Where he knew he was heavy-handed, she was subtle and diplomatic. She could get people on side and doing things her way without them even knowing they were being stage-managed. She had been doing it to him for years.

Jane reversed into a space outside the Rose and Crown pub in Nether Stowey and turned off the engine. She twisted in her seat and looked back at the white cottage next to the pub. The front door was painted a glossy black with a rusting number 10 screwed on at a jaunty angle above a large round brass knocker.

'We're fifteen minutes early,' she said. There was no answer. Not that she was surprised. The drive over from Express Park had been no different.

She took out her phone and typed a message to Lockyer. He was meeting her here after he was done at the Farmer's Arms, where Pippa had been working in the kitchen and behind the bar. Combe Florey, the village the pub was in, was on the other side of the Quantocks off the A358 out of Taunton. She was glad he had offered to interview the landlord; at least it meant Jane was spared another trip up and over the hills. Yesterday and this morning had been enough to put her off for life.

When she had left Fyne Court after meeting Derek Cooper this morning, she had ended up coming off the hills on the opposite side to Bridgwater and heading into Taunton, a market town ten miles or so south of the Quantocks. It had been more of a mercy mission than a jolly, after her mother had called to say Peter was running a fever. Jane had wondered if he was sickening for something at breakfast, but Lockyer had dragged her out of the house before she could check. She had left DC Pimbley in her car, the engine running, as she ran down the high street and into Boots to get some Calpol. Peter loved Christmas, but the excitement made him fractious and he was often ill as a result – a physical manifestation of the stress. She had known, without needing to be told, that her mother's call had been a cry for help. Jane had as good as tipped Pimbley out of the car at Express Park and headed back up the M5 to Clevedon.

By the time she arrived, Peter and her mother were beside themselves. She had left her mother in the kitchen, muttering to herself about the evils of sugar, and gone to rescue her son from himself. He was bent over an Ordnance Survey map of Somerset, tears fat in his eyes. It seemed he had quizzed his grandmother on the county only to discover that Bridgwater and nearby towns, Taunton being one of them, were surrounded by four hill ranges: the Quantocks, the Mendips, the Blackdowns and the Brendons. This information, to anyone else, would have been noteworthy at best, but Peter was different. Her mother had put him in front of a film while she prepared lunch. It was the second in the *Ice Age* franchise. The storyline revolved around the main characters finding their way out of a valley before the ice melted, the valley was flooded and they were, in turn, drowned. Peter had somehow merged fiction with fact and decided Jane was in danger. He imagined the snow that had been falling on and off since their arrival from London would thaw and flood the bowl in which his mother was working, and she would drown.

As bizarre and incomprehensible as this idea might be to most people, to Peter it was real, as was his distress. It had taken Jane an hour to calm him down. She had left him watching an episode of *Friends* and given her mother strict instructions not to be drawn into any more discussions about where Jane was working. It was ironic that something so abstract had been the cause of his upset, given that his grandmother had been filling his head with talk of dragons and blood-soaked earth since their arrival.

She had been almost back to the station when her phone had started to ring. Her mind had been elsewhere as she pulled off the motorway, her eyes drawn to the Willow Man – Somerset's equivalent to the Angel of the North. The huge sculpture was striding across the fields between a supermarket depot and a new housing estate. She was too busy questioning the placement of the piece of artwork and admiring the ample curve of its arse to anticipate the reason for her mother's call. It seemed Peter had found a coffee-table book about Somerset. His grandmother had thought nothing of it, until he came to the section on the levels and how they flooded each year.

Jane hadn't even attempted to pacify her distraught son over the phone; she had just turned around and headed back up to Clevedon. Before she left again, Peter had extracted promises that she would take him to Alton Towers and make him up a bed on the floor in her room.

Her phone beeped. She looked down at the screen. It was Lockyer:

You've got the chuckle brothers. My guy's MIA. Be with you as soon as. M.

She smiled at his sign-off and then looked at her passengers. Neither of them was looking at the other. Neither was looking at her.

The Night Stalker

DS Abbott was in the passenger seat, staring out of the window, and DC Pimbley was sitting in the back seat to Jane's left. Pimbley was one of the Daniels, but she couldn't remember if he was *the* one or *the other* one. She would have asked, but her attempts at conversation both this morning and during the drive had been met with monosyllabic answers. She had hoped the addition of DS Abbott to their troupe might improve the situation, but it seemed he was as taciturn as his colleague. She cleared her throat and went back to staring out the window.

The rain had melted the majority of the snow on the motorway and the main road into Bridgwater, but not here in Nether Stowey. The cobbled pavements that ran the length of the village were still covered in snow. She ran her hand through her hair, catching her finger on a knot she must have missed. She hadn't slept well. She pulled the tangle loose as she rested her elbows on the steering wheel. Lewisham didn't look like this in winter. The plethora of concrete, brick and asphalt all took on the same dull appearance whatever the weather. Somerset was like another world. Even though the trees were bare, there was a sparse beauty to the place.

Abbott had mumbled directions out of Bridgwater, leading her onto the A39, the road she had seen the night before when she was out with Barney. It cut right through the landscape, rolling farmland to her left, the Bristol Channel – now dark blue rather than black – to her right. As she had turned off at the signpost for Nether Stowey, she had been able to see the Quantocks off to her left. From a distance, the naked woodland looked almost purple. She shivered. Even thinking about the place gave her the willies. She rubbed her hands together as the temperature dropped in the car now the engine was off. She looked again at her silent passengers. She had tried to engage them by talking about the area, asking for recommendations when it came to pubs or places to eat, but to no avail. She looked at the clock on the dashboard. It was ten minutes to three. 'I reckon we should give it another five minutes, guys,' she said. 'What do you think?'

From the back seat, Pimbley said, 'I guess that's up to you.'

She decided to let the dig pass, given the utterance was at least progress in the conversational standoff. 'Given they weren't expecting us 'til Monday, I think arriving early is poor form,' she said, more for her benefit than theirs. 'Besides, it'll give me a chance to get to know you two better.' She hid her smile with the back of her hand.

'Soooo,' she said. 'Have you guys been with CID long? The Express Park building is amazing, isn't it? Must have cost a fortune.'

More silence.

'Townsend said he'd only been with you lot for six months. Seems like a decent DI.' She heard Pimbley scoff from the back of the car. She was used to cajoling an eight-year-old into conversation. If she could crack Peter, these guys didn't stand a chance, not now they were a captive audience. 'I guess it takes a while for a team to gel. Who was your DI before Townsend?'

'Waters,' Pimbley said.

'Where did he . . . she go?' With Peter, she could usually break his silence with a well-placed question about dinosaurs. These guys were a little different.

'She,' Abbott said. 'She's had a baby.'

'So Townsend's just covering her maternity leave.'

'We wish,' Pimbley muttered.

'And here I was thinking it was *us* you didn't like.' More silence. She decided to wait and see if one of them would fill the void. She kept her eye on the rear-view mirror, watching Pimbley's expression. People didn't show this much dislike for their boss for no reason. Perhaps Lockyer was right to be wary of the guy.

'No one has a problem with you or your boss,' Abbott said from the passenger seat. His voice was quiet. His tall and lanky frame was folded into the passenger seat like damp tissue paper, but his face was hard.

'Well, that's good to know,' she said. 'So what's the problem with Townsend?'

'He—' Pimbley started to speak, but Jane saw Abbott glance in the rear-view mirror.

'There's no problem,' Abbott said.

'OK.' She tried to think of another way in. 'Are you guys local?'

'Abbott is,' Pimbley said. Jane felt Abbott shift in his seat. 'I live past Cannington way.'

'Where do you live, then?' she asked, turning to Abbott.

'Doddington.' She could see he wasn't happy divulging the information. 'So you must know Barney, then. He's a—'

'I know Barney,' Abbott said.

'He's his neighbour,' Pimbley added from the back.

'Small world,' she said, watching as Abbott flared his nostrils. 'I was out with him yesterday. He took me up to the crash site and was showing me the hills . . . you know.'

'He's the best one to do it,' Pimbley said. His demeanour

had changed beyond recognition. He looked relaxed, his eyes bright and smiling.

Jane thought about what Barney had told her – and what he hadn't. 'Did either of you know Pippa Jones?'

Abbott turned in his seat to face her. 'No,' he said. 'Barney said you'd been asking him about that too.'

'Why, is that a weird question to you?' she asked, frowning. 'Seems to me this is a pretty small place. Who knows who is kinda relevant, don't you think?' Abbott shrugged. 'Barney was telling me he went to school with Pippa and her brother, Aaron.' She caught Abbott's eye. 'What about you?'

He reddened. 'As it happens, yes, but she was a year below me, so we were never in any classes together or anything.'

'But you knew her . . . saw her in the playground or whatever,' Jane said, thinking Abbott couldn't have been a DS very long if he was only twenty-six. She glanced again at the clock.

'I guess,' he said.

'Did you see anything of her when she moved back?'

'We've seen her in here a fair few times, haven't we?' Pimbley said, nodding to Abbott and then the pub outside the window. He received a hard look from Abbott for his disclosure. 'Once or twice over the other side, I s'pect.'

'Would this be your local?' Jane asked, turning to look at Abbott, exploiting the division that had sprung up between the two officers.

'No,' he said.

'Does Townsend know? Did you tell him you knew the victim . . . that you knew Pippa?'

'No,' Abbott said, 'because we didn't. I didn't.'

'Still,' she said, 'I think he'd want to know.' Abbott folded his arms and turned away from her. The conversation was over.

'Everyone knows everyone around here,' Pimbley said from the back. He seemed oblivious to Abbott's annoyance. 'No one really knew her or anything . . . she hadn't been staying here long, but most people know her aunt. Well, the girls on the team do.'

'Why's that?' she asked.

'Claudette runs a spa place over in Taunton.'

'Pippa's aunt?'

'That's right,' he said. 'And most folk know *of* her uncle.'

'Why? Who's he?'

'Well, I guess he must be an ex-uncle now,' Pimbley said. 'Him and Claudette split up years ago. He wasn't DCC then. His mother didn't approve of the marriage, apparently . . . something about them being Catholic and Claudette's lot being C of E, who knows. Shame. She died a while ago now. Choked on a Brazil nut.' He put his hand to his throat.

'Sorry, who? Whose mother are we talking about? Who wasn't DCC?'

'Hamilton's mother,' Pimbley said, as if that alone should suffice.

Jane rolled her lips over her teeth and shook her head. 'You've lost me.'

'Claudette's late mother-in-law. Les Hamilton was her eldest. He's DCC now.'

'Hang on,' Jane said, trying to wrap her brain around the plethora of names and random pieces of information Pimbley had just dumped on her. 'Who's DCC?'

'Hamilton, Les Hamilton,' he said. 'Claudette's ex-husband.'

'So you're saying Pippa's uncle is a deputy chief constable?'

'For Avon and Somerset, yeah,' he said, 'but like I said, him and Claudette have been divorced years now. He remarried not long after. Someone his mother approved of, I guess. She died too, a few years after his mother . . . cancer, I think. Her folks used to own Pepperhill Farm, I think, but . . .'

Jane nodded along as Pimbley continued his impromptu and baffling genealogy of half the population of Nether Stowey, but she wasn't listening. Only one name had stuck. *Hamilton.* DCC for Avon and Somerset. Pippa's uncle. DCC was the second highest rank in the Country.

The mystery surrounding Lockyer's secret mission had come into sharp focus. Although she was surprised and somewhat impressed that this was the first she had heard about Hamilton. She had worked with Aaron for over two years, and he had never said a word about his powerful uncle. Not a word.

CHAPTER FIFTEEN

12th December – Saturday

Lockyer pulled in to the side of the road at the Carew Arms in Crowcombe Village to let a string of cars pass him. It occurred to him as he raised his hand in response to the numerous thank yous that this would have been the last point of civilization Pippa Jones encountered before she died. In the fading light it was unremarkable, but at night, on an icy road with the rain pouring down? It couldn't have been a pleasant journey. He sighed and focused instead on each car, trying to decide how best to describe them.

Before his meeting with the paint nerds, he had only ever thought in terms of straight colour: red, blue, white, black and so on. Now, though, he realized each vehicle had a different tint, a different accent. The palette was as varied as the cars themselves. The red Fiat at the back of the line was in fact maroon, which would appear on the 'red with blue tones' range on a colour chart. Whereas the Ford Focus, two from the front, was a warmer orangey-red, so it would appear within the 'red with yellow tones' spectrum.

It had been a fascinating couple of hours. He had dealt

with paint fragments numerous times in his career, but he had never really paid attention to the science. Larry and Linda Mason were a husband and wife team who owned and ran South West Forensics. They offered a mind-boggling list of services, from examining trace evidence, including fibres, glass and paint samples, up to and including DNA analysis. In fact, their company was handling the footwear and tread marks found in and around the crime scene. He somehow doubted the impressions would be from the other driver, given the whole idea of a hit and run was to 'run' afterwards, not stand around and watch; but it was worth a shot.

As a couple, Larry and Linda were an odd pairing. She had to be a good twenty years his senior. Larry was a fresh-faced science geek with glasses, gelled hair and a Seventies dress sense, whereas Linda reminded Lockyer of Joanna Lumley's character Purdey from *The Avengers*. Lockyer guessed she was in her late fifties, but she was well put together. She had explained, in husky tones, that the contact paint fragments taken from Pippa's car would be examined using their three main components: the carrier, the binder and the vehicle. Linda would then input the data using the PDQ – the international forensic automotive paint data query database – and with any luck be able to identify the make, model, year and even the factory the other vehicle had come from. Her lips were like two plump cushions. When she said 'paint pigment', Lockyer could swear he had blushed.

He nodded to the guy in the maroon Fiat, put his car into gear and started up Crowcombe Hill. The scenery looked different as the light grew dim. Either side of the car were grass-covered verges peppered with snow and thick undergrowth leading up to dense woodland. The hill itself was steeper than he remembered. He thought again about the conditions on the night Pippa Jones had died. There was no way he would be happy about his daughter making this journey.

A gateway to his left showed an open vista beyond, the rolling farmland cast in shadows. He glimpsed it for a second and then it was gone as the car was enclosed by woodland again. He shook his head. Of course, Megan *was* here and could very well be using this road, day or night, and as per usual he could do nothing to stop her. 'Kids,' he muttered to himself as he accelerated, his engine rumbling with the effort. It would take about fifteen, maybe twenty minutes to get to the Joneses'. He would have been earlier, but his discussion with John Mills, once he had found him, had taken longer than expected.

It transpired Mills was the chef as well as the landlord, so Lockyer had ended up conducting the majority of the interview in the kitchen. The guy had a lot to say for himself, all whilst browning meat and par-boiling a dizzying array of vegetables. He was, by his own admission, the eyes and ears of the place. Mills claimed to know who was screwing whose wife, who had a drink problem, who was about to be made redundant – but he wouldn't name names. He was 'a man of discretion', he had said more than once. Lockyer huffed out a laugh as he flicked on his headlights. Within five minutes of this statement Mills had proceeded to tell Lockyer the life story of everyone south of Bristol, it seemed. And he wasn't kidding. He appeared to know his customers' lives in minute detail.

One example of clandestine goings-on involved the skittles team. On an away match in Minehead three of the team had got so drunk, they had ended up swapping wives at the end of the night. The three couples never breathed a word and still played together – skittles, that was – every Sunday night. Lockyer had asked how it was Mills himself knew. He had tapped the side of his nose and moved on to the next poor sod to have their life put under his microscope. Lockyer pulled at his seatbelt and knocked the heated seat down a bar. His arse was beginning to roast.

Mills' knowledge of Pippa was no less detailed. According to him, despite growing up in Somerset, Pippa had hated the South West. She was a London girl through and through. It was her intention, so Mills said, to earn as much money as she could while staying with her aunt, Claudette Barker, over in Nether Stowey. All she needed was enough to cover her room in London until one of her many job applications came to something. When Lockyer asked how Mills knew all this he had just shrugged and said, 'It's a gift. The tail end of a conversation here and there, talking to her, reading between the lines. It's all there. You just have to have the right ear . . . and I do.' Lockyer had thought he would make a pretty good detective, but he had kept that nugget to himself. Let Mills decipher it with his mind magic.

Lockyer's car rumbled over the cattle grid as he passed onto the Common, as the locals called it. He was struck, as he had been this morning, by how barren it was up here: the trees blown sideways, the grass and heather buffeted into submission. It was bleak. How must Pippa Jones have felt navigating this tiny lane at night as a pair of headlights loomed large in her rear-view mirror? The thought reminded him of the old Spielberg movie *Duel* where Dennis Weaver was pursued through the American Midwest by an unknown, unseen driver of an oil tanker. The film was as understated as it was unnerving. Had Pippa known who was behind her? It was a question Lockyer kept putting to himself, but so far he didn't have an answer. He tapped his brakes, slowing enough to avoid a herd of sheep ambling by the side of the road.

From what Mills had said, Pippa had made few friends. She had been out with some of the AONB lot a few times, Barney among them, but other than that Mills said she kept herself to herself. Lockyer thought about Jane's earlier text. Cooper, Pippa's boss at Fyne Court, had said the same. He would send Jane up here tomorrow night. Sunday was skittles night. She could speak to the regulars and get their impressions of the girl. Jane was better at tackling a group than he was. No doubt she would say that was because she could multi-task and he couldn't. He flicked on his windscreen wipers at the first drops of snow. She could bring a few of Townsend's team with her: Crossley with the big bum and the other one, with the grey hair, Nicola something-or-other. His phone started ringing, blinking from the passenger seat next to him. He had left his hands-free in Jane's car. 'DI Lockyer,' he said, touching the speaker button, picking up the handset and balancing it between his collarbone and chin.

'It's Bill Townsend.'

'Bill,' Lockyer said, his surprise genuine. 'Good to hear from you.'

'Where are you?'

Lockyer noted the lack of preamble and the edge to

Townsend's voice. 'I'm on my way to the Joneses' now,' he said. 'Should be there in five, ten minutes. Did you get my email? Are you back in the office?'

There was a long silence before Townsend said, 'I'm not in the office, no. I called to see who was and Crossley advised me that you, DC Pimbley, DS Abbott and DS Bennett were all out running interviews.' A silence hung in the air. What could Lockyer say? Everything Townsend had said so far was true. 'In future I would appreciate it if you and your colleague would speak to me *before* you arrange or *rearrange* any interviews relating to *my* investigation, not to mention having the courtesy to ask before you requisition *my* officers.'

'Fair enough,' Lockyer said, going for sincere and failing. He wanted to add that maybe next time Townsend should consider being in the office when he had a murder investigation to run.

'I understand you told Maureen Jones that you would be *seizing* her daughter's laptop?' Townsend was almost growling.

Lockyer found himself nodding, his neck heating. He wasn't sorry, but it was embarrassing. If anyone had done to him what he had done and was continuing to do to Townsend, there's no way he would have remained so magnanimous. 'That's right,' he said. 'I thought it best to get a jump on her known associates . . . chase down any issues. You know how these kids are today – they live their lives online.'

'I'm not sure that's necessary. The Joneses are trying to cope with the death of their daughter.'

'Bill,' Lockyer said, measuring his tone. 'You know as well as I do that every second counts in a murder investigation.'

'If that's what this is.'

Lockyer debated challenging him for a second, but then decided he needed some answers, and now was as good a time as any to get them. The guy had been MIA all day – who knew when he would resurface again? 'Either way, she's still dead, Bill. Murder, manslaughter, what's the difference? *Someone's* still to blame.'

'There's a difference,' was all he said.

'Shit, maybe I'm wrong here, Bill, but you seem more than a little reluctant to see this incident as a deliberate act – that it could have been premeditated.'

'Deliberate and premeditated are two different things, Mike,' Townsend said. 'I'm still inclined to think we're looking at manslaughter – someone driving drunk. It wouldn't be the first time . . . or the last.'

Lockyer was shaking his head. He felt like he was pushing jelly up hill. 'Look. I don't disagree that drink could be a factor,' he said as he passed over the cattle grid where Pippa Jones had lost control of her car, 'but the evidence from the crash investigation team clearly shows it was a sustained attack – incident – made worse when whoever they were fled the scene and left her to burn.' His phone slipped and dropped to his lap. 'And another thing,' he said, grabbing it and shoving it to his ear, 'you said Pippa Jones died on impact.'

'Yes.'

'That's not what Dr Reed said yesterday.' Lockyer braked and pulled into a passing space. The line was crackling. He wasn't going to risk losing the connection. Now he had Townsend cornered, he wanted some answers. 'He said there's evidence she tried to get out of the vehicle after the fire took hold.' An image of Pippa's wrecked hand flashed in front of his eyes.

'I haven't had a chance to look at Dr Reed's full report,' Townsend said.

'But you were there, Bill. Reed said the two of you discussed it.'

'Dr Reed is mistaken,' Townsend said. Lockyer thought he could hear an electronic announcer in the background. Where was he? 'I trust you won't be burdening the Joneses with this *new* information?'

'Of course not. For Christ's sake, Bill, we're on the same team here.'

'Are we?' Townsend said. 'Superintendent Atkinson advised me earlier that DS Bennett has requested to review a file I handled when I first came down to Bridgwater. The Chloe Evans case?'

It was Lockyer's turn to be on the back foot. He was going to kill Jane. His mind ground to a halt as he reached for a plausible explanation. He saw a black 4x4 coming up the hill towards him. He spotted the AONB insignia. 'That's right,' he said, feigning nonchalance. 'I'm pretty sure I mentioned it in my email – the one I sent this morning?' If Townsend was going to put him on the spot, Lockyer was going to return the favour. 'DS Bennett was out at the crash site with one of the rangers, Barney Gill, yesterday,' he said. 'He mentioned that the local community were distressed about the incident . . . that they were fearful of driving through the area.'

'I'm sure,' Townsend said, his voice thick with disdain.

Lockyer decided to let the dig go – for now. 'Anyway,

Barney was telling Jane about the local legends – Dead Woman's Ditch, et cetera?'

'I wouldn't believe everything you hear from Barney – or the locals, for that matter,' Townsend said with a snort. 'In my experience they will say and do whatever's necessary to maintain the status quo. They protect their own.'

'Meaning?'

'The Evans case,' Townsend said with a heavy sigh. 'I'm sure you have cases you'd rather not . . . revisit. Well, the Evans case is mine.'

'What happened?' Lockyer asked, raising a hand to the two guys in the passing AONB truck. Both looked to be a regular size, so he assumed neither was Jane's BFG.

There was a pause before Townsend spoke. 'I was dragged down from Bristol and thrown in at the deep end,' he said. 'The DI was pregnant – Atkinson felt it was inappropriate for her to handle the case.' He made a harrumphing noise. 'I had zero cooperation from the team. They were kicking off because Waters had been taken off the case – against her wishes, I gathered. Like it was my fault? Like I had anything to do with it? As for the *locals* . . . the people who knew Chloe, who supposedly cared for her – they were belligerent, secretive and downright obstructive. By all accounts they had sat back and watched this girl go off the rails and done nothing.' He was breathing hard. 'She was murdered on their doorstep and they were far too busy spewing nonsense about legends and superstitions to care.'

'Why, Bill?' Lockyer asked. 'And why didn't you tell me?'

'Because they could,' Townsend said. 'Because they were protecting one of their own, that's why.'

'Who . . . ?'

'And why on earth would I tell you about it?' Townsend said. 'Chloe Evans's murder was six months ago. It has no bearing on the Pippa Jones case . . . legends and superstitions, even less so.'

'This ditch place – where Evans was found – it's less than half a mile from the crash site, Bill,' Lockyer said, looking in his rear-view mirror at the cattle grid and the tree where Pippa Jones's journey had ended. Again he heard the tinny voice of an announcement in the background.

'Look, Mike,' Townsend said, 'I really don't have time for this. You'll have to trust me. One has absolutely nothing to do with the other.'

'How can you be so sure?'

'Because I know who killed Chloe Evans.'

CHAPTER SIXTEEN

12th December – Saturday

Steph rinsed the basin again and again. It was clean. There wasn't a trace of soap or hair, or anything. She was stalling.

'Come on, Stephanie,' Connie said. 'Don't you have a home to go to?'

She turned off the tap and looped the shower attachment around her hand several times before dumping the coil in the basin. 'Didn't you want me to get the towels out of the dryer?' She looked up when she heard her boss laughing.

'Talk about a transformation,' Connie said, dragging a piece of tinsel out of her ponytail. She had made all the girls wear a different colour to give the salon a festive feel. Steph's was green. She had it tied around her neck like a choker. 'You've done more than enough today. You should have been off two hours ago. It's quarter to five.'

'I don't mind,' she said. 'Save anyone having to worry about it. The girls are going out for drinks over at the Quay tomorrow night for Paula's eighteenth. They'll be hanging come Monday morning.'

Connie chewed the edge of her lip. 'That's true. Paula is

the worst when she's got a hangover,' she said before looking at her watch. 'Trouble is, I'm meeting Archie in Sainsbury's car park in a sec. We're heading up to Cribbs for a bit of late-night shopping. If I'm much later, he'll just be sat there . . .'

'You go. I can lock up,' Steph said, her heart leaping in her chest. She saw a frown wrinkle Connie's forehead. 'Stacey showed me how the other day.'

'I'm not sure . . . the snow's getting pretty heavy out there. I don't want you getting stranded . . .'

'Please, Connie,' Steph said, trying not to whine. 'I really want to prove to you I've changed – that things have changed. I can do this.' She could see by her boss's expression that she was softening. 'I think the responsibility would be good for me, don't you?'

Connie nodded, her mouth turning down at the edges, as if she was weighing up her options. 'OK,' she said. 'You show me you know what you're doing and you've got a deal . . . and you text me the second you get home, OK?'

'Of course,' Steph said, feeling elated – feeling relieved. The longer she could stay in the salon, the better. More time here meant less time out there. She didn't care about the snow. It could snow all night for all she cared.

'Come on, then,' Connie said. 'Here are the keys. This is my spare set so don't, for God's sake, lose them. Now show me what needs doing.'

Steph had to stop herself from snatching the bundle of keys. She turned on her heel and went to the alarm panel at the back of the salon. She opened the clear plastic cover and looked over her shoulder at Connie. 'I press 1, 8, 8, 1 and then the A for away. There'll be a long beep. I have thirty seconds to get to the front door, go outside and lock it.' She rushed on before Connie could raise any doubts. 'If I needed to come back in, for whatever reason, I unlock the door and again I've got thirty seconds to get to the panel. There's a long beep. I press 1, 8, 8, 1 and C for cancel. There'll be three quick beeps and then it's unset.'

'And you need to—'

'I know,' she said, interrupting. 'I need to switch off the main lights, unplug the tree lights and the display in the window. Make sure the dryers are off, unplug the straighteners and make sure all the internal doors, like the toilet door, are shut tight.'

Connie chuckled. 'Are you sure you don't have a twin?' she asked. 'You're certainly not the same girl I had working here, or rather not working here, last week.'

Steph forced herself to smile. 'I really want to do this, Connie.'

'OK, OK,' Connie said. 'Sort the towels and if you want to you can set up for tomorrow, but then home, OK?'

'Sure,' she said. 'Thanks, Connie. I won't let you down.'

It looked like her boss was going to say something else, but instead she gave Steph a quick hug and then turned to leave. 'See you . . . Tuesday, is it?' she said.

Steph nodded. 'In the afternoon, yes,' she said, already dreading it. 'Say hi to Archie.'

'Will do.'

As soon as Steph heard the bell jingle and the door to the salon close, she collapsed into one of the chairs by the basins. She had gone beyond tired. Every bone, fibre and tendon of her ached from hours of worrying. Last night had been all right in the end. Her dad had relented and not only dropped her at work, but picked her up too. The downside to his generosity was that it meant he wasn't working today, so she was on her own. She had to drive in and she *had* to drive home and, of course, it was dark. When she had gone to bed last night she had lain there fully clothed and stared at the ceiling, thinking about the girl she had seen in the paper. *Local woman dies in hit and run.* Ten hours later she was still staring at the same fleck of paint on the ceiling. Hit and run. Those three words had stopped Steph's breath. She had read them over and over. The police were investigating. Anyone with any information should come forward, it said. According to Paula, whose sister was dating one of the response team over in Bridgwater nick, the car had been rammed off the road – on purpose.

The sound of a car racing past outside startled her. She looked around the salon. She was surrounded by decorations and lights. At least the endless Christmas music had stopped. If she had to listen to Slade screaming 'It's Christmas' one more time, she thought she would go mad. She looked at the sofa in the window. She could move it, drag it back here. No one would know if she slept here. No one would care. All she had to do was phone her parents and say she was staying with Stacey or Paula. She felt her cheeks heat and tears prick in her eyes as the realization hit her. She had her mother's house keys. She had to go home. Her tears felt hot against her cheeks.

Anyone with information should come forward.

She shook her head, pushing away the tears on her cheeks. What was happening to her was different. Someone was just trying to mess with her head, to scare her. *Hit and run.* It might even be one of the boys having a laugh. Whatever had happened to that girl, Steph was different. Why would anyone want to hurt her?

CHAPTER SEVENTEEN

12th December – Saturday

Jane's hand was on the latch of the Joneses' front door when it swung inwards, connecting with her knee. She sucked in a breath.

'Hey, sorry I'm late,' Lockyer said, ducking his head as he stepped over the threshold, forcing her to step back, unaware of the pain he had caused. His head and shoulders were peppered with snow. 'Mills took an age and then I got stuck on the phone with Townsend.' She opened her mouth, keen to find out where the guy had been all day, but Lockyer held up his hand. 'Don't ask.' He shrugged out of his jacket and threw it over his arm, covering her with a fine spray in the process. 'I parked at the top end of the village,' he said, stamping his feet on the doormat. 'It's really coming down. Didn't want to end up stuck out here.'

She craned her neck to look outside. The road was covered with about an inch of unbroken snow. 'Shit, I didn't realize it'd started again,' she said. 'Should I move mine, do you think?'

'Nah, I wouldn't worry,' he said, sniffing and rubbing his hands together. 'I'll get it out if need be.'

'Me man, me move car in all weathers,' she said in her best caveman voice.

'That's about the size of it,' he said, pulling a face. 'So what's been happening with you? How are the chuckle brothers?'

'Better,' she said. 'I've managed to get whole sentences out of them. What's happening with Townsend? Where's he been today?'

'I never established that,' he said with a shake of his head. 'I'll tell you about it later.' His expression changed. 'Is Megan here?'

'No,' she said, lowering her voice and moving closer. 'She and Aaron went to the supermarket. They'll be back later.'

'You saw them?'

She nodded. 'Only briefly. They were on their way out when I arrived.' He ran his tongue along his bottom teeth. 'What?'

He shook his head for a long time before he spoke. 'I hate that she's here with him,' he said. 'And before you say it, I know this isn't Aaron's fault, and yes . . .' He narrowed his eyes. 'I know he's a good lad and all that, but still – the association – having Megs this close to a violent death . . . again. It's driving me nuts, if you want to know the truth.'

She put her hand on his arm and waited for him to stop chewing his cheek and look at her. 'She's fine, Mike. She knew you were coming, so she made herself scarce. She understands this situation isn't . . . ideal.'

'She spoke to you?' He looked hurt.

'We had a five-minute chat before they left, if that,' she said. 'From what the vicar tells me she's been a whirling dervish, taking care of them all. You've done a great job. She's a very mature, caring young woman.'

He snorted. 'Not sure I can take credit for that.' He took a deep breath, shaking his shoulders as he blew it out. 'Anyway, enough of my crap. How are the Joneses?'

She paused, thinking of the best way to describe them. 'I'd say they're an enigmatic bunch, circumstances aside.' She held up her fingers to count off the Jones family. 'We've got Reverend Anthony Jones. He hasn't moved from his seat by the fire but he's quick to chime in on other conversations – a passive patriarch. Abbott's been talking to him. He'll update us when we get back to the station.' Lockyer rolled his hands, one over the other. He had a cheek, given he was the one who had rocked up late. 'Pimbley has been talking to the twins' sister, Cassie Jones. She flew back from Australia the week before it happened but hadn't been down because she was visiting friends in London.'

'Shit,' he said. 'So she was in the Country but never saw her sister before the accident?'

She shook her head. 'No . . .'

'God, that can't feel good. How's she handling it?' he asked with what seemed like genuine sympathy.

'I'm not sure she *feels* much,' Jane said, stepping back and up onto the bottom stair. Her neck was aching from looking up at him. 'I asked her plans . . . you know, is her work being good about the time off and the delay getting back to Oz, that kind of thing?'

'And?'

'Her boss told her to take all the time she needs,' she said, pausing to ensure she had his full attention. 'So she's planning on using that time to fly off to the States before Christmas so she can visit friends out there.' She was satisfied when she saw his expression. He was as shocked as she had been.

'That's cold,' he said. 'Any clues as to why?'

She conjured an image of Cassie Jones. Despite the tan and golden hair, there was no warmth to the woman. 'Not sure. There's a definite distance between her and the family, though, and maybe even an underlying animosity towards Pippa, but I wouldn't swear to that.'

'Survivor's guilt?'

'Could be.' Jane pursed her lips. 'She'd have been a teenager when Pippa and Aaron were born. I'd imagine she did her fair share of childcare. The mother's pretty dedicated to her husband . . . and the church. That could have built up some resentment.'

'What about the mother? What's she like?'

'Maureen Jones,' Jane said, taking one foot off the stair and bouncing her heel against the mauve runner. 'I've been talking to her. She's pretty reserved, like her husband, but I'd say she's more detached. She looked the part, if you know what I mean. If she feels the distance with her eldest daughter, she doesn't show it, and neither parent had spoken to Pippa in several weeks due to a falling out.'

Lockyer's eyebrows shot up in a question.

'They'd been helping her with her rent for her flat-share in London so she didn't lose it, but they had ended up paying the lion's share because Pippa said she didn't have any money. The aunt, Claudette Barker – Maureen's sister – told Maureen that Pippa was in fact out a lot, a bit disrespectful and wasn't contributing to her house funds either. So, to cut a long story short, there was a row and the parents stopped paying at the beginning of last month.'

'Interesting,' Lockyer said.

She sighed. 'I'm not sure it is. You'll appreciate how benign they are when you meet them.'

He shrugged. 'OK, what else?'

'This is the family home,' she said. 'Anthony Jones was offered a . . . vicar-ship, or whatever it's called, when Aaron and Pippa were twelve, and so the family relocated to London. Cassie had already flown the nest. Father, Aaron and Pippa love the city – Maureen hates it, and wants to be back here.' She leaned forward and lowered her voice again. 'Her sister Claudette has been living here since her divorce . . . a messy business, by the sounds of it. His family didn't approve. Some religious differences or something, but I'll tell you about that in a second. I think, reading between the lines, that Maureen finds it hard being here because she still sees this place as her home. Cassie has made a few comments about it not being *her* house, as if maybe it should have been.' She shrugged. 'You know how families are. There's always more under the surface than on it.'

He looked at her like she had just landed from another planet. 'Well, that is fascinating,' he said in a mocking whisper, 'I'll have to tune in next week to find out what happens next.' He rolled his eyes. 'They're not the Archers, Jane.'

'All right, all right, I was just saying.' She felt peeved to be ridiculed, but he had a point. Why was she wasting her time and his with family gossip, when she had far more important information to give him? 'The person I really wanted to talk to you about was Claudette Barker, the aunt. You'll never guess who her ex-husband—' Before she could finish, the door to the lounge opened.

'Everything all right out here?' Cassie Jones said, beckoning Jane and Lockyer into the room, sweeping her hair over one shoulder as she pulled the door wide. Jane couldn't help but feel envious, which was obscene given the circumstances. She hated her own hair. It was the colour of watered-down tar, her fringe an unmitigated disaster. Cassie's hair, on the other hand, was the colour of sand on a tropical beach. She looked more Swedish than British. In fact, seeing her again, Jane realized she looked just like the girl in the Timotei adverts from when she was a kid. 'All we can hear is you two whispering,' Cassie said, screwing up her face. '*Pss wss wss wss.*'

Jane stepped down from the stairs. 'Sorry,' she said, gesturing for Lockyer to go first. 'This is Cassie Jones, Pippa and Aaron's sister.'

'Good afternoon. I'm Detective Inspector Lockyer,' he said, ducking his head as he entered the room.

Maureen Jones appeared from behind her daughter. 'Hello,' she said. 'Please come in. I was just about to make a pot of tea.'

'Thank you, Maureen,' Jane said. 'This is DI Lockyer.'

'So *you're* DI Lockyer,' Cassie said. 'My brother has told me a lot about you.' The look she gave him told Jane none of the things Aaron had said were complimentary.

'Right,' he said, extending his hand. Cassie turned away as if she hadn't seen the offer and went and sat down on the arm of the sofa, crossing her long legs, one foot swinging.

Maureen Jones, in contrast, was moving in a slow circle, asking in a quiet voice who wanted tea, who wanted coffee and did anyone take sugar. She didn't appear to be focused on the answers, just asking the questions, over and over.

'For God's sake, leave it, Mum,' Cassie said. 'Claudette'll sort it. It's *her* house.'

Jane glanced at Lockyer and then the reverend to gauge his reaction to his daughter's choice of words and manner, but he didn't appear to be listening. His eyes were almost closed, and his hands were clasped together as if in prayer.

'Maybe I'll just go and check—'

'Sit down, Mum,' Cassie barked. 'I'll do it.' She turned to Jane and then to Lockyer. 'I'll just do a pot, shall I?'

'Thank you, Cassie. I'll help,' Jane said, thinking she could use the opportunity to ask Claudette to show Abbott and Pimbley Pippa's room, so they could take some photographs and collect her laptop and any other relevant hardware. She assumed the two of them were hiding in the kitchen after Cassie had bollocked Pimbley for calling her 'Casey'. *You might want to work on that bedside manner, mate,* she had said. Abbott had hidden a grin, but Pimbley had looked mortified.

'Fine,' Cassie said, turning to leave the room. 'Is it appropriate to offer biscuits?'

'We're fine,' Lockyer said. Jane looked at him. His eyes flicked to hers for not more than a second but she got the message. *Yes, I think she's weird too.*

'I wasn't thinking of you, detective,' Cassie said with a sneer. Jane heard the reverend sigh as he clasped his hands tighter. If his daughter heard him or recognized his exasperation, she showed no sign. Her overall demeanour was just so aggressive. It must be exhausting to be around her for any length of time. Jane turned at the sound of raised voices, followed by a loud bang coming from the kitchen.

'What now?' Cassie said, not making any move to find out.

Lockyer pushed past Jane and opened the sliding doors that led to the dining room. He stopped, blocking her view. She stepped around him to see Abbott and Pimbley wrestling with someone on the floor. They were halfway under the dining-room table. It took her a second to realize the third person was Aaron. He was struggling as the two officers tried to pin him down. 'What the hell's going on?' Lockyer said.

'Stop fighting,' Abbott said. 'Just relax, mate. For Christ's sake, relax.'

'I don't know what happened,' Claudette said from the doorway to the kitchen, her hand to her mouth. 'Aaron was . . . listening to his voicemail, I think, and then . . . I don't know – he threw his phone and it hit her, and these two just jumped on him.' A man Jane didn't recognize was standing behind Claudette, his hands on her shoulders. Who was he and where did he spring from?

'All right, that's enough,' Lockyer said, pulling Abbott up by the arm. Pimbley sat back on his heels, panting. Aaron sat up and shuffled backwards, hanging his head between his knees. 'Aaron, are you all right?'

'I'm fine,' he said, swiping his hand under his nose.

'What happened?' Lockyer asked.

'I'm sorry, sir,' Pimbley said. 'There was an altercation in the kitchen. I stepped in to calm things down. However, things escalated. DS Abbott was just trying to assist.'

'Danny wasn't to blame, sir,' Abbott said, folding his arms, tipping his chin up. 'The guy was going nuts, lashing out and then he lobs his phone – hit his girlfriend square in the face.'

'It was an accident.'

Jane turned. Lockyer's daughter appeared in the kitchen doorway, holding a tea towel up to her face. When she dropped her hand Jane saw blood and a livid mark on her right cheek, just under her eye. She reached out for Lockyer as understanding dawned, but she was too late. He had already launched himself at Aaron.

CHAPTER EIGHTEEN

12th December – Saturday

'I'm fine,' Aaron said, although he didn't feel fine. 'It was my fault.' He felt like his head was full of swarming bees, the high-pitched drone driving him mad. He looked up at Abbott and the other officer who had gone for him. They were standing with their backs against the windows of the dining room, shoulder to shoulder, arms folded across their chests. They looked like a couple of bouncers outside a sleazy nightclub. Where Abbott was tall and lanky, the other one was stocky and short, his head shaved. Lockyer was nowhere in sight.

'I think you might need a couple of stiches,' Jane said, dabbing a tissue over his right eye. He winced when she made contact.

'I'm fine,' he said again, wondering if anyone could hear him. If they could, they weren't listening. His parents were huddled at the far end of the dining table, his mother's arm linked through his father's. Neither spoke. Neither moved. Their expressions were blank. He noticed the cups of steaming tea. Claudette, aka Cinderella, must be in the kitchen.

'I've got some steri-strips in my suitcase,' Cassie said,

barging Jane out of the way, grabbing hold of his head and pulling it towards her. He almost came off his chair. 'Bit of antiseptic and a few of those and you'll be fine. The skin's just split. It's not deep.'

'Maybe we should take you to A&E just to be on the safe side,' Megan said, squeezing his hand. Her face was a mess. 'I can drive. It won't take long, I'm sure. Better to get it checked, don't you think?' Aaron figured she wasn't really addressing him, so he didn't bother answering. What could he say? The mothers' union was in full effect surrounding him, suffocating him: his sister, his girlfriend and his boss.

'I think Megan's right,' Jane said. 'It might do everyone some good to have some breathing space.' He sighed and let his shoulders sag. He couldn't tell if Jane's concern was about his well-being, or that he might decide to have Lockyer up on assault charges. He figured given her allegiance, it was probably the latter.

'He said he's fine.' Aaron pulled his head out of his sister's grip and looked between the gaggle of women to see Lockyer stalking into the room from the lounge. 'Stop fussing over him.'

Aaron felt his sister tense. He dragged his tongue off the roof of his mouth. 'I'm OK, Cass,' he said, catching her eye. 'It was a . . . misunderstanding.'

'I wouldn't go that far,' Lockyer said, 'but you can break the circle, ladies. He's quite safe – for now.'

Aaron pushed himself up, shrugging off his sister's hands. He turned to Megan. 'Are you OK? I'm so sorry.' He looked at the bruising coming out over her right cheek and eye. He couldn't see the cut, but she pulled back when he reached up to touch her face. 'If we're comparing injuries, you came off much worse than me, Megs.'

'I second that,' Lockyer growled from the other side of the dining table.

'This is nothing,' Megan said, pulling her hair over her eye. 'It's a graze. It'll be healed by tomorrow.'

'I doubt that,' Lockyer said. He took a step towards the table and Aaron felt the circle of women tighten around him.

'Let it go, Dad,' Megan said. 'It was an accident. I got in the way . . .'

'Of him throwing his phone?' Lockyer said.

Aaron felt heat rising in his chest. His phone. He saw it bouncing off Megan's cheekbone and flying through the air until it landed with a thud on the kitchen floor, the back coming off and the battery skittering across the lino. 'Where's my phone?' he asked. 'I need to . . .' Before he could finish, he felt his centre of gravity shift. He reached out to the table to stop himself falling. He didn't have the words to describe what was happening to him. All he could hear was her voice. She was inside his head, pleading with him. He retched, but nothing came up.

'Aaron, sit down,' Lockyer said. 'Jane, can you take everyone into the other room for a moment. Megan, you go with them. Cassie, you too.'

Aaron looked up at his sister. He could see she was angry. She held out her hands as if waiting for him to say something, but he couldn't. He just shrugged. There was no fight left in him. He blinked his eyes once, then again. When his vision came back into focus Cassie was gone. Jane and

Megan too. He felt his eyes starting to roll, but then a steadying hand gripped his elbow.

'Come on,' Lockyer said.

Aaron felt his body sag. He had forgotten how to make his feet move.

'It's all right. I've got you.' The low timbre of Lockyer's voice vibrated through Aaron's head. 'You're all right. You're all right.' Aaron felt his body moving, but he was no longer in control. His legs bent on reflex as the chair touched the back of his knees. He closed his eyes. 'Just take some deep breaths.' He heard a chair scuff the carpet as Lockyer took a seat next to him. He tried to look at his boss, but found he couldn't make his eyes focus. He dragged in a breath, trying to pull himself back into the room. Her voice was everywhere. It was in the air he was breathing. He was choking on her.

'Let it go,' Lockyer said, putting a hand on the back of Aaron's neck and pulling his head to rest on his shoulder.

He took one breath, then another, his lungs squeezing in his chest. He felt as if he was pulling the oxygen up from his toes and through his body, each breath saturated with memories of his sister. He felt the strength of Lockyer's grip. His own father had never hugged him – never comforted him. Aaron heard someone crying – a desperate, keening sound, like that of a wounded animal.

It took him a second to realize it was him.

CHAPTER NINETEEN

12th December – Saturday

Lockyer pulled open the back door and stepped out into the gloom of a courtyard garden. Snow or no snow, he needed some air. Jane, Megan and the rest of the Joneses were still in the lounge. He had left Aaron half sitting, half collapsed at the dining room table. The poor kid was hanging on by a thread. Lockyer was all too accustomed to seeing people in pain, but with Aaron he could feel it – *feel* being the operative word.

'Hi.'

Lockyer turned to find a bloke huddled under a garden umbrella, smoking. 'Hi.'

'Pathetic, isn't it?' he said, gesturing first to the cigarette then to his shelter. 'Every winter I think, that's it – this is the year I'm going to quit.'

'Sure,' Lockyer said, not knowing what else to say. He pulled the kitchen door closed behind him and flattened himself against it, avoiding the snow.

'I'm Lester Hamilton,' the man said, extending his hand. 'Les.'

'Hi, Les,' Lockyer said, shaking his hand, realizing he was the guy who had been in the house before. He had been standing with the aunt. He looked like a rugby player gone to seed. His ample frame, still thick with muscle, was also covered in a layer of fat.

'How's Aaron doing?'

'OK . . . considering,' Lockyer said.

'He's not a violent kid, but I guess you already know that.'

'Sorry, you are . . . ?'

'I'm his uncle,' Hamilton said. 'Claudette's ex-husband. I'd hoped to get a moment of your time. It's Lockyer, isn't it?'

He reached for the doorknob. 'DI Lockyer, yes,' he said. 'If you'll excuse me, I need to—'

'Escape?' Lockyer looked at him. 'Don't worry, we're on the same team,' Hamilton said. 'Although I'm not technically here in an official capacity.' He ran a hand over his head, smoothing his hair. It was jet black. Lockyer wondered if it was natural or the stereotypical over-fifties' dye job.

'I didn't realize anyone in the family was on the force, other than Aaron, of course,' he said, thinking this was yet another detail Townsend had either missed or neglected to pass on. Not that Aaron had mentioned anything about his uncle, either. 'Where are you based?'

'Somerset,' he said. 'I'm DCC for the area.'

Lockyer opened his mouth, then shut it again. Roger's mystery phone call wasn't so mysterious any more. 'You're DCC for Avon and Somerset?'

'Yes.'

'And you're Pippa's uncle?'

'And Cassie's and Aaron's too,' Hamilton said. 'Though I

doubt he'd have told you that. Keen to make his own way. Worried people will think he had a hand up.'

'I'm sure,' Lockyer said, his forehead crumpling. 'So . . . are you here to see *me*?'

'No,' Hamilton said. 'My ex-wife asked me to come over for moral support. It's a difficult time for the family . . . as I'm sure you can imagine.'

'Right,' Lockyer said with a nod.

'What?' Hamilton asked.

Lockyer realized too late he was still frowning, replaying his conversations with Roger over and over in his mind. 'No, it's nothing. I'm just not sure I'd be my ex-wife's first call in the same situation, that's all.'

Hamilton shrugged. 'Anyway, I would have given you a heads-up about being here, but today's meeting was rescheduled, as I understand it, so when Claudette called it was all very last minute.' Lockyer could sense a rebuke. 'But as I said, I'm not technically here in an official capacity, so I thought I'd just keep my head down.'

'You succeeded,' Lockyer said.

'How's the investigation coming?'

'Are you asking me as Pippa's uncle, or in an official capacity?' Lockyer asked.

Hamilton looked at him. 'Both.'

'Forgive me, sir,' Lockyer said, conscious now who he was speaking to, 'but you *are* the one who wanted me here, aren't you?'

'Yes and no,' Hamilton said, taking a long drag on his cigarette, the burning embers making his face glow red. He had the look of Desperate Dan, minus the plaid shirt and meat pie. 'Superintendent Atkinson was the one who started that particular ball rolling at our end the second he realized who Pippa was. Or rather, as soon as he realized who she was in relation to me.'

'Why?' Lockyer asked.

Hamilton took another drag on his cigarette before flicking the butt into the snow. 'I think Terry felt the case warranted outside assistance to ensure it was dealt with expediently, so he called your boss in London, asked for the Met's best and . . . well, you know the rest.' The dismissal in Hamilton's tone was evident, the meaning implied. *You haven't proved you're the best . . . yet.*

'And this is because of who you are – your position, your relation to the . . . victim?'

'Partly, yes,' Hamilton said, 'but Terry was also concerned about issues with the press and, of course, the DI in charge. He was Townsend's SIO on a previous case so he knows what *can* happen with that guy at the helm.'

When he didn't say more, Lockyer decided to just ask the question straight out. 'Sir, if you'll forgive me. What exactly *is* the problem with DI Townsend?'

'What isn't?' Hamilton said, widening his stance and shoving his hands in his pockets. 'It's a long story.'

Lockyer looked at his watch. 'I'd say we've got time, sir, but as it happens we don't. Can you give me the short version . . . the highlights?'

'Can I trust that this will be just between us?'

'Of course,' he said. Hamilton didn't need to know that Lockyer would in fact tell Jane and no doubt Roger as well.

'DI Townsend was brought down from Bristol six or

seven months ago to replace another DI who'd had to leave on medical grounds,' Hamilton said. 'She was pregnant.' Lockyer knew this part. He had heard Townsend's version. He was curious to see how Hamilton's would differ. 'A girl had been murdered. Someone had made a right mess of her by all accounts. Her body was found in woodland up on the Quantocks . . .'

'This is the Evans case, right?'

'How do you know about that?' Hamilton asked. He looked agitated.

'It's come up,' Lockyer said, realizing the position he was in. He was stuck between someone he was trying to work with and someone who could get him fired before the day was out if he put a foot wrong. 'I've spoken to Townsend about it.'

'What did he say?'

Lockyer paused. He had no choice. Whatever little loyalty he had for Townsend, Hamilton was the senior officer – senior by a very long way. If he said, *jump*, Lockyer would be saying, *how high*? But that didn't mean he needed to tell him everything. 'He just said the case hadn't gone well. That he'd been unable to press charges against the guy he thought did it.'

'Not thought,' he said, '*did*. Ashworth was the victim's ex-boyfriend, and he would have been charged if Townsend hadn't dropped the ball. He made a complete cock-up of the investigation; arrested the suspect too soon, with too little evidence. He pissed the locals off to such an extent, no one would make a statement, incriminating or otherwise. He'd also pissed his team off with his officious working methods, so they weren't inclined to help him either. Evidence was lost . . . Oh, and of course, I mustn't forget: he attacked the suspect.'

'Townsend attacked a suspect?' Lockyer couldn't believe that.

'Yes,' Hamilton said. 'The lawyer had a field day with that one. The case should have been a slam-dunk.'

'What actually happened?' Lockyer asked.

'Chloe Evans was dating this lowlife, Kevin Ashworth. He's from the Sydenham Estate.' He waved away Lockyer's confusion. 'If you lived here, you'd know it,' he said. 'Ashworth was a low-level drug dealer. Chloe's parents were very vocal about their desire for her to end the relationship. As so often happens, Chloe got pregnant. Whilst I hate to be indelicate she wasn't what you'd call fussy. She already had two kids from different dads, Ashworth being one of them. Anyway, according to her friends the kid she was carrying wasn't Ashworth's, despite the fact that they were dating. Ashworth was, perhaps understandably, upset, but the two of them stayed together. However, within a few months Chloe was persuaded by her parents to break it off with Ashworth, with them saying they would help her with the baby. So she breaks it off. Next day, she's dead,' he said. 'She was found by a local school group a week later. Some kids tripped over her body.'

'So I heard,' Lockyer said.

Hamilton raised his eyebrows. 'Anyway, even without the assault, Townsend was a disaster. He let the locals run all over him. They were feeding him disinformation . . . ghosts and legends . . . how the Quantocks was haunted.'

'Why would they do that?'

'God knows,' Hamilton said, 'but it took the guy a week to even get one statement on record.'

Lockyer couldn't help thinking Townsend was on the same path with the Jones case.

'Townsend said he thought the locals were trying to protect their own.'

'Bollocks,' Hamilton said. 'Ashworth wasn't local. No one wanted him around. He was nothing but trouble. Why would they want to protect him? If they'd wanted to protect anyone, it'd be Chloe. She'd lived there all her life.'

'This legend stuff,' Lockyer said, not sure how to proceed. He didn't want to make matters worse for Townsend – or himself.

'Don't tell me he's still on about that?'

'Not him,' Lockyer said, 'but I've heard the locals are pretty unsettled, given what happened with your niece.'

'What the hell does any of that have to do with Pippa?'

'Well, as far as I can gather, the locals are under the impression the incidents are somehow linked.' Lockyer felt like he was in the head teacher's office getting a bollocking. Hamilton had a way of speaking that suggested he was used to being surrounded by idiots.

Hamilton started shaking his head. 'No, no, no, no, no,' he said. 'This is why you are here. You've got to take control, DI Lockyer. Chloe Evans wasn't killed by some ghost, and neither was my niece.'

'Sir, I'm not suggesting that's the case. But has it occurred to you the two could be linked, purely by proximity?'

'No, detective,' Hamilton said, raising his head and looking at him. 'My niece died in a car wreck. Chloe Evans was almost decapitated by her ex-partner, Kevin Ashworth. They are in no way related, and you would know that if you knew the Evans case or . . . knew my niece.' He let out a shuddering breath. 'Ashworth should be in prison, and he would be if Townsend hadn't fucked things up. What happened to my niece . . : what happened to Pippa . . ' He stopped. 'Whoever did this . . ' He looked close to tears.

'Understood,' Lockyer said, looking away to give Hamilton time to compose himself. By the time he turned back the DCC had lit up another cigarette, his mouth pulled into a tight line.

'You said Atkinson was worried about the press, sir?'

'Hence the low profile,' Hamilton said, gesturing to where he was standing.

'You're not worried about Abbott and Pimbley? I'm assuming they know who you are?'

Hamilton waved his hand. 'I'm not worried about them,' he said. 'They know who I am . . . who I am to Pippa, but they know better than to say anything to the press. They'd be under as much scrutiny as me . . . if not more.'

'So what's Atkinson's concern?' Lockyer asked.

'*If* the press sniff out my association, it'll attract a lot of attention, and I assume Terry wants to make sure his team . . . look good. That it's apparent he's gone above and beyond.' He rolled his eyes. 'Your presence being one of those measures.'

'Yes, sir, but that only works up to a point,' Lockyer said.

'Meaning?' Hamilton said.

Lockyer sniffed. His toes were starting to go numb. 'I can understand the superintendent wanting outside help to . . .

cover his arse, shall we say?' Hamilton nodded but didn't speak. 'But if the press *do* find out who you are to the victim . . . to Pippa, then I would have thought my presence would do more harm than good. Local officers not up to the job, would be the headline, I'd imagine.'

'Quite,' Hamilton said. 'And I can assure you I wasn't thrilled when I found out Terry had gone ahead with this without speaking to me first. He was, as you say, covering his arse and in a way, I suppose, trying to cover mine. I'm sure you can appreciate the kind of stuff that goes hand in hand with an investigation of this type – DCC uses undue influence, would be the headline.'

'Correct me if I'm wrong, sir,' Lockyer said, hoping he wasn't about to talk himself out of a job, 'but isn't that exactly what you are doing?'

Hamilton put his tongue in his cheek and looked at him 'That's one way of looking at it.'

'And the other way?'

'I'm damned if I do, damned if I don't, detective,' Hamilton said. He was fingering his cigarette packet despite being only halfway through the one he was smoking. 'If the press find out who I am and the investigation into my niece's death goes as it should . . . her attacker is caught and brought to justice. Then there'll no doubt be talk of undue influence and preferential treatment, which could be damaging to me and the force. However, if the investigation falls apart, then the press will ensure Townsend, the team, Avon and Somerset . . . and me, look like a bunch of incompetent idiots who can't even look after their own.'

'So *that's* where I come in,' Lockyer said. 'To make sure

Townsend doesn't make a mess of it, whilst also making sure that no one knows why I'm here . . . oh, and that the press don't find out who you are?' He wanted to add, *and I'll take the fall if it goes tits up.*

Hamilton threw away the rest of his cigarette. 'No, detective,' he said. 'You are here for one reason, and one reason only. You are here to find out who killed my niece.'

Lockyer almost fell back as the door behind him opened. He turned. It was Megan. 'Megs,' he said. 'Can you give us a minute, please?'

'Aaron wanted me to give you his phone,' she said, ignoring his request. She held out the mobile phone like it was coated in acid.

'Thanks,' he said, taking it and putting it in his pocket. 'Now if you can—'

'No, Dad,' she said. 'You need to listen to his voicemail now.'

'Why?' he asked, noticing for the first time how pale his daughter was.

'There's a message from Pippa,' she said.

'What do you mean?' Hamilton said, approaching Megan in two strides. 'What did she . . . ? What did she say?' he stammered.

'It's a voicemail from the night she died,' Megan said, looking at Hamilton and then back at her father. 'It was recording when she died.'

CHAPTER TWENTY

12th December – Saturday

Jane pulled the bedroom door closed and tiptoed back along the hallway. She and Lockyer had arrived twenty minutes after Peter's bedtime. It was now an hour past that, and she had only just managed to get him calm enough to sleep. She crept into her bedroom and changed out of her work clothes into a pair of leggings and a baggy grey hoodie. She shoved her feet into her slippers.

When she walked into the dining room she found her father sitting alone at the head of the table. He had the shadow of a smile on his face. 'You all right, Dad?' she asked, planting a kiss on his cheek. His skin felt dry and warm beneath her lips.

'Your boss is helping your mother in the kitchen,' he said with obvious amusement.

Jane sucked in a breath. 'Ooh, that can't be good.'

His expression changed. 'How's Pete?'

She blew out a long breath. 'He's . . . asleep,' she said, smiling and sitting down next to him. 'What are we having?'

'A heart-healthy curry,' he said with a shake of his head.

'Oh, bloody hell,' she said. 'So that's basically tofu and a curry sauce made predominately with coriander, then?'

'That's the one,' he said, reaching for his glass. His movements were still slow but she noticed there was less of a tremor in his hand.

'Do you think I should help?' she asked, giving him a mischievous look. 'Or maybe let him suffer?'

'Let him suffer,' he said. 'They deserve each other.'

'How's that?' she asked, breaking a poppadum with her finger and offering her father one of the pieces.

'Well,' he said as he shoved it in his mouth. 'He drives you nuts and yet you spend almost all your time with the guy, right?' Crumbs fell from the corners of his mouth. She nodded. 'Your mother's the same. Let them drive *each other* nuts for a bit. It'll make a change – give us a break.'

She nodded and yawned. She had worked longer days than this, but she felt ready to drop. 'So how are you finding it, Dad?' she asked, realizing it was the first time they had been alone since her arrival on Thursday night.

'Clevedon?' he said. 'It's a nice place.'

'Don't go overboard, now,' she said, breaking another poppadum and giving him the larger piece. 'You miss London?'

He covered her hand with his. 'I miss you, Jane. You and Peter.'

'Dad,' she said, doing her best not to cry.

'You're so far away,' he said with a sigh, his shoulders dropping. 'Clevedon's fine, honey. It's a lovely place, tons for us old fogeys to be getting on with. There's the beach, the pier, enough antique shops to bankrupt a fat cat – and there's this place.' He gestured around him. 'We would never have been able to afford this in London . . . never. I've got the garden, my shed, the conservatory . . .'

'You've got Mum,' she offered, cocking her head on one side.

He chuckled. 'That is true, Jane . . . painfully true. I will live a long time if she has anything to do with it . . . but it's not the same without you and Peter.'

'Oh yeah,' she said, wanting to lighten the mood. She was too tired for this. 'Peter I believe, but me? I'm not buying that. You just need me as a buffer. If she's on my case, she can't be nagging you to death.'

'We both miss you, poppet,' he said, squeezing her hand. 'Your mother will never say it, but she's worried sick about you being up there on your own.'

'I'm fine, Dad,' she said, taking her hand from beneath his and patting it.

The door to the kitchen opened and Lockyer walked in carrying an enormous bowl of curry, the smell of coriander overwhelming. 'Hey,' he said.

'Having fun?' she asked. 'Nice pinny.' Lockyer put the bowl down in the middle of the table on the waiting heat mats and looked down at himself. He was wearing a blue apron with a daisy pattern on the front.

'Your mother was worried about my clothes,' he said, raising his eyebrows.

'It's very fetching,' her father said with a snort.

Jane could see that Lockyer was unsure how to react to her father's amusement. He had been the same since they arrived. It was as if he was worried John Bennett might keel over at any moment with another stroke.

'It's OK,' she said in a whisper. 'Dad understands your pain.'

'Your wife is very concerned about your health,' Lockyer blurted out.

Jane looked at her father and they both started to laugh. 'It didn't take her long to have you dancing to her tune,' her father said.

The door swung open again. Celia Bennett strode into the room carrying dishes in each hand, one filled with naan bread and the other samosas and onion bhajis. 'Here we are,' her mother said in a sing-song voice. Lockyer moved to sit down opposite Jane. 'No, no, Michael. You go and sit over there. The view's better.' Lockyer looked at Jane, and then turned to look at the view from her side of the table. As they were in a room with no windows, she could imagine what he was thinking. Her mother pointed to the picture hanging over the sideboard. 'We got that in an antique shop in town,' she said, adding in a whisper, 'They didn't know what they had,' and giving Lockyer a nudge as he passed her. He took his seat next to Jane.

'How's Peter?' Lockyer asked.

'Oh, he's fine,' Jane's mother said with a wave of her hand.

'He's fine,' Jane whispered, leaning into Lockyer, nudging his shoulder with hers. 'Thanks for asking.'

'He's just unsettled, Michael. That's all it is. He isn't often like that, is he, Jane?'

'He struggles with change,' Jane said. 'Even small changes to his routine or surroundings can throw him off. We normally eat in the kitchen when we're here.' She gave her mother a pointed look.

'Oh, don't be ridiculous, Jane,' her mother said, not looking at her, ladling curry onto her father's plate. 'What child isn't a little . . . frazzled this close to Christmas?'

'I understand,' Lockyer said. 'My brother's autistic.' His statement dropped into the conversation like a boulder into a bowl of rice. Jane had never known him to mention Bobby, not without serious coercion. He looked at her and returned the shoulder shove. She smiled.

'Don't stand on ceremony,' her mother said, as if Lockyer hadn't spoken. 'Dig in.' She offered the spoon to him. He took it without comment. Jane looked at her father. It was clear he was enjoying the show as he tried and failed to hide his smile.

'Soooo, you two,' her mother said, sitting down. 'You have been busy. I can't believe this is the first time we've actually been able to sit down together properly since you arrived. Did you have a good day?'

Jane glanced down at Lockyer's right hand. A bruise ran across his knuckles. 'It was a . . . long day,' she said. He seemed to sense her looking as he put his hands in his lap.

'Aren't they always?' her mother said. Jane ignored the dig. These moments, however surreal, were to be savoured.

Over the next twenty minutes Lockyer was cajoled and then forced into eating two huge helpings of Celia Bennett's over-herbed curry. He tried to say no to the fourth bhaji, but it was clear Jane's mother wasn't listening. The novelty of having a healthy middle-aged man in the house was having quite an effect. Jane spent the majority of the meal exchanging looks with her father at her mother's bizarre behaviour.

Now that they were on to dessert, she could feel Lockyer's desperation to flee. 'That was amazing, Mum,' she said with as much sincerity as she could muster. 'Leave the dishes and I'll do them later. Mike and I have got some work we need to do before tomorrow.'

'I don't know,' her mother said, shaking her head. 'You never stop. Do *you* work as hard as my daughter?' she asked, her tone veering towards accusatory.

'No one works as hard as your daughter,' Lockyer said, giving Jane a look that said he wanted to laugh and cry, in that order.

'Do you mind if we use the conservatory, Dad?' Jane asked, pushing back her chair. Lockyer followed her lead.

'Yes, yes, that's fine, dear,' her mother answered for him. 'Your father and I will be off to bed very shortly. We aren't the night owls we used to be.'

'When were we ever night owls?' Jane's father asked, leaning on the table as he stood.

'Oh, shush,' she said. 'You go and sit yourself down. I'll bring you through a cup of tea.' She put on a big show of rolling her eyes. 'Waited on hand and foot, this one,' she said, gathering up the plates.

'Leave them, Mother,' Jane said. 'Honestly. I'll do them after we've finished.'

'And have the whole house smelling of curry?' Celia said. 'No, thank you. I'll do it. You go on now and get your work done. I can look after your father.' With a pile of dishes in her hands, she disappeared into the kitchen.

Jane knew a dismissal when she heard one. She gestured

to Lockyer to follow her, and put her hands on her father's shoulders as she passed. 'We'll see you in a bit.'

'That's right,' he said. 'You leave me with your mother . . . I'm used to it.'

'I'd feel sorry for you, Dad, but you married her.' She kissed his cheek.

'Your mother's . . . interesting,' Lockyer said, as he closed the door that separated the conservatory from the lounge. 'And is it just me, or has she got posher?'

'She's just trying to impress you,' Jane said, sitting down on a wicker armchair with navy blue cushions edged in yellow piping. Her mother had decided on a jungle theme. All the lampshades were different animal prints, and there was a big bear throw draped over a matching wicker sofa. Peter (or rather, her mother at Peter's instruction) had strung multi-coloured paper chains all around the room and going up to the centre of the conservatory like an indoor maypole. The flower pots and windows had been sprayed with a liberal helping of fake snow. Jane shifted, trying to get comfortable. 'How's your hand?'

'Fine,' he said, looking at the sofa and the throw as if it might come to life and attack him.

'Just toss it on the floor,' she said.

'It's OK,' he said, positioning himself at one end of the sofa before reaching for his laptop bag. Jane waited while he logged on.

'Anything?'

He shook his head. 'Not yet.'

'Tech said it might take a while,' she said. They had tried

to listen to Pippa's message back at the station. The phone would turn on, but it wouldn't dial out to the voicemail.

'They'll be lucky to recover it, I think,' he said. 'Especially as Aaron cracked the sim card when he broke the phone on my daughter's face.'

'OK,' Jane said, raising her hands. 'Let's not get all worked up over that again. Pass me the Evans file, will you?' He reached into his bag again, took out the file and tossed it to her. 'Thanks.' She opened it and scanned the first page. 'Who was the guy they had down for this again?'

'Kevin Ashworth. He'd dated Chloe on and off. They had a kid together.'

'But the one she was carrying wasn't his?'

'Apparently not.'

'Is there anything to suggest Ashworth knew Pippa?'

'No,' he said. 'No reason why he should. I was going to ask Hamilton earlier, but he was upset. I figured it wasn't the best time to imply his recently deceased niece might be associated with a known drug dealer and low-life.'

'Probably wise,' she said. 'We'll have to find out for ourselves.'

'Exactly,' he said. 'And I thought you were just the woman for the job.'

'Oh, yeah? How so?'

'Mills said all the locals would be in tomorrow night. It's skittles night. I thought you could go . . . maybe take one of Townsend's lot with you and get some background on Pippa, but at the same time do some surreptitious digging on Chloe and Ashworth, and whether there might have been any way Pippa could have run into the guy.'

'And *I'm* doing this because . . . ?'

'Because, Jane, you're good at talking to people,' he said, 'and I'm . . .'

'Not,' she offered.

'I'm going to pretend I didn't hear that.'

Jane smiled, flicked forward a few pages to the post-mortem and read the transcript. 'Blimey, Chloe's blood alcohol level was high,' she said, 'especially for someone who was seven months pregnant.'

'She had some issues with alcohol,' Lockyer said with a sniff.

'Not a lot of defensive injuries.'

'Looks like he knocked her out and then slit her throat,' he said with a shrug.

'What's this?' she said, holding up one of the photographs.

He looked up from his computer. 'It's listed as charcoal on the pathology report,' he said.

'What is it?' She looked at it again, moving the photo from side to side, trying to decipher the image. There was a dark ring on Chloe's stomach, almost like a target drawn in the centre of her distended belly. 'What do you see?' He was tapping away on his computer, only half listening to her. 'Mike?'

'I don't see anything. Just looks like a smudge to me,' he said, still focused on his screen.

'But it's been put there deliberately?' she said.

'Who knows?'

She decided to cut her losses and read in silence. When she had gone through the interview section, which was sparse to say the least, she said, 'I still can't believe Townsend assaulted a suspect.'

'I know,' Lockyer said. 'Although having said that, I was talking to Crossley earlier when we got back to the station, and she happened to mention that Townsend also had a run-in with another officer.'

'Really?'

'Yeah, some scuffle over an interdepartmental football match,' Lockyer said, pulling at his eyebrow. 'Apparently Townsend lost it and went for some DS on the opposing team.'

'He doesn't seem the type,' Jane said, flicking through the file. It wasn't as thick as she would have expected. There were photographs of the scene. She glanced at them, but didn't linger.

'I made a call to a superintendent I know in Bristol earlier,' Lockyer said, glancing up from his screen. 'He couldn't speak highly enough of Townsend – said he was one of their best DIs. An asset to the department.'

'Until the Evans case,' she said, biting her lip. 'But then, everyone has their trigger – the death of a pregnant mother . . . and therefore the baby. It can't have been easy. Something made him attack Ashworth.'

'According to Hamilton, Townsend alienated himself from his team and the local community. The initial interviews were delayed, or not completed.' Lockyer shook his head. 'There's nothing systematic about the way it was handled. Even basic information is missing. I'd expect these types of errors from a trainee, maybe; but someone of his seniority? By the time Townsend got Ashworth into custody,

the case was already in trouble. He didn't even have statements from Ashworth's known associates – nothing to
support the spurned lover motive. There was DNA evidence
on the body, but as far as I can see, he never even attempted
to match it to Ashworth. And he didn't bother to get the
DNA back, to prove or disprove whether Ashworth was the
father of the baby. The whole investigation was a shambles.'

She read through the exhibits page. 'Was any of this trace
evidence utilized once Ashworth was in custody?'

'No,' Lockyer said. 'Ashworth voluntarily provided DNA,
but he was released without charge before the samples even
made it to the lab. CSI had recovered footprints, not to mention tyre tracks from the nearby road. None of them were
ever matched to Ashworth or his vehicle. It was all too late,
so they just got shelved.' He dragged his hands down his face.
He looked as tired as she felt.

'Well, Hamilton did tell you the guy wasn't up to the job.'

'I know, and from what I've seen it would be hard to disagree.'

'But you do?'

'It just strikes me as odd that someone with his level of
experience would drop the ball like that . . . out of nowhere.
That he could go from invaluable to inept overnight.'

Jane looked at him. 'You think he deliberately screwed up
the Evans case?'

'No, no,' Lockyer said. 'I just feel like I'm dealing with two
different people: the respected DI, and the guy who doesn't
seem to know his arse from his elbow.' She heard his phone
buzz. 'That's me,' he said, shifting in his seat and reaching
into his trouser pocket. He took out his phone. 'I put it on

vibrate.' He looked at her. 'I figured your mother wouldn't appreciate an interruption to her dinner.'

Jane laughed. 'You're right there.'

'It's through,' he said, reaching for the laptop. 'It's just downloading.' He stared at the screen. 'You ready?'

'Yes and no,' she said, knowing it wouldn't make easy listening if Aaron's reaction was anything to go by.

The sound of static filled the conservatory. Jane felt her stomach tighten. There were times when she wished she had chosen a different profession. Now was one of those times. The static cleared, and there was a crunching sound.

What the fuck? Jane could hear Pippa's breathing over the sound of the engine. *Try leaving more than an inch next time, mate.*

A shiver ran down Jane's back as Pippa's disembodied voice filled the room. She heard a sharp intake of breath.

Anything else? Jane looked at Lockyer. He shrugged. *What with deer, dickheads and now sheep, I'm about done for the night.* They both nodded in understanding, just as there was a loud bang on the recording. Jane heard Pippa grunt. *Jesus.* Jane could hear the sound of metal on metal. Pippa's breathing was jagged, but it was drowned out by the sound of the engine as she accelerated away – away from whoever was behind her. Jane could hear Pippa muttering, but couldn't make out what she was saying. She looked over at Lockyer, and then at the door to the lounge to make sure her mother was nowhere in sight. The sound of the next impact made Jane jump in her seat. There was a sickening thump and the sound of Pippa's breath being forced out of her lungs. The next thing Jane heard was a fast rumbling sound.

'The cattle grid,' Lockyer said.

She nodded. There was more static, the sound of the engine revving, and then a gurgling sound. The sound of rapid breathing. Then another impact, this time much louder, much closer. She heard the dull crack before realizing what it was. It was Pippa's head hitting the driver's-side window. Her skull fracturing. She was coughing and retching. Jane put her own hand to her mouth. The noises Pippa was making didn't sound human. There was yet another bang, and then silence.

'That must be when she hit the tree,' Lockyer said.

Jane let out a long breath. 'Thank God it ends there,' she said. 'I couldn't bear to hear . . .' Before she could finish, the recording sprang back into life. There was the sound of static. It crackled.

Careful, it's hot.

Jane frowned. 'What's she talking about?'

'God only knows,' Lockyer said.

She listened as the static continued; it popped, crackled and sizzled. Pippa's voice was muffled now, but Jane could hear her moaning. It was then that it hit her. She wasn't listening to static; it was fire. 'How long do you think she was conscious?'

'Too long,' Lockyer said.

CHAPTER TWENTY-ONE

13th December – Sunday

'I really don't want to have to listen to it again,' Jane said, walking away from the conference table. 'Why can't you just tell me?'

'Because you need to hear it,' Lockyer said, looking at his watch. 'Where the hell is Townsend? Is that guy ever in the office?'

'It is Sunday,' she said, turning her back to him.

He was about to launch into a rant about why 'it's a Sunday' was not a good excuse when he thought better of it. She had been subdued all morning. She hadn't said a word at breakfast and had then excused herself to go for a walk, to get some fresh air. He knew that was bollocks. Jane was like him – she went everywhere at a run. The only times he had ever known her to go for a walk were when something was eating away at her. The Andy fiasco meant she had been going out for a lot of 'walks' of late. He decided to leave her to her own thoughts. She had a lot to process – they both did.

When the recording had ended Jane had left the conservatory in a hurry – to be sick, he assumed. When she returned neither of them had said a word for a good fifteen minutes. She went back to studying the Chloe Evans case file as if nothing had happened. When she did speak, it was to ask a question or make a comment. He watched as she leaned against the window, the low winter sun silhouetting her shape. She looked knackered. There was a knock at the conference room door. Lockyer waved for DC Pimbley to come in.

'Yes?' he said.

'Sir, DI Townsend said he'll be with you in a few minutes. He's just on the phone with the superintendent.'

'Fine,' he said. 'Thanks, Pimbley.'

Pimbley turned to leave but stopped, staring at his shoes. 'Sir . . .'

'Yes?'

'I just wanted to apologize for yesterday,' Pimbley said. 'I think maybe I went a bit overboard with Aaron.'

'You and me both,' Lockyer said. Pimbley paused for a second, nodded and left the room.

As Lockyer turned he caught sight of himself in the window of the conference room. If Jane looked haggard, he looked a lot worse; like a cartoon character who had just stuck a finger in a plug socket. Jane's mother had insisted on opening the skylight in his room to let him hear the sea. *Don't worry. It won't let the rain in, but the sound of the sea is magical. It soothes the nerves like nothing else,* she had told him in a sing-song voice, opening the window with such force he was surprised it hadn't come off its hinges. However, Lockyer's nerves hadn't been soothed; in fact, he had found the precise opposite to be true. He would have shut the bloody thing, but couldn't find the pole Jane's mother had used. The constant smashing of water on stone had done nothing but give him a headache and make him want to pee every five minutes.

He ground his fists into his eye sockets. He would have to get Jane to close the window tonight. There was no way he was going to ask her mother. That woman was like no one he had ever met. Although she did have one thing going for her: she was brilliant with Jane's son. The two of them were like a weird double act. Neither stopped talking. Neither seemed to realize or care that no one was listening. Lockyer had never met Peter before, other than for maybe a few minutes here and there at work barbecues and other social events. He had imagined him to be a mini version of his brother. Bobby was quiet and, for the most part, locked away in his own world. Peter was nothing like that. For a start, he talked non-stop. His vocabulary would rival that of most adults, and if this morning's discussion was anything to go by, he had an encyclopaedic knowledge of dinosaurs, velociraptors being his favourite.

A familiar pain rippled across Lockyer's chest. It was always the same when he thought about Bobby. His oh-so-wise daughter, who was halfway through some online psychology course alongside her degree, had told him that he was grieving. When he pointed out that his brother was in fact still alive, she had rolled her eyes, something she had picked up from her mother, and said, *Not that kind of grief, Dad.* She talked to him as if she were the parent and he the child. *You're grieving for the brother you lost when your parents sent him to live with your aunt when you were little. And . . . you're grieving for the brother you can't have because of Uncle Bobby's condition.* His daughter had become his emotional caretaker, whether he liked it or not.

He moved his head around his shoulders, resisting the urge to pull a face. Psychobabble drove him nuts. The occupational health woman he had been forced to see earlier in the year had sounded just the same – talking at him in soft, patronizing tones. She had spoken a lot about grief too. However, the kind of grief she was talking about was real and only happened when someone had been ripped out of your life. He sniffed. The emotions he felt about his brother came in waves, but when it came to *her*? Thoughts of her knocked him off his feet like a tsunami. He would be tossed around in its wake, kicking for the surface, only to be sucked down again by the current of his memories. Even when he resurfaced, gasping for air, it could take hours, sometimes days, for the pain to subside.

He had spent over ten years with Clara. She was the mother of his child. Their split had left a scar, no doubt, but nothing like this – not like with *her*, and they had been together less than two weeks. She had left an indelible mark in his head and on his heart. It was a relationship that should never have happened, that had changed his life and ended hers. In the early hours, when he couldn't sleep, he would find himself worrying that he was forgetting her face. He had one picture on his phone. It was a blurred shot of the side of her face. He remembered taking it. She was rolling away from him in bed, laughing, her arms and legs caught up in the sheet. He sighed. There were other photographs on file, but he didn't want to look at those.

The sound of the door opening broke his train of thought. It was Townsend. Lockyer took a deep breath and pushed the pain away, back into its lair where it would lie dormant until the next time. This was why he didn't like shrinks. No good could come from dwelling on the past.

'Sorry to keep you waiting,' Townsend said. 'I just got this from Basil.' He held up a tan paper file. 'It's his full post-mortem report.'

'Great,' Lockyer said, reaching out for the file. Townsend handed it over without comment. 'Be good to check I didn't miss anything.'

'I'm sure you haven't,' Townsend said.

Lockyer slid the file over to his right and dragged his laptop towards him. 'Thanks for coming, Bill,' he said.

'Of course,' Townsend said, taking a seat at the head of the table. Jane remained by the window. 'I would have been in yesterday, but I was . . . circumstances kept me elsewhere.'

What the hell did that mean? Lockyer rolled his lips over his teeth and bit down hard to keep himself from asking the question out loud. Now wasn't the time. Hearing Pippa's last moments on the recording had changed everything – in his mind, at least. She wasn't just a victim any more. She wasn't just Aaron's twin sister. She had a voice. He couldn't even begin to comprehend how Aaron must be feeling.

He had called Megan this morning to check on her eye, but he couldn't deny that part of the reason he had phoned was to ask after Aaron. Lockyer had been witness to the ravages of grief throughout his entire career. It was tough, a harsh reality of the job, but he had become practised at compartmentalizing. But with Aaron it was different. His pain was tangible, and the closer Lockyer got, the more it seemed to transfer to him.

'Can we get this over with, please?' Jane asked, walking back to the table as if her feet were encased in concrete.

Lockyer nodded as Townsend took a seat next to hers. He pressed play on his laptop. The recording crackled into life. 'You won't have to listen to the whole thing,' he said, talking over the static. 'It's only the last minute or so I want you to hear.'

'That's precisely the part I *don't* want to listen to,' Jane said, putting her head in her hands.

'Just listen,' he said, turning up the volume until it was at maximum. The sound of Pippa moaning filled the conference room. Jane seemed to shrink into herself. Townsend, in contrast, was focused, which made a change. His eyes were glued to the laptop. Lockyer held up one finger. 'Here,' he said. 'Listen.'

'This is after the car has caught fire, of course,' Townsend said, his face impassive.

Lockyer nodded, but didn't speak. 'Don't listen to that and don't listen to Pippa.' Jane looked up at him. 'OK,' he said. 'Try to put the sound of the fire and Pippa to the back of your mind. What else can you hear?'

Jane was shaking her head. 'All I can hear is her,' she said.

'The noise from the fire is pretty loud, Mike,' Townsend said. 'I can hear crackling, spitting . . . I can hear what I guess would be the air being dragged into the vehicle by the flames, but other than that, I can't hear anything.'

'Me neither,' Jane said.

Lockyer let the recording play on for a couple more seconds before stopping it. 'OK, hang on,' he said, dragging the icon back to the same starting place on the recording. He looked at them both. 'Try again. I want you to listen to the sounds beyond the fire, beyond Pippa. Try closing your eyes.

That's what I did earlier when I listened to it again.' They both stared at him. 'Indulge me,' he said. 'Just close your eyes and listen. Push the noises you know are there to the side and listen for what else you can hear.' Townsend closed his eyes. Jane rolled hers but then closed them, holding her hand to her mouth. 'And try not to throw up on the conference table, Jane,' he said in an attempt at levity. He was trying to break the spell that was fixing her mind in place. She was so focused on what she didn't want to hear that she wasn't picking up what he needed her to hear. 'Here we go.' He pressed play. Again Pippa's moaning filled the room. It was soon accompanied by the sounds of the fire igniting and then taking hold. He tried to increase the volume, pressing the button in vain. He could hear it, but could they?

'The fire's much louder now,' Townsend said.

'She's quieter,' Jane said.

'What else?' Lockyer said, willing them to hear it.

'Her engine is still running,' Townsend said.

'Keep listening,' he said.

Jane frowned. 'That's not Pippa's engine,' she said.

'Keep listening.'

For the remaining thirty-five seconds of the recording, none of them made a sound. The conference room was silent but for the sound of the flames, Pippa moaning and a car engine, idling in the background. There was a crunch as gears were engaged, and the clear sound of a vehicle accelerating away.

'They stayed to watch,' Jane said, shaking her head. 'They knew she was alive – and they stayed to watch.'

CHAPTER TWENTY-TWO

13th December – Sunday

Lockyer followed the ancient-looking Land Rover down the rutted path towards an old stone farmhouse. The snow made it near impossible to avoid the ruts. He cringed as the underside of the squad car scraped along the ground; and this was going downhill. How was he going to get back out? The lane looked a lot steeper now he was halfway down it than it had from the gateway at the top, where he had almost knocked down Robert Goodland.

He had been forced to find an alternative route around Nether Stowey when he came up against a 'road closed' sign. It made sense. They were forecast for more snow, and given the plethora of lanes around the Quantocks and its surrounding villages, it was unrealistic to expect the gritter lorries to keep them *all* clear. It was on his detour that he met Goodland. The ancient farmer had all but jumped out in front of the squad car. Lockyer had managed to brake and swerve to the left, sliding into a snow-covered verge rather than Goodland's legs.

'You one of them London coppers?' Goodland had asked,

approaching the driver's-side window like nothing had happened. He had a chicken slung under one arm. When Lockyer had said he was indeed 'one of them London coppers', Goodland had introduced himself and said, 'You'd better follow me,' disappearing into a field only to reappear moments later in the clapped-out Land Rover Lockyer was now following.

He looked at the clock on the dash. He was meant to be meeting Jane in twenty minutes. She had somehow managed to change his original plan – to send her and a couple of Townsend's team to speak to the regulars at the Farmer's Arms in Combe Florey – into the two of them going in, with the BFG as their 'guide'.

Goodland pulled his 4x4 adjacent to the house and sign that read 'Pepperhill Farm'. Lockyer watched him get out with the chicken still under his arm and proceed to walk away from the farmhouse, towards the barns. He sighed, dragging his hand down his face.

Of course he could have travelled over with Jane and avoided this bizarre interlude, but then he would have missed the call from Linda at South West Forensics. She had an update on the paint samples taken from the Jones crash site. When he answered her call he had told Jane to go without him. Linda's voice would have been better suited to radio presenting than geek work. It was low and husky. He had found himself listening without hearing until he remembered the reason for her call. She had managed to identify the other vehicle from a paint fragment. She had done the work herself to ensure Lockyer got the results he needed ASAP. He had promised to buy her a drink to say thank you.

The car they were looking for was a 'Chawton White'

Land Rover Defender, 1999, from the Solihull plant up near Manchester. It had been a big production year – over fifty-six thousand had come off the line, spread across fifteen colours. Lockyer skidded to a stop behind Goodland's white Land Rover Defender and blew out a breath. He had seen almost as many Land Rovers as sheep since his arrival from London. If he didn't know any better, he would swear Somerset was sponsored by the British 4x4 manufacturers. The expression 'looking for a needle in a haystack' sprung to mind. He turned off his engine, got out and half walked, half jogged to catch up with Goodland, the sun setting behind him. Jane would be pissed. He was going to be late – again.

'I know, honey,' Jane said as her son protested her absence. 'It sounds amazing . . . I'm sure Grandma's photos are ace . . . yes, and I can't wait to see your picture.' His voice was rising with each plea. 'I'll come in and give you a big kiss when I get home.' He wasn't convinced. 'Yes, of course I'll wake you.' She wouldn't, but now wasn't the time for honesty. The signal kept dropping out: his voice drifting away and then screeching out, loud in her ear. She tugged at her hands-free. 'Piece of shit,' she said to her car as it grumbled up the hill. Thank God the gritter lorries had been out, otherwise she would have been in real trouble. 'Sorry, honey,' she said. 'Yes, I'm still here . . . why don't you ask Grandma to help you write a story all about your day? I would *love* that.' The back end of her car slipped for a second as her tyres lost purchase. Her jaw tightened. She had been forced to come through Doddington after encountering a very snowy lane and a lopsided 'road closed' sign on the only route she knew. She wasn't happy, but she had no one to blame except herself. She should have gone down the motorway to Taunton and come up to Combe Florey that way. But no, she had chosen to come over the hills – the way she knew, the way she hated – and now she had to listen to her son waxing lyrical about the place.

To combat Peter's 'Christmas fever', as her mother called it whilst indulging his love of dinosaurs and all things reptilian, Celia Bennett had driven Peter all the way down here so they could do the 'Dragon Walk' – something to do with the story of Gurt Wurm and a woodcutter. Jane rolled her eyes. She felt like she was up to her neck in legends. The result of her son's 'awesome' day was that he was now beside himself because he had all this 'brand new information' to share with her and he wanted to do it *now*, not later.

'I would love to, honey, but I can't. I have to work,' she said. 'I know . . . I know you want me to come home, and I will . . . later on. You'll see me later on.' She could hear the disappointment and anxiety in Peter's voice. 'OK, honey . . . I keep losing you . . . my phone isn't working so well . . .' His voice rose by an octave. 'Put Grandma on,' she said, surprising herself. The line crackled and fell silent in her ear. She didn't know if she was still connected or not, but she couldn't look. She daren't take her eyes off the road or her hands off the wheel. 'Good choice, Jane,' she mumbled to herself, and then to her mother: 'Oh, it's nothing, Mum, I was just talking to myself . . . yes, I know, first sign of madness, yes . . . that's right.' The familiarity of the conversation made Jane's shoulder relax a little. It came to something when she courted a reprimand from her mother, but right now it was a welcome distraction. 'I know, Mum,' she said. 'Because it's my job . . .

and I love it, yes.' She nodded to herself. 'And I love Peter, too . . . of course I love him more than work.' She was still nodding, no doubt resembling the dog off the insurance adverts. 'I'm doing my best . . . that's right,' she said. Up and down, up and down. The movement was almost soporific. 'It's all I can do . . . well, thank you . . . yes, I couldn't do it without you . . . or Dad, yes.' She could feel her eyes wanting to close. 'No, of course I won't wake him up . . . I know, he just needed to hear that . . . no, I don't consider it lying.' She exaggerated the nodding motion until she was rocking back and forth in her seat. 'No, I don't make a habit of it . . . of course . . . kiss him goodnight from me . . . yes, you're right. Mm-hmm. Yes . . . mm-hmm, yes . . . yes, Mum . . . OK . . . I will . . . yes . . . Mum? Are you there? I think I've lost you. Are you there?' She listened, but there was nothing but silence in her ear; no static, no rebuke, nothing. 'I'll see you later,' she said to the empty line, pulling the hands-free earpiece out of her ear and throwing it and her phone onto the passenger seat.

She could see the cattle grid ahead, the sign for Quantock Common on the left asking her to drive carefully. If she hadn't already arranged to meet Barney at the pub, she would have been half tempted to call him so they could drive over the hills in convoy. Her original plan had been to come with Lockyer, but he had insisted she go ahead without him because he had to take a call from the paint specialists with an update.

She flicked her windscreen wipers up to the next setting, and turned on her full beam. The snow wasn't heavy but it was settling on the glass, obscuring her view. She could feel the temperature changing as she climbed. This was a mistake.

She should never have come this way after listening to the recording again. She needed time to process things – to recover. She didn't need to be driving over the Quantocks in the pitch black, passing the place where Pippa had died, where Chloe's body had been found and where Walford had killed his sodding wife all those years ago. The muscles surrounding her spine tightened. 'This was a mistake,' she said aloud. She resumed the rocking, and began humming the *Friends* theme tune to herself.

At first, listening to the recording of Pippa's last moments had made her nauseous. To identify a person with the sounds she was hearing had turned her stomach. But she didn't feel sick any more. Instead her mind was overrun with pity for Pippa and what she had gone through, and anguish for Aaron and what he was going through. But the overriding feeling was one of anger and disbelief. What kind of person could watch another human being burn? With one hand she pulled her hair back and held it in a stubby ponytail for a moment, then dropped it, returning two hands to the wheel as her car rumbled over the cattle grid. The revelation had also put a fire under Lockyer's arse. The veil of 'assisting' in the investigation was slipping as he all but took the lead. He had called the team into the conference room without even a look in Townsend's direction. He had them chasing up results from the crash investigation team, the paint specialists and any and all trace evidence that was yet to be logged and cross-referenced on the system. He made no reference to the Chloe Evans case to anyone, including her, but she knew that was where his head was at.

It all came back to her own question: what kind of person

could watch another human burn? It had to be someone with no respect for human life. Perhaps the same kind of someone that could snuff out not one but two lives when they murdered Chloe Evans.

She braked as a hare dashed across in front of her, its eyes shining like marbles in her headlights. What were the odds that there were two people of such depravity stalking the same area? Her foot hovered over the accelerator.

Even with her lights on full beam the blackness was overwhelming, surrounding her on all sides, but for the slice of road and snow-covered landscape they illuminated. She could feel Shervage Wood looming large to her right as the incline increased. The trees seemed to jump out, their branches reaching for her. With her elbow she pushed down the lock on her door, which in turn locked all the car doors. She was being ridiculous. She was being hysterical, but she couldn't stop. Every fibre of her being was screaming for her to turn back, but even that made her pulse quicken. She didn't want to stop. She had started something and now she had to finish it, no matter what the voices in her head were telling her to do.

The road seemed to melt away in front of her. She sniffed and kept her eyes forward. She couldn't look to her right. She didn't want to see the scorch marks on the road. She didn't want to see the rips and tears in the big oak. She didn't need to. Since listening to the recording, Jane was seeing those things all the time. The images were just there, occupying a part of her brain she couldn't switch off. She could hear the flames. She could see the bright orange contrasted against the black of the night. They were licking up her driver's side window, tasting her, wanting more.

She heard a noise off to her right, a deep crack within the forest.

'There is no fire. They are just trees,' she said to herself. 'This is just a road. There is no one here but me.' As she spoke, the calm she had hoped to instil vanished. What if she wasn't alone? What if there was someone watching, waiting for their time to strike?

'Jane,' she said, startling herself with the forcefulness of her voice as it echoed around the car. 'Stop it now.'

'Mr Goodland?' Lockyer called, looking around the stables for any sign of the man.

'In 'ere, son,' a voice said.

Lockyer veered to the left, to the sound of rustling and the low rumble of Goodland talking – he assumed not to him. The chicken he had seen before was tied up outside by a length of twine. Lockyer brushed the falling snow off his head as he passed through clouds of hot breath billowing out from the other stables. He stopped at the farthest one, where the chicken was, and looked in. A large head came up to great him, almost sending him onto his arse as he staggered backwards.

'This 'ere's Toffee,' Goodland said, appearing at the side of the horse. 'And that down there is Dolly. She likes a walk afore bed.' Lockyer opened his mouth but found he had nothing to say. He had seen and heard some things in his time, but walking a chicken beat the lot.

Goodland pointed up to the sky. ''Tis forecast to get colder overnight so I wanted to make sure Toffee here had plenty of hay and she had her rug on good and snug.'

'What about the others?' Lockyer asked, gesturing to the other long faces that had come out to greet them.

'None of them's mine,' Goodland said, stroking Toffee's brown neck. Lockyer was pretty sure brown wasn't right, but he had no idea of the correct vernacular. 'Their owners lodge them here. They come up and look after them the'selves, though I expect I'll be getting some calls given the weather.'

Lockyer racked his brains for a horse-related follow-up, but drew a blank. 'You wanted to speak to me, I take it, Mr Goodland?'

Goodland looked puzzled for a moment, but then his eyes cleared. 'Oh yes,' he said. 'I was down at the Farmer's last night and I run into Barney. He's a ranger up on the hills.'

'I've spoken to Barney, yes,' Lockyer said. Jane had spent the majority of the drive home on Saturday trying to convince him that the guy was an asset whose local knowledge could help them. Given he had been blabbing to the locals, Lockyer was less inclined to feel the same way.

'Well, 'e was telling me that you been talking a good deal about what happened back in the summer and . . . and what happened not so long ago.' Goodland raised his substantial eyebrows.

'I'm not at liberty to discuss an ongoing investigation, Mr Goodland,' Lockyer said, backing away from the stable.

'No, no, 'course not,' Goodland said, waving a large working man's hand in Lockyer's direction. His fingers were like pork sausages. 'I didn't mean to *get* information, I meant to give it.'

Lockyer stopped. 'OK,' he said, still wary of the guy's

motives. Gossip must be worth its weight in gold in a place like this – knowledge was power, and all that.

'Well, Barney and me were talking about what goes on up in them hills when no one's looking, right,' he said, leaning on the stable door and lowering his voice. Lockyer looked around. They couldn't be more alone if they were on the moon. 'He'd been telling the lady copper about what the kids get up to and whatnot.'

'My colleague mentioned it, yes.' Lockyer stamped his feet. It was freezing out here, yet Goodland was in a body-warmer and shirtsleeves. 'I believe there's been a problem with drugs, graffiti and . . . other anti-social behaviour.'

'I don't think it's kids,' Goodland said, flattening his mouth out like a toad. He started nodding. 'I mean, yes, I'm sure some of it 'tis kids, the condoms and beer cans no doubt, but not all. Not all.'

'Can you give me an example of what you mean?' Lockyer asked, dodging the snuffling mouth that seemed to have taken an interest in his left pocket. The horse nudged him in frustration. He stepped back.

''Bout a week afore the accident up on the Common, I was driving through Doddington and I just happened to be stopped near the memorial and I noticed someone'd been messing with it.'

'The memorial?'

'Yes, 'tis for Jane Walford,' Goodland said.

Lockyer felt the hairs that had been standing to attention on his arms lie down again. 'Right,' he said. 'I should tell you I'm not a superstitious man, Mr Goodland.'

'You would be if you lived round this way,' the farmer said, sliding one of his sausage-like fingers under his nose. 'My grandfather used to sit me and my brother on his knee and tell us the story of John Walford, of all the bad things he done, and just when he had us, when we were hanging on every word, he'd drop down his legs and send us both sprawling on the floor. If we was bad, my mother would send us to bed and say, "Think on what you done else John Walford will come for ye in the night."' Goodland chuckled. 'I'm not ashamed to say I wet my bed more 'an once for fear of Walford.'

'Stories, Mr Goodland,' Lockyer said. 'They're just stories.'

'But folk *did* go missing,' he said, furrowing his brow. 'Well, not folk as much as sheep and cattle – I've lost a horse afore now.'

'I'm afraid I don't see the connection,' Lockyer said, shoving his hands in his pockets, ready to make his excuses and get out of here. He pictured the woodburner at the Farmer's Arms. 'Now, if you'll excuse—'

'That land up there is cursed,' Goodland said, raising his hand like a preacher. Dolly had begun pecking at Lockyer's boot. 'Has been ever since Walford did what he did. O' course his family claimed *he* was the victim, not Jane – that she had bewitched him, possessed him somehow and made him do what he did. The local folk back then tried everything to rid the place of the whole lot of them: chased them out, set a fire running through the ditch, put a hold on the land so no one could own it after the Walfords was gone. But it made no difference. Fifty birds dying all at once, just falling to the ground stone dead. Animals gone missing and either found dead with no cause, or never seen again – and that's just what I've known to happen. You ask anyone, anyone, and they'll tell you same as me. There's some that say the place was cursed even before Walford, and that's why it's called Dead Woman's Ditch.' His eyes were wide. It was clear he was caught up in his story, even if Lockyer wasn't. 'Don't know if Barney told you but t'was called that before Walford killed his missus. Some say it drove him mad. Him and his family, they'd been colliers from way back, lived and worked the land for years; ate, slept and breathed it 'til it blackened his soul.' Goodland stopped. He was out of breath. 'When I seen what they done to Jane's memorial, I just thought . . . there's another thing.' He tutted and slapped his open palm on the horse's neck, making it and Lockyer start. ''Course, I know now I shouldn't have moved it, given what happened to that girl, but people go walking that way all the time, little 'uns and all. I didn't want them stumbling on it and frightening themselves half to death.'

The hairs on Lockyer's arms flickered. 'Sorry, what did you move, Mr Goodland?'

Jane blew out a couple of breaths as she followed the road around to the right, passing the sign for Walford's Gibbet. She couldn't remember the last time she had felt so unglued. She knew things must be bad when she had asked Peter to put his grandmother on the phone just now. She wasn't just hysterical – she was desperate. There was movement to her right. She let out a yelp, but managed to stop herself from screaming. She put her foot down on the accelerator. There was no way in hell she was looking to her right. Whatever was there, she didn't want to see it. She started humming again, relieved when the woods began to thin, to retreat behind her.

She forced her shoulders down as she drove out onto the

open moorland. Her lights swept across the snow-covered grass, heather and gorse bunched together as if for warmth. A herd of sheep was huddled by the roadside. She took her foot off the accelerator, glancing in her rear-view mirror as she did so. Her eyes snapped back to the road. 'Nope,' she said, 'not looking. I am *not* looking.' She didn't know what was frightening her more: the thought of seeing another set of headlights or of seeing the ghost of John Walford coming for her, dragging her into the woods and leaving her there to draw her last breaths. 'Oh, come on,' she said. What was it about the dark? What was it about this place? 'Oh, great,' she said, as her lights illuminated the road in front of her. Dead Woman's Ditch was just up ahead. Her chest was hurting. She rubbed it until she realized she was holding her breath and her heart was hammering away at her ribs, begging for some oxygen.

She focused on a spot in the road at the very edge of her headlights. She wasn't going to look anywhere but there. But she couldn't stop herself. Her eyes kept flicking to her right over and over again. She could see the car park. She could see the beginning of Dead Woman's Ditch. Her foot came off the accelerator without her knowing. Her breath stopped without her being aware. There was a man standing at the edge of the ditch. Jane's brain turned to mush. She reached and reached, but she couldn't hold on to a coherent thought. All she could hear in her mind were the words, *it's Walford. It's Walford. It's Walford.* Her car drifted to a stop as she mounted the verge to her left. She couldn't take her eyes off the man, but she couldn't move. All she had to do was put her foot on the accelerator pedal and she was out of here. She would be away in seconds. Ghosts couldn't outrun a car, could they?

She felt a tear roll onto her face. She reached up. Her cheeks were hot to the touch. He had seen her. He was looking at her. He was walking towards her. Jane's fight-or-flight response stalled until all she could do was shake, mid-fright, mid-flight.

''Twas a sheep's head,' Goodland said with a grimace. 'Someone had hacked it off and left it there. And mind, they hadn't done a good job. It was a right mess, blood and whatnot all over the place.' He shook his head, putting his hand to Toffee's mouth and letting it snuffle his palm, the horse's breath filling Lockyer's nostrils. 'It wasn't dumped there,' Goodland said, his expression serious. 'It had been stood on its neck right in the nook of the memorial, right where her name would have been if it hadn't rubbed off years ago now.'

Lockyer folded his arms. He wasn't sure how or where to put what Goodland had told him. What did it add to the investigation? He didn't know that it added anything. Like Chloe Evans, he could see no correlation with the sheep's head and Pippa's death other than, again, the proximity. Doddington was less than a mile from the crash site. 'What did you do with the head?'

'Brought it home and put it on the bonfire,' Goodland said. 'Didn't think no one would want to see something like that. But,' he said, his bushy brows rising again, 'I never heard another word about it. I asked a couple of farmers I know if anyone was missing any livestock, and they all said no. So where did the body go, eh? It's not every day you see a sheep with no 'ead. Reckon someone would've spotted it.'

'Did you tell Barney or any of the rangers?' Lockyer asked, as a pathway opened up in his mind.

''Course,' Goodland said, 'but like I told you, he reckoned it was kids. I mean, I know the younger generation aren't like I was at their age. 'Tis all different, with drugs and what have you, but even so. Whoever did it was off their 'ead, if you ask me, like one of those Hannibal Lecter types. Killing animals then rubbing themselves down with the blood when they's naked . . . whooping it up in the moonlight like some animal.'

'Jane?'

He was talking to her. He was reaching out to her. Without thinking, she lunged for the door handle and held onto it with both hands as Pippa had, but Jane wasn't trying to get out. She was trying to stop him coming in.

'Jane?'

'No, no, no, no,' she said, shaking her head and closing her eyes. She didn't want to see. She didn't want to see any more.

'Jane? Are you all right?'

Her panic stopped dead, the rest of her terrified thoughts crashing up against it, piling up with nowhere to go. She opened her eyes. The breath she was holding came flooding out in one big rush. 'For fuck's sake, Barney,' she said. 'Are you trying to kill me?'

CHAPTER TWENTY-THREE

13th December – Sunday

'What were you doing up there?' Jane asked, her breathing yet to return to normal. She took a step towards him and felt her foot go from under her. Barney's hand wrapped around her bicep and held her firm. His face changed from red to green in the glow of the colour-changing Christmas lights illuminating the Farmer's Arms car park. She had driven here in a daze, his truck in her rear-view mirror the entire way.

'If you must know, I was having a pee,' he said, putting her back on her feet but keeping hold of her arm as they walked towards the pub. 'No law against that, is there?'

'No, Barney, there isn't,' she said, 'but you're lucky we don't live in the States. If I was armed, I'd have shot you with your dick in your hand – no questions asked.'

He rolled his lips inward, which made the beard around his mouth stand out like whiskers. 'That would have been unfortunate,' he said.

'Somewhat,' she said, feeling her shoulders relax a little. 'But why there? Could you really not hold it?'

'I was just checking the area . . . you know, making sure the gritter had done enough so the main routes were passable,' he said with a shrug, the action lifting her off the floor for a second. 'I'm not strictly working but I'd never go by without making sure all's as it should be.'

'I think I can manage, Barney,' she said, shrugging off his hand.

'You'd think so,' he said with a wry smile.

'Don't push it,' she said, straightening her coat. 'You're already in my bad books.'

'Hey, it's not my fault you got yourself in a bit of a state,' he said.

'I was not in a state,' she said, looking behind her.

'You was saying "Walford, 'tis Walford",' he said. 'Round here we call that a bit of a state.'

'I never was,' she said, taking on his accent and speech pattern without intending to.

'White as a sheet,' he said. 'I thought I was gonna have to give you mouth to mouth for a second there.'

Jane felt her cheeks heating. 'I wasn't . . . I think . . .'

'Don't worry,' he said, giving her a gentle nudge – not so gentle that she didn't lose her footing again. He steadied her, but then released his grip. 'I promise I won't tell anyone.' He mimed pulling a zip across his mouth.

'I appreciate that,' she said.

'Come on, let's get you inside before you freeze to death. Wouldn't look too good on us lot if we killed off one of the London coppers, now, would it? John'll have the burner lit so you'll soon warm up.' The flashing lights illuminated the long thatched roof and tiny windows nestled under the eaves.

'It's a beautiful building,' she said.

'Dates back to the fifteenth century, though after the fire I'm not sure what's original and what's new. Place near burnt down back in the eighties.' He pulled open a heavy oak door painted the colour of fresh olives. 'After you,' he said.

'There's not a lot you don't know, is there, Barney?' she said.

They both turned at the sound of crunching gravel as a set of headlights swung into the car park. It was a squad car.

'This'll be my boss,' she said. 'You go on; I'll see you in there.' He nodded, ducked his head and let the door close behind him. Jane crossed her arms and walked back across the car park towards the squad car. 'Hey,' she said as Lockyer climbed out.

'Are you late or am I early?' he said, frowning.

Jane looked at her watch. 'I'm late,' she said with genuine surprise. 'Not sure how, though.'

'Shall we?' he said, reaching out for her arm.

She pulled away. 'I can walk, you know.' Since when was she a damsel in distress? First Barney, now Lockyer.

'You say that,' he said, turning her while holding her elbow, 'but it seems to me you're not cut out for country living. You move like Bambi on a new set of pins.' He pulled open the door and ushered her inside.

The heat hit Jane like a hairdryer. 'That feels good. You never know how cold you are until . . .' She stopped when she realized she was the only one talking. Almost every head in the bar was turned in their direction. In contrast, the diners in the room beyond seemed oblivious to their presence, their conversations a low background hum.

'Looks like John gave people the heads-up that you lot'd be coming,' Barney said, appearing beside her. He held out his hand. 'DI Lockyer, I'm guessing? We spoke on the phone.'

Lockyer shook his hand. 'Barney,' he said, looking him up and down. 'Good to meet you. And thanks for your help . . . so far.' Jane cringed at the insincerity in his voice.

'You picked a good night,' Barney said, either unaware or unfazed; she couldn't tell which, though she admired both. 'All and sundry comes down on skittles night.' He turned and raised a hand in greeting, and at least half a dozen hands were raised in return. 'Come on, they'll stop gawking in a minute.'

Jane followed Barney over to a long oak bar, Lockyer at her left shoulder. She spotted the wood burner blazing at the far end of the room beyond the diners. Beads of sweat popped out on her forehead, although she wasn't sure if that was from the heat or the stares she and Lockyer were getting.

'They don't look very friendly,' she said out the corner of her mouth.

'Don't mind them,' Barney said. 'They're not keen on coppers, and they're not keen on outsiders. So . . .'

'They're not keen on us?' Lockyer said.

'They'll warm up in a bit.' Barney raised his hand again. 'All right, Trim? Where's the wife?'

'She'll be up in a bit,' said a man sitting at the other end of the bar, a glass of what looked like whisky in his hand.

Behind the bar was a half-sized window with two stags' heads mounted either side, and three shelves containing bottles of every type of alcohol imaginable. There must have been twenty beer pumps. 'What can I get you?' Barney asked, turning and putting his hand in the small of Jane's back, bringing her forward until she was standing next to him.

'Do you think they'd do me a cup of tea?' she asked, rubbing her hands together.

'Course,' he said. 'I'll introduce you guys to John. John,' he called, waving to a man wearing chef's whites talking to the whisky drinker.

'All right, Barney?'

'John, this is DS Bennett,' he said, gesturing down at Jane, 'and this is DI Lockyer . . . the boss.' He hooked his thumb over his shoulder at Lockyer.

'Pleasure to meet you,' Mills said, reaching over the bar and shaking Jane's hand. 'You'll be the other London copper. I met your boss, here, yesterday.'

'Good to see you again, Mr Mills,' Lockyer said from behind her.

'Can I get a cup of tea for the lady, John, and a pint of Angry Orchard for me . . . and you?' he said, turning to Lockyer.

'I'll have the same.'

'Two Orchards then.'

'Coming right up,' John said, grabbing two pint glasses from a shelf above his head.

'Looks busy tonight?' Barney said.

'Always,' John said. 'The restaurant's fully booked. I've had to turn down business. We've got three Christmas parties in.'

'Ours isn't 'til January,' Barney said. 'Never made sense to me to leave it 'til after the New Year. What's the point? The festivities are all done by then and everyone's broke.'

'They do the same up in London,' Jane said, relieved to hear the murmur of conversations starting up behind her. For all she knew they were talking about her and Lockyer, but at least they were talking.

'Well, it's hard to find places that can accommodate a big group,' John said. 'I gave my staff the night off and took them all out bowling down at the ten-pin bowling alley out by junction twenty-five, back in November. There was no way I'd have been able to do anything this month . . . or next, for that matter.' Mills handed Barney a pint, which he passed back to Lockyer, and another one, which he took himself. 'I'll bring the tea over, OK?'

'Sure,' Barney said. 'Why don't you two get settled over there.' He pointed to an empty table near the door. 'I'll give you a guide to who's who, and you can then get to mingling?'

'Thank you, Barney,' Jane said. 'We really appreciate it. You're saving us a lot of time.'

'Who wants the Hugo seat?' Barney gestured to the bench on the left of the table, facing into the pub. 'Or are you gonna brave it and sit side by side?'

'What's a Hugo seat?' Lockyer asked, ushering Jane into the bench before coming in to sit next to her. He had made the decision for her, it seemed.

'You're in it,' Barney said, sitting down opposite them. He made the two-person bench look like a child's seat. 'It's the seat that faces out so you can see everyone and have a nosey at what's going on.'

'That would work,' Jane said, 'if you weren't a wall of a human being.'

He smiled and shuffled to the edge of the bench closest to the wall. 'Better?'

'Do you know Kevin Ashworth?' Lockyer asked. Jane turned to look at him, as did Barney. 'Jane tells me you knew Pippa Jones and you knew *of* Chloe Evans, so I was wondering if you knew Ashworth.' He was talking as if they had been in the middle of a conversation. Jane felt her face flush. As an interviewer Lockyer had only ever had two settings: hard and harder.

Barney seemed to pause for a second as he no doubt caught up with Lockyer's change of pace. 'I know Ashworth . . . when I say know, he's not a mate, but I definitely know who he is.'

'Go on,' Lockyer said.

Barney glanced at Jane before resting his arms on the table, spinning his pint glass with the tips of his fingers. 'I know he's a piece of work,' he said. 'You'll be hard pushed to find anyone around here or Bridgwater way who has a good word to say about him.'

'Hold that thought,' Lockyer said as the waitress approached with Jane's cup of tea.

'Milk and sugar,' the girl said, putting down a bowl of white and brown sugar lumps and a tiny jug filled to the brim with milk.

'Thank you,' Jane said. The girl turned to leave.

'So tell me about Ashworth,' Lockyer said, his voice loud and clear. Did he really want the entire pub listening to their conversation? Half the bar was already leaning in their direction. The whisky drinker looked about ready to fall off his stool.

'He was wrong right from when we was young,' Barney said. 'He was a bully then . . . still is, by all accounts.' He took gulps of his pint, swilling the contents around his mouth before swallowing. 'He was growing weed by the time he was fifteen . . . selling it, but he didn't make enough . . . not enough to cover how much he pissed away on booze.'

'He was drinking at fifteen?' Jane asked, realizing as she said it that if the kid was smoking weed, drinking alcohol wasn't really shocking. In Lewisham, being involved with either by the age of thirteen was commonplace in areas like the Aylesbury Estate.

'Course,' Barney said. 'His mum wasn't up to much. She wasn't well. Had some disease or other, meant she couldn't walk or something. Anyway, it weren't long before he moved on to harder drugs: cocaine, ecstasy, and I hear he's dealing heroin now.'

'He's never been caught dealing?' Lockyer asked. He had taken a notepad out of his coat pocket, shrugging out of the coat as he spoke.

'Sure,' Barney said. 'He's been caught hundreds of times . . . even been inside once or twice, but never for very long.' He looked at Jane, and then at his pint. 'Everyone knew it was him when they found Chloe up in Shervage.'

'Not Walford, then?' Lockyer asked, his voice thick with sarcasm.

Barney stopped and sniffed. 'Do you want me to answer that, or are you just talking?'

Jane could have kissed him. It wasn't often someone put Lockyer in his place, but right now he deserved it. She had no idea what his problem was with Barney, but if he hadn't said something, she would have. It was the guy's weekend, his Sunday night off to chill out away from all these people, and yet he had come over here in hideous weather for them – well, for her, at least. Barney was an above and beyond kind of guy. He continued: 'Because if you ask me, you'd have to be dumb to dismiss it outta hand.'

She could see Lockyer was wrong-footed. He hadn't expected to be challenged. 'You were saying people had a good idea it was Ashworth, Barney?' she said, hoping to break the tension. She knew what her mother would have said: *Rutting males. You can't have two stags on the same turf.*

Barney seemed to hold Lockyer's gaze for a few more beats before he said, 'It was expected . . . not that he'd kill her, I mean, but they were a disaster right from the off. Chloe wasn't up to much herself, poor girl. Her folks did their best, but she just wouldn't be told. She took teenage rebellion to another level. She was trying to get clean, to get back on track when she met Ashworth, and then, well, that was it for her. He had her over a barrel. He helped pay for her kids with the money he got from drugs. At the same time he got her hooked on the hard stuff and there was nothing her mum or dad could do about it. Ashworth treated her like she was nothing. He used to beat her something awful.'

'How do you know?' Jane asked.

'I saw the bruises,' he said, 'but she never would do nothing about it. She loved him.' He shook his head. 'She came in here a fair bit . . . and I'd see her at the Carew Arms and the Hood Arms over Kilve way. She was a regular all over the place. Rumour went round that the kid she was carrying wasn't Ashworth's. So when she turned up dead, well . . . it didn't take a brain of Britain to figure that one out.'

'Who said the baby wasn't Ashworth's?' Lockyer asked.

Barney shook his head. 'I don't know. 'Twas just a rumour. A place like this lives and dies on rumours.' His face fell. 'Sorry . . . I didn't mean that like it sounded.'

'It's fine, Barney,' she said.

'Did the police ever talk to you?' Lockyer asked. Jane noticed his pint remained untouched. She was surprised he had ordered it in the first place.

'Not about her murder, no,' Barney said. 'A couple of officers came round the pubs once or twice, a bit like you are, I guess, but they never spoke to me about Chloe. I wish they had done. I'd have told the guy in charge what was what.'

'Who?' Jane asked, knowing the answer she would get.

'Townsend,' he said. 'Same guy from Pip's accident. You'll pardon me for saying, but he doesn't seem too . . . switched on, if you ask me.' Jane resisted the urge to look at Lockyer.

'What about this lot?' she said, nodding at the crowd behind them. 'Did Townsend talk to them?'

'Enough to piss 'em off, yes,' Barney said, draining the rest of his pint. 'He's lucky they didn't lynch 'im. I was half tempted meself.'

'Piss them off how?' Lockyer asked.

Barney shrugged. 'The way Chloe died . . . the fact she was pregnant and that she had two little 'uns at home. It really shook everyone up, and . . .' He looked at Lockyer. 'You obviously don't wanna hear about Walford and what happened there, but after Chloe you'd have been hard pushed to find someone who wasn't . . . thinking about it.'

Lockyer pushed his pint away from him. 'You'll pardon me for saying,' he said, using Barney's words, 'but you can't have it both ways. Either it's Walford or it's Ashworth. Stands to reason it can't be both.'

'I'm not sure this is constructive,' she said, feeling like she was in the middle of a pissing contest, although Lockyer was the only one taking part.

'It doesn't have to *be* Walford,' Barney said. 'But that doesn't mean it's not still *about* 'im.'

'Because Chloe was found in . . . Dead Woman's Ditch?' Lockyer asked. Jane could see his mind was working on something, but she was damned if she knew what it was.

'Sure,' he said. 'Stands to reason, given what happened. People stopped driving over the Common for a good couple of months after Chloe . . . same as now.'

Jane saw Lockyer open his mouth to argue. 'You were talking about Ashworth,' she said, catching Barney's eye, determined to stop the conversation going any further off track.

Barney looked down into his empty glass. 'The whole place was devastated,' he said, his voice quiet. 'I think people felt guilty. Guilty they hadn't helped Chloe before . . . you know, stopped her hooking up with Ashworth. I know I did.'

'That's understandable,' she said. 'Someone well known being murdered in circumstances like that – it's bound to affect everyone who knew her, whether they had a close association or not.' She took a sip of her tea while deciding how to phrase her next question. 'Barney, while I understand how upset people must have been, and I definitely *see* the similarities in location with Walford, et cetera, I'm afraid I don't get why Townsend's investigation would have got them so riled up?'

Barney sighed. 'Because,' he said, stretching out the word, 'Townsend came in here like some copper off the telly. He was trying to be all good-cop-bad-cop – 'cept he was doing both. He was nice to folk one minute, then the next he was accusing them of knowing more than they were saying. *He* was the one that asked about Dead Woman's Ditch and all about local legends, Walford, Gurt Wurm and all that . . .' He stopped, turned in his seat and held his empty pint glass in the air until the landlord caught sight of him and nodded. 'He even called me,' he said without missing a step. 'Didn't realize it was him at the time, but he wanted all the lowdown on what went on back in the day, or whatever. So he comes up here asking folk about it and then turns on a halfpenny and says people are . . . I don't know, saying about the legends to cause trouble . . . to waste time and muck up his investigation into Chloe's murder.' Barney raised his eyebrows. 'Seems to me that guy could fuck up a salad. S'cuse the language,' he said to Jane. She couldn't help smiling. It had been a while since someone had apologized to her for swearing. 'He basically made out like we was protecting Ashworth. Folk were furious. No one here would ever, then or now, dream of protecting a piece of shit like Ashworth.' He looked at Jane and shrugged another apology. 'Folk were frightened – *genuinely* frightened.'

'At least the looks we're getting are starting to make sense,' Lockyer muttered. 'Can you give me a quick run-down on who's here?' he asked, as if dismissing everything Barney had just said. Jane felt her cheeks heat. 'If you can start with those who might have known Pippa Jones or her family best, and work your way out from there.' He was talking to him like an employee. It was mortifying.

'If you've got time?' Jane added.

'Sure,' Barney said. 'That's why I'm here.' He smiled at her and rolled his lips in as he had before, his beard standing up around his mouth. A girl arrived with his second pint. He thanked her and took a big gulp the foam, wetting his whiskers. Lockyer had yet to start his own pint. Jane looked at him. She had spent the time they had been sitting here taking in their surroundings; looking at everyone in the pub in turn. But it seemed Lockyer had eyes for only one person, and that person was Barney.

'You don't like him, then,' Jane said, as soon as the BFG was out of earshot.

'Whereas you do,' Lockyer said, disturbed to hear a childish whine in his voice. It had been his idea to speak to the locals, to find out more about Chloe Evans and Ashworth and whether there was any real connection with the Jones case, but so far it just felt like a distraction. For all the time he was here getting the three-line whip from the BFG, he wasn't out following up on actual leads, tangible evidence that could lead them to Pippa's killer. He already had the team cross-referencing the make and model of the vehicle, traffic were keeping an eye out for any and all white Land Rovers and Crossley, who was fast becoming his favourite, was trawling through hours of traffic-camera footage. Lockyer wanted to be with them, to be chasing down this bastard, not stuck here in la-la land.

'He's an asset, Mike,' she said, frowning. 'He just saved us about four days' background work.'

'If he's telling the truth, yes.' Again Lockyer's tone was more infantile that he would have liked. 'So, are we going to do this together or split up?' he asked. 'I want to get back.'

She looked at him for a second, her eyes searching, but then her face cleared. 'Let's split up,' she said. 'You take the skittles team and I'll take the lot over by the dart board.'

'Don't trust me to talk to Chloe's dad?' he asked, looking over at a guy in his sixties wearing a faded yellow jumper, dark green trousers and wellies. He was one of the first people Barney had pointed out.

'If we end up looking more into Chloe's murder, then we might need him. I figured a softly-softly approach would be best at this stage,' she said.

'I can do soft,' he said, knowing he couldn't.

She waved away his comment. 'What level of official do you want to go?'

He gestured to his pint. 'Friendly,' he said.

'I'd better get a drink, then,' she said, standing and side-stepping out of the bench.

'You're driving,' he said.

'So are you,' she said, giving him a look that said she had picked up on his tone and wasn't impressed.

Jane put her cup and saucer on the bar. The young girl who had brought her tea over was serving. 'Could I get a lime and soda?' Barney was at the other end of the bar. He raised his glass in her direction. She smiled. If Lockyer's attitude had bothered him, the feeling had been short-lived.

'Sure,' the girl said, reaching for a glass and a bottle of lime cordial in one smooth motion. When she added the soda she swore under her breath. 'Sorry, I just need to change over the pump. This stuff is flat.' She showed Jane the glass.

'Thank you,' Jane said, glad of the extra time. She needed to prepare. From what Barney had told them, they had one chance to get this right.

She looked over her shoulder at Lockyer. He was sitting down at a table with two men, both in flat caps. They looked guarded, but they appeared to be talking, so to give Lockyer his due, he hadn't pissed them off – yet. If they thought Townsend pushed hard when he interviewed, they were in for a shock.

'Hello.'

Jane turned to her right. A small man wearing a tweed jacket, white shirt and green corduroys was standing next to her. He was halfway through a pint of Guinness. 'Hello,' she said.

'You're from London, I hear,' he said.

'News travels fast.'

'Always.'

'I'm Jane,' she said. 'DS Jane Bennett.'

'Simon. Simon Jenkins.' He shook her hand. 'It's nice to meet a lady detective.'

'Thank you,' she said. 'Are you from around here?'

'Crowcombe. Just up the road.'

She nodded. 'I know the place. What's the pub there . . . the Carey Arms?'

'Carew Arms,' he said.

'Not your kind of place?'

240

'It's fine,' he said. 'I just prefer it here nowadays. I don't know as many folk.'

'Looking for some peace and quiet?' she asked.

'Something like that,' he said, picking up his pint and downing the remaining half in one. He waved the glass at the girl, who was now serving at the other end of the bar. She tipped her chin. He set down his glass. 'How are Pippa's folks doing?'

'They're doing OK,' she said, thinking he had just made her job a whole lot easier. 'Do you know the Joneses well?'

'Used to,' he said. 'Used to know the reverend before the family moved up your way.'

'Did you know Pippa?'

'Yes,' he said. 'I mean, knew her when she was little. Her and Andrea went to Sunday school together. We had Pip over to play sometimes after church. She was such a sweet girl.'

'Andrea is your daughter?'

'That's right. They could be little buggers when they got together,' he said, smiling. 'My wife had a devil of a time keeping them in the house.'

'Is your wife at home?'

'No,' he said. 'She passed on fifteen years ago now. She had cancer . . . breast cancer.' He whispered the word breast.

'I'm sorry,' she said.

'That's all right,' he said. 'I don't mind talking about her.'

'Did you speak to Pippa much when she was working here?' she asked, feeling a tug of guilt at changing the subject from his dead wife.

'A bit,' he said. 'I don't think she really remembered me – or if she did, she didn't know what to say.' He shook his head whilst fiddling with his glass. 'I know how her folks must be feeling, the reverend especially. After all he's done – all he's given to the church.'

'He's dedicated,' Jane said, more as a statement than a question.

'Always was,' he said. 'How does a man of God make sense of this kind of thing?'

'The same as anyone, I guess,' she said.

'You'd think he'd get a . . . I don't know, a pass or something,' he said. 'That all his good would be repaid to him somehow, but . . . having his daughter taken away. He must feel betrayed . . . I know I do.'

Her drink had arrived without her noticing. She swilled her glass, dispersing the lime cordial. 'It must be very hard,' she said.

'I haven't been to church in years,' he said.

'I can understand that,' she said, picking up her drink. 'You must miss her.'

'Every day. After my wife passed it was just the two of us. Andrea was all I had in the world.' His eyes filled with tears. He swallowed, turning away from her, and sniffed.

'That must be . . .' She stopped. 'I'm sorry, I didn't realize. You've lost your daughter too?'

'Yes,' he said. 'It'll be two years tomorrow.'

'Gosh, I am sorry,' she said, feeling like she had really put her foot in it. She turned, looking for Barney. A heads-up on this guy might have been a good idea. 'How did she die? If you don't mind me asking?' She whispered the question.

Simon pushed a tear away with the back of his hand.

'Doctor said it was from being outside,' he said. 'He put something like "exposure" on her certificate.'

'I'm sorry,' she said. He seemed to get smaller the longer she talked to him. He had lost his wife and his daughter. He was alone in a bar avoiding talking about any of it, and here she was, ripping open all his wounds.

'We usually walked home together,' he said. 'She would sit at one end of the pub with her friends and I'd be t'other end with mine, and when we were done we'd walk home arm in arm. She'd sing.' Jane pressed her lips together and nodded in sympathy. What could she say? 'But I'd done my back in over at the stables. I was laid up for a week. Andrea took care of me. She was off work making sure I was all right – bringing me my tea and supper in bed.'

'She sounds like a good daughter,' she said.

'Oh, she was, she was,' he said. 'Don't get me wrong, she had her troubles, we fought like mad when she was a teenager; but she'd changed. She'd grown up – she wanted more from her life, but then . . . then it was all taken away.' He sighed. 'We live up Crowcombe Hill,' he said. 'She was walking back from the Carew. It must have been gone midnight and whoever . . . well, I guess they didn't see her.'

Jane's mind had been wandering as she tried to think of a way to extricate herself without offending the poor guy, but his words stopped her, made her focus. 'Sorry, who didn't see her?'

'Whoever hit her,' he said. 'The police reckoned someone clipped her with their car . . . didn't realize and drove off.'

'And this was two years ago?' she asked, looking around

for Lockyer but catching Barney's eye instead. Why the hell hadn't he mentioned Andrea Jenkins?

Lockyer nodded, tapping his fingers on the side of his glass. Jane had been throwing him looks for the past twenty minutes. It wasn't clear what she wanted but he wasn't about to cut his conversations short to run over to join her, the BFG and some bloke who appeared to be weeping into his pint. 'You were saying you lost some livestock?' he said with a feeling of déjà vu. First Robert Goodland and his stories of sheep's heads and cursed lands, and now these guys.

'That's right,' Harry Garfield said. 'I kept my ewes on the Quarry side in the main but the same six or so kept wandering. God knows why, the grass is much better where I put 'em, but I kept finding them in Shervage. I found six first time, then five, then three – then none.'

'They couldn't have gone elsewhere on the hills?'

'If there's one thing you can't keep in, 'tis sheep,' Norman Grace said. 'They might be thick as pig swill but when it comes to get'in out they's like Houdini.'

Lockyer had taken to saying their full names in his head every time they spoke in order to commit them to memory. He didn't think this lot would respond well to a notepad and direct questions. Mind you, he didn't really need to ask questions. They seemed to move from one topic to the next without his help. All he had to do was put them on the path. He had mentioned Pippa's crash and Dead Woman's Ditch, and there hadn't been a break in their conversation yet.

'I'd have found 'em,' Harry said. *Harry Garfield*, Lockyer

repeated in his mind. 'I know my animals and I'm tellin' you, something or someone took 'em.'

'Great Worm?' Lockyer said.

'It's Gurt Wurm,' both men corrected him at the same time.

'Gurt as in hurt,' Norman said, 'and Wurm as in worm, but with a u.'

'The dragon?' Lockyer said, trying hard not to smile. He had received quite the history lesson already, but while he didn't believe in dragons or tales of missing animals and bloodshed in the woods, he was prepared to concede that the legends must have come from somewhere.

'Who's to say *what's* up in them hills?' Harry said, opening his hands.

'Or *who*,' Norman added. He pulled on the loose skin under his chin.

'I was up at Wayland's Pool yesterday,' Lockyer said. 'Although I couldn't find a pool per se.' He shivered at the memory. One of his little toes was still recovering from his sub-zero hike into the woods with Jane. She had tried to hide it, but it was obvious the place gave her the creeps. He supposed it made sense given the history and the landscape; tall bare trees, creaking branches, the ground beneath their feet hidden by leaves and snow. He pinched the bridge of his nose with his thumb and forefinger. They had him at it now.

Norman shook his head, still holding the piece of skin under his chin as he spoke. 'You wouldn't see the pool this time of year, no,' he said, ''specially not in this weather, but come the spring floods it's there.'

'Barney was saying the ditch runs pretty much past it,'

Lockyer said, taking a sip of his pint. It was warm but it still tasted good. He had made a mental note of the brewery.

'The big fella's barely out of shorts,' Harry said, 'yet he knows as much about these 'ere hills as the rest of us. His daddy brought him up on 'em – used to take him up to Seven Sisters and leave him with a map and a compass and make him find his way home.'

'Jesus,' Lockyer said. 'How old was he?'

'About six foot,' Norman said with a laugh. 'We don't know Barney by his age, we know him by how tall he'd got.'

'So how old would six foot have made him?'

'Ooh,' Norman said, looking at Harry. 'He was six foot by the time he was what, fourteen, fifteen?'

''Bout that, yeah, I'd say,' Harry said. 'His father knew he was safe from the kiddie-fiddlers and what-have-you. It's not like they could bundle a kid that size into their car, was it?' Both men laughed and took a drink.

'You were telling me about the ditch,' Lockyer said, leading them back onto the subject. As much as he was loath to indulge the legend conversation, he was beginning to think Barney was right. He would be foolish to dismiss out of hand something that drew this much focus. Goodland had been adamant that the land was somehow cursed, and of the six people Lockyer had spoken to so far, every single one had brought up Dead Woman's Ditch without him saying a word. They did appear, as Barney had said, unnerved, but Lockyer knew better than to take that at face value. He was thinking about Townsend and Hamilton. Both had said the legends had proved a distraction on the Evans case; Townsend had said it was deliberate. Hamilton blamed Townsend for allowing himself to be diverted by extraneous information. Lockyer had to admit, whether by design or by accident, the tactic was working on him too.

He turned at the sound of a loud bang. He half rose out of his seat as some kind of scuffle broke out at the bar. All he could hear was someone effing and blinding, and all he could see was Barney's back and someone's arms and fists flailing about just out of view. Barney appeared to have hold of whoever was kicking off. The rest of the people at the bar, Jane included, seemed to have taken a step back in a 'leave them to it' attitude. Of course Barney would intervene. Someone his size must like to throw his weight around. Lockyer stood up. 'Back in a sec, gentlemen,' he said, cracking his neck.

As he approached, he saw the punch land square on Barney's jaw. The walking wall didn't seem to register the impact, but to his credit he didn't return the blow. Instead he grabbed the other bloke by the collar and lifted him clean off his feet. Lockyer stepped in, took one of the guy's arms and shoved it up his back. 'I've got this,' he said to Barney, who obliged by setting the struggling piss-head back onto his unsteady feet.

Lockyer turned the guy where he stood until his arm was halfway up his back. There was the usual squeal he would expect from such a manoeuvre. That's because it hurt. It was meant to. 'That's enough,' he said. 'Calm it down, now.' Barney was already at the door, holding it open. 'Come on,' Lockyer said as he released the guy's arm for a second, regretting it just as quick. The kid spun round and threw a punch. The flying fist darted past Lockyer's face as he dodged out of the way. 'You don't want to be doing that,' he said, holding his hand out as the boy stepped back, his face puce. Lockyer stopped when he realized who it was, but the recognition was not mutual. His opponent was way too pumped up to see or care who he was hitting. The next punch found its mark on Lockyer's chin. He stumbled backwards, his hand to his mouth. 'You have got to be kidding me,' he said, spitting blood in his hand. '*You* have got a death wish.'

CHAPTER TWENTY-FOUR

13th December – Sunday

Aaron blinked once, then again. He was looking at Lockyer. Of all people – Lockyer. He couldn't seem to escape him. 'Boss,' he said as the grip on his arm tightened. 'I didn't realize . . .'

'Clearly,' Lockyer said, almost taking him off his feet as he frog-marched him out of the pub. Aaron tried to find his feet, to break free of his boss's grip, but he couldn't. 'Pack it in. I don't want to hurt you.'

Aaron heard the words, but the meaning sounded very different. It sounded like Lockyer did want to hurt him – a lot. And who could blame him? He had just punched the guy in the face. He had punched his boss. He had punched his girlfriend's father. Not his best day.

'What the hell do you think you're doing?' His sister sounded angry, but then, she was always pissed off about something. She had thrown a wobbly when Claudette asked her to tidy up after herself. Cass was staying in a hotel, but half her stuff seemed to be dumped all over his poor aunt's ever-shrinking house.

'Miss Jones, I'd appreciate it if you would keep your distance,' Lockyer said as Aaron felt himself being manhandled
into a sitting position, the edge of a picnic bench banging
into the back of his legs. 'Sit.' Aaron did as he was told. He
wasn't sure he could have stood unaided even if he wanted
to. The bottle of whisky at his aunt's house was beginning to
feel like a bad idea; the half-empty bottle in his car, an even
worse idea.

'Don't patronize me, detective,' Cassie said.

'Look, I need to have a word with your brother here. I'm
guessing . . . hoping you drove him up here, so please, go
inside for now. You'll be able to take him home shortly –
where he should have stayed.'

'I—'

'I wasn't talking to you, Aaron,' Lockyer shouted.

'What's going on?'

Aaron looked up. What was DS Bennett doing here?

'Nothing much,' Lockyer said. 'PC Jones is out of his
head, and just assaulted Barney for some reason . . . and me.'

'I didn't mean to—'

'No one's talking to you, Aaron,' Lockyer said. 'Jane, can
you do me a favour and take Miss Jones inside, please?'

'It's Cassie,' she said, 'or did you forget?'

'Fine, Cassie,' Lockyer said. 'Please . . . go with Sergeant
Bennett.'

Aaron tipped his head back and looked up at the night
sky. There was a hole in the clouds right above him, revealing
three bright stars. 'Orion's Belt,' he said.

'Do shut up,' Lockyer said. Aaron blew out a breath, his
lips as they vibrated making a sound like a horse. He started

to laugh. 'Barney, you too. Off you go.' Aaron felt his fists clench at his sides as he heard his voice. He was up and pushing towards him. He wanted to kill him. His legs felt like they were moving, but he wasn't getting anywhere.

'Piece of shit,' Cassie said.

'Everyone inside . . . now,' Lockyer barked.

Aaron decided it might be best to sit down again. He looked around for his sister, but she was gone. All he could see was gravel and cars changing from green to red and back again. Lockyer pushed him back down on the bench with a thump. He looked up at his boss's face, Lockyer's eyes and mouth moving like a Picasso. His mouth felt dry. He needed a drink. He pictured the half-empty bottle of whisky he had left in the car. 'I just need my keys,' he said, trying to push himself to his feet, but his legs wouldn't hold him.

'Aaron?'

He turned and looked up again at Lockyer's moving face. 'Evening, sir,' he said. 'How's things?'

'Good, Aaron,' Lockyer said. 'I'm having a splendid evening. How about yourself?'

'It's still early,' he said. 'Who knows what can happen. Cass and me are doing a . . . doing a pub crawl.'

'The crawl part I can see,' Lockyer said, 'but can I ask what made you physically assault a guy who is easily twice your size?'

Aaron frowned, his head thumping as his flesh crinkled on his brow. 'You're not twice my size, boss.'

'Christ,' Lockyer said, hanging his head. 'Not me, Aaron. Barney. What's the issue with Barney?'

'He's a piece of shit,' Aaron said.

'So I hear,' Lockyer said, 'but why?'

Aaron closed his eyes and tipped his head back, his stomach flipping over, making him shiver. 'He'd been messing around with my Pip. He dumped her. *He* dumped *my sister*. Can you believe it?'

'Actually, I can,' Lockyer said, lowering himself onto the bench beside Aaron. It bowed under their combined weight.

'You're heavy,' Aaron said. 'He's an arsehole.'

'Right,' Lockyer said. 'And who told you this?'

'Some bloke up at the Hood Arms told Cass,' Aaron said, resting his hands on his knees as the red and green lights flashed, making the ground in front of him appear to move. 'He said Dickster-von-arsehole took Pip out and then dumped her after they'd . . . after they'd . . .' He didn't want to say 'fuck' in front of his boss – or about his sister, now that he thought about it. 'After he got what he wanted.'

'I see,' Lockyer said. 'Wasn't he a friend of yours?'

'Fuck, no,' Aaron said. 'Did you get a whiff of his breath?'

'Barney's?'

'Yes, Barney's,' Aaron said, nodding his head and then regretting it when the bench started to move beneath him. 'His breath was rancid.'

'I'm not sure you're one to talk right now, Aaron,' Lockyer said, shifting on the bench next to him.

'Maybe not, but at least I'm not fuck ugly.'

'That's a matter of opinion.'

'Your daughter thinks I'm hot,' Aaron said, swaying forward, only to be righted by Lockyer's palm against his chest.

'I would quit while you're ahead, Aaron.'

Aaron felt all the air leave his lungs in a great rush,

emptying him out. He could feel the tears burning the backs of his eyes. When would it stop? He couldn't stand thinking about her any more. It was too much. It was all too much. 'Who did this, sir?' he asked as his last reserves of energy drained out of him.

'I don't know, Aaron, but trust me, I will find out . . . But will you do me a favour?'

'Anything, sir,' he said, turning and trying to focus on Lockyer's face. 'I'll do anything.'

'One,' Lockyer said, holding up a finger. Aaron tried to follow it as it moved in and out of his vision. 'Stop drinking. And two: for Christ's sake, stop hitting people. Me especially.'

'I just wanted to . . .' He searched for the words.

'Hurt someone,' Lockyer said, finishing his thought for him as he dragged him to his feet. Aaron nodded, but he couldn't speak; standing was taking all his energy right now. 'I'd probably feel the same way if it was my sister.'

Aaron locked his knees. 'I didn't know you had a sister, sir.'

'I don't, Aaron.' Lockyer pulled him forward, and out into the car park. 'I was empathizing, for God's sake.'

'Oh.'

'Anyway, as much as I'm enjoying listening to you try and string a sentence together, Aaron, I think it's about time we got you home, don't you?'

'Yeah, I wanna see Megs,' he said, trying to hold his head steady. 'I love her soooo much.'

'Great,' Lockyer said. 'This evening just keeps on getting better and better.'

CHAPTER TWENTY-FIVE

13th December – Sunday

Her mother had texted twice, asking Steph when she would be home. She was driving through Williton when her phone beeped again. She braked and looked down at the screen as the traffic lights changed to red, then picked up her mobile and tapped out a message:

I'll be home in half an hour x

She read and re-read her message. She deleted the kiss and added 'I love you', but then she deleted that and replaced the kiss. She turned and looked out at the snow floating down and landing on her windscreen. It was a light flurry, the snowflakes dancing in the night air. They seemed to be melting before they reached the ground.

The road was wet, a shiny black lake rippling beneath her. She picked up her phone again. She was about to delete the kiss as the lights changed – the green light shining down on the bonnet of her car. Her last drink – or three – was making it hard to focus. A horn blared from behind her, making her jump. She looked in her rear-view mirror, feeling the beads of sweat in the curve of her back, her mouth dry. The street lights illuminated a woman in a Land Rover gesticulating for Steph to move. She pressed send on her message with her thumb, raised her hand in apology and put her car into gear, her breathing easing as she joined a line of traffic. She looked at the lights strung above the high street. She used to love Christmas, but when she had realized it wasn't Santa at the end of her bed come to fill her stocking but her parents, the magic had disappeared overnight.

She blinked as a few cars left the snake of traffic to head out of town, the lights disappearing behind her. She heard a horn blare again, but when she looked in her rear-view mirror there was no one there. It was just her. She was at the back of the snake now – the tail. She put her foot down and crept closer to the car in front. She wouldn't lose them. The tail couldn't survive without the body.

When she had found the courage to leave the salon last night, she had driven home sandwiched between two cars for the entire journey back to her parents' house. She wasn't fool-ish enough to think it was over, but for one night at least, she had a reprieve. She had even slept after her mother insisted they watch a scary movie and Steph had fallen asleep on the sofa. The film hadn't frightened her, and even now, despite her determination to stay with her snake chaperone, she didn't feel fear. Something had changed. She had changed.

When Ash had texted to say they were all out in Dunster drinking, she had not even hesitated. What was the point? Even if it didn't happen tonight, it would happen another night. She couldn't outrun her fate. She sighed, turned on her stereo and set it to CD mode. There was a mechanical whir-ring from the boot as her CD changer selected and loaded her chosen album. It was Prince's *Purple Rain*. She skipped forward to track six, 'When Doves Cry'. The sound of the electric guitar filled the car. She increased the volume to twenty, then to thirty as the drums kicked in and he started to sing, his voice rough and deep.

She felt a sense of calm and hazy euphoria as she was pulled along by the line of cars in front of her. There must be six, no, seven cars including hers, their brake lights shin-ing out behind them, guiding her. The snow was heavier, but Steph didn't care. She looked to her left at the black expanse that was the Bristol Channel. For the first time in days her breathing was slow and rhythmic. The inevitability of her situation had steadied her pulse. Two cars turned off at the Hood Arms: the snake's forked tongue and fang-filled mouth. But the mechanical reptile didn't stop. It continued forward despite not being able to smell or taste. She tapped the fingers of her right hand on the steering wheel as the song reached its crescendo. Her left hand was hovering near the stereo, waiting to skip back so she could listen to the track again. Three more cars left the line at Kilve: the throat, the lungs and the belly. As she watched them leave, three beats were added to her pulse. The snake could no longer swallow, breathe or digest its prey, and yet it kept going; but its pace was slowing, its strength fading. She knew how it felt. How much fight did she really have in her? Her eyes were drawn to a pair of shining lights in her rear-view mirror.

Her stomach clenched and she swallowed, forcing back a

tide of whisky and coke. The road narrowed as her wounded animal limped its way down the hill. She felt the tears come when the final car, the bowels, abandoned her at Holford. She was alone. A tail being chased by gaping jaws. They would eat her whole. She gripped the steering wheel as if in anticipation but there was no impact, no squeal of metal on metal. She looked at the shining white lights behind her. They seemed to blink at her.

'Come on, then,' she said, her voice low and quiet. 'If you want me, you're gonna have to catch me.' She started to accelerate, watching the speedo as it went past forty, fifty, fifty-five, sixty, until she was doing seventy-five miles an hour. Her car seemed to fly over the bends and humps in the road. She raced down the hill, her full beams cutting a path through the darkness. Her engine was screaming. She realized she was still in third gear. She saw a turning up ahead, a road off to the right. She took her foot off the accelerator, hovered over the brake and pulled her steering wheel to the right. As she shot down the lane at a speed that would, on any other night, have terrified her, she realized she wasn't ready to give in – not yet. The hedges whipped by in her peripheral vision. Her car seemed to lift off the road as she crested the brow of a hill and then she was going down, trees crowding in around her – to shelter her – to protect her. She braked, allowing her engine some respite. Her hands felt glued to the wheel. Her car rolled to a stop, a bare oak above her, snow everywhere around her. She looked back. No lights. She rested her head back and concentrated on her breathing. She felt light-headed, delirious; neither happy nor sad but numb, her head void of all thoughts.

She peeled her hands away from the leather of the steering wheel. How long had she been here? Five, ten minutes maybe? She could see the glow of street lights ahead of her. She tried to locate herself, but the map in her head was jumbled. She must be on one of the back roads to Nether Stowey or Doddington.

She took a deep breath, drawing comfort from the darkness around her. Her phone beeped as the screen lit up beside her. It was a text from her mother.

I'm here. Fire's lit, mince pies in the oven, brandy snaps at the ready. Thought we could watch that film you recorded last week ☺ see you soon. Drive safely. Love Mum xx

Steph smiled and let the tears run down her cheeks unhindered.

Her headlights lit up the road and the woods to her right. The snow was lying like a blanket at the base of the trees. As she began to pull away she saw the truck up ahead, tucked into the side of the road. She pulled her car forward a few feet until her headlights illuminated the 4x4. She braked. It looked parked. She hadn't noticed it before, its white paint camouflaged by the snow. Her pulse jumped in her neck. She couldn't take her eyes off it. She held her breath, waiting for the lights to come on, to blind her as the car raced towards her – but nothing happened. The car remained dormant, its owner nowhere in sight. She let out the breath she was holding and reached for her phone. She tapped out a reply to her mother:

I'll be home in ten. Love you too xx

She pressed send and tucked her phone into her handbag.

Her door was open and she was being dragged out by her hair before she knew what was happening. She could feel the snow and mud soaking into her jeans as she slid along the ground. She twisted and thrashed, trying to free herself but the hand gripped the top of her head like a vice, her hair straining at the root. The pain was excruciating. She flipped over until she was looking down at the road. It was soon replaced by a grass verge buried deep in snow. It covered her face, water trickling into the corners of her mouth, and then she was in the wood. She could see the tree roots passing her, the leaves bunching up at her waist as her body cleared a path behind her. She opened her mouth and screamed with every ounce of energy she could muster. The punch came hard and fast into the side of her head. The ground blurred beneath her. She could taste blood. Another blow rang in her ear, sending pain right down her spine. She reached up and held on to the hand that was holding her. Her scalp was on fire. She pulled herself towards the hand and felt a moment of relief as her hair slackened, but then she was flying through the air, landing on her back with a thud, the air rushing out of her lungs. Before she could take a breath he was on top of her, his knees pinning her upper arms to the ground, his body sitting heavy on her chest, crushing her. The blows came one after the other after the other, until she lost count and consciousness.

When she tried to open her eyes she found she couldn't. She couldn't breathe. His hands were around her neck, pushing her throat into the ground. She kicked and bucked, her hands finding his face, her nails raking the soft skin of his cheeks over and over. He cried out as he shifted his weight. She could feel his legs entwining with hers as he tried to restrain her. His grip around her throat loosened. A voice inside her head screamed at her, *it's now or never, Steph. It's now or never. Fight or die. Fight or die.* She balled her hands into fists at her side, taking as long a breath as his hand allowed as she brought her knee up hard into his crotch. He grunted like a wounded animal and rolled off her. She willed her body to move, but she felt welded to the floor. *It's now or never, Steph*, the voice said again. *Fight or die.* She pushed herself up and onto her side. He was curled up in a ball next to her, moaning. She took a breath, then another, then another. She could almost feel the oxygen filling up her red blood cells, reviving her. She turned onto her knees and used a tree to drag herself to her feet. She took one step and steadied herself. Her head felt like a bowling ball weighing her down. She felt his hand around her ankle. She didn't think. She didn't look back. She just kicked and kicked until her foot fell free.

And then she was running and stumbling between the trees. The sound of her feet was deafening but she wouldn't stop. She pushed herself to keep going, to put as much distance between her and the devil as she could. She slipped and fell to her knees. She could hear him grunting somewhere off to her right. He was calling out to her but it wasn't her name he was calling.

'Annie,' he growled. 'Annie.'

Steph turned away from his voice and kept going, slipping and tripping over and over again. She wanted to cry out, to scream her name, to tell him she wasn't Annie, she wasn't the one he wanted, but her mouth felt welded shut, her tongue swollen and useless. His shouts were angrier and more insistent. Whoever Annie was, Steph realized she was going to die in her stead. Her knee struck something, a pain shooting into her hip. She pushed herself up but collapsed back down, lying on her side, her left leg useless. She held her breath and listened. She could hear him cursing, spitting and sniffing. He was coming for her.

She pulled herself back towards the base of a large tree, another lying dead on its side next to it. There was a gap between them of a few feet. She pushed her legs in first and then wriggled and shuffled backwards, the pain in her leg making her bite down on her lip, drawing fresh blood. She couldn't make a sound. She couldn't give away her position. That's all he would need. She was injured. She couldn't run and she couldn't fight him.

She tucked her head under the roots of the fallen tree and dragged leaves and snow around her as best she could. She kept her breathing shallow and quiet. She was trembling, her eyes wide with terror. She could hear him.

He was hunting her.

CHAPTER TWENTY-SIX

14th December – Monday

'This is a nightmare,' Lockyer said, dropping his head in his hands. He had hoped time and distance from this morning's breakfast revelation would make him feel better. It hadn't. 'Townsend is meant to be the clueless one . . . not us and yet it took an eight-year-old to tell us how to do our jobs.' Jane's son had proved himself quite the historian. His fascination with the Quantocks had involved, up to now, endless tales of dragons and sightings of the ghost dog that was meant to haunt the hills at night. Lockyer had, for the most part, tuned the kid out. That was until Peter had mentioned John Walford. Peter knew every gory detail. He knew more than they did, and therein lay the problem. Lockyer sat back and looked out the conference room window at the winter sun bathing the NHS depot. 'I still can't believe you didn't check.'

'Why didn't *you* check?' she shot back. 'I thought you *did* check. You were the one banging on about local legends.' He could see that her mood was almost as black as his, so perhaps now wasn't the time to pass the buck or cast aspersions on her son. 'You looked up all that stuff about Wayland's Pool, didn't you? I assumed if there was something more on Walford, *you'd* have found out then and told *me*.' He could see by her expression that even she didn't buy her last statement.

'You're the one who brought it to me,' he said. 'Barney told you about the Evans case and you passed on what I assumed was all the information – all the information, Jane, not just what Barney-bloody-rubble had *told* you.' He gritted his teeth as she opened her mouth to argue with him, but then her shoulders dropped.

'This is pointless, Mike,' she said, reaching up and pulling on the back of her neck. 'The fact is, *neither* of us looked any more into the Walford murder because we assumed . . . *wrongly assumed* that what Barney had told me and what Townsend told you was the full story – all we needed to know. It's not like we didn't do anything about it. We might not have had *all* the facts but we still did something. We're looking into the Chloe Evans case in connection to Pippa's. We've spoken to the locals about both girls, about Ashworth and Dead Woman's sodding Ditch.'

'Small mercies,' he said, feeling his anger dissipate. Besides, blaming Jane wasn't making him feel any better. 'No wonder the bloody locals were . . . are shitting themselves. If I thought some nut-job was stalking the sodding hills carrying out some sick homage to a two-hundred-year-old murder, I think I'd be more than a bit perturbed as well.'

'Maybe,' she said, 'but I think the question here should be, why didn't Townsend tell us?'

'Why would he?' he said, feeling his anger rise again. 'As far as Townsend's concerned, Pippa was killed by a drunk driver—'

'Who stayed to watch?' Jane was incredulous.

'That fact seems to have passed him by, Jane,' he said, huffing out a breath. 'He thinks we're wasting time even looking at the Chloe Evans case, and as far as the legends and John Walford goes? Townsend thinks they're the very reason his case against Ashworth fell on its arse, so . . .' The door to the conference room opened before Lockyer could finish. Townsend bustled in, looking sweaty and harassed. His day was about to get worse.

'Sorry I'm late,' he said, out of breath. 'I was just on the phone with South West Forensics. They've sent through the results on the tyre tracks and footwear casts taken from the Jones crash site. I've got Abbott and Pimbley doing a cross-check on the off chance we get a hit. I had a brief look at the data. The impressions left were from a 4x4.'

'We already know we're looking for a 4x4,' Lockyer said, balling his hands into fists in an attempt to keep his temper. 'I emailed you and the team with the update I got from Linda at South West Forensics . . . yesterday.' He bit down hard. Now was not the time to go off the deep end. Depending on what Townsend said, though, it might be soon. 'I went over it again in the briefing this morning. But of course, you weren't here.'

'Traffic was terrible,' Townsend said. He pulled out a chair and sat down, running his hand through his greying hair. He seemed oblivious to the atmosphere in the room. Lockyer looked at Jane. She opened her hands, palms up in a 'search me' gesture.

'How's Aaron this morning?' Townsend asked. 'I heard there was trouble over at the Farmer's Arms last night?'

'He's very hung-over,' Lockyer said, not grateful for the reminder of his second run-in with PC Aaron Jones – though what Cassie was playing at, taking him on a pub crawl in the first place, was anyone's guess. She was asking for trouble. According to Megan, Cassie had as good as dragged Aaron out of the house. 'I spoke to my daughter on the way down from Clevedon this morning. She said she'd be keeping him in bed for the foreseeable.' He frowned as the dual meaning of his statement hit home. He pushed away his jam dough-nut. He had lost his appetite.

'I was more concerned with the man he assaulted.'

'It'd take a bigger man than Aaron to "assault" Barney,' Lockyer said. 'You could run that guy down and end up with more damage to your car than him.'

'An unfortunate analogy, Mike,' Townsend said, brandishing a cardboard folder. 'Anyway, I've got the Jenkins file here. It took me a while to get the paper copy because it was in the coroner's archive rather than CID's.' Jane held out her hands and he tossed it across the table to her. She fell on it like Oliver on a bowl of gruel. 'Pimbley tells me Barney dated Jones?'

'They went on *one* date,' Jane said without looking up. 'The thing with Aaron was a misunderstanding – gossip from another pub his sister had . . . embellished.'

She dragged her eyes away from the Jenkins file for a moment. It was clear from her expression that the information she was providing was to be taken as fact and not questioned further. Lockyer had tried to play devil's advocate in the car this morning as to why Barney had underplayed his relationship with Pippa, but Jane wouldn't have it.

'He didn't say anything before,' she said now, 'because for one thing, he didn't see the relevance and for another, he didn't see the point in wasting police time with something and nothing.' Neither Townsend nor Lockyer spoke. 'I made it *very* clear that it is not *his* place to decide what is and what isn't important in a murder investigation. He has apologized and I've made an appointment for him to come into the station later today to give a full statement.' She resumed her appraisal of the Jenkins file. End of discussion, it seemed.

Townsend looked at Lockyer and scratched behind his ear. 'Right,' he said, raising his eyebrows. 'I guess we'll have to take his word on that.' Lockyer saw Jane flinch. 'I was just in with Superintendent Atkinson. He was telling me you wanted the Jenkins file in relation to the Jones case?'

'Yes,' Jane said. 'We were hoping to take a look at it last night, but Atkinson felt it best to wait for you . . . given you are the DI in charge of the Jones investigation.' She sounded as pissed off as Lockyer felt, although he knew he had no one to blame for his own irritation. Despite Townsend's title, Lockyer was the DI in charge in all but name. He should have looked into the Walford connection. It was his responsibility, not Jane's – not even Townsend's.

'I know,' Townsend said. 'I must have just missed you. I left right after a meeting with Atkinson. Sorry about that.' He didn't sound contrite. 'What's the issue? Where does it fit in with the Jones case?' His inquiry appeared genuine.

'So you've not heard of the Jenkins case before?' Jane asked, sitting back in her chair and crossing her arms. She was wearing her faux-indulgent face. Lockyer was more used to seeing it directed at him.

Townsend turned down his bottom lip. 'No, should I?'

'Andrea Jenkins was killed two years ago,' Lockyer said.

'Two years ago today, as it happens,' Jane said, flicking through the file and throwing Townsend occasional looks of disapproval. Lockyer thought she would have made an excellent headmistress. She had that kind of reserved anger that could still a schoolboy's blood.

'She was walking home from the Carew Arms in Crowcombe,' Lockyer said. 'According to the father, the police said Jenkins was clipped by a passing vehicle . . . it was assumed a 4x4, as they might not have felt the impact and therefore wouldn't have stopped. She fell into a ditch before climbing out and crawling halfway across a field before she succumbed to her injuries and eventually died of exposure from hypothermia.' Townsend was nodding as Lockyer spoke, but if anything in what he had said had sparked his interest, it didn't show on the guy's face. 'This happened less than half a mile from where Chloe Evans's body was found, and just over that distance from where Pippa Jones's car left the road.'

'Right,' Townsend said, frowning.

'We're thinking there could be a connection,' Jane said, not even trying to disguise her irritation.

Lockyer held up his hand. 'I wouldn't go quite that far,' he said, feeling Jane's eyes turn on him. 'However, given the proximity, age and sex of the victims, et cetera, we certainly think it warrants further investigation, especially given what we *now* know about the Evans case.' There was no getting away from his mistake. If Lockyer didn't own it now, it would come out later – the truth always did. 'We only found out the *full* details of the Jane Walford murder this morning.'

'I'm afraid you've lost me, Mike,' Townsend said, looking from him to Jane and back again. A ray of sunlight shone through the windows of the conference room and seemed to put the bewildered DI in a spotlight.

'No surprise there,' Jane said under her breath as she turned another page in the Jenkins file. Even Lockyer was surprised by her attitude. He wasn't having the best morning, but she seemed livid. He was more used to being the hothead. He wasn't sure how to handle this new side of her. It was unnerving.

'Bill, given what happened to Jane Walford, the manner and method of Chloe Evans's death was at best a cause for concern, at worst, evidence of a ritualistic killing . . . a copycat,' Lockyer said, choosing his words with care. He didn't know why, but he felt like he wanted to at least give Townsend the chance to explain himself. 'It's standard procedure with a case like that, like Chloe's, to cross-reference for any similar deaths to ensure you're not looking at some kind of serial offender.'

'Serial offender?' Townsend said. 'Are you being serious?'

'Of course,' Jane said, unable, it seemed, to hold her tongue any longer. 'Chloe Evans's murder wasn't just similar to Jane Walford's back in . . . seventeen-whatever-it-was.' She held up her index finger on her right hand. 'Chloe was heavily pregnant.' Another finger shot up to meet its neighbour. 'She had a contusion on the back of the head –' and another – 'and her throat was cut.' The final finger made four. 'And . . . she was dumped in Dead Woman's Ditch. It's damn near identical.'

Townsend closed his eyes for a second, and then opened

them again. 'Detective Bennett, I *know* who killed Chloe Evans,' he said, 'and I assure you it wasn't John Walford or someone trying to emulate his work.' It was clear he was now the one trying to control his temper. The sun disappeared behind a cloud and his face was thrown into shadow. 'Ashworth is a local boy and despite playing the fool, he's anything but. I've no doubt he knew what would happen when he set that poor girl up . . . staged her body as if it was some kind of sick tribute or copycat, as you put it.' He turned his gaze on Lockyer. 'Trust me when I tell you it was all theatre. I've met the boy.' He sighed, closing his eyes again. When he opened them he seemed to have regained his composure. 'I know, I know, you've been out to speak to the local residents. I understand. The same exact thing happened to me. I suppose you've heard about strange goings-on . . . that the land is cursed – animals disappearing, or dropping down dead for no reason?' he asked, raising an eyebrow. Lockyer thought about Goodland's sheep's head story. 'I can see by your face, Mike, that you have. You are being dragged into the same dead-end Bermuda triangle nonsense I was.' He huffed out a laugh. 'It's a relief, if I'm honest.'

'A relief?' Lockyer asked, feeling the tendrils of doubt creeping into his mind. Jane, in contrast, was so focused on the Jenkins file it was as if Lockyer and Townsend weren't even in the room.

'Yes,' Townsend said with a smile. 'I thought it was just me. But if they can throw two seasoned London detectives off with their tales of the supernatural then at least it goes to show I'm not crazy.' He paused. 'Do you seriously think there's someone prowling the Quantock Hills wreaking Walford's revenge, seeking out victims, Mike?' Lockyer sniffed and pushed his tongue against the back of his teeth. The way Townsend put it, it did sound ludicrous. 'I looked at the file. Andrea Jenkins died of exposure after being knocked down, no doubt pissed, on her way home from the pub. Hardly the stuff of legends. And Pippa Jones?' He raised his eyebrows even higher. 'She was run off the road by another car. Not very eighteenth-century, is it?' He held up his hand as Lockyer opened his mouth to speak. 'The recording,' he said. 'You're going to tell me I'm ignoring the fact that we heard the other vehicle in the background . . . that whoever it was appears to have waited, to have watched.' Lockyer found himself unable to interject. In spite of himself, he wanted to hear what Townsend had to say, as so far the guy was making sense. He didn't sound crazy. If anything, he was the calmest one in the room, if Jane's huffing and puffing was anything to go by. 'If you had just driven someone off the road either in a rage or pissed, Mike, wouldn't you stop? Wouldn't you sit in your car thinking, *fuck, fuck, what have I done?*' He stopped, as if waiting for Lockyer to agree. With reticence, Lockyer nodded. 'So he drove off?' Townsend said. 'He – or she – realized what they had done, and drove off. Even pissed out of their minds they would know that death by dangerous driving carries a prison term. How many people have you arrested in your career, Mike, who panicked and left the scene of a crash . . . a fight, a murder?'

Lockyer took a deep breath. 'More than one,' he said.

Townsend nodded. 'More than a dozen, I'd bet,' he said, without a hint of judgement. 'Look. I don't blame you. When I was brought in on the Chloe Evans case I had Ashworth in my sights from the get-go. I was so cocksure I knew what was what, I didn't stop to think. I let a team that didn't want me here and a community who wanted Chloe's death off their conscience get under my skin and throw me off my game. When things started to fall apart, they fell apart quick. I knew I was losing a hold on it and I just . . . lost it. I assaulted the main suspect, for God's sake.' He shook his head. 'I've been a senior DI for over ten years, Mike, and I let some supernatural mumbo-jumbo derail my case. Because of that, Chloe Evans's family were left without justice for their daughter. Two children have been left without a mother, and a baby died before it even had chance to draw its first breath.' He stopped, his face flushed. He was panting. The conviction in his voice was obvious. This was the Townsend Lockyer had met back in London, the one he had respected – liked, even.

'OK, Bill, you've made your point,' Lockyer said, sitting back in his chair and looking up at the ceiling. The only sounds were Jane rustling through the pages of the Jenkins file, and the hum of the offices beyond. He felt foolish, not for the first time today. 'It's *possible* we've jumped the gun on the Jenkins case.' He dragged his hands down his face.

'I don't think so,' Jane said. He wasn't surprised. She had been the one who had Simon Jenkins crying all over her. She wasn't going to let go of this without a fight. 'There's a statement here from her father, and another,' she said, holding a page in her hand, 'from her case worker. Andrea lost her mother to breast cancer. It was just her and her father after that. She went off the rails . . . understandably.' She fixed first Lockyer and then Townsend with a look that seemed to dare them to interject. 'She started skipping school. She had an abortion.' She looked at Lockyer. 'She was fifteen.'

'Tragic,' Townsend said, shaking his head.

'Statutory rape,' she said.

'Who was the father?' Lockyer asked. 'Were they ever prosecuted?'

'It doesn't say, but that's when social services got involved. She was assigned a case worker.' Jane closed her eyes. 'She had another termination at eighteen . . . and who knows how many after that. She was in and out of trouble, some petty theft, problems with alcohol . . .' She gave him a pointed stare. 'She had treatment for substance abuse.' He guessed she was thinking about Ashworth and whether, as with Chloe, he had played a role in Andrea's life or perhaps even her death. 'By nineteen she was getting her life back on track. She'd trained as a beauty therapist. Her father told me she wanted to make something of herself.' She shook her head. 'Why the hell was the file passed back to the coroner so quickly?'

'Because Jenkins' death was listed as accidental, I'd imagine,' Townsend said in a not unsympathetic tone.

'So why was she half-naked, tell me that?' Jane asked, her eyes wide, her finger jabbing at the pages in front of her.

'I'm no expert,' Townsend said, 'but as I understand it people suffering hypothermia can become very confused, delirious almost . . . removing their clothes, believing themselves to be too hot.'

'OK, OK. But that would only have happened after she'd been out in the elements for a good while. So tell me, why did she crawl *away* from the road when she first fell?' Jane said. 'Why wouldn't she try and crawl back to the pub to get help? Tell me that?'

'I can't tell you that,' Townsend said. 'I wasn't there – I

wasn't even here when she died. I simply don't know.' He looked at Lockyer, and then at Jane. 'I'm sorry I can't give you the answers you want, DS Bennett, but you have all the information there. I can see you want there to be a connection . . . that you want to give some resolution to Mr Jenkins, but I'm not sure this is the way to go about it. You and Mike are here to assist with the Jones inquiry – not to go off half-cocked looking at past cases with little or no connection . . . other than geography.'

'We know Andrea and Pippa knew each other,' Jane said, her expression defiant.

'When they were kids, Jane,' Lockyer said, unable to believe he was coming down on Townsend's side of the argument. Ten minutes ago he had wanted to tear the guy a new one. 'What were they, five, six?'

'All right,' she said. 'What about this? Walford killed his wife because she was a drunk and slept around – with his brother, no less.' She held up the file, pages dropping out as she waved it in their direction. 'We know Chloe drank. We know she was promiscuous. Andrea was the same. The transcripts from her case worker could've come from Chloe's file, they're that similar.'

'And Pippa?' Lockyer asked, knowing she would not appreciate him blowing a hole in her theory, but she wasn't listening – she hadn't been listening. Like Townsend had just said, she was heading off on a certainty based on nothing but conjecture. 'Have you heard or seen *anything* to suggest she was a drinker, or put herself about?'

Jane folded her arms. 'No. Not yet,' she said, 'but we don't know her. We don't know enough about her.'

'You will get no argument from me there,' he said, 'but Bill's point was valid. We are here . . . *I* am here to assist in the Pippa Jones investigation.' He hoped she would get his point. It was the first time today he had thought about Hamilton, and it made him uneasy. Lockyer was here to keep the investigation clean, unfettered by the Walford nonsense, and yet here they were looking for *more* fuel to add to the metaphorical fire. 'Whether or not Ashworth killed Chloe . . . it's simply not our problem. It's not our case. What happened to Andrea? We *don't* and *can't* know,' he said. 'Her body was cremated. I already checked.'

She sat back in her seat, a piece of paper in her hand. She wasn't looking at him.

'Jane, are you even bloody listening to me?'

'Have you got Chloe's file with you?'

He hated it when people ignored him. Clara used to do it all the time when they were married. She did it when he was saying something she didn't want to hear. 'Yes,' he said.

'Can I have it?' she asked, holding out her hand.

He reached for his bag and dug around until his fingers closed around the file. He took it out, resisting the urge to throw it at her. She was almost as bad as him when she fixated on an idea – almost. 'Here,' he said, putting it on the table and giving it a shove.

Without speaking she pulled it towards her, opened it and started flicking through until she came to a stop. 'Look at this,' she said, turning the file around and pushing it back halfway across the table.

'I've seen it,' he said, looking down at Chloe Evans's postmortem.

'And this?' she said, holding up a photograph.

It was a close-up of Evans's torso where charcoal had been smeared onto her naked skin. 'If you're going to ask me again if I see a pattern or some kind of circle, I don't,' he said. 'It still just looks like a smudge to me.'

'This isn't Chloe Evans,' she said. 'This photograph is from Andrea Jenkins' post-mortem. Evidence of charcoal was found on her stomach and back.' Lockyer opened his mouth and shut it again. 'Still think I'm barking up the wrong tree?'

'Shit,' he said, putting his head in his hands. It hadn't escaped his notice that he had started out this discussion in the exact same position. 'John Walford was a collier.'

'A what?' she asked.

'A collier – he made charcoal,' he said, wondering how bad this day was going to get. 'I looked it up this morning after we got schooled by your eight-year-old son.' He saw Jane flinch. He raised his hands, palms facing her. 'Sorry,' he said. 'Anyway, Walford's whole family were in the business – the technique was passed down from father to son and so on. That's why Walford lived on the hills. He would collect a load of wood, bury it in a pit, set it alight, cover it and then let it burn for half a day or whatever. The result was charcoal. He'd then sell it. That's what he did. It was his job.'

'So it was deliberate . . . a sign,' Jane said. 'A brand of some kind?'

'Or a tribute,' he said without enthusiasm.

'Was charcoal listed anywhere in Jones's post-mortem?' Jane asked.

'Christ, Jane, I don't know. The poor girl was practically

cremated. She could have been rolled in charcoal and I wouldn't have known.' He looked at Townsend, who was bent over his phone, his face pulled into a grimace. 'What is it, Bill?' he asked. 'Or should I say, what now?'

Townsend looked up. 'It appears I owe you an apology, Detective Bennett,' he said with a heavy sigh. 'We've had a hit on the tyre impressions taken from the Jones scene. Casts were taken from a pull-in on the road closest to where Chloe's body was found. They match.' There was an edge of desperation to his voice. 'Obviously just because the same vehicle was present at both crime scenes, it doesn't necessarily mean it was involved in either of the murders, but . . .'

'But who are you kidding?' Lockyer offered.

'Quite,' Townsend said. He pushed back his chair and started pacing up and down the conference room.

'I'm afraid it gets worse,' Jane said, holding up her phone. 'I've just had a text from Barney. A girl was found this morning at the southern end of Shervage Wood. Some hikers found her. She's been taken to Musgrove Park Hospital in Taunton. Her name is Stephanie Lacey. Next of kin have been informed.'

'She's alive?' Lockyer said.

'Yes,' she said.

'Fuck me,' Townsend said, slapping his palm against the window, a dull thud reverberating around the room.

The implications of the last few minutes had sent Lockyer's brain into a tailspin. 'We are in deep shit,' he said. 'We are all in very deep shit.'

CHAPTER TWENTY-SEVEN

14th December – Monday

'You've had a week, Bill,' Atkinson shouted, his face the colour of ripe cherries. He had listened without comment as Townsend explained how his one murder case had turned into three – or four, if you counted the attempted murder of Stephanie Lacey. Five if they factored in Jane Walford. Lockyer had interjected once or twice, but on the whole he had kept his mouth shut. Atkinson was angry enough without his help.

'According to members of your own team, who shall remain nameless, half the bloody trace evidence didn't go to South West Forensics until Friday . . . after the London lot arrived,' Atkinson said, throwing a dismissive hand in Lockyer's direction. 'I just got off the phone with the crime scene manager and he tells me his team had the evidence logged and ready to go on the eighth, and yet it took you until last thing on the eleventh to get anything sent over to Linda and Larry.' He was shaking his head back and forth, his mouth hanging open. 'I've spoken to Larry this morning as well. He said his wife has been working overtime to get their findings back to us ASAP. And why?' He didn't leave suitable pause for Townsend to respond, although his expression suggested a reply could prove fatal at this point. 'Because DI Lockyer called to expedite things.'

Lockyer had thanked Linda for her help, but he hadn't realized she had worked out of hours to get him the information he needed. Maybe he would offer her dinner with the drink he had promised.

'Last time I checked this was a *murder* investigation, Bill. What are you playing at?'

'We've been working on the assumption that Jones's death was manslaughter, sir,' Townsend said, his voice lacking conviction. 'Our time and resources have been directed towards locating the other driver.' Lockyer didn't appreciate the 'we', but decided now wasn't the time to break ranks.

'By what?' Atkinson said with a grimace. 'Doing nothing in the hope they would turn themselves in?' Townsend flinched. 'To say this investigation has been mishandled is an understatement. I had no idea.' He turned his attention to Lockyer, who had so far escaped Atkinson's wrath. 'I assure you, DI Lockyer, this is not how we usually run things.' He pushed his fingers against his eyebrows. 'Jesus, Bill, at the very least we could have got a warning out to motorists.'

'Saying what, sir?' Townsend asked. He must have a death wish.

'Fuck, I don't know, Bill,' Atkinson said, almost jumping up and down on the spot, 'but if I'd have known last week that Jones and Evans were linked – that we had some sicko murdering girls and watching them burn in their cars – you can guaran-fucking-tee I would have done *something*.'

'But we still couldn't have known—'

'Save it,' Atkinson said, closing his eyes and holding up one finger to silence Townsend. 'If you're even thinking of telling me you couldn't have done anything to prevent the attack on Stephanie Lacey, don't bother.' He dropped into his chair with a thud. 'If you had done your job, Bill, we *would* have known that the person responsible for Chloe Evans's death was in all likelihood responsible for Pippa Jones's death. If you had done your job, Bill, we *would* have known that Andrea Jenkins was not only murdered, but murdered by, it seems, the same guy as Chloe *and* Pippa. From that, Bill, we *would* have known that there was a serial predator who has been active in the area for, as far as we know, over two bloody years. How many other disappearances, unsolved rapes, abductions might be linked back to this guy? With all of that, Bill, we *would* have known beyond a shadow of a doubt that the public was at risk, and we *could* have put out an alert, and we *could* have stopped Stephanie Lacey driving across the Quantocks at night, by herself, before being beaten half to death.'

'How is she?' Townsend asked, as if Atkinson's bollocking had been directed at someone else. Lockyer had been in his place more than once, but he had never remained this calm.

'She's alive, Bill,' Atkinson said. 'That's about all we can be thankful for right now.'

'The case hasn't been straightforward,' Lockyer said, surprised to find himself defending Townsend for the second time this morning. 'The information on Evans and Jenkins has come up quite by chance. We—'

'I fucked up, sir,' Townsend said, dropping his head, his

voice quiet. It was only the second time Lockyer had heard him swear. It didn't suit him. 'DI Lockyer and DS Bennett floated the idea of the Chloe Evans case being linked at the start of the weekend. I didn't listen. It's no secret I had some . . . issues on that case, that it . . . dented my confidence. So when DI Lockyer approached me about it, I'll admit I didn't give it my full attention. If I had handled the case better in the first instance, it's possible I would have made the Andrea Jenkins connection back then.' His shoulders seemed to sag further with each admission. 'As for Jones – I was, until this morning, adamant it was a simple hit and run. A drink driver. I didn't push the trace evidence through because . . . because I didn't appreciate the urgency. I take full responsibility. It was my oversight.'

'Sir,' Lockyer said, already regretting what he was about to say. 'It's not all DI Townsend's fault. You brought me in to assist with the Jones case. When DS Bennett brought information to me regarding the location where Chloe Evans's body was found, I didn't realize at the time the severity of the situation.' He took a deep breath. He could be about to commit professional suicide. 'It was my understanding that Evans's body had been found in Dead Woman's Ditch, the same site where John Walford had killed Jane Walford in 1789. However, I didn't go much further than that.' He swallowed his desire to cut and run and leave Townsend carrying the can. 'I only discovered the full story of the Walford case this morning.'

'What are you babbling about, DI Lockyer?' Atkinson said with a sigh.

'Sir,' he said. 'I have dealt with serial offenders. If I had realized that Chloe Evans had been killed utilizing the same exact MO as Jane Walford, my handling of the situation would have been very different, I assure you, but . . .' He stuttered to a stop, opening and shutting his mouth like a bloody goldfish struck dumb by his own carelessness. He had been so focused on what Townsend *wasn't* doing, he had lost sight of what he *should* be doing.

'I can hardly hold you to account for something *we* should have picked up on,' Atkinson said. The look he gave Townsend made Lockyer turn away.

'We've got a witness, at least,' Lockyer said, 'not to mention another crime scene with potential forensic evidence. I'll speak to Lacey as soon as she's conscious.'

'What about Ashworth?' Atkinson asked, looking at him rather than Townsend. 'I assume you'll be speaking to him?'

'He'll be our best starting point, yes, sir,' Lockyer said. 'We know Andrea Jenkins had a substance abuse problem, so it's possible she crossed paths with Ashworth. Nothing yet on Jones, but we'll keep digging.'

'Who knows, Bill,' Atkinson said, sitting back in his chair, 'you might yet be able to redeem yourself on not one but two of your cases, and maybe even solve a third.' He sat up, pulled himself closer to his desk and started tapping away at the keys on his laptop. 'Although I've gotta say, Ashworth didn't strike me as much of a historian. I'd be surprised if the boy could read.'

'We're assuming the correlation to Jane Walford's murder is more of a diversionary tactic rather than a straightforward copycat, sir,' Lockyer said, realizing he was voicing something Townsend had said. It made more sense, and if he was honest, he was more comfortable with the idea that the person he was pursuing was devious rather than the alternative – someone who was emulating a centuries-old murderer. Townsend was nodding. He looked relieved to have Lockyer on his side – in some form. And no wonder. As Atkinson had said, if they could nail Ashworth with all three murders, Townsend would not only be vindicated for two legendary screw-ups but he would no doubt be commended for solving such a complex case.

Lockyer ran his tongue along the front of his teeth. The fact that the guy had so far had bugger all to do with solving this or any other case was beside the point. Lockyer knew he wasn't going to get any credit at the end of this. There was only one scenario where his true reason for being here would be revealed – if things went wrong, really wrong, and Hamilton and Avon and Somerset Constabulary needed a fall guy. 'They've taken scrapings from under Lacey's nails, and Ashworth's DNA is on file, so assuming we get a match, we'll bring him in. If we can link him to any of the victims before that's back from the lab, we'll bring him in sooner.'

'No you won't,' Atkinson said, turning his laptop around and looking at Townsend. 'Your friend Ashworth was nicked for aggravated assault. He's been on remand for the past month, so Jones and this girl . . . Lacey are out.'

'Yes, sir, but that doesn't mean he isn't still a fit for Chloe's murder . . . or Andrea Jenkins,' Townsend said. He had taken a step towards the superintendent's desk. Lockyer could see it was a desperate gesture, but he could also feel the aggression coming off Townsend in waves. He might be desperate, but he was also angry.

'No, no, no,' Atkinson said, taking back his laptop and wagging his finger at Townsend. 'You can't have it both ways, Bill. You and DI Lockyer have just made an excellent case for a serial offender. Jenkins and Evans share the charcoal residue. Evans and Jones share tyre tracks. Jones and Jenkins knew each other, and Stephanie Lacey . . .' He looked up at the ceiling. 'She was attacked at the southern end of Shervage Wood, this guy's hunting ground. That's good enough for me. There's one guy, and it isn't Ashworth.'

'But, sir . . .'

'It isn't Ashworth,' Atkinson said again. 'Bill, drop it. Move on.' He straightened his tie. 'So, now he's out of the picture, tell me, detectives, what's next?'

Lockyer cleared his throat. He couldn't say he was all that surprised about Ashworth. From what he knew about the guy, he was a bottom-feeder with more baggage than brains. To get away with murder was no mean feat. To get away with it more than once?

'Your silence is not reassuring, gentlemen,' Atkinson said. 'Here's what I suggest.' He held up his index finger. 'You can start by getting a statement from Miss Lacey. She's seen this guy. With any luck she can give you a description, and with a good e-fit you might just be able to catch this guy before someone else ends up in that Dead Woman's sodding Ditch.'

'Well, that went well,' Lockyer said, as he and Townsend walked back to the CID offices. His phone was vibrating in his pocket. He took it out and looked down at the screen. 'Excuse me, Bill,' he said. 'I'll be back in a second.' He turned and walked back the way they had come, heading for the stairs at the far end of the atrium. He didn't recognize the number, but thought he knew who it might be. 'Hello,' he said as he put the phone to his ear.

'Lockyer,' Hamilton said. 'I'm outside, back of the station, black BMW.'

'On my way, sir,' he said, taking the stairs two at a time. He wondered if he needed to prepare himself for the second dressing-down of the day. He paused as the automatic doors slid open. The car park was a mess of snow and slush, cars parked askew or just abandoned where they ended up. The snow had eased, but they were forecast for more. It wouldn't be helping the CSI guys at the Lacey crime scene. He would guess they would need more than a few footboards to maintain any kind of evidence trail.

As he rounded the building he spotted Hamilton's car at the far end of the car park. It was one of those huge dual-fuel hybrids, an X5. He broke into a jog, careful not to slip. He put his hand on the door handle and looked in. Hamilton waved him inside. 'Sir,' he said as he climbed in and shut the door behind him.

'Thank you for coming,' Hamilton said, without turning to look at him. He was smoking a cigarette, his window open an inch for him to flick his ash. 'Do you mind?'

'No, go ahead,' Lockyer said.

'So I hear things have progressed somewhat since we last spoke,' Hamilton said, taking a drag of his cigarette, staring out the windscreen at something of unknown interest.

'Yes, sir.'

'Want to tell me your take on it?'

'Of course.' Lockyer decided to tell Hamilton the same as he had told Atkinson. 'Ashworth is out of the picture.'

'On remand, I understand.'

'That's right,' Lockyer said, thinking news travelled fast.

'So he's not around to pin it on.'

'So it appears,' Lockyer said.

'So what direction is your merry band heading in now, then?'

He took a deep breath. 'Well, sir, it is beginning to look as though the . . . Walford issue could have more bearing on the case than previously thought.'

'So *now* you think the nutty locals are right? The ghost of John Walford is back . . . and this time, he wants revenge,' he said, putting on a dramatic voice. Townsend had used the exact same phrase.

Lockyer dragged his finger and thumb down the sides of his mouth. 'Something like that, sir, yes,' he said. 'Although I very much doubt we're looking for a ghost.'

'An apprentice, then? A killer seeking legendary status?'

Lockyer shook his head. 'Not exactly, sir,' he said. 'More like someone who wants us to *think* that's what they're doing . . . to throw us off . . . keep us chasing our tails.'

He snorted. 'Like our friend Townsend on the Evans case?'

'Yes, sir.'

'I'll tell you the issue I have with this new . . . theory.' Hamilton rested his head back against the headrest.

'Please do,' Lockyer said, hoping it didn't sound like he was kissing arse.

'John Walford took a knife to his wife's throat for three

285

reasons. One, she spread her legs for anyone. Two, she drank like a fish, and three, she spent all his money.' He took another drag of his cigarette and rolled his head to the right as he blew the smoke out of the gap in the window. Lockyer was as good as talking to the back of the guy's head now. 'Chloe Evans, God rest her soul, was by all accounts not fussy when it came to guys. What did she have, four kids?'

'Three,' Lockyer said. 'Two and one on the way.'

'Upsetting,' Hamilton said, 'but as we know, almost identical to Walford's wife.' He looked down at his cigarette and threw the remainder out of the window. 'I also understand that Chloe liked a drink.'

'That's right,' Lockyer said.

'Do we know if she was a spender?'

'No.'

'Fine,' Hamilton said. 'Two out of three ain't bad. Now to the next one. What was her name?'

'Andrea Jenkins.'

Hamilton paused. 'That's right, the hit and run you're now trying to prove wasn't accidental,' he said. 'Jenkins had been pregnant when she was what . . . ?'

'Fifteen, and again at eighteen,' Lockyer said.

'The world today,' Hamilton said. 'And she was a drinker too, but again, we don't know if she spent her daddy's money.'

'That's right.'

'What do we know about Lacey?' he asked.

'Nothing yet, sir,' he said. 'I'm heading over to the crime scene after this and then hoping to get in to see the girl later on today, with any luck.'

'I thought she was critical?'

'She was, but she's improved enough to come out of the high dependency unit.'

'Small mercies,' Hamilton said, looking at his watch. 'Fine. So you'll find out more about her in due course, but I hope you can see the point I'm driving at, Lockyer. If your suspect is picking his victims with deference to Walford and his pet peeves – and given what we have just discussed, that does appear to be the case – then you, detective, are suggesting that my niece was something of a drunken hussy. Is that right?'

'No, sir, not at all,' Lockyer said, knowing he had done just that. If Hamilton wanted to remain under the illusion that his niece was whiter than white, he wasn't about to argue with him. It was clear Atkinson was feeding the case information back, but he seemed to have had the good sense to withhold Pippa's failed pregnancy. Without that knowledge, Hamilton's reticence to see her case attached to the others made sense. 'However, it *does* appear that your niece may have drawn the attention of our suspect, for whatever reason . . . perhaps a case of mistaken identity?' Hamilton sniffed, then nodded. 'I want to assure you, sir,' Lockyer said, putting on his best arse-kissing voice, 'your niece remains my *first* priority.'

'I'm glad to hear it,' Hamilton said, shifting in his seat and putting both hands on the wheel. It seemed their conversation was over. 'You have my full support to throw as many resources at the Walford girls as you deem fit: money, manpower, whatever it takes to catch the person responsible. But I want it made clear that Pippa's case, her death, is different. I won't have her memory tainted by this . . . mess.'

'And if she was killed by the same man?' Lockyer posed

it as a question, despite knowing it was as good as fact given the tyre impressions hit.

'Then I will happily rip the guy to pieces with my bare hands,' Hamilton said. 'No one sullies my family's name and gets away with it.'

CHAPTER TWENTY-EIGHT

14th December – Monday

'I don't know if they're going to let me in to see her yet,' Jane said.

'So why are you calling me again?'

'Because I wanted you to know I was waiting to speak to the consultant,' she said. 'And I've spoken to her parents.'

'Oh yeah – and?' he said, cracking his neck and using his shoulder to hold his phone up to his right ear while he pulled on the gloves being handed to him by one of the perimeter officers.

'She doesn't drink much, doesn't have time for boys, no boyfriend . . . the usual.'

Lockyer huffed out a laugh. 'So in reality she drinks like a fish, spends all her time with boys and there's not one boy-friend but ten.'

'I'd say that's a fair assumption . . . within reason,' Jane said.

'OK, well let's see what she has to say,' he said. 'It'd be good to get a statement while the incident is still fresh in her mind.'

'You don't say?' she said. He didn't need to see her face to know she was rolling her eyes.

'No one likes a smartarse, Jane,' he said, lifting up his feet as the officer bent down and helped him into some booties. He didn't get this kind of service in Lewisham. 'Is it snowing there?'

'No,' she said, 'raining. What about with you?'

'Snowing,' he said, ducking his head down so he could look out from underneath the awning. 'It's bucketing down.'

'That won't help,' she said.

'No.' He sighed. 'Well, I'd better go and show my face.'

'No one knows your face.'

'Jane, what did I say about—'

'I know. No one likes a smartarse.'

'Precisely. I'll text you in a bit,' he said. 'Keep me posted on Lacey.'

'Will do.'

'Good luck.' He ended the call and dropped his phone into his jacket pocket just as it rang again. 'I am popular,' he said to himself, pulling it back out and looking at the screen to decide whether to take the call. He saw Roger's name flashing up at him. He would be taking the call.

'You got my message, I take it.' He had sent an email to Roger's private Gmail account this morning to give him an update, or a heads-up, depending on how you looked at it. *He can't know that I know that you know,* Roger had almost squeaked down the phone when Lockyer had called over the weekend to tell him he knew Hamilton was the secret bene-factor. He guessed it was only natural for Roger to be on edge. He had been superintendent for all of five minutes. The last thing he needed was trouble with a DCC.

'You know how to pick 'em,' Roger said.

'You picked me, sir, remember?' he said, shoving his free hand as far into his jacket pocket as it would go.

'You really think you've got a serial offender?'

Lockyer shrugged, the gesture letting the cold wind up and under his coat. He shuddered. 'Not many other ways to look at it,' he said. 'Like I said, I've got trace evidence linking a six-month-old unsolved murder case with an accidental death dating back two years, and tread impressions linking the same case back to the Jones murder scene. And . . . the Jones girl knew our accidental death victim.'

'Shit,' Roger said.

'You said it.'

Roger cleared his throat. 'You need to play this one . . . carefully,' he said.

'You're telling me,' Lockyer said with a snort.

'I'm being serious, Mike. Hamilton called me this morning.'

'What did he want?' he asked, knowing it wouldn't be a chat about old times.

'He didn't say explicitly,' Roger said, 'but he was beside himself with this Townsend situation. I also got the impression he's none too pleased with his niece being associated with the other two victims. Some issue with their sex lives?'

'They had them, Rog. I think that's the problem,' Lockyer said, feeling his shoulders stiffen. What did Hamilton want? His niece had been murdered. What did it matter who she had or hadn't slept with?

'Just *try* and stay on his good side. He's not the kind of

guy you want to piss off, DCC or not. He's worked his arse off and fought hard to get to where he is. He spent years moving all around the Country to move up the ranks – taking on the shittiest cases – you name it . . . all while nursing a wife with dementia and terminal cancer.'

'His second wife?' He had heard about Hamilton's marriage, or rather his divorce from Claudette, but nothing much else. Under normal circumstances he wouldn't care, but as Hamilton was holding Lockyer's career in his meaty hands, he figured the more he knew about the guy the better chance he had of keeping his job.

'Elaine, yes,' Roger said. 'From what I've heard, the woman was a nightmare. Their marriage was on the skids when she was diagnosed but Hamilton stood by her – moved heaven and earth to get her the best treatment. Family and the force. That's about all he cares about, and so I don't imagine he will appreciate having his niece's – or his – reputation smeared all over the press when this comes out. Which it will.'

'A public advisory is going out tonight,' Lockyer said. 'I've spoken to the press office and they're keeping it loose, but we can't keep this quiet. Someone else could . . . will get hurt.'

'Jesus, Mike,' Roger said. 'This is going to get big quick. Where are you on the vehicle?'

'Nothing yet. Traffic's looking. We're pulling DVLA records left and right and half the team are sifting through weeks' worth of traffic cam footage. We'll get something, but it's gonna take time.'

'What about the girl, the one who was attacked last night?'

'Stephanie Lacey. Jane's at the hospital now,' Lockyer said.

'We're hoping for an ID, an e-fit at least – that's if she's conscious.' He shook his head, despairing at his own offhand language. Politics, power and position. It was always the same. When a case went national the game of 'quick, quick, cover your arse' began. 'I'm doing my best, Roger. I'm doing my job.'

'I know that. Hamilton knows that. And he *is* grateful to have you there . . . he said as much, but you have to appreciate that this situation with Townsend is a PR nightmare. If it gets out that he missed this charcoal residue link,' Roger said, 'all because he didn't do a simple cross-check, Avon and Somerset are going to be in serious trouble.'

'Why doesn't Hamilton just get shot of him?' Lockyer asked, feeling, of all things, disloyal. He had left Townsend back at the station licking his wounds. The poor guy looked broken.

'I think that's inevitable now,' Roger said, 'but not on this case. Not on something this high-profile. All I'm saying is, Hamilton is gunning for Townsend, with good cause. Just make sure you don't inadvertently add yourself to his shit list.'

'You know me,' Lockyer said, feeling far less flippant than he sounded.

'Yes, Mike. I do.'

Lockyer had already ended the call before he thought to ask how things were back in Lewisham. He couldn't wait to get back – to sleep in his own bed, deal with his own team and be allowed to take credit for his work, or at least fight his corner if the blame shifted his way.

He stepped forward and looked at the circus going on around him. If he had to guess, he would say this was the most people ever to visit this part of Shervage Wood since the first tree sprouted root. The lane was packed with cars tucked up against the banks of snow covering the verge. He had counted eighteen, plus two CSI vans. He would be making the suggestion that the bulk of them got out of there before it started to get dark, otherwise he could foresee people getting stuck. The temperature was expected to drop well below freezing this evening and the section of road where Stephanie Lacey's car had been found was on a steep incline.

'We've had to chase off a few folk already,' the perimeter officer said, coming to stand next to him half under the awning. He had been trying to engage Lockyer since he arrived. With reluctance Lockyer shifted sideways to allow the guy to shelter from the snow.

'People are just curious,' he said.

'People are sick,' the officer said, walking away. 'Lucky we've had help.' He pointed towards the woods.

Lockyer followed the officer's extended finger and saw Barney standing at the edge of the wood, his arms folded. He looked like a giant stone sentry. 'Well, of course he's here,' he muttered to himself. Was there a crime scene in Somerset this guy didn't frequent?

'Making friends, I see.'

He turned to find Dr Basil Reed standing behind him, stepping into a pair of wellington boots. 'Nice to see you again, doctor,' he said. 'You must have had one helluva journey down from Flax Bourton?'

'It was all right,' Basil said with a shrug. 'I've got a four-wheel drive. Besides, Barney parked her up at the top of the hill so I won't get stuck.'

'Of course,' Lockyer said, rolling his eyes.

'Have you been over yet?' Basil asked, either not caring for or not understanding Lockyer's joke.

'I was about to.'

'Then we'll go together,' Basil said. 'I can introduce you to the faces you don't know.'

'That would be great, doc.' Lockyer had never called a doctor 'doc' in his entire life, but for some reason Basil's personality fit the tag.

'I'm surprised they had enough boards to cover an area this size,' Basil said, pointing down at the beginning of a series of footboards leading from the road all the way to where Stephanie Lacey was found.

'I'm not sure they need've bothered,' Lockyer said. 'With this weather I can't imagine they're going to find much of use.'

'You'd be surprised,' Basil said. 'This lot are accustomed to dealing with outdoor environments. I bet they turn up more than you think.'

Lockyer nodded. He wondered if he should offer Basil an arm to steady him, given how slippery the road surface was. It wasn't that he looked infirm. On the contrary, he was the picture of vim and vigour for a guy of his age, whatever that might be; but Lockyer had been brought up to respect his elders. 'You all right there?'

Basil turned and looked at him over the top of his glasses. 'I'm fine, thank you, detective,' he said. 'I don't need a rug to put over my knees either.'

'Point taken,' Lockyer said, following behind as the doctor headed for Lacey's car just off to their left.

'Have they done the car already?' Basil said, speaking to the perimeter officer Lockyer had managed to offend.

'Yes,' the guy said, pulling at his hat. 'They've done four sweeps of the vehicle, four where the girl was found, two of the area leading up to and leading away from the crime scene, and they're on a third sweep of the crime scene itself, where the bulk of the attack took place.'

'They've not wasted any time,' Basil said.

'No,' the officer said, throwing Lockyer a look. 'People have been coming by all morning trying to get a look-see. They realized if they didn't get the evidence now they'd be hard-pressed to get anything decent once Tom, Dick and Harry have been through there with their iPhones and cameras.'

'Thanks, Ian,' Basil said, waving Lockyer over to join him. 'Shall we walk it and talk it?'

'Sure.'

Basil cleared his throat and took a Dictaphone out of his coat pocket. 'Do you mind?' Lockyer shook his head. 'Good. Let's get started, then.' He approached the driver's-side door, bent forward and leaned in. 'The girl was inside the vehicle. Her attacker approached from . . .'

'The front of the car,' Lockyer said. 'There's evidence of another vehicle over there.' He pointed to an area sectioned off by yellow crime scene tape. 'They've made casts of a few tyre treads. I'm hoping there's a match to ones I've already got; that's *if* they're useable in these conditions.'

Basil pushed out his bottom lip. 'Oh, ye of little faith,' he said. 'So our attacker approaches from there, opens the door here and grabs our girl with their . . . ' He mimed the action as he was talking. 'Left hand, I'd say.'

'We think she was dragged by her hair.'

Basil sniffed and nodded his head up and down. 'That would make sense,' he said. 'Hair is easy to hold on to.' He looked down at the door handle. 'Any prints here?'

'Not that they've told me,' Lockyer said, though he didn't like to admit that they hadn't told him much. Maybe if he had been nice to the perimeter officer, he might know more.

'I'm sure they've taken samples of what they can,' Basil said, turning and walking in a slow zig-zag across the road and over to the verge. It was like watching a butch Miss Marple putting together the clues. 'Drag marks here, here and here,' he said. 'The victim was facing down . . . you can see the impressions here.' He pointed to some indentations in the verge. 'These are from the front of her shoes, not the back.'

'How do you know?'

'They're rounded,' he said, curving his hand as he spoke. 'I'm sure we have hair, saliva, blood perhaps, but I'd imagine all will be from her. We're assuming the attacker wore gloves?'

'I think that's a safe bet, although it looks like she scratched him,' Lockyer said. 'There was a good amount of what looks like skin in with the mud, et cetera, under her fingernails.'

'Well, that's good,' Basil said, looking down as he stepped forward.

Despite the heavy snow, the struggle was evident once they passed the verge and entered the woods. Leaves, snow and mud had formed a sort of mulch. The new snow was settling in depressions that looked like the imprints of knees, elbows and one of the victim's whole body, as if she had been picked up and dropped. It was disturbing to look at, to visualize what it must have been like while she struggled to break free. When Jane had called earlier she had relayed Stephanie Lacey's injuries like she was reading from a shopping list – there were that many. They approached a section of undergrowth that had been marked out, and yellow plastic markers put in place. Each had a letter. The resulting file would detail each letter and what, if anything, had been found. Lockyer stopped when he thought he saw a shadow to his left. He looked, staring deep into the wood. He shook his head. He was getting as bad as Jane. In fact, he was worse. At least she had the decency to only get scared when she was on her own.

'Looks like there was some impact here?' Basil said. 'Could be an arm . . . or perhaps a leg. The blood loss is minimal so I'd say ankle, knee, elbow or . . .'

Lockyer dragged his thoughts back to reality. 'The victim has a broken patella,' he said. 'It's an open fracture.'

'Fine, fine,' Basil said, moving away. 'So she's still being dragged. Still struggling. Oh, and here?' He stopped beside a single yellow marker. 'There is a significant amount of blood here.'

Lockyer came and stood next to him and looked down. He didn't know what Basil could see, but all he could see was a mess of the mulch and fresh snow. 'Where?'

'Here,' Basil said, pointing to a section of turned earth. 'The blood has soaked into the ground here. Look at the colour change between this, say –' he looked around him – 'and over there. Do you see it's darker?'

'Good eye,' Lockyer said.

'The best.'

Lockyer turned at the sound of Barney's voice. 'Barney, my boy,' Basil said. 'You keeping the weirdos away?'

'Someone has to, doc,' Barney said. Lockyer resolved not to use the shorthand again. 'You know better than most what people can be like.'

'True, true,' Basil said. He turned to Lockyer. 'Do you know—?'

'Yes, we've met,' Lockyer said.

'How's the chin?' Barney asked, rubbing his giant hand over his giant bearded chin.

'Fine,' Lockyer said.

'What happened to your chin?' Basil asked, a curious look on his face.

'Nothing,' Lockyer said. 'Nothing important.' He looked at Barney. 'We should get back to it, doctor. I have places to be.'

'Of course, detective,' Basil said. 'Keep up the good work,' Barney.'

Lockyer turned away. 'You were saying?'

Basil looked down at the ground and put his gloved hand to his mouth. 'That's right,' he said. 'I'd hazard a guess this was a bleed from the scalp. Head wounds bleed like hell.'

'Part of the victim's scalp was missing,' he said. 'We're assuming it came away with a chunk of her hair.'

'Do we have that?' Basil asked, unmoved, it seemed, by Lockyer's revelation; but then, this was his business. He dealt with injury and death every day. Maybe nothing shocked him any more.

'Not so far,' Lockyer said. 'I told the CSI guys to keep an eye out after I spoke to my colleague earlier.'

'Townsend?'

'No, one of my colleagues from London.'

'Ahh, DS Bennett,' Basil said.

'That's right.' Lockyer frowned. 'Have the two of you met?'

Basil shook his head. 'No, no,' he said, looking back to where Barney was still standing guard. 'I've just heard her name mentioned, that's all.'

'And?'

'It's all right, detective,' he said, smiling. 'I've only heard good things.' Lockyer wasn't sure what made him more uncomfortable: people talking about Jane, or Barney talking about Jane – *good things.* 'And so on to the main event,' Basil said, pointing up ahead to a large group of CSI all bent over the scene they were examining.

Lockyer picked his way through the undergrowth, using the footboards where needed. He had to resist the urge to keep looking over his shoulder. 'Did you get my email about . . . ?'

'Jenkins, yes,' Basil said.

When he didn't say more, Lockyer asked, 'So what did you think?'

'I think it shouldn't have been handed back to the coroner so soon,' Basil said. 'I did the post-mortem on Chloe Evans. Need I ask *who* missed the link with the charcoal residue?'

'Townsend,' Lockyer said with a sigh.

'He's not having a good week, is he,' Basil said, looking over his glasses at Lockyer. The rumour mill appeared to be as well-oiled down here as it was in Lewisham.

'So you think it's possible Jenkins could have been attacked?'

'Not *could*, detective, *was*,' he said. 'The injury to Jenkins' shoulder was, as the pathologist said, a glancing blow, but it would have been enough to knock her off her feet . . . drunk or not.'

'So you're saying the pathologist was right,' Lockyer said. 'But you just said—'

'Those were the only injuries described in detail in the post-mortem, but they were by no means the only ones present,' Basil said. 'I didn't have the body to examine, of course, but just from the photographs I could see she had defensive wounds on her forearms and hands. She had a broken nose, and what looked like a fractured eye socket . . .'

'How was this not . . . ?'

'It's all been lumped in with the head injury and the fall,' Basil said. He turned and looked at Lockyer. 'All I can say is my colleague, Dr Michaels, is no longer practising. I was brought in to take over the area when he was given . . . mandatory retirement. Trouble with the drink, I'm afraid.'

'Great,' Lockyer said, thinking that with the catalogue of screw-ups surrounding these cases, he would be lucky to catch anyone at this rate. 'So you're happy to confirm she was attacked . . . amend the documentation?'

'Absolutely,' Basil said.

'Even drunk, surely, Michaels should have picked up on this.'

'Of course,' Basil said. 'However, this isn't the first mistake of his I've seen. It's come to the point where I dread even the mention of the man's name.'

'I'm not surprised,' Lockyer said, thinking the only upside, at least for Townsend, was that Michaels's incompetence took at least some of the heat off his catalogue of errors. If the good doctor had laid off the booze and done his job, Avon and Somerset would have started the search for a killer two years ago, not two days ago.

Jane walked into the private room and shut the door behind her, taking care to be as quiet as possible. The consultant had explained that Stephanie Lacey had a burst eardrum, so she would be very sensitive to sound.

She looked over at Stephanie. The girl was a sorry figure to behold.

The curtains in the room were drawn and the lights were down low. Jane picked up a chair and placed it next to the bed. She sat down, crossed her legs, rested her hands in her lap and waited. Stephanie was awake. She had stirred when Jane came in, but she had turned her face away. Jane took this as a sign that she wasn't ready to talk – not yet.

Her phone buzzed in her pocket. Thank God she had put it on vibrate. It was a message from Lockyer:

Confirmation from pathologist – Jenkins was attacked.

Jane re-read the message. Any doubt she might have had evaporated. So that made three: Chloe, Pippa and Andrea. Stephanie made four. She looked back at the girl, glad she couldn't see Jane's reaction as she took in the devastation of her broken face.

The eye she could see was swollen shut. A thick bandage covered the other side of her face. The skin on her cheeks and around her mouth was pink and red with flecks of white, like raw steak mince. Her neck was a myriad of bruises, purple, burnt orange and yellow. Her ear was black, a dry crust of blood on the lobe. And that was just her face. The consultant had told Jane the extent of Stephanie's injuries from top to toe: a tear in her scalp, a fractured eye socket, a split lip, a broken jaw, severe swelling around her throat and windpipe, a punctured lung, multiple lacerations and contusions covering her entire body, a broken kneecap, a torn quadriceps tendon, and she was hooked up to a warm saline drip to treat hypothermia. The doctor had said she was lucky to be alive. Jane had to agree. The broken body in front of her was the kind she was more used to seeing at the mortuary, not the hospital. The courage and strength it must have taken for Stephanie to escape was unfathomable – almost. Jane reached up and held her own throat, memories of her own ordeal tightening her windpipe.

It wasn't so long ago that she had been in a similar position: throat swollen and bruised from the hands that had tried to squeeze the life out of her. It wasn't the first or, she imagined, the last time that her life would be threatened because of her job, but it was the first time it had been at the hands of a friend. She closed her eyes and tried to remember how she had felt; to come so close to dying, and yet survive. The memories were a jumbled mess of thoughts, emotions and physical pain. 'I was attacked,' she said, before she realized she was going to speak. Stephanie turned her head. 'I remember how helpless I felt, lying in a hospital bed, relying on strangers to fix me.'

Stephanie's tongue poked out of her mouth. It was almost purple. She licked the edge of her torn lip. 'I'm not broken,' she croaked, her face contorting in pain.

'Can I get someone? Do you need some water?'

Stephanie rocked her head from side to side on the pillow. 'He wanted me dead,' she said, 'but I survived.' The defiance in her voice was astonishing.

Swap places, and Jane had been a wreck. It had taken her weeks to come to terms with what had happened, but what came next had been, in a way, worse. There was a void. She had felt thrown off her axis. Her life would be forever split into two parts: before the attack and after. But Stephanie Lacey seemed to defy her position. Despite her appearance, she wasn't a victim.

'How are you feeling?' Jane asked, knowing it was a stupid question but feeling compelled to ask.

'The painkillers are good, but . . .' Stephanie swallowed, her eyes searching.

'Water?' Jane asked again.

'Please.' Her voice was a hoarse whisper. Jane was finding it difficult to focus, difficult to remain detached. She was here to do a job, not rake up old wounds. This wasn't about her. It was about Stephanie.

'Stephanie,' she said.

'Steph.'

'OK. Steph. My name is detective sergeant Jane Bennett . . .'

'Knew you were a copper,' Steph said, her words distorted by her swollen tongue and lips.

'I'm here to find out what happened . . . to find the person who did this to you with, if you're up to it, your help.'

A single tear rolled down Steph's cheek. Jane resisted the urge to wipe it away. 'I don't remember anything once he hit me.'

Jane opened her pad and rested it on the edge of the bed, leaning forward so the girl wouldn't have to speak above a whisper. 'So you were attacked by a man?' There was a second's delay before Steph nodded. 'Can you tell me what he looked like? Hair colour . . . the clothes he was wearing . . . anything you can remember. The smallest detail could make all the difference.'

Steph closed her eyes. She was very still. Jane held her breath. She knew what Steph was doing; she had done it herself. She had closed her eyes so she could remember. What Steph couldn't know, what Jane wouldn't tell her, was that in the coming days, weeks and months the images would come back to her over and over again, to the point where she would be afraid to close her eyes. She would be afraid to sleep, because that would be when her attacker would come again. For months Jane had woken in the night, her mouth open in a silent scream as she tried to escape the feeling of his hands around her throat. She looked at Steph, at what was left of her young face.

'He was big,' Steph said.

'Tall? Fat?'

'Tall,' she said, her t's distorted to d's.

'What else?' Jane said.

'Boots . . . army ones, with laces.' Jane jotted down every word Steph said. 'Combat trousers . . . tucked-in socks, army socks.'

'What about his face, Steph? Can you remember anything about his face?'

She rocked her head from side to side again. 'I never saw his face,' she said as another tear washed down her battered face. She reached up with bruised fingers and touched the side of her head, where a thick bandage was hiding what Jane knew was a fractured eye socket and a broken jaw.

Jane rested a hand on hers. 'It's OK,' she said. 'You rest, I'll come back. We'll talk again.' Steph managed to shrug, tears now running down her face, soaking into her bandages. 'We will find him,' Jane said as she retreated to the door. She reached out for the handle as she remembered her pad was still on the bed. She crept back and picked it up. Steph's breathing had already deepened. Jane tiptoed back and opened the door without a sound.

'He didn't want me.'

Jane turned. 'What do you mean? Who did he want, Steph?'

Steph was shaking her head. 'It wasn't me he wanted,' she said. 'He kept calling her name, *Annie, Annie*. He said it over and over. It was *her* he wanted . . . but she wasn't there.' She closed her eyes. 'I took her place.'

When they reached the main group of CSIs, Lockyer noticed Abbott was standing with them.

'Sir,' he said, giving Lockyer a nod.

'Abbott,' he said. 'This is—'

'I know Ben,' Basil said. 'Known him since he was a boy. His father and I were golf buddies.'

'All right, Basil,' Abbott said. 'You keeping well?'

'Can't complain, Ben,' Basil said, 'can't complain. How's that gorgeous mother of yours?'

'She's well, thanks.'

'Still single?' Abbott nodded. 'It's a crying shame,' Basil said. 'Your father would have wanted her to move on . . . to find someone to have fun with.'

'I think she's tried,' Abbott said, 'just hasn't found anyone she likes.'

'You tell her if I wasn't married, I'd be beating a path to her door.'

'Will do,' Abbott said.

Lockyer stood by and observed this intimate display. The CSI team didn't appear to have noticed, let alone tuned in, but he was all ears. It was fascinating what you could learn about people in a two-minute conversation. The insight into Abbott's life was interesting. He wondered if the surface aggression Lockyer had witnessed came from losing his father after some protracted illness. And he wondered if he was an only child, and if so, whether he now felt responsible for his mother's happiness?

Lockyer cringed as he felt the pull of his daughter's influence. He would be glad when her psychology course finished and she stopped filling his head with psychobabble, but for now Lockyer couldn't help himself. He was looking at Abbott through different eyes – more sympathetic eyes. It was annoying. Although he could hear Jane's words in his head: *There is always a deeper reason behind someone's behaviour: hurt people hurt others.*

His phone beeped in his pocket. He took it out. It was a message from Jane.

Dr said Lacey will be in for couple of weeks. Extensive injuries, life changing not life threatening. Re lifestyle — she has UTI and STD. Spoke to her. No ID on attacker. Some details. Not enough for e-fit. Heading back to station now.

He frowned as he read the next line of her text.

Attacker was calling out another woman's name: Annie.

The name rang a bell, but he couldn't think why.

'This looks pretty good,' Basil said. Lockyer sniffed, pocketed his phone and turned to look where he was pointing. 'That looks like a good print to me.' One of the CSI officers was pouring a mixture that looked like Yorkshire pudding mix into the depression in the mud. 'You're a big guy,' Basil said. 'What size feet are you?'

'Twelve.'

Basil looked down at his feet, and then over to where the CSI team were working. 'That's bigger,' he said. 'Thirteen, fourteen maybe.' A line from a film flashed into Lockyer's mind: *You know what they say about men with big feet? Big feet . . . large shoes.*

CHAPTER TWENTY-NINE

15th December – Tuesday

Jane took another bite of her smoked salmon and cream cheese bagel despite the fact that she couldn't taste anything. Her throat was on fire and her nose had transformed into a dripping tap. It was no wonder, given her excursions over the weekend. The most unfortunate part was that she had given it to Peter. He had spent the night in her bed, kicking her in the stomach on the hour every hour. She had given up and got up at five thirty, only to be prodded awake by Lockyer offering her a cup of coffee twenty minutes later. She had collapsed on the sofa, which had resulted in a crick in her neck. She covered her mouth with the back of her hand as she yawned, her mouth wide. The snow outside was heavy. It had eased off overnight but started again in earnest this morning. The drive down from Clevedon had been slow, made slower by Lockyer's mood. She knew, given what had happened, that he must be thinking about the Stevens case. The ripples of Lewisham's first and, with any luck, last serial killer were still being felt in Lewisham murder squad – by Lockyer more than anyone.

She looked around the office, listening to the hum of conversation, telephone calls and the tap-tapping of numerous fingers on computer keyboards. In contrast to Lockyer, the discovery of a serial offender on their patch had brought the CID team alive. Their apathetic, unhelpful faces had been transformed by flushed cheeks and clear, focused eyes. Amalgamating three, no, four cases was no easy task. Extra officers had been drafted in from the response teams to help. There was an almost tangible buzz around her. No one *wanted* to deal with violent crime, but she couldn't help admiring Townsend's team for their gear-change. This was new to them – something so out of their field of expertise that a few nerves would be forgiven, if not expected. But as far as Jane could tell they were raring to go, determined to catch the newly dubbed 'Hill Killer', or HK for short. She was impressed with them, at least.

As for Townsend? He was a different matter. Her phone beeped on the desk. She glanced at the screen. It was a message from Lockyer:

Arrived at hospital. Townsend said he'll meet me here. I'll believe that when I see it. Will call in a bit.

She tapped the reply icon.
'DS Bennett?'
She paused and looked up as Pimbley came to a stop next to her desk. He appeared to be coveting her lunch. 'You're welcome to it,' she said, 'but I should warn you I've got a stinking cold.' Her t's were still coming out as d's. She

saw him wrestle with his hunger and good sense. 'I really wouldn't, Pimbley.'

His eyes lingered for a second before snapping up to meet hers. 'I'm through about half of the DVLA reports,' he said, taking a step back. 'Believe it or not, I've found five "Chawton White" Land Rovers in Devon and Somerset so far. Figured you'd want to check them and seize or rule them out before we carried on with the rest of the list.'

Jane could tell by his expression that his desire to get the vehicles checked was more for his own benefit than hers. She had done some shitty jobs in her time, and checking through page after page of DVLA records with their tiny print had to be right up there with watching paint dry. She gestured for him to go on.

'We've got three here, and two over the border. I've forwarded the details of the Devon ones to the relevant stations and asked them to liaise with you.'

Jane pursed her lips. 'Great, well done,' she said, sensing again that there was subtext to Pimbley's statement – referring work to her was easier than dealing with the whole Townsend/Lockyer/who was in charge debacle. 'I can't believe there are so many,' she said. 'Who'd buy a white car down this way? They show up all the dirt.'

Pimbley's lips flattened as he shrugged. 'People who don't care, I s'pect.'

'You said there were three here,' she said, taking the folder he was offering her. 'Where are they?'

'All the details are in there,' he said, gesturing to the folder. 'There's one registered to a guy out in Holford. Another in Doddington, and the other one's at a garage in

Taunton.' He looked down at the piece of A4 paper he was holding. 'The Devon ones are in Exeter – both residential – forty-odd minutes away.'

'Taunton, Doddington and Exeter I know,' she said, opening the folder. 'Where's Holford?'

'It's past Stowey out on the A39.' His hand entered her field of vision as he pointed to and then slid out a sales prospectus. 'I found this online. The house is called Hunter's Moon.' He looked sheepish.

'Hey,' she said, stifling another yawn. 'Never apologize for being proactive . . . unless you're doing something expensive. Then wait to find out if it's been beneficial before you own up to your boss.' She looked at a clutch of black and white photographs, a detailed plan of the property and a map. There were two buildings: a single-storey four-bedroom house that looked like sixties architecture, surrounded by a mature garden, and a one-bedroom flat at the bottom of a steep driveway. The flat was an uninspiring white box, a shuttered garage underneath. Both properties sat in just under an acre of land. Her pulse quickened as she spotted the cattle grid at the end of the driveway separating the two buildings. What was it with this place and cattle grids? She would never be able to drive over one again without thinking about Somerset, without thinking about this case. 'Have we got a name?'

'Mr L. Rice,' Pimbley said. 'Don't have a first name.'

She swallowed, feeling like each ring of cartilage in her throat had been replaced with razor blades. 'And who are the others?' She could almost feel her temperature rising.

'The Taunton one is for sale at a local garage,' he said.

'Could be interesting,' she said, thinking that if she had

run someone off the road she would get rid of the car she did it with.

'The Doddington one's at Pepperhill Farm. A Robert Goodland,' Pimbley said, walking behind her, leaning over her shoulder and pointing to the corresponding batch of papers. 'Managed to get an old sales brochure for this one too – mind, it's pretty old.'

She looked at the cover image showing a quintessential English red-brick farmhouse with three chimneys and a slate-tiled roof at the bottom of a winding, rutted lane. No wonder they needed a 4x4. She flicked to the map at the back and stopped. At least a third of the land backed onto or was at least within a stone's throw of Shervage Wood. 'This one's Goodland, you said?'

'That's right,' Pimbley said, pulling out a chair, sitting down and rolling himself over until he was almost in her lap.

'It might be an idea to do a—'

'Priors check?' he asked, looking pleased with himself.

She snorted a laugh. 'Yes,' she said. 'You are keen.' He straightened and puffed out his chest. 'And?'

'None,' he said. 'Not for any of them.'

'Right,' she said, with a tinge of disappointment and a dose of *get serious*. Did she really think it was going to be that easy? Find a white Land Rover, link it to an owner with a record as long as your arm, and wham, suspect found; job done. She had a reputation in Lewisham for being Ms Positive when it came to cases, but thinking they would find their guy and have this over within a day was pushing it even for her.

'I don't get the feeling he'd be local. Not *local* local,

anyway,' Pimbley said. 'People'd know him, for one; and not only that, he'd have to be pretty dumb to be doing what he's doing if he lived here.'

'Meaning?' she asked, tapping away at her computer as she pulled up a map of the Quantocks and looked at the proximity of the two Land Rovers to each other, to Shervage Wood and the four crime scenes.

'If you were going round killing people, would you do it on your doorstep with a vehicle *registered* in your name where you live? Talk about shitting where you eat.'

Jane's mind boggled at Pimbley's mix of expressions, but he had a point. 'I'll need to get teams out to . . .'

'I thought me and Crossley could check out the Taunton one,' he said before she could finish her sentence. 'I'm due to head over there anyway, to get another update from South West Forensics for DI Lockyer and drop off and pick up some more samples. They're doing the DNA prep work on the stuff they scraped out from under Lacey's fingernails, so we can get it run through the database.' He sniffed. 'They've got some good business out of Avon and Somerset this past week.'

'That they have,' she said, opening an action log on the computer. 'Fine. You and PC Crossley head into Taunton.' She looked up at Pimbley's keen expression. His left leg was jiggling with, she guessed, a combination of excitement and adrenalin. 'You're to locate the vehicle and, if appropriate, speak to the registered owner . . . but bear in mind the kind of guy we're looking for here. If you get a feeling you're on the right track, call it in immediately and wait for backup before seizing the vehicle or even contemplating an arrest.'

She could see he wasn't listening. 'Pimbley, I'm serious. Armed response is on standby as and when we find this guy. In the meantime, you keep your distance and keep it casual. The last thing we want is to spook this guy into running, or worse, having an officer in the firing line if he panics. OK? Atkinson would have a fit.'

'Yes, boss,' he said with an enthusiastic nod. 'Of course.'

'Abbott,' she called across the office. He looked up. 'Can I borrow you for a second? You too, Nicola.' Both pushed back their chairs and crossed the office to Jane's desk. Where Abbott was tall, dark and lanky, Nicola Chandler was short, grey and sturdy. They made an odd pair, but together Jane figured they portrayed just the right balance of subtlety and strength. What Abbott lacked in girth he made up for in height and shoulder width, and Chandler might be small, but she had the physique of a rugby prop. Jane wouldn't mess with either of them. But then, she hadn't killed three women and tried to kill a fourth. She felt a seed of doubt start to germinate. Should she speak to Lockyer before she sent them out? She paused for a second, then shook her head. The likelihood that any of the Land Rovers were *the* Land Rover was slim to none. Like Pimbley had said, the guy they were looking for would have to be crazy or stupid to shit so close to home. 'We've got a vehicle over in Doddington I need you two to check out. DC Pimbley and PC Crossley are headed into Taunton, and I'll head over to . . .' She looked at Pimbley.

'Holford,' he said.

'I'll head to Holford with . . .'

'Me,' a voice said behind her.

She turned. 'DI Townsend,' she said. 'I thought you were going to the hospital?'

'On my way now,' he said, looking at his watch, 'but I shouldn't be gone long. If you can hold the fort here, I'll be as quick as I can and we'll head over to Holford in my car. We'll need a four-wheel drive in this weather.'

'Fair enough,' she said, feeling thwarted. Despite what she had said to Pimbley, she couldn't deny she was keen to get out there – to be doing something. The quicker they could act on the new information, while it was still fresh, the better chance they had of catching the guy unawares. A public announcement had gone out on last night's evening news warning motorists, hikers, walkers and the like to be extra vigilant in and around the Quantocks due to the recent hit and run incident, but there was no mention of historical cases or murder. The brief had been to keep it general in terms of facts. There was nothing to tip the girls' attacker off that they had made a breakthrough and were, at this very minute, hunting him down.

'I'll buzz you when I'm leaving Musgrove,' Townsend said.

He was gone before she could agree or disagree. She had intended to update him on their progress, but it was clear he had more urgent business to attend to. The business of being seen doing his job, no doubt. She blew out a breath as she updated the action logs of who was going where. Abbott, Chandler and Pimbley had made themselves scarce and looked to be getting their stuff together to head out. She tipped her head on one side, trying to stretch out the crick in her neck that was making her head thump. Did Townsend really think he was going to keep his job after his latest cock-up? Was he really that deluded? Her phone skittered across the desk as it started to ring. It was Lockyer.

'Hey,' she said. 'Townsend's on his way to you now.'

'Great,' he said, without sincerity. 'I just wanted to run something by you.'

'OK. How's Steph doing?' she asked, plugging in her hands-free. She wanted to text her mother to find out how Peter was doing. If she felt this shit, he would be worse. She was dreading tonight already.

'I spoke to her briefly,' Lockyer said. 'She's definitely start-ing to remember more, so I've managed to arrange for a sketch artist to come over and help her with an image. Should be here within the hour. Even if it's rough it'll be better than nothing.'

'Absolutely,' she said. 'Fingers crossed.'

'Any news on the DNA from under her fingernails?'

She shook her head despite the fact that he couldn't see her. 'Pimbley is heading over there in a bit,' she said. 'I'll ask him to ask, but to be fair, they've had the samples for all of five minutes. We'll have to be patient.'

'Not my favourite word,' he said. 'I'll try Linda in a bit and see if I can't get things moving.'

She snorted. 'Of course.' It hadn't escaped her notice that he appeared somewhat enamoured with the sultry-voiced scientist. Jane's voice was low and husky as a result of her cold and red-raw throat, but she didn't sound sexy. She just sounded full of phlegm. 'I'm heading out in a second.'

'Where to?'

She looked out and across the road at the snow covering

the car park of the NHS depot. The lorries coming in and out were leaving giant slalom skids. There was no way she was waiting for Townsend to resurface. The sooner she was out, the sooner she would be back. 'Pimbley's come up with some names and addresses from the DVLA data. There are three vehicles matching the description in the local area. Two this side of the hills, and one down in Taunton.'

'Who's going where?' he asked, an edge to his voice. 'Have you talked to armed response?'

'I'll speak to them before I leave,' she said, 'but I've told the guys that are going to keep it casual – to get a look at the vehicle and speak to the registered owner if it's appropriate. I've said there's to be no heroics if they think it's our guy.'

'So who's going?' he asked again. He sounded impatient, but that was nothing new, not when a case kicked up a gear like this one had. Not when lives were at risk.

'Abbott and Chandler are headed to a farm over in Doddington; Pimbley and Crossley to a garage in Taunton, and I'm driving over to Holford to a house out there.'

'With who?'

'Well . . .' she said, looking at her watch. It was only two o'clock, but the light was fading. 'Townsend wanted me to wait for him to get back from the hospital, but I'm not going to. I was due to meet Barney later over in Doddington, because I wanted to check out that Jane Walford memorial you mentioned yesterday.'

'What for?' he asked. She could hear the beep of a heart monitor somewhere in the background. 'CSI have already been over this morning and taken samples. I told you. The guy who told me about it was just some nutter with a chicken.'

'Still,' she said. 'I spoke to Barney last night, and he said he'd be happy to show me where it was. I don't want to *assume* something's not relevant. We made that mistake before.' Silence greeted her statement.

'I'd prefer you waited for Townsend,' he said. She could almost hear his jaw clenching. 'You can take his 4x4 up there. Barney isn't a police officer, Jane, and you seem to be forgetting that he knew more than one of the victims. I'm not happy about him being involved.'

'It's already arranged,' she lied. If she was going to be in the middle of nowhere in the snow to have a look at a vehicle that could belong to a killer, then having Barney with her could only be a good thing – not least because of his size. She wouldn't tell him, but Lockyer had a point, and under any other circumstances she would be wary of someone with Barney's connection to a case; but if it came down to a choice between him and Townsend, she would pick Barney any day of the week. 'What did you want to ask me?' she said, hoping a change of subject would help.

'Fine,' he said, 'but I want you to keep in contact. OK?'

'Of course,' she said. 'Now what did you want to run past me?'

There was a pause before he spoke. 'Something has been bothering me.'

'Mm-hmm,' she said, getting up and shrugging into her coat, her phone wedged between her ear and shoulder.

'When I spoke to Hamilton yesterday, after my meeting-slash-bollocking from Atkinson . . . he knew about Andrea.'

'What do you mean?' she asked, taking her keys out of her handbag and dropping them into her coat pocket.

'I mean, he knew about Andrea's background, her pregnancies, that she drank – stuff like that.'

'I know,' she said, wrapping her scarf once and then twice around her neck. 'You said Atkinson was keeping him in the loop.'

'Of course,' he said, 'but I never talked to Atkinson about Andrea Jenkins in detail. Not then, anyway.'

'So how did Hamilton know?' she asked, pausing in her search for her gloves.

'Exactly,' Lockyer said. 'Hamilton must have got the information from someone else.'

'But who?' she asked, sitting down again as her mind worked. 'The only people who had access to Andrea's file were you, me and . . .'

'Townsend,' Lockyer said.

CHAPTER THIRTY

15th December – Tuesday

Aaron lay back on the sofa and groaned. His whole body ached, although he suspected most of his discomfort was coming from his liver. He hadn't had a hangover like this in years. He hadn't been able to get out of bed at all yesterday. As if on cue, his stomach grumbled. Older guys at the station were always saying the older you got the longer the hangover would last. He remembered when a pizza and a pint of Coke would sort him out. Not this time. He couldn't face eating.

He rested his chin on Megan's head. She was sleeping. Her hair smelled of shampoo. If he closed his eyes, he could pretend they were back in London – maybe in their own place. He was relaxing into the daydream when the cat dug its claws into his bare feet, as if determined to bring him back to reality.

He felt in limbo between the past and the present. His chest ached every time he thought about Pip; that he would never see her again. Was he the only one who missed her? He felt like it. His parents had gone over to the Hendersons' for Christmas drinks, and Claudette had 'popped off' to join

321

them. They were all returning to normal. His aunt still looked pale and pinched, his father's expression was fixed and his mother's over-zealous demeanour was unnerving, but it was clear they were moving on. His mother most of all. The emotional door that had been opened by Pippa's death was closing. She had morphed back into the vicar's wife, her life filled with do-gooding and baking. He sighed.

'Close your eyes,' Megan murmured.

'They are closed,' he said, kissing the top of her head.

'Try and sleep.'

'I can't.'

She pushed herself up on her elbow and looked at him. 'Do you want me to get you something to eat? A drink, maybe . . . tea, coffee?'

He smiled as she added his choices of beverage. Whisky was not a choice. Neither was vodka. It was fair to say she had gone off Cassie after their impromptu pub crawl. 'What am I going to do when we get back to London?'

She reached up and held his face, resting her thumb against his lips. 'We'll take it one day at a time.'

'I meant, what am I going to do when I don't have you to look after me?' he said, stroking her hair.

'I'm not going anywhere,' she said, resting her head back on his chest.

He wrapped his arms around her and squeezed her as tight as he dared. How could he be so happy and so sad at the same time? His life was full yet empty. He lifted his head at the sound of his phone, craning his neck to locate it. It was on the mantelpiece. 'Sorry,' he said, slipping out from under Megan's arm. He stretched his back as he stood up, a dull ache settling in his spine. 'Maybe I will have a cuppa,' he said. She started to sit up. 'No, no,' he said. 'I meant *I* would make it. Stay where you are.' She sank back down and smiled at him. He picked up his phone. 'Hey, Cass,' he said, putting the phone to his ear.

'Aaron, Aaron . . .' The panic in his sister's voice made his heart falter.

'What's wrong?'

'I can't find Casper,' she said.

'Christ, Cass,' he said, his breath rushing out of him, 'he's a dog. He'll come back.' He shook his head. 'Who walks someone else's dog anyway?'

'I wouldn't be fucking doing it if Claudette hadn't volunteered me for the job,' she said. 'I'm meant to be *helping out*, remember?'

'You should have said no. She could have—'

'Listen, Aaron, forget about the bloody dog,' she said. 'Look, this is gonna sound . . . stupid . . . hysterical, maybe. I don't know, but . . . I think someone's following me.'

'What? Where are you?' The air around him seemed to cool in an instant.

'I'm about halfway up Hack Lane.'

'What the hell are you doing up there?' The news bulletin had been general and benign, but Cassie, more than anyone, should know it was anything but.

'I chased the fucking dog up here.'

'Jesus. I'm coming now,' he said. 'Get back to Castle Hill. Knock on a door, anyone's door . . .'

'I don't think I can,' she said.

'Cass, what is going on?'

'I don't know,' she said. 'I heard a car. I got scared . . . then Casper ran off. I think I can hear someone.' Her voice had dropped to a whisper. 'I can. Aaron, there's someone back there.'

Aaron felt glued to the spot. He didn't know what to do first – go to his sister, or call his boss. Megan was standing next to him now, her mouth open in an unspoken question. He needed to get to Cassie but he didn't want to hang up on her. 'Hold on,' he said, 'just talk to me, keep talking.' He ran to the lounge door, almost taking it off its hinges as he flung it open. 'Meg, where are the keys?' He turned. She was gone. 'I'm coming, Cass, I'm coming. Just keep walking.'

'Aaron, I'm scared,' she said, a hitch in her voice. This wasn't the Cassie he knew. Cassie was the strong one. She was the one who looked after him; looked after Pip.

'Can you see anyone?'

'No,' she said.

'Here,' Megan said, appearing behind him. 'Let's go.'

'We're getting in the car now, Cass,' he said. 'Meg, call your dad. Cass, we're coming . . . we'll be two minutes.' She didn't reply. 'Cass, Cass, are you there?'

'I'm here,' she said.

'Just keep moving,' he said. 'Keep walking, and keep talking to me.' He ran over to Megan's car, slipping on the snow and slush covering the road. He turned and pointed at the driver's side. Megan ran behind him and opened the car. He climbed into the passenger seat as she landed with a thump on the driver's side. 'Christ, Megs, are you all right?'

'I'm fine,' she said, opening the door as she dragged herself up. Her trousers were covered in snow.

'Let's go,' he said. 'Let's go. Cass, you OK?'

'Yes,' she said.

'Just keeping talking, OK?' he said. 'Just keep talking.' He watched as Megan turned the key, fumbling with her phone in her other hand. The car turned over but it didn't start. 'Oh my God, come on, Megs.' She tried again and again. She was pumping the accelerator, her eyes wide.

'It won't start,' she said. 'The battery must be dead.'

Aaron flung open the door and was out and running. 'I'm coming, Cass,' he said, trying to hold the phone to his ear as he ran, slipping and sliding as the ground seemed to move beneath him. She couldn't be more than a mile away, but that was a mile too close to where he had lost Pippa. He could hear Megan shouting, running, trying to keep up, but he couldn't stop. He was not going to stop until he saw his sister.

CHAPTER THIRTY-ONE

15th December – Tuesday

Lockyer stopped and looked at the floor plan for the Duchess wing of Musgrove Park Hospital. The place was more like a small town than a hospital. There was an exit and A&E to his left, and a Marks & Spencer's to his right. He headed off in that direction, his shoes squeaking on the pastel-coloured linoleum. He looked at his watch. The sketch artist was stuck in traffic on the M5. He figured he had a good half an hour before he needed to be back at Stephanie Lacey's room. And right now he needed caffeine, more for his brain than his body. He could deal with a headache by popping a handful of paracetamol, but this wasn't your standard ailment. The pain wasn't being caused by dehydration, or even stress. His brain was just at capacity, and letting him know further information and revelations would not be tolerated. How had a simple hit and run morphed into a behemoth of four cases in under a week? He had never worked a case that had transmogrified to this extent.

Despite Townsend's reluctance, Lockyer had always believed that Pippa Jones's death was murder, though he could never have guessed the motivation – still couldn't. When they had found the voicemail message confirming Pippa's attacker had waited to either watch or check she was dead, Lockyer had been surprised, but not very. His years on the murder squad made the unusual usual, the unimaginable commonplace. Even the introduction of Dead Woman's Ditch, legends, loopy locals, men walking chickens, drug-dealing exes and the unsolved murder of Chloe Evans hadn't thrown him off his stride – not really. But never had he imagined he would now be dealing with the murders of three women, plus the attempted murder of a fourth, by an individual who had managed to operate under the radar for two years – if not more. The portrait specialist should do a sketch of Lockyer's face so he could frame it for posterity, because for the first time in a long time he was not just surprised – he was shocked to shit.

His phone rang loud in his pocket, its trilling reverberating off the sterile walls of the endless corridor. He looked at the screen as he took it out. 'Hey, Megs,' he said. 'It's not a good time, honey. I'm—'

'Dad, I need you . . . Aaron needs you,' she said before he could finish.

He stopped walking and hung his head. 'What's he done now?'

'He's . . . she's. I couldn't keep up . . .'

'Megs, you're breaking up . . . where are you?'

'We were at home . . . at Aaron's house,' she said, the line crackling and popping in Lockyer's ear. He cringed away from the static hiss. 'Cassie . . . I mean, what she's doing out I don't . . . She saw the news the same as we did but . . . I don't even know if it's serious but . . . she sounded scared, Dad. She heard a car. Now she says there's someone following her.'

Lockyer turned on his heel and started running back along the corridor, heading for the exit. 'Where are you now?'

'Outside the house. Aaron's run off. She . . . his sister said she was on Hack Lane. I don't know where that is . . .'

He knew where Hack Lane was. It ran adjacent to the lane where Stephanie Lacey had been attacked, dragged into the woods and left for dead. 'I'm on my way. How long ago did Cassie call?'

'A few minutes,' she said, 'maybe more than that. I don't know.'

'OK, OK,' he said, his mind racing.

'Dad, what shall I do? What can I do?'

Lockyer slowed to a stop. He couldn't believe what he was about to say. 'Megs, knock on doors,' he said. 'Get someone with a car and go.'

'I don't know where—'

'They'll know,' he said. 'If they're local, they'll know. Just find someone now . . . get in a car and go.'

'OK, Dad,' she said.

He could already hear her pounding on a door. 'Honey, I've got to go. I've got to call it in. Megan . . . Meg . . .'

'Yes,' she said, coming back on the phone. He heard a door open, a voice asking what was wrong.

'Megan, whatever happens you *do not* get out of the car, do you understand me? You get up there. You find Cassie and get her *in* the car. You *do not* get out of the car yourself. Understood?'

'OK, Dad, OK,' she said. 'I've got to go . . . there's a man here. He's going to help.'

The line went dead in his ear. He could feel the father in him starting to panic. What had he just done? It was his job to keep her out of harm's way, not direct her to it. He stared at his phone. Should he call her back, tell her to stay away? His car was bloody miles away in an overflow car park, no doubt getting papered with fines for not displaying a valid ticket. He needed to call the station for backup. He needed to tell Jane. He looked up just as Pimbley walked through the automatic double doors opposite him.

'Sir,' Pimbley said. 'I was just coming to find you. Me and Crossley were just over at South West Forensics so I thought I'd give you an update before we—'

'Tell me later,' Lockyer said, running to meet him. 'Where's your car?'

'I just left it in the—'

'Never mind,' he said, grabbing Pimbley by the arm and spinning him around. 'Let's go. I'm driving.'

'Where are we going?'

'Nether Stowey,' Lockyer called over his shoulder as he ran towards the exit. When he got there he stopped and turned. 'Where?' he said, gesturing one way then the other.

'I left it in staff parking over there,' Pimbley said, pointing to the left.

Staff parking. Why hadn't Lockyer thought of that? He was off and running again, shouting for Pimbley to hurry up, when he spotted the squad car, a quizzical-looking Crossley sitting in the passenger seat. Lockyer jumped over the low hedge surrounding the car park. 'Come on,' he shouted. 'Give me the keys – get in the back.'

Pimbley threw the bundle of keys over the bonnet and climbed in behind PC Crossley. 'What's happened, sir?' Crossley asked as Lockyer jammed himself into the driver's seat. Pimbley was somewhat shorter than he was.

He felt under his seat for the release lever, his chair flying backwards until his feet didn't even reach the pedals. 'Bloody hell,' he said, yanking himself back towards the wheel, putting the keys in ignition and starting the car all in one smooth motion. 'Cassie Jones is in trouble.' He rammed the car in gear, put his arm behind Crossley's seat and reversed out of the space. He mounted the kerb behind them, but didn't stop to see what damage he had done to either the kerb or the car. He pushed down on the clutch long enough to get the car into first gear and raced out of the car park, his wheels spinning as he rounded the corner. He leaned on the horn to stop some people who were about to cross in front of him. 'Out of the way,' he shouted. He yanked the steering wheel to the right, drove straight over the mini-roundabout and put his foot down. 'Aaron's on his way,' he said, 'but he's on foot.'

'It'll take half an hour to—' Pimbley began.

'Just tell me the way,' Lockyer said. 'It won't take me half an hour. I guarantee it.'

Aaron pumped his arms, but he couldn't run any faster. His muscles were screaming at him to stop. He kept bringing the phone to his ear every few strides. 'Cass?'

'I'm here,' she said. 'Where are you?'

'I'm coming, Cass, I'm coming.' He tried to keep to the centre of the road, but the snow was so deep it was hard to know where he was.

'I can hear them,' she said. 'They're on the other side of the hedge.' Her voice was a strained whisper.

Aaron swallowed as he was sick in his mouth. 'Cassie, *run*,' he said, coughing. 'Don't look back, just run. I'm coming. I'm coming.' He clutched the phone in his hand, gritted his teeth and ran harder. His legs didn't hurt any more. He couldn't feel them any more. All he could hear was his sister's voice. Then he heard Pippa. He heard her grunting and crying out in pain as her car burnt around her. He pushed himself faster still. He had lost one sister. He couldn't lose another.

'Straight on,' Crossley said. 'We'll go up and over . . . it's quicker.' Lockyer accelerated over the junction and changed down into third gear as they shot up the hill on the other side. The engine screamed in protest, but he couldn't slow down. It was his job to save Cassie, but all he could think about was Megan. He lost the back end of the car for a second but managed to hold on as the tyres found purchase again. He took his foot off the accelerator but not by much. It wasn't the first time Megan had ended up in the middle of one of his cases. It wasn't the first time she had been in danger. What happened back then had damn near broken him, but at least his daughter had been safe. Would he be that lucky again? 'Where?' he said, seeing a junction up ahead.

'It's straight all the way,' Crossley and Pimbley said in stereo.

'But it's give way, so . . .' Pimbley said.

Lockyer flew over the intersection. The only way some-one was going to stop him now was if they crashed into him, which he realized was a distinct possibility. At the top of the hill he passed over the cattle grid. 'Is there any way over these godforsaken hills without having to pass that bitch in the ditch?'

'No, sir,' Crossley said. Lockyer could see she had her arms braced against the dashboard.

'Well, I'm telling you now,' he said, cutting the corner, peat and snow spewing up behind him. 'If John Walford or any other fucker jumps out at me now, I'm going to mow him down and ask questions later.' He skidded, bounced off a snow-laden hedge to his right and glanced a stone wall to his left.

Aaron passed the row of houses at the end of Hack Lane, his eyes searching the road ahead of him. He couldn't see Cassie. He couldn't see anyone. He stopped for a second to catch his breath. He tried to listen, but his pulse was banging in his ear and his breathing was loud and hoarse. He took a deep breath, held it for a moment and tried again. Nothing. He couldn't hear anything.

He set off running again. 'Cassie?' he yelled at the same time as he heard what sounded like a shout. He set off across a snow-covered field in the direction of the sound. He strained his ears, listening for her. Off to his left, something else. A car – an engine rumbling into life. He was running towards the sound, unwilling to comprehend what it might mean. There was a crunching of gears before it roared away.

Without stopping he launched himself up and over the hedge, using the fence buried deep within it to give him purchase. He came crashing down on the other side with a thud. He felt the brambles ripping at his clothes, tearing at his skin. He was wet through. The car was gone. But where was his sister?

'There,' Crossley said.

Lockyer jumped out of the car and followed the direction of Crossley's outstretched finger. He saw someone disappearing over a hedge not fifty yards from where he had stopped the car. He ran up a lane to the left of it, his arms pumping at his sides. The snow was deep under his feet, but he wasn't in one place long enough for it to be a problem. He could hear either Crossley or Pimbley behind him; he didn't know which, but whoever it was, they didn't sound like they had been quite so lucky with their footing. He rounded the hedge and saw the shadow of a man. He realized it was Aaron. He was looking left and right, shouting his sister's name over and over.

CHAPTER THIRTY-TWO

'How's she doing?' Lockyer asked, though what he wanted to ask was, *what the hell was she doing up here in the first place?*

Cassie Jones was sitting in the back of the ambulance, her legs hanging out over the edge, her feet not even touching the snow. Aaron was standing in front of her, holding her hands. Megan was off to one side, an elderly gentleman at her elbow. The Good Samaritan who had driven her up here, no doubt. Her face was ashen.

'She'll be OK,' the paramedic said, pulling off her surgical gloves. Lockyer took a second to process she was talking about Cassie, not Megan. 'We've managed to get hold of the aunt. A Claudette . . .'

'Barker,' he said.

'That's right. She's coming to collect them both.' She gestured back at Aaron and Cassie. That suited Lockyer. He would take Megan back himself. He knew he couldn't keep her away from Aaron, but he felt the need to create some space, however brief, between his daughter and – whatever had happened here. 'Other than some cuts and bruises, Cas-

334

sie's physically fine. Obviously the shock will come later, but for now, I'm happy to release her into her aunt's care.'

'Looks like he came off worse, if you ask me,' Lockyer said, looking at a long rip running down the side of Aaron's shirt. His skin looked raw, as if it had been raked.

'It's all superficial,' the paramedic said, turning to leave. 'It looks worse than it is.'

'Thanks,' Lockyer said as she walked back to the ambulance, gesturing to her colleague that it was time to go. They needed to be ready for the next emergency – although he doubted the rest of their shift would turn out to be this tame.

'Cassie's lucky Aaron was able to get here in time,' Jane said, appearing beside him, her face obscured behind a fog of condensed breath. The temperature had dropped enough for it to stop snowing. *Brief respite*, Lockyer thought. 'From what Cassie's said, it sounds like Aaron scared our guy off.'

'We don't *know* it was our guy, Jane. Aaron didn't *see* the vehicle. He didn't *see* anyone. Neither did his sister, for that matter.'

'Oh, come off it, Mike. She's terrified.' Jane held up two gloved fingers. 'We've got tyre tracks . . . we've got footprints back there,' she said, throwing her arm in the direction of the hedge Cassie had hidden in and Aaron had launched himself over. 'What more do you want?'

'I'm not saying it *wasn't* our guy, Jane, but I don't think we can say for definite that it *was*. Can we?' She didn't answer. 'Well, can we?' She shook her head, her chin tipped downward. He rubbed his hands together, the wool of his gloves crackling beneath his fingers. 'How come you're here, anyway? I thought you were off somewhere with Ranger Boy.'

'Oh, grow up, Mike,' she said, not looking at him. 'I was

meant to be meeting Barney over in Doddington, yes, but he got called out on a job. I couldn't get hold of Townsend . . . no surprises there, and I didn't want to attempt the drive out to Holford on my own, so I was about to head back to the station when I heard about what had happened up here.'

'What did happen?' he asked, running a gloved hand under his nose. 'Not much, as far as I can tell.'

Jane threw up her hands. 'For God's sake, what more do you want, Mike? Would a body make you feel better? Would that be enough to convince you?'

Steph opened her eyes. She couldn't see much, but the swelling must be going down because she could see a sliver of light coming through the gap in the curtains. She could just about see to the end of the bed. There was a cabinet to her left with a water jug and glass on top, and spare pillows tucked underneath. She tried to blink to clear her vision, but it was still blurred, tinged with red. The swollen tissue was pushing her eyelashes into her eyes, making them itch, but she wouldn't scratch them. She reached up and used her fingertips to touch the mess that was her face. She blew out a breath as she felt tears swell in her eyes and fall, bathing her raw skin. She swallowed hard, closed her eyes and turned her face into the pillow, trying to clear her mind.

She had to get him out of her head. She couldn't stand it.

The snippets of memory were coming back to her in painful flashes. She could see his hands, his skin rough and cracked. She could see his face, his eyes staring down at her, piercing in the darkness. She shook her head. She didn't want to see him any more.

The feel of cotton was cool against her cheeks. She moved her head to the side and tried to take a breath, but found she couldn't. The pillow moulded to her face, touching every part of her. She tensed for a moment, panic coursing through her.

He was back.

'Forensics are here,' Crossley said.

'Great, thanks, Emma,' Lockyer said. 'Get them to focus on any and all footprints behind the hedge here . . .' He pointed to the section where Cassie claimed to have heard her stalker. 'And we'll need impressions of the tyre tracks to the side lane there.' As Crossley turned to walk away he realized she must have been the one slipping in the snow behind him when he had been racing to get to Aaron and his sister. Her ample arse was covered in mud. 'Emma,' he called after her. 'Get the car warmed up and get my daughter,' he said, pointing Megan out. 'We may as well get back to the station and leave response to it. Little point in half of CID being out here.' She nodded, and broke into a trot as she headed off towards Megan, who looked for the first time like a spare part. Claudette was fussing over Cassie, wrapping her in a blanket and clucking like a mother hen as she manhandled her niece into the back of her car.

'Get in the other side, Aaron,' she was saying. 'It's all right, honey. Aaron'll sit next to you. We'll be home before you know it. The fire's lit. It's all warm and cosy. Your mum and dad are on their way back now. There's nothing to worry about. Nothing at all.' Aaron was now in the back seat. Claudette pushed the door closed with so little force, Lockyer was surprised the latch caught. She was still talking in soothing soundbites as she ran around to the driver's side and climbed in. Aaron turned and looked out the back window, first at Megan, then at Lockyer. He raised his hand. Lockyer did the same.

'You may as well get off, too,' he said, turning back to Jane as if their previous conversation hadn't happened. *Would a body make you feel better?* It was a stupid question. If in doubt, ignore. It was his failsafe. 'With any luck my sketch artist will have turned up by now.' He pushed up his sleeve and looked at his watch. 'If Lacey can give us a useable e-fit, we've got somewhere to start.' His phone buzzed in his coat pocket.

'You're not taking this thing with Cassie seriously, Mike,' Jane said. 'She could have been—'

'Hang on,' he said, taking his phone out and checking the screen. It was a mobile number he didn't recognize. 'One sec.' He held up a finger to silence her. 'DI Lockyer.' He listened, unsure how to process what he was being told. He said *yes* over and over in a monosyllabic tone. What else could he say? He could see Jane was stewing, just waiting for him to end his call so she could make her point again. 'And this was when?' he asked, closing his eyes. 'I understand, sir. I'm on my way.'

He hadn't even taken the phone from his ear when she started up again.

'Cassie could have been killed, Mike.'

'No, she couldn't, Jane,' he said, feeling numb, but not from the cold any more. 'It comes down to physics.'

'What are you talking about?'

'Physics,' he said again. 'You can't be in two places at once.' He hung his head as the implications hit him like physical blows. 'While we've been out here chasing a figment of Cassie Jones's imagination, our guy was busy waltzing into Musgrove and putting a pillow over Stephanie Lacey's face.'

Even Jane didn't have a comeback to that.

CHAPTER THIRTY-THREE

15th December – Tuesday

'Where is he?' Lockyer asked.

'Your guess is as good as mine,' Atkinson said. 'I've left messages on his mobile . . . with his wife. I've tried to keep our presence here low-key, but security have already had to block two camera crews from getting in, so the press know something's up. One of the staff must have blabbed. When I couldn't get hold of Townsend or you, I thought it best to come myself. Although I feel like I've done little more than stand here with my thumb up my arse, guarding a door after the horse has well and truly bolted.' The veins in the side of Atkinson's neck pulsed in his efforts to remain composed.

'Jane called when I was on my way here,' Lockyer said, his jaw tensing at the mere memory of their conversation. 'She's with Barney Gill, the Quantock ranger. He's driving her over to Holford to check out one of the registered vehicles that came up on the DVLA search.'

Why was he surprised? Of course the BFG had swept in at the last moment and called Jane to say he could take her over to Holford after all. What a hero. Lockyer had been less than thrilled and more than vocal about his concerns, but as per usual, Jane had ignored him. Yet again, it seemed the guy was gaining unfettered access to another potential crime scene. Lockyer was about to tell the superintendent just that, but managed to hold his tongue. Atkinson looked like he had all he could handle with Townsend going AWOL.

'She had a message from Townsend about –' Lockyer looked at his watch – 'ten minutes ago, saying he was on his way to meet her. They'd arranged to meet over there earlier today, so I'm guessing, sir,' he said, loath to anger the superintendent more, 'that he isn't aware of the situation here.'

'The situation here? The *situation* here,' Atkinson said, his voice strained, his cheeks flaring red. 'That is underplaying it somewhat, don't you think? The *situation*, as you call it, is in fact attempted murder, DI Lockyer. Attempted murder.'

'Of course, sir,' Lockyer said. 'I only meant . . .' He wasn't sure what he had meant. He was still trying to process the fact that Stephanie's attacker had come back to finish the job. He could understand the motivation. Unlike the others, she had survived – she might be able to identify him. But still; to stroll into a hospital teeming with patients, personnel, members of the public, not to mention half of Bridgwater nick?

He stopped mid-thought. But of course the police presence *hadn't* been here then. Nor had Lockyer. Cassie's imaginary stalker had seen to that. Like he had told Jane, it couldn't have worked out better if the guy had planned it himself. While Lockyer and half the team were off buggering about in the snow, he was free to stroll into Musgrove unchallenged and put a pillow over the poor girl's face. The fact that she had survived was beyond astounding. Like a cat, Stephanie Lacey had nine lives – or at least two.

'Christ, if Townsend doesn't give me a stroke, I don't know what will.' Atkinson held his hands together as if hoping for divine intervention. He took a deep breath in through his nose and blew it out again, his lips pursed. 'What did the consultant say about Lacey?'

'She's been taken up to intensive care,' Lockyer said, stepping back as a fingerprint technician ducked under the crime scene tape and into the hospital room beyond. Here, more than anywhere, Stephanie should have been safe. 'She's been put into an induced coma to prevent further damage.'

'I don't suppose—'

'I'm afraid the sketch artist arrived *after* the attack, sir,' Lockyer said.

'Anything from the CCTV?' Atkinson asked. 'I spoke to security briefly when I arrived, but they didn't seem to know their arses from their elbows.'

'We're seizing all the footage for the entire building and surrounding area, sir,' Lockyer said. 'The team will be going through it ASAP, but as I'm sure you'll appreciate, that's going to take time, given they have no idea who they're looking for.'

'I suppose someone in a balaclava carrying a pillow would be a bit much to ask,' Atkinson said in a failed attempt at levity. He looked ready to either cry or kill.

'I'm afraid it gets worse,' Lockyer said. He would have some choice words for Townsend when he got his hands on him. *He* should be the one here taking the roasting from Atkinson. *He* should have stayed at the hospital when

Lockyer left to go and deal with Cassie Jones and her shadow – but no, *he* had swanned off and left Lockyer carrying the can and in the shit. 'The system has blind spots, sir.'

'Blind spots?' Atkinson said, as if the words were an infectious disease.

'Yes, sir. It seems some areas are covered, some aren't. The main door on this floor . . . covered. The lift to this floor . . . covered. The back stairs to the fire exit?' Lockyer gestured to the hallway behind them. 'Not covered.' He pushed his hands up his face and through his hair. 'From the footage I've seen, it's just hospital and cleaning staff coming in and out of here. They all have name tags and fobs for certain areas, but the fire exit isn't secured.'

'Jesus, this is supposed to be a *sealed* unit,' Atkinson said, his mouth hanging open. 'What's the point in securing the house if the back door is left wide fucking open?' He rolled his eyes, his forehead wrinkling. 'This is a nightmare. A nightmare.'

Lockyer wanted to ask if Hamilton had been made aware of what had happened, but knew he couldn't. And he knew the answer. Of course he had. Half of Avon and Somerset would know what Bridgwater CID had allowed to happen.

'What about security?' Atkinson asked.

Lockyer said nothing as a guy he recognized from the CSI team passed them. His expression said what everyone on scene must be thinking. Two attacks on the same girl in as many days: *nice going, pal.*

'I'd left hospital security on the door,' he said, 'but there was some shift-change confusion . . . apparently. She's got three officers on her room now, sir.'

'Nightmare,' Atkinson said again, hanging his head.

Lockyer decided silence was the best course of action, so he stepped off to one side to give the superintendent some space to breathe – or have a nervous breakdown, whichever came first. He looked in at what had been Stephanie Lacey's hospital room. It looked more like the domain of a chimney sweep than a doctor now. Fingerprint dust was on almost every surface – even the windows. As if her assailant had somehow shimmied up to the outside of the building to the third floor in order to make good his attack.

As he looked at the blackened soot, a thought that had been opaque in Lockyer's mind came into focus. A name he had heard but dismissed. 'I'm wondering, sir,' he said, 'if I might not have been a bit off in my assumption that the suspect was using the legacy of John Walford as a diversionary tactic.'

'I daren't ask,' Atkinson said, squinting his eyes as if to protect himself from whatever liquid atrocity Lockyer was about to dump over his head.

Lockyer tipped his chin up and looked at the ceiling as each thought shifted into position like the blocks of a puzzle. 'The MO of Chloe Evans . . . the charcoal on her and Jenkins,' he said. 'I figured it was all theatre; something purposefully done but with no *real* connection to the legends themselves.'

'If you were aiming for obtuse, Lockyer, congratulations,' Atkinson growled.

'Sorry, sir.' He paused, unsure how to vocalize what he was thinking. 'I'd assumed the guy we're looking for was clever . . . manipulative – that he was using the local superstitions surrounding the Quantocks to his advantage. I've been reluctant to take any of the talk about legends seriously, other than of course considering their influence on the local community, which can, as you know, have an impact on an investigation.'

'Will you be arriving at a point this side of Christmas, detective?'

Lockyer felt like he was back at school, justifying why his homework was late again. Although it wasn't Atkinson he was worried about. It was Hamilton, and the career he held in his hands. 'Stephanie Lacey said her attacker kept calling her Annie. Anne was the name of the woman John Walford was meant to marry before he got the other one . . . Jane . . . pregnant.' He stopped short of telling Atkinson his source was an eight-year-old boy. 'By all accounts, Anne was the love of Walford's life.'

'Give me strength,' Atkinson said, holding his hand over his mouth. Lockyer didn't blame him. He couldn't believe he was thinking this stuff, let alone saying it out loud, knowing full well Atkinson would no doubt be relaying it to Hamilton within the hour. 'So we're dealing with a nut-job.' Lockyer hesitated to correct him, given what he now thought.

'I think we may well be dealing with someone obsessed with Walford, perhaps determined to walk in his footsteps, yes. I think Chloe was his best attempt,' Lockyer said. 'Whereas I think Andrea Jenkins may well have been his first, but he never got to see it through. She was found close to the road. Maybe he got spooked.' The motivation was madness, but the logic felt undeniable. 'I think he expected Pippa Jones to stop – to get out of the car. Most people would if they had a shunt, wouldn't they? But she didn't. She sped off – so he was forced to chase her and when he hit her, she slammed into that tree. According to the crash investigation guys, the fire started pretty much on impact. A fire is conspicuous. Maybe that's why he stayed and watched – he was thinking – realizing he couldn't do what he wanted to do.' The blocks of the puzzle had melted into bubbles of liquid mercury. They moved and slid together without effort. 'Stephanie was his next attempt, but she fought him off – she hid. If she hadn't escaped, I think we'd be looking at a crime scene not unlike that of Chloe Evans.'

'So a nut-job,' Atkinson said again. 'Well . . .' He flattened his mouth. 'It makes sense. To come into a hospital of this size? To take that risk, the guy would have to be certifiable?'

'And desperate,' Lockyer said.

CHAPTER THIRTY-FOUR

15th December – Tuesday

Jane looked up at the main house, thankful that the sky was clear, at least for the moment. The driveway was on a forty-degree angle, as were the surrounding lawns, not that she could see them. The snow was deep and untouched, like a plump pillow. Peter would love it. It was a perfect toboggan run. 'That'd be fun,' she said to Barney, pointing to the snow-covered slope.

'Other than that,' he said, nodding his head towards a knot of brambles at the bottom of the hill.

She looked back at the flat. There were no signs of life, and the garage beneath it was locked tight. She turned and ventured over the cattle grid – yet another cattle grid. There wasn't a gate or walkway, so she had to pick her way over, taking care where she put her feet given the snow was so deep it was almost impossible to tell the difference between the bars and the gaps in between. She looked to her right. The perimeter of the garden was marked out by a thick hedge, though as Barney had pointed out, it was more bramble

346

than hedge, weighed down by great mounds of snow. It was a beautiful property, even if the style was a bit dated.

'Let's go up,' she said. 'It looks like someone's here.' The tyre tracks in the snow had to be recent – today, even. Any earlier and the snow would have covered them. Barney grunted as he lost his footing. 'And I thought I was the clumsy one,' she said.

'It's ice under there,' he said, reaching out to her.

'You've got to be kidding. If you go down, you're on your own,' she said as he arrived behind her with a thump, holding his arms out to steady himself. She had to resist the urge to laugh and remind herself that this wasn't a jolly. They were isolated up here. The private lane that led up to the property was over a mile long; a post box jutting out of a hedge the only sign of civilization. There was no way her car would have made it up here.

They walked up the driveway in silence. Jane wondered if it had occurred to Barney, as it had to her, that they could be walking towards someone very dangerous. She felt her pulse flicker but then swallowed, telling herself to get a grip. How many routine vehicle checks had she done over the years? Two dozen, three? As Lockyer had pointed out, the likelihood that a quick DVLA search had turned up *the* Land Rover they were looking for was minimal. Besides, Townsend would be here any minute. Between him and Barney, she figured she was safer than most. She sniffed and rooted around in her coat pocket for a tissue.

'I can't believe you don't know who owns this place,' she said, wiping the end of her nose.

'I don't know everything . . . or everyone, Jane,' he said.

'Could've fooled me,' she said, giving him a sideways glance but keeping her main focus on where her feet were. She did not want to end up on her arse – again.

'This is not the car you are looking for,' he said, putting on the voice of Obi-Wan in *Star Wars*. Jane craned her neck to see what he was looking at, the cold wind chilling her skin as it found its way down her back.

It was a red Fiat Panda, and judging by the slalom-shaped tracks leading up to it, the driver had struggled to get it under the car port at the side of the house. The front bumper was resting against a substantial log pile. 'How did they get that up this hill?' She had struggled on a flat road.

'With a bit of a run and experience, it's not hard,' he said. 'The trick is not to brake or try and turn – just let the tyres do the work. They're designed to cope with this kind of road surface.'

'I feel like I've just stumbled into an episode of *Top Gear*,' she said, 'and you should know, I don't like *Top Gear*.' Barney smiled, his wind-burnt cheeks squishing his eyes into slits.

As they reached the rear of the car Jane held up her hand. Despite Barney being three times her size, it wasn't his job to put himself in danger, and she had no intention of letting him do so. 'Just hang back here, OK? I won't be a second.' She looked over her shoulder at Barney. His eyes flickered. It was as if she could see his brain working – figuring out how long it would take him to get to her if there was any trouble. He widened his stance and crossed his arms.

'I'll be just here,' he said.

'No shit,' she hissed, ringing the bell.

*

Lockyer tried again, but the call still wouldn't connect. He held up his phone, staring at the bars in the classic signal search position. 'I've got full signal,' he said to the phone and anyone passing who might be wondering why he was holding it aloft like Excalibur. 'Oh come on, you piece of shit.' He looked out the window as the snow fell, heavy and thick. No doubt it would be heading Jane's way if it wasn't there already. The roads would be a nightmare. Of course, Wonder Boy was with her, but still. Lockyer wanted her off the hills before it was dark – darker than it was already. The moon might not be high, but the sun was gone for sure.

He pocketed his phone and walked down the corridor, keeping his eyes lowered. The press didn't know him here, but he wanted to make sure he looked as un-cop-like as possible. He shoved his hands in his pockets and slowed his pace. As he passed the nurses' station he could feel the hospital staff looking at him. He clenched his jaw. Let them look. This was as much their fault as it was his. He had passed through several security doors on his way up to Stephanie's room. Not one had been shut. No one had stopped him, asked where he was going. And what was the point in having cameras if they covered everywhere but where they were needed? He crossed the hallway and took the main stairs two at a time. He needed caffeine. His head was about ready to explode.

'DI Lockyer,' a voice called from behind him.

He cringed at the volume of her voice. 'So much for keeping a low profile,' he muttered as he turned, pasting a smile onto his face. One of the nurses who had been looking after

Stephanie Lacey was half walking, half running to catch up with him, her keys jangling in the pocket of her dress.

'Sorry,' she said, seeming to realize her mistake. 'I didn't mean to shout.'

He waved away her apology. 'It's fine. What can I do for you . . . ?' If he knew her name, his brain wasn't delivering it up, so he shut his mouth.

'It's Janice,' she said as she did a weird little bob, almost like a curtsey.

'Janice,' he repeated.

'I just wanted to apologize for not letting your boss in before,' she said, her cheeks turning the colour of ripe tomatoes. 'I didn't know who he was – he didn't have ID, so I just . . .' She trailed off. She looked mortified. 'I mean, given what's happened I'm glad I didn't now. I'd have lost my job for sure, but you know how it is. They're always going on at us to be vigilant. I've got a review coming up. They send people in – like secret shoppers to test us. I figured it'd be just like management to send in someone posing as a copper to prove we weren't up to the job when it came to security. I just felt so embarrassed.'

Lockyer held up both hands, hoping to stem the torrent. 'You're apologizing to the wrong guy,' he said. 'My boss is upstairs. Superintendent Atkinson.'

'No, no,' she said. 'I knew who he was. He showed me his warrant card without me even having to ask. Even the Pope'd have a hard time getting in this place now.'

'Sorry,' Lockyer said, pulling at his ear like a kid with toothache. He was beginning to wonder if the pain in his head might not be caffeine withdrawal. Cassie Jones and her phantom stalker had thwarted his earlier efforts to reboot, and now Nurse What's-her-name was doing it as well. 'You've lost me.'

'Your boss,' she said again, leaning on the word like she was angry with it. 'You'd gone tearing off wherever it was – I saw you running out in the car park.' She held out her hand as if she were carrying a tray. 'You ran off. I'd been on lunch. He said he was there to replace you.'

'Replace me?'

'You know,' she said, now waving both hands, 'take over. He said he was taking over from you . . . like a shift, I'd guess.'

'I'm sorry, who was this?'

'Err, I forget. It was . . . Downton . . . Town . . .'

'Townsend?'

'That's it,' she said, the relief evident on her face. 'Detective Inspector Townsend.'

'But you didn't let him in? When was this?' he asked, unsure if Atkinson would be pleased Townsend had a good excuse for not being at the hospital, or angrier still that he had turned up without his ID.

'Not long after you left – I mean, right after. I'm surprised you didn't see each other,' she said, nodding her head with such gusto that strands of hair were coming loose from her ponytail. 'Like I said, he didn't have his warrant thingy with him, so I said no . . . you know, the computer says no.' She laughed. Lockyer felt like he had missed the joke. 'Anyway,' she said. 'I just wanted to pass on my apologies and . . .' Her cheeks, which had up until now been pink, lost their colour. 'You don't think . . . Was this my fault?' He was alarmed to see tears in her eyes. What was it with him and crying women? Did he attract them somehow? 'If I'd let him in, then someone would have been with her, wouldn't they? She wouldn't have been on her own and she wouldn't have got hurt.' A tear spilt out onto her cheek.

'It's fine,' he said, although she made a good point. If she had let Townsend in, Stephanie Lacey might not have been attacked for the second time. 'You did the right thing. DI Townsend would agree with me. Don't worry. Listen, I've got to go. I need to make a phone call.' He held up his phone as if he needed proof. He started walking backwards. 'Thanks again. You did the right thing.' He turned and headed for the exit. He would speak to Jane first. Coffee second.

When the door opened, Jane had to do a double take. Her mind stumbled for a second. 'Claudette?' she said, turning and looking back at the car and then Barney. 'Do you know, I thought your car looked familiar.'

'It's Sergeant Bennett, isn't it?' she said, opening the door wider.

'That's right,' Jane said. 'How's Cassie doing?'

Claudette looked around Jane. 'Hey, Barney.' She raised her hand. 'She's fine,' she said, turning back to Jane. 'She's all tucked up by the fire. Maureen is making a big fuss of her.'

'Hi, Claud,' Barney said, coming to stand next to Jane. He looked almost as bemused as Jane felt. 'You look nice.'

'Christmas drinks at the Hendersons',' Claudette said, cupping her bobbed hair before smoothing down her dress. 'Not had time to change, what with Cassie and everything.' Barney nodded.

'Sorry,' Jane said, feeling like she was missing something.

'I'm confused. What are you doing here? I mean, is this your house? I didn't realize . . .' The cottage in Nether Stowey was cute and cosy, but there's no way Jane would take it over this place.

Claudette laughed. 'I wish,' she said with a raise of her eyebrows. 'No. I'm just up here turning the heating on. Barbara's a client of mine. She's away in the States at the moment . . . lucky bugger. She was worried the pipes might freeze in this weather.'

'Barbara?' Jane asked, taking her notepad out of her inside jacket pocket and pulling off her gloves with her teeth. 'Do you know her surname?'

'Downs,' Claudette said. 'This is her place. Hers and her partner's . . . Allison . . . I don't know her last name.'

'Do they own it, do you know?'

Claudette was shaking her head. 'They wish,' she said with a smile. 'They're renting. They've been here about a year now, I'd guess.'

'Do you know the owner, by any chance?' Jane asked. 'Surname Rice?'

Claudette's mouth pulled up to one side. 'Mmm, the name doesn't ring a bell,' she said, 'but then, I've always been hopeless with names. I've only been up here once before when I was feeding their cat.' Jane looked down, half expecting to see a cat winding itself around Claudette's legs. 'It died,' Claudette said then, when Jane looked at her. 'Not on my watch, I hasten to add.'

'Does the flat come with the house, do you know?'

'No clue,' Claudette said. 'She's a potter on the side, so maybe she uses it as her studio?' Her expression changed.

'Bugger, do you think maybe I'm meant to put the heating on down there as well? I never even thought of that.'

'Have you got keys?' Jane asked, hopeful now that the drive up here wouldn't have been a total waste of time.

'To the flat? I don't know,' Claudette said, 'but Barb's got more keys than she knows what to do with in here. Do you want me to see what I can dig out? I'm sure Barbara wouldn't mind.'

'I couldn't use the bog, could I?' Barney asked, giving Jane an apologetic grimace when she gave him a disapproving look. 'Unless,' he said, 'you'd prefer me to go in the hedge?'

'I'm here to sort the heating, not water the plants, Barney,' Claudette said, reaching out and pulling him inside. 'It's at the end of the hall opposite the kitchen.' He turned to leave. 'Shoes, Barney,' she added, gesturing at the thick baby-pink carpet. 'And take that jacket off while you're at it. You'll soak the place otherwise.' She turned to Jane. 'Let me find those keys.' She disappeared off down the hallway.

'You couldn't hold it?' Jane said when Claudette had gone.

Barney perched on the edge of a radiator as he bent double and started to unlace his boots. The military needed to get with the times and convert to something more time-efficient, like Velcro. 'It's not good for guys to hold it,' he said, looking up at her under his long dark eyelashes. He pulled off one boot before using that foot to work the other boot free. He stood up, unzipping his coat and fleece in one go.

'Here we are,' Claudette said, shaking a bundle of keys in her hand. 'There's a truckload back there, but this bunch looks promising to me.' She held out a bundle of keys and plastic labels. 'We've got flat, garage, back door, front door . . . you name it, there's a key for it.'

'Great,' Jane said, reaching out to take the proffered keys.

'I'll come with you,' Claudette said, pulling a coat off a hook by the door. Barney shrugged out of his jacket. He was wearing a T-shirt, his arms thick and tanned. Jane could feel a blush starting at the base of her neck, but then something stopped the heat in its tracks. 'The door's on the latch, Barney,' Claudette said, 'so just pull it to, keep the heat in and we'll see you down there?' She was out the door, taking Jane in her wake as she filled the air with clouds from her breath and an endless stream of chit-chat.

Jane felt like she had been punched in the stomach. He had lied to her. Barney had lied to her.

'She's mistaken,' Townsend said again. 'I left right after you.'

'Why?' Lockyer asked, moving his phone to his other ear and picking up his cup of coffee. It was a double espresso macchiato. He didn't go in for the fancy stuff, but today he had decided to treat himself and see what all the fuss was about. The M&S cafe was packed. You could always rely on a hospital to keep trade brisk: death and taxes. The line crackled in his ear. 'Bill, are you still there?'

'I'm here,' Townsend said, some of his words lost in the ether. 'I'm meeting Jane over in Holford. I'm stuck in traffic on the motorway, but I should be there . . .' The static ate his words.

'Hello – hello,' Lockyer said, looking at his screen to see if the call was still connected. 'Bill, are you there?'

'. . . spoke to . . . back at the office,' Townsend said. 'They filled me in on what had happened with Cassie Jones *and* with Stephanie Lacey. It's . . . unfortunate.'

'Unfortunate? That's not really the word, Bill,' Lockyer said. 'Besides, if you left right after me, that's . . .' He pulled up his sleeve and looked at his watch, almost tipping his coffee into his lap at the same time. 'That's almost two hours ago.'

'I had to head home,' Townsend said. 'Family emergency. I've just got back now. I'll be with Jane in twenty, thirty minutes with any luck, and then I'll come straight in to the hospital. I've tried to get hold of her, but she's not answering. The signal is terrible up there, so that might be why.' The line fizzed and crackled again.

'Atkinson isn't happy,' Lockyer said, unsure why he was giving the guy a heads-up.

'I spoke to Terry before I called you,' Townsend said, his voice clear as their connection settled. He must be near a mast. 'I've explained the situation. Listen, Mike, the traffic's moving, I've got to go.'

The line went dead in Lockyer's ear. He put his phone on the table and stared at it as he took a big gulp of his coffee and held it in his mouth. He could almost feel the caffeine charging his blood. He half tuned into the conversation on the table behind him. Things weren't looking good for Uncle John, it seemed, made worse by the fact that Aunty Jacky was already hooking up with someone else. Lockyer smiled, gratified to know other people weren't perfect either. He pulled on his bottom lip. A feeling was taking up residence in his gut; a squirming irritation that he knew, unless he discovered the cause, would only get worse. What was bothering him about his call with Townsend? He couldn't put his finger on it, but something didn't add up.

'Typical,' Claudette said, stamping her feet. Her shoes were thin leather pumps. Her feet must be freezing. 'There's got to be half a dozen keys with some derivative of "Flat", but none of them fit.' Jane's mind had yet to find suitable traction to speak to Claudette. The woman had talked non-stop down the driveway, over the cattle grid and over to the garage door below the flat. Jane would hear the jangle of keys, a pause and then a sigh as yet another key failed to do the trick.

Jane's eyes had, she would admit, been tracking up Barney's generous bicep with interest when she had seen it. Her brain had taken half a second to process the image and attach it to its mate. The deep black ink, the wings spread wide in flight. Pippa Jones had the exact same tattoo on her ribcage. The same Pippa Jones who Barney said he had known as an acquaintance. The same Pippa Jones he had then admitted to taking on *one* date, but nothing more. The same Pippa Jones whose body was still lying waiting to be released for burial. One date? No way. No one got matching tattoos after one date. Why did he lie? The question was circling her mind like that same bird of prey. The natural follow-up question made Jane's stomach flip with anxiety. What else had Barney lied about?

'It's none of these,' Claudette said. 'I'll just run up and get the box. I should have brought it with me in the first place. Typical.'

'I'll go,' Jane said, her voice dull, her tongue leaden in her mouth.

'Don't be silly, I know where—'

'I will go,' she said. 'You stay here. I won't be long.' She held Claudette's gaze for a few seconds. 'Stay down here, OK?'

'All right,' she said, her expression confused. 'The box is in the kitchen.' Jane turned and walked away, her thoughts jumbling like knotted yarn in her head. 'Next to the micro-wave.'

Jane didn't look back. She crossed the cattle grid, words and images filling her mind. The tattoo drew the most focus, but there was more. *He was big.* Steph's words were loud inside Jane's head. *Tall.* Her blood seemed to have slowed down in her veins as if it had turned to treacle. *Combat trousers . . . tucked in socks, army socks.* How had Jane not seen it? It was as if Steph was describing Barney. She stopped; her feet unwilling to take her any further up the drive, any closer to the house.

Steph *was* describing Barney.

Lockyer dialled the Express Park CID number. It was answered on the second ring.

'DS Abbott, Bridgwater CID.'

'Abbott, it's Lockyer,' he said. 'Have you heard from Sergeant Bennett at all?'

'Not for a while, sir, no,' he said.

Lockyer showed his ID and walked through the double doors. The takeaway coffee he had brought back for Atkinson was heating the inside of his hand. He felt as if he was carrying molten lava and any moment it would break through the cardboard cup and deprive him of a couple of fingers. 'Have you got an address for where she is?'

'Yes, hang on . . .' Abbott said. Lockyer heard a rustling of paper and a hushed question. He stopped at a nurses' station and mimed a request for pen and paper. The nurse took a few sheets of paper out of the printer and passed them to him before handing over a pen.

'Don't walk off with it,' he said.

Lockyer nodded as he got Abbott to repeat the address and jotted it down. He handed back the pen and turned away, folding the paper and putting it in his jacket pocket. 'How far is it from here . . . from the hospital?'

'Twenty minutes, half an hour,' Abbott said. 'Depends on the roads, I guess . . . and how fast you're going.'

Lockyer found himself looking at the exit sign. 'I've called her a couple of times. Is there reception up there?'

'Doubt it, sir,' Abbott said. 'Most of Kilve and Holford way is a dead zone.'

'Have we got a number for the property? A landline?' More shuffling and the tapping of computer keys greeted his question. 'So?'

'The owner is Mr L. Rice,' Abbott said. 'There's a number here, but it can't be right, the area code is for Exeter. Hang on, let me do a search.' *Tap, tap, tap.* Lockyer walked over to a bank of windows and leaned his elbows on a windowsill as he looked out. The roads were still pretty clear, given the heavy traffic around the hospital. He doubted the lanes around the Quantocks would be the same. 'I can't find one, sir. Looks to be ex-directory. Have you tried DI Townsend?'

'I spoke to him not long ago. He's stuck on the M5. I think I'm gonna head up there myself,' Lockyer said, surprising himself. 'Jane's there on her own. Well, she's with Barney, but still, I'm not happy about it. I reckon if I left now, I could beat Townsend there.' The squirming doubt in his stomach had stepped up a gear.

'Do you want me to go, sir?' Abbott asked.

'No, no, it's fine,' Lockyer said. 'I want everyone working on the CCTV.' He was about to hang up when a thought occurred to him. 'Abbott?'

'Sir?'

'Do me a favour, will you?' Lockyer asked. 'I'm trying to get a timeline sorted in my head. I think I left the hospital about two, after Aaron called. Can you check the CCTV at the front entrance of the Duchess wing and look out for me?'

'Sure,' Abbott said. Lockyer could hear the fast tapping of keys and the familiar swoosh and click of a mouse. 'Shall I call you back?'

'No, it's OK. I'll hang on.' He waited in silence, the gentle *tap, tap* of the snow on the window accompanying Abbott's *tap, tap* on his computer.

'Got it,' Abbott said. 'It's time-stamped two ten, sir.'

'Great, great,' Lockyer said. 'Now just move it on frame by frame, and talk me through who you see.'

'OK. Am I looking for anyone in particular, sir?'

'I'm not sure yet.'

Lockyer listened as Abbott commentated the comings and goings of the Duchess wing entrance. 'Two nurses, in,' he said. 'Three . . . no, four doctors and a . . . looks like a cleaner out. Oh no, the cleaner's back. No one . . . no one,' he said, sounding bored. 'A nurse coming in . . . and a guy in a suit. He's now talking to the nurse . . .' Abbott paused. 'It's Townsend.'

'What's the time-stamp?' Lockyer asked, feeling a lump forming in his throat.

'Two twelve, sir.'

'Thanks,' he said. 'If DS Bennett calls in, tell her to call me.' Lockyer hung up the phone before waiting for a response.

Without thinking he started to increase his pace as he approached the exit, dropping Atkinson's coffee in a bin as he passed. Townsend *had* talked to Janice. So why did he say he hadn't – that she was *mistaken*? Either the guy had a severe case of short-term memory loss or he was lying. But why would he lie? Lockyer swallowed the lump in his throat. It solidified, getting heavier and heavier until it hit his churning stomach like a stone. Why would Townsend lie? There was a simple answer to that question, but it wasn't good. In fact, it couldn't be worse.

Jane stood at the open door to the house and tried to steady her breathing. She should wait for Townsend. He had to be here soon, and if she waited, they could confront Barney together. She knew she should do that, but she also knew she wasn't going to. Why? Because Barney had made a fool of her. She wanted to ask him straight out, and dare him to lie to her again. It wasn't so long ago that she had got it wrong, and it had cost her on both a professional and personal level. She had promised herself then that she would never be taken in again – that she wouldn't let a handsome face fool her.

And yet, here she was: a fool and a failure. She stepped over the threshold. He wouldn't try anything. Not with Claudette there.

The hallway was quiet. 'Barney?' she said, her voice steady. When there was no response, she tried again. 'Barney.' His name seemed to bounce back at her from the flowery wallpaper around her. She willed herself to keep moving, to keep breathing. She passed a bedroom, a bathroom and on her left, the kitchen. 'Barney, I need you to . . .' Her words shrivelled to useless pips in her mouth. Just inside the entranceway to the kitchen were two large, sock-covered feet.

Her instinct took over. She was through the door and on her knees next to him before she had a chance to think about what she was doing. He was lying motionless, the skin on his face pale and waxen. 'Barney?' She put her head to his chest. He was breathing. 'Barney?' She looked for the injury, the blow that could have felled a man of his size. Her knee felt damp. She looked down at the pool of blood soaking into her trousers. 'Shit, Barney, no.'

She was searching for something to stem the bleeding when her phone started to ring. Startled, she dropped it, unaware that it had been in her hand this whole time. She snatched it up. It was Lockyer. 'Mike,' she said. All she could hear was static. 'Mike?'

'. . . you there?'

'I'm here,' she said, standing, lifting the phone, staring at the screen as she looked for a signal. 'Hang on.' Leaping over Barney's prostrate figure, she ran down the hallway and out onto the driveway. A bar appeared, then disappeared. The screen was empty. She had lost him. 'Shit, shit, shit,' she said, darting one way and then the other. She opened her mouth to shout to Claudette for help when her phone rang again. She stabbed at the green answer icon and crouched down, not wanting to move her phone an inch in case she lost him again. 'Mike?'

'Jane.'

'Barney's been attacked,' she said. 'You need to get an ambulance up here now.' She listened but only heard static. She bobbed around, searching for a signal. 'Are you there? Shit, Mike, are you there?' The crackling stopped. 'Mike?'

'Jane, listen—'

'Did you hear me before?' she said. 'Barney's been attacked.'

'I heard you,' he said. She could hear the sound of an engine. He was in the car. 'Where are you now?'

'I'm up at the main house – well, on the driveway. Barney's out cold in the kitchen. He's bleeding. Claudette's down at the flat waiting for me. She was here when we got here.' She put her hand to her cheek. Her skin felt hot to the touch. 'I thought it was him, Mike. I thought it was Barney. I remembered Steph's description, saw his boots . . . I put two and two together and came up with ten. I mean, he does have the tattoo, so why wouldn't I think that, but . . .' The line crackled. 'Oh Christ, did you hear any of that? Are you there?' She held her phone out like an unexploded bomb, shifting it one way and then the other. She dropped to her knees to keep the phone steady. Her hands were shaking, but the signal held.

'Where's Townsend?' Lockyer asked, his words punctuated by the crunch of gears.

'He's not here yet,' she said, craning her neck. She couldn't see the flat crouched down like this. She would have to stand to be sure, but if she did she might lose Lockyer again.

'He's there,' was all he said.

'What? How do you know?' She strained to hear voices. She heard none.

'Trust me, he's there, Jane,' Lockyer said. 'He must still be in the house. You've got to get out of there and take Claudette with you.'

'What? Why?'

'*It's Townsend, Jane,*' he said, accentuating each word. 'He's been *lying*. He lied about where he was Sunday night – the night Steph was attacked. He lied about trying to get into the hospital – about not having ID.'

'What ID? Mike, you're not making any sense.' Her brain felt sluggish, unable to catch up. 'Why would Townsend lie?'

'My guess would be that he has something to hide,' Lockyer said, each of his words weighted – like darts hitting a dartboard, only she was the board. 'Now get out of there.'

'What about Barney?' she asked, her brain serving up more questions than she could handle – than she could ask. 'He's still in the house. I can't leave him. Do you think . . . I mean, is Townsend dangerous?' The question felt stupid the second she said it aloud. If she understood Lockyer right, he was saying Townsend was the one who had attacked Barney.

He was more than dangerous. He was a killer.

CHAPTER THIRTY-FIVE

15th December – Tuesday

Lockyer put his foot down as far as he dared. He couldn't be more than a few minutes away. He could see the chequered flag on the satnav. His windscreen wipers were going full pelt trying to keep the flurries away.

Of course Townsend was there. All that bullshit about being on the motorway, being stuck in traffic? That's what had been bothering Lockyer about their conversation. The line had been terrible, static, breaking up – the same as it had been with Jane. Townsend hadn't been on the motorway. He had been in Holford all the time. Had he already taken Barney out when Lockyer spoke to him on the phone? The second he ended his call with Jane, another part of the puzzle had slid into place assisted by the information he had gleaned from Peter and since verified. The name – Rice. It had landed in Lockyer's head like an anvil, crushing any and all other thoughts. The house in Holford, the 'Chawton' white, 1999 Land Rover; they were both registered to Mr. L Rice. Rice was the maiden name of Anne. Anne was the woman John Walford had been in love with – the woman he wanted to marry. It was her name Stephanie Lacey's attacker had been calling over and over – Annie. If Annie was the original Mrs, what was the betting Townsend was playing at being Mr Rice? Lockyer resisted the urge to shake his head for fear of taking his eyes off the road. And all this because of Walford – because of some long-dead piece of shit who killed his wife. Lockyer hated him. The guy might have been dead for two hundred years, but Lockyer still hated him. If Walford was here right now, he would hang him all over again. He would have to make do with Townsend. He wasn't going to hang him, but if he laid a finger on Jane, he *was* going to kill him.

Jane felt frozen to the spot, Lockyer's words still ringing in her ears. The snow had been replaced by a fine drizzle, soaking her hair and face. Not a sound disturbed the silence, which bothered her. She looked up at the house. There was no sign of Townsend. Unless he came out the front door there was no way he could see her. Was he waiting for her to go back in? To do to her what he had done to Barney? She shuddered just as she heard a car in the distance. Could that be Lockyer? She raised her eyes upward and prayed it was.

The lone bar on her phone had disappeared. She took a deep breath and pushed herself up and into a crouch. She looked left and right, deciding which was her best option. She didn't want to go back the way she had come, down the drive and over the cattle grid. If Townsend came out, he would see her straight away. She moved crab-like to her left until she could no longer see the house or the driveway. With her heart in her mouth she inched upward, craning her neck until she was standing. She let out a breath. She couldn't see Claudette. She turned. She couldn't see the house. 'It's OK,' she said to herself. If she couldn't see the house, then Townsend couldn't see her. The snow silenced her footsteps as she followed the line of the hedge. There was a gateway leading to a field beyond. She broke into a run, only stopping when she reached it, her breath clouded in front of her. With a skill from childhood she put her left hand on the third rung down and her right on the top. She dropped her head to the ground, put her weight on her left arm, her elbow coming into her chest as she threw her legs up and vaulted over the gate. She landed on the other side with a soft thump.

Again she followed the line of the hedge to another gate that led to the lane, the flat visible to her left. She stretched her neck, looking over the gate left and right. No one. She held up the latch and opened the gate just enough to squeeze through, flattening herself against it as it clanged shut. She was about to call out to Claudette when she stopped. Off to her left, out of her field of vision, she could hear voices; a woman's and then, without question, a man's voice, low and rumbling. 'Shit,' she whispered to herself. How did he get down here without her seeing him? She remembered going into the house, calling Barney's name. There had to be a back door. He must have legged it when he heard her come calling. The voices were moving in her direction. She couldn't make out what they were saying, but Townsend appeared to be doing most of the talking. She took a deep breath.

She knew she had to go in hard and fast if she was going to take Townsend out. Surprise was her only leverage. She felt the weight of the stone in her hand. When had she picked that up? She closed her eyes for a second and took a series of quick breaths, adrenalin driving her forward. 'It's now or never.'

'Turn right,' the satnav said. 'Turn right soon.'

'There is no fucking right,' Lockyer shouted at the same time as he saw a postbox and the beginning of a lane. He slammed on his brakes, pulled the wheel to the right and skidded into the hedge. There was a thud as his bumper made contact, followed by another thump as a drift of snow dislodged from the top of the hedge and landed on his bonnet. He rammed his car into reverse and started to back the car up, resisting the urge to floor the accelerator, which would just cause his tyres to lose purchase and skid. His lights were on auto, so sprang to life in the descending gloom. He could see several pairs of tiny red eyes staring out at him from the hedgerow. The animals scattered when he revved the engine. He waited until the nose of his car was level with the right turning, then put the car into first and started up the lane, building momentum as he went. The speedometer crept upward as the snow-covered hedgerows slipped by faster and faster.

'Your destination is ahead,' the robotic woman said in a drawling Australian accent. It had never bothered him until now. The incline increased, forcing him to accelerate to maintain his speed, which was now up to forty-five miles an hour. He would worry about how he was going to stop when the time came. 'You have reached your destination,' she said. 'Windows up, grab those sunnies and don't let the seagulls steal yer chips.' He wrenched the satnav off the windscreen and threw it over his shoulder into the back seat.

Up ahead and to his left he could see a squat red-brick bungalow. It was a much higher elevation than the lane he was on, and as he crested a rise in the road he saw the flat up ahead and on his right. Barney's 4x4 was in a pull-up just beyond the flat. Lockyer was still looking at the truck when he saw two people appear from around the side of the building. The snow was heavy, obscuring his view even with the wipers at full pelt. He narrowed his eyes. The two figures seemed bound together, slipping and sliding into the middle of the road. It had to be Townsend, but who was with him? Who was he wrestling with? Was it Claudette, or – Lockyer's stomach flipped – was it Jane?

He realized too late what was going to happen. He had nowhere to go. The lane was narrow, a car's width. He could veer to one side, but his car would keep going, and neither of the struggling figures seemed to have registered his presence. He began pumping the brakes, gentle taps to take his speed down without the wheels locking, and he leaned on the horn. The effect was immediate. The two figures turned their heads in his direction, their eyes wide. He couldn't tell who was who. They separated, each jumping away from the oncoming car, but it was too late. Lockyer yanked the wheel to the right, forcing his car into the hedgerow. There was a shrieking sound as the brambles tore along the side of the car, but as he had guessed, his efforts were in vain. The front end of the car made contact with one of the fleeing figures at almost the same time as the back end took out the other. The corresponding thuds and screams made Lockyer's throat close as both went flying over the snow-covered tarmac like skittles after a strike.

The figure on his left was thrown clear, but the one on his right came down in slow motion and, with a sickening noise, disappeared under the car. Lockyer bounced in his seat at the impact. A voice inside his head was screaming, *Don't let it be Jane,* over and over. *Please don't let it be Jane.*

CHAPTER THIRTY-SIX

18th December – Friday

'How is she?' Atkinson asked, pushing back from his desk and leaning back in his chair. The strain of the past three days seemed etched on the superintendent's face.

'She's doing well,' Lockyer said. 'She'll be out before Christmas. She'll make a full recovery . . . thank God.' No one was more grateful than him. His car had been doing well over forty miles an hour when it had ploughed into Claudette Barker, but other than a few broken bones and concussion, she was recovering well.

'And we've got her statement?' Atkinson asked, the thudding of the rain on the atrium roof punctuating his words.

Lockyer nodded. 'Yes. Jane went in to see her this morning. Claudette confirmed Townsend arrived on foot. At least, she never heard or saw a vehicle.' Townsend's car had been found on a lane north of the property, his footprints hugging the boundary as he crossed a frozen field to get to the back of the main house. The shortcut would have bought him precious extra time. His keys to the house and flat had also been found close to his body. 'Claudette said she was standing in front of the garage, her back turned, when Townsend arrived. Apparently he was stumbling and almost incoherent and then, without provocation, he grabbed her and put his hands around her throat. He was calling her Annie, sir.'

Atkinson sucked in his cheeks as he shook his head. 'It doesn't matter how many times I hear it, I still can't believe it. I mean, Christ, I had the guy down as incompetent . . . not crazy.'

'You're not alone there,' Lockyer said. 'If you'd have told me two weeks ago that the Jones case would go from a simple hit and run to a triple murder bound up in legend and superstitions, I wouldn't have believed you. If you'd said Townsend would end up in the frame, I would have laughed in your face . . . sir.' He cleared his throat. 'Anyway, I also got a contact number for the tenant – Barbara Downs. She and her partner aren't due back from the States until after the New Year, according to Claudette, but I've left a message for them to contact me ASAP.' Lockyer felt as if he had been relegated to admin, which, in a way, he had.

There was a knock at the door as it opened. 'Room for one more, Terry?' Hamilton asked, coming into the room, shutting the door and pulling a chair up next to Lockyer. 'I thought I'd check in before the press conference later today.'

'I really appreciate you doing this, Les,' Atkinson said.

'Not a problem,' Hamilton said, although Lockyer knew the DCC had, at first, flat-out refused to hold the press conference. According to office whispers he was none too happy about having his name associated with the Townsend debacle. Who could blame him? However, word had come down from above in the form of the Assistant Commissioner and representatives from the IPCC – the Independent Police Complaints Commission – that the public needed to be reassured, and Hamilton, in his full dress uniform as he was now, was the man for the job. Lockyer didn't envy him the dubious honour, but he didn't feel much sympathy for the guy either. 'Avon and Somerset is a team, Terry. We stand together, we fall together.' Hamilton folded his thick arms over his chest.

'DI Lockyer was just filling me in on Claudette's statement. DS Bennett was over at Musgrove earlier, establishing the events leading up to the accident,' Atkinson said.

'Yes, I spoke to her on the phone this morning,' Hamilton said, turning to look at Lockyer. 'I suppose I should thank you, detective.'

'Thank me, sir?' That would be a first.

'If you hadn't turned up and flattened my ex-wife and Townsend, then Claudette could be the one in the morgue right now instead of him,' Hamilton said with a sardonic smile. 'As much as I would *love* to hear Townsend try and talk his way out of this one – rather him than her, I say.'

'Of course, Les,' Atkinson said.

'Has your team got anything more from the property?' Hamilton asked, looking at his watch. The press conference wasn't due to start for another hour, but Lockyer figured he must be apprehensive. As DCC it would be Hamilton's job to confirm Detective Inspector William Townsend's involvement in the murder of three women and the attempted murder of another. Either that, or he didn't want to look Lockyer in the face.

'I've had confirmation this morning that the Land Rover recovered was the vehicle used in both Pippa Jones's and

Chloe Evans's murders, as well as the attack on Stephanie Lacey out at Shervage Wood,' Lockyer said. 'The car Townsend left to the north of the property has also gone off to be forensically examined.' He had spoken to Linda at South West Forensics this morning. She had bent over backwards to expedite the results so far. He owed her more than a drink now, for sure. 'We're still trying to trace the purchase of Hunter's Moon back to Townsend. Along with the false name, the money goes back through a maze of third parties, so it'll take time. As for the flat itself – the place was like a library. To be honest, sir, it's been kinda hard to manage this whole thing *off-site*.' He knew he should keep his mouth shut, but his patience was running thin.

'I'm sure, detective,' Hamilton said, still not looking at him, 'but as I think I made clear before, I had no choice but to agree to a full investigation of the incident, and you being on scene would only serve to further muddy the water. A senior officer died and a civilian was injured . . .'

'And a killer was stopped,' Lockyer said, feeling his neck beginning to heat. He balled his hands into fists to keep his anger in check.

'No one is disputing that, Mike,' Atkinson said, his face the picture of sincerity. 'As Les said, you probably saved Claudette Barker's life, not to mention Barney's . . . and Jane's.' Even the thought made Lockyer's stomach turn. 'But with the IPCC getting involved, we need to keep you out of . . . out of harm's way.'

'To be quite frank,' Hamilton said, 'the sooner you are back in London, the better – for you and us.' He sniffed. 'I myself have been on site as often as my schedule will allow, to ensure the team have all they need to expedite the evidence recovery process.' It hadn't escaped Lockyer's notice that *his* team had morphed into *the* team. 'Obviously the urgency with which we'll need to examine the documents is no longer there, not with Townsend in the morgue; however, all that can be handled in-house. Your help has been invaluable, but . . .'

'I'm surplus to requirements?'

'Hardly,' Hamilton said. 'Your assistance has been, as I said . . . invaluable. And believe me, I do understand your frustration, DI Lockyer, but I assure you, keeping you clear of this mess is by far the best course of action for your career and this case.'

Lockyer stayed silent. He knew the guy was right. If he had been given the choice, he would have removed himself from the on-scene team to prevent issues with cross-contamination of the accident site – but that was just it. He hadn't been given a choice. He had been told what to do. And for as long as he could remember, Lockyer had never relished being told what to do.

'Anything else Les needs to know, Mike, before we send him off to face the wolves?' Atkinson said, in a vain attempt at levity.

Lockyer took a deep breath and relaxed his hands. 'As I said, the flat was more like a library than anything else,' he said with a sigh. 'Detective Bennett and the team are cataloguing a raft of documentation, books and photographs – all relating to the murder of Jane Walford and John Walford's subsequent hanging. From the genealogy documents recovered so far, it appears Townsend was – or believed himself to be – a direct descendant of John Walford.'

'Quite a claim to fame,' Hamilton said. 'Go on.'

'There are numerous files relating to land titles, applications and so on,' Lockyer said as his pulse returned to normal. 'Townsend had spent years trying to break a heritage clause on the land in and around Shervage Wood in order to buy it, so—'

'Back,' Hamilton said.

'Sorry, sir?'

'Back,' Hamilton said again. 'He was trying to buy the land back. I assume the land was originally owned by the Walford family . . . way back when, so I can only assume Townsend was trying to reclaim his . . . what would you say, birthright?'

Lockyer nodded. 'I guess, sir, yes. I hadn't thought of it like that, but it would make sense. Townsend used the name Mr L. Rice on the Land Rover registration, as well as his *many* applications.'

'That's the bit I don't get,' Atkinson said, getting up from behind his desk and beginning to pace back and forth. 'Walford's children were bastards – the first two, at least – so why would Townsend *want* to associate, or *re-associate*, himself with that?'

'I'm not sure you're going to find a logical explanation for this, sir,' Lockyer said, picking at a thread on his trousers that had come loose.

'It seems to me,' Hamilton said with a sniff, 'that as illogical as it sounds, Bill was trying to right what he *perceived* to be a wrong against his family. There are those in Nether

Stowey who believe John Walford was wrongly hanged, that the facts of the case were twisted – that his wife . . . Jane . . . was the one who had trapped him with her second, or was it third pregnancy? She was, by all accounts . . . correction, by *some* accounts, a very difficult woman, and there are those who think she drove Walford to kill her; that she emasculated him and mocked him for his infatuation with the other one – Anne Rice. From what I've read, John Walford's family were hounded out of the community after he was hanged. Their lands were burnt, and then taken away from them. They were punished for what Walford had done, and I suppose if you look at the land as a legacy, then in a way, Bill was punished too. The stigma must have followed his family for generations.' Hamilton looked at Lockyer. 'I did *my* homework, detective,' he said, his inference clear. 'It seems to me this might have been resolved somewhat earlier if other people had done theirs.'

Lockyer bit the inside of his lip. Had he really thought Hamilton was just going to let his oversight pass? He had been summoned from London to give Townsend and the case the benefit of his experience – make sure no stone was left unturned. And what had he done? He had swanned in and neglected to look under the first sodding stone. 'I take full responsibility for—'

Hamilton held up his hand. 'Relax, DI Lockyer,' he said. 'This isn't a witch-hunt. As I said to Terry, we stand together at Avon and Somerset. Errors have been made at all levels,' he said. 'But with Townsend on the slab, this is all a moot point. The whys and the wherefores are irrelevant. No point wasting any *more* of the team's valuable time on the man, or his . . . library.'

'I couldn't agree more,' Lockyer said, wishing it was that simple. With Townsend dead, there was no case to build for the CPS – no prosecution – but given Townsend's rank and years on the force, the IPCC were opening their own inquiry. It would be the team's job to prepare the evidence for them, and he somehow doubted the IPCC folk would be impressed with a dozen boxes just marked 'stuff'. He ran his fingers up the back of his neck and over his head. But then, that wasn't his problem any more, was it? As Hamilton said, Lockyer was better off out of it, and right now that suited him fine. London, Lewisham and his own bed were calling.

'Well, I'd better be getting on,' Hamilton said, pushing back his chair and standing up. 'Good work, gentlemen. I'll leave you to wrap things up while I go and give these press boys and girls something to write about, eh?' He raised his eyebrows and left the room with a flourish.

'You get used to him,' Atkinson said, the colour returning to his cheeks.

'I'm kinda glad I don't have to,' Lockyer said.

'I just think it's odd, that's all,' Jane said, dragging her hands down her face, remembering too late that she had put mascara on this morning. 'Panda?' she said, looking at Lockyer.

'You're fine,' he said, turning his Costa Coffee takeaway cup in his hands.

'Walford killed Jane,' she said. 'He loved Anne.'

'So?'

She could see he wasn't interested. He had spent more

time looking at his watch in the past hour than anything else. He was heading back to London tonight, due to a development in the Bashir case. Jane knew that was bollocks, but Lockyer had refused to say any more. It seemed he could keep his mouth shut when it suited him.

She pushed a finger into her temple. He was leaving. She was staying. That was the long and short of it. The powers that be had decided Jane should stay behind, for the time being, to ensure a smooth transition when a replacement DI was found and to oversee the case handover to the IPCC. If they hadn't been in a team briefing when Lockyer had dropped his mini-bombshell, she would have thrown something at him. She was just as keen to get back to London as he was. Well, maybe not *as* keen. She wasn't sure that was possible, but she had a life and cases to get back to. However, as the consummate professional, she would suck it up and get her revenge later. 'So,' she said, waiting for him to look up. 'Townsend called Steph and Claudette "Annie" when he was attacking them, yes?'

'Yes, ma'am,' he said in mock deference.

'Well, wouldn't it make more sense for him to call them Jane?' she asked.

Lockyer's eyes moved from side to side, then up and down before coming to rest on hers again as he processed what she had said.

'From what we know, Townsend saw himself as some kind of avenger, carrying on Walford's legacy, or whatever,' Jane said, uncomfortable with how ridiculous it sounded. 'So if that's the case, why wasn't he calling the women he killed Jane? Jane was the one who tricked him into marriage. Jane was the one who slept around . . . with his brother, no less . . . and she was the one who spent all his money and drove him nuts – so nuts he killed her. Surely Townsend should be killing "Janes", not "Annies". She waited. The mirth in Lockyer's eyes had gone. He frowned, but didn't speak. She held his gaze.

'I've got everything from Townsend's place, boss,' Pimbley said from behind her. Jane saw Lockyer look up, but in fact when she turned she realized Pimbley was talking to her. She resisted the urge to laugh. The look on Lockyer's face made staying almost worth it. 'We've taken his toothbrush, hairbrush and razor for DNA,' Pimbley said, counting the items off on his fingers. 'And I bagged up all his footwear and clothes for trace evidence.' He stopped and pursed his lips. 'Angela's in a bad way.'

'No bloody wonder,' Lockyer said. His words lacked sympathy, but Jane knew better. She had been with him when he spoke to Angela Townsend. He had made a point of going to see the woman himself to reassure her that she wasn't to blame for her husband's actions. Jane had found it hard to look at Angela as she confirmed, in between sobs, that her husband had been absent for the past six months, if not longer. She said he was often away from home, sometimes overnight, and it was always the same excuse: he was working. Of course Jane, Lockyer and half of Bridgwater CID knew different. He had lied to everyone.

With an exact timeline from Janice Ward, the team had the footage proving that, despite Townsend's denial, he had been challenged by Janice when he tried and failed to get into the hospital without ID. They were yet to find his second, successful attempt – the one where he had gone on to try and suffocate Stephanie Lacey – but Jane had no doubt it was there. But as with everything else, it was buried in hours of work. And the lies didn't end there. The family emergency he had told Lockyer about was fictional, too. He had, it seemed, used his time to get over to Holford, park up and make his way down to the house without being seen. He had felled Barney with a large rock from the garden before heading down to the flat to finish the job. Jane's stomach did a small flip as she remembered the blood soaking into the knee of her trousers.

She had been to see Barney in Musgrove yesterday. He had been back to his cheerful self in spite of his pallor. He was due to be discharged later today. If Jane hadn't been driving Lockyer back to her parents' to collect his stuff, she would have offered to pick him up, though perhaps it was wise to keep her distance for now. She was happy he was OK, but he had still lied to her, and that would take time to forget, to move past. He had admitted to sleeping with Pippa once, but was adamant he knew nothing about the tattoo that matched his own. His ink had been an impulse purchase when he got the job as ranger for the AONB.

If he was telling the truth – and Jane believed he now was – Pippa had been reluctant to leave the relationship at one night. Barney had told Jane that he had ended up blocking Pippa's calls when she didn't get the hint. Jane would guess the tattoo had been an impulse on Pippa's part too, before she realized one night didn't equal lasting love.

Her phone beeped. It was a text from her mother – well, Peter, via her mother.

Peter says to say he knows all the words to 'Pease Pudding Hot'.

That was it. No kiss. No explanation. But then, Jane didn't need one. Her son's message was clear: he had learned the song off by heart. Whether she liked it or not, Jane would be walking around Clevedon carolling this evening – end of discussion.

The extension on Lockyer's side of the partition rang. 'DI Lockyer,' he said in a dull voice. He really was working on half-measures. But then his face brightened. 'Doc . . . good to hear from you. I knew you wouldn't let me down. What have you got?'

Jane was yet to meet Doctor Basil Reed, but if he brought out this response in Lockyer, he must be something special. Or maybe her boss just had a thing for pathologists, given Dave Simpson, Lewisham's resident slicer and dicer, was Lockyer's closest friend. She wondered if their collective lack of experience with living, breathing people drew them together. She smiled, picked up her mobile and sent a text to Peter via her mother saying she would indeed be back in time for carolling. The response was almost instant.

You promise?

As her mother's technical knowledge was limited, Jane knew this message was from Peter himself. She tapped out a reply, confident, for once, that she could keep her word.

I promise. Love u x

She looked up as Atkinson walked out of his office and over to the water cooler. Lockyer was right. The guy looked like shit. He glanced up as if hearing her thoughts. He finished filling his cup and then smiled. 'Can I borrow you for a minute, Jane?' he asked, motioning for her to follow him into her office.

'Of course, sir,' she said. 'Mike's just on the phone with Doctor Reed about the post-mortem, but he shouldn't be long, so shall I . . . ?'

'That's fine,' Atkinson said. 'I'm sure we can manage without him.'

Jane pushed her chair back and walked across the office, looking over her shoulder at Lockyer, willing him to look up. When he did, his face said it all. He had heard the exchange between her and Atkinson and like the prize git he was, he was going to let her deal with it while he stretched out his phone call and watched the clock. She wouldn't be at all surprised if he was gone by the time she came out; he was that keen to leave. If she wasn't driving him back to her parents' and then on to the train station, she was sure he already would have.

CHAPTER THIRTY-SEVEN

18th December – Friday

Lockyer crossed his arms against the cold. The rain was washing down the windows at the front of the station in giant rivulets, dissolving the snow and ice and leaving the tarmac of the car park shiny and black. It was as if the downpour was washing the landscape clean so it could start afresh. That's just how he would feel the moment his train pulled into Paddington. He nodded to one of the team as they joined the huddle of officers gathered outside Express Park.

The press conference was in full swing, and despite the freezing temperatures and rain Hamilton was holding court, sheltered only by a makeshift awning. He looked the part in his dress uniform. If he hadn't been a copper, he would have made an excellent politician. He was using the classic David Cameron move – closed sideways fist with a slightly protruding thumb – to accentuate his point. Pointing wasn't allowed when you were in politics; it was seen as too aggressive. Hamilton used the gesture well and looked every bit the statesman. 'A full and through investigation is under way . . .'

Lockyer tuned out. His phone buzzed. He slid it out of

his pocket but kept it down at his side, chancing a glance every few seconds to see what he had missed. Janice Ward had called to speak to him twice. He sniffed, using the back of his hand, still clutching his phone, to wipe under his nose. The snow might have gone, but the wind felt bitter against his cheeks. He returned his hand to his side and opened the next email. It was from Abbott, with a message to call a Doctor Richard Raynor as a matter of urgency. He narrowed his eyes. The name didn't ring a bell. Could be London-related, he guessed. The final email was from Roger, with an update on the Bashir case. It had been the faux reason for his departure, but it seemed Roger had no intention of letting Lockyer 'settle back in' when he got back to London. An interview under caution had been set up for Monday morning with the main suspect. Lockyer would be taking the lead. Despite his surroundings, he found himself unable to keep his smile under wraps. He wanted to do a bloody jig. *Gun crime, gangs and lies, oh my.* He couldn't wait.

'. . . Of course, reviews of William Townsend's cases past and present will be necessary, but unless evidence can be found to confirm beyond a doubt that errors were made, any and all convictions will be upheld . . .'

Lockyer resisted the urge to say, 'yeah, right'. Hamilton knew as well as he did that lawyers the length and breadth of Somerset would be fielding calls at this very moment from gleeful clients demanding to have their files reopened, their convictions overturned, verdicts quashed, records cleared or anything else that would get them off the proverbial hook.

'DI Lockyer?' a voice whispered behind him.

He turned and took a step back, a scrum of CID bodies taking his place in the line-up. Unlike him, they wanted to be there. This would be the most high-profile case they had ever seen. 'Janice,' he said, remembering the nurse's missed calls. 'Sorry I haven't had a chance to get back to you.' He kept his voice quiet. It was amazing what a stray journalist's mic could pick up.

'I'm sorry to bother you,' she said, blushing. 'I was just passing and thought I'd see, on the off chance, if you were here.'

'Here I am,' he said, spreading his arms as wide as the crowd would allow.

She looked around her. 'I just . . . I wasn't sure but I thought I ought to . . .'

'Would you rather talk inside?' he asked, gesturing to the double doors behind them. 'We can go up to the office and—'

'Oh no,' she said. 'I honestly don't want to be a bother. I wouldn't want people to think I was . . .'

He realized she was about to cry. 'What's on your mind, Janice?' he said, going for sympathetic but aware he sounded on the edge of impatient.

She seemed to consider him for a moment, her eyes darting back and forth over his face. 'I was watching telly last night,' she said, her words clipped, 'and I caught the end of the news. I don't like the news. I never watch it, but I did . . . I don't know why, but anyway, they were talking about her . . . about Stephanie Lacey, and they showed a picture of . . .' She leaned in and looked up at him from under her fringe. 'The detective – Townsend, that they say killed all those girls and tried to . . . well, tried to kill Stephanie.'

'Right,' Lockyer said.

'Well, the thing is . . . it wasn't *my* Townsend.' Her forehead creased. 'I mean, the Townsend they showed wasn't the Townsend I met.'

'Sorry, Janice. Can you run that by me again? Your Townsend isn't our Townsend?'

She nodded as he spoke. She appeared relieved that he understood. He hated to burst her bubble, but he wasn't sure he did. 'They showed a picture of him,' she said. 'He looked a bit like . . . I thought Phillip Schofield, but I don't know. Anyway, the man I spoke to – the man who *said* he was DI Townsend, and that he'd just forgotten his warrant card . . . Well, they aren't the same person. They're *not* the same person.'

Lockyer felt the creeping fingers of doubt crawling up his spine. 'We have CCTV footage of you talking to Townsend at the entrance to the Duchess Building. I've seen it myself.'

Janice looked thrown for a moment, but then she opened her mouth in a wide O. 'I know why that must be,' she said. 'You're looking at the wrong entrance.' She seemed reassured. Lockyer wasn't. 'I may well have talked to *your* Townsend – I talk to hundreds of people a day. I didn't remember him . . . not from the picture on the news, but anyway, the man I *did* speak to. The man who *said* he was DI Townsend, but obviously wasn't . . . I spoke to him at the south entrance to the ward. It's on the M&S side of the building.' Her words were quiet and clear now she seemed in control of her subject. 'The place is like a maze to the uninitiated, so I can understand you looking where you were looking, given where I spoke to you, but . . .'

Lockyer felt an icy wind behind him. He glanced over his shoulder. The line of CID officers had parted. Hamilton's 'our nation' address was over, it seemed. He was waving a thick hand to dismiss the gathered press. Lockyer turned back.

'That's him,' Janice said, her jaw tight, her voice distorted like that of a ventriloquist. He followed her wide eyes. 'He told me his name was Townsend.'

Lockyer snorted. 'I'm afraid that's not possible, Janice,' he said, already manoeuvring her towards the double doors. The press were packing up, but their mics could still be live. The last thing he needed was for Janice to make her accusation a little louder. That would bring attention – very unwelcome attention. It was a miracle Lockyer had managed to get this far without a Hamilton-shaped axe falling on his career-shaped head. He wasn't about to let Janice screw that up, but she refused to move. Her eyes were fixed on Hamilton, the recognition obvious. What was making Lockyer's pulse jump was that Hamilton was looking back – the recognition appeared to be mutual. A question that had been dogging Lockyer for the past week flashed into his mind. How had Hamilton known Andrea Jenkins' background when they had spoken in the car that day? The answer came to him on another gust of icy wind.

It was not, as Lockyer had thought, because either Atkinson or Townsend had told him. He knew now that they couldn't have. Atkinson didn't know, and Townsend had been in Lockyer's presence the entire time.

No. The only way Detective Chief Constable Les Hamilton could have known about Andrea's difficulties – her pregnancies, her alcohol abuse – was if he *knew* her. If he had *chosen* her. If he had *killed* her.

He had killed them all.

CHAPTER THIRTY-EIGHT

Christmas Eve

Lockyer bent down and read aloud. 'Twenty minutes per kilo, plus ninety minutes.' He looked at the turkey. 'Fifteen pounds is about . . . seven kilogrammes, so that's . . . four hours? That can't be right.' He went back to preparing the vegetables, wondering, as he cut crosses into the Brussel sprouts, if Maureen Jones would bother with Christmas lunch. Claudette was just out of hospital, but with three broken ribs, she wouldn't be eating much. Megan and Aaron were staying in Somerset tonight, but driving back in the morning, and Cassie was flying to the States today; so really, it would only be Maureen and the vicar eating. 'Poor sods,' he said, looking out at the rain. He had never been happier standing in his kitchen peeling spuds, though how he had ended up hosting Christmas lunch was still a mystery. He threw a pale spud into the pan of salted water. *You salt the pan before you boil the water,* Celia Bennett had said.

He hated to admit it, but he missed the Bennetts. That said, he wasn't missing Bridgwater CID, the Hamilton shit-storm he had left behind or, in fact, any part of Somerset. He didn't envy Jane her task of overseeing 'the transition', as Atkinson kept referring to it, over the weekend while the bigwigs of Avon and Somerset tried to manage an unmanageable situation. He opened the fridge, took out another beer and twisted off the lid. It gave a satisfying hiss.

It had been Saturday afternoon before Lockyer spoke to Doctor Richard Raynor. He shook his head as he took a gulp of ice-cold beer. He still couldn't believe it. Townsend had been neither incompetent nor insane. He had been ill. Droplets of water splashed back as Lockyer threw another spud into the pan. He wiped his hand on his apron. Townsend had been suffering from early-onset dementia, of all things. He had been taking part in a medical trial Raynor was supervising. Patients were required to attend residential clinics, so their vital statistics could be monitored before and after they took the new combination therapy.

Lockyer swallowed another mouthful of beer. Raynor had reeled off a veritable banquet of symptoms common with the condition: memory loss, changes in behaviour, personality changes, poor judgement, issues with balance, depression, confusion, difficulty with times and numbers. No wonder Townsend had been all over the place – body and mind. At one point Lockyer remembered thinking the guy was abusing alcohol, he was that erratic, and even Claudette had said in her statement that Townsend was stumbling and incoherent before he attacked her. According to the doctor, the freezing temperatures and stress could have exacerbated Townsend's confusion and disorientation. Lockyer finished another spud and threw it in the pan. How many should he do? He counted in his head how many people were coming, but kept losing count. He would do the whole bag just to be on the safe side – better too many than too few.

Townsend had been the perfect patsy. His symptoms had been intermittent and slow to progress, helped in part by the treatment he was having – but he *had* been affected. It *had* affected his decision-making, and someone had noticed. Someone who had nursed his own wife with the same disease. Hamilton. It had been a piece of piss for him to pass the poor guy off as incompetent. Once Townsend was away from his colleagues in Bristol, he was isolated. None of his team appreciated his arrival, so they only ever looked for the bad in their new DI. Lockyer was guilty of the same apathy. He had been spoon-fed a line and swallowed it whole. Jane, too.

He sniffed and shook his head again. Hamilton must have thought all his prayers had been answered when Lockyer had blundered in and killed Townsend. He remembered something Hamilton had said. *If you hadn't turned up and flattened my ex-wife and Townsend, then Claudette could be the one in the morgue right now instead of him.* Lockyer didn't doubt that to be true. Claudette had been lucky – on more than one count. Townsend had been unlucky on too many counts to number. Lockyer sucked in a breath as he nicked the end of his finger with the knife. *You should have used a peeler,* Celia would have said. She was providing a weird inner monologue for him. He was used to Jane in there, but her mother too? He sucked the blood from the end of his finger as his mobile rang. He dropped the knife on the chopping board, grabbed a tea towel off the rack and walked through to the lounge. His phone was on the arm of the sofa. It was Jane.

'Hey,' he said. 'What's up?'

'Not much,' she said. 'Just called to give you an update . . . that's if you care, but mainly to check your pipes haven't burst and you are enjoying being back under your own roof.'

'The pipes were fine,' he said. 'I'd left the heating on so it was roasting in here when I got back.'

'That's going to cost you,' she said.

'I know.' He wiped the starch off his fingers. 'So how's it going?' She was right. He didn't want to know. Once he had read Hamilton his rights, Lockyer had wanted nothing more but to wash his hands of the whole case. But for Jane, he would listen and at least pretend to care.

'I went in this morning,' she said. 'He's been charged with Chloe and Pippa's murders. There's a second charge for the attempted murder of Stephanie Lacey.'

'What did you use in the end?' he asked, perching on the arm of the sofa.

'Lacey was pretty much cut and dried,' she said. 'Forensic accounts had successfully tracked the money used for purchasing Hunter's Moon and the Land Rover back to Hamilton. Plus we've got a DNA match from the scrapings taken from under Steph's nails . . . and Janice's ID – hopefully Steph will be able to back that up once she's out of hospital. They brought her out of the induced coma late yesterday. She's doing well.'

'That's great news,' he said, flooded with relief. He hadn't wanted to be responsible for yet another death. He went to take another swig of his beer before realizing the bottle was empty. 'And the others?' He stood up and walked back through to the kitchen.

'For Chloe and Pippa we've got the Land Rover, but I'm sure we'll find more, given time,' she said.

Hindsight was a wonderful thing, but Lockyer realized now that Pippa had been their biggest and best clue, right from when they found out about the Dead Woman's Ditch connection. She had never fitted the profile. Andrea, Chloe and Stephanie all had commonalities with Jane Walford. Pippa hadn't. He heard Hamilton's voice again. *No one sullies my family's name and gets away with it.* Family meant blood. Pippa hadn't qualified. Which left a question: why Pippa? Why risk killing someone with direct links to him? There was only one answer. Pippa must have found out the truth about her uncle, or at least enough for him to need to silence her. Lockyer ran his hand over his chin and down his neck as he opened the fridge and took out another bottle. 'And Jenkins?'

'Not enough to charge yet,' Jane said. 'Michaels' bungled post-mortem isn't helping.'

'Michaels was an absolute gift for Hamilton,' Lockyer said, twisting off the cap and tossing it into the bin. 'Basil said everyone knew the guy was off his head half the time. Hamilton would've known he could call the guy's findings into question down the line if he needed to.'

'It won't be enough to save him,' Jane said. 'He's off down to Exeter to wait on remand until the CPS can get all their ducks in a row. Forensics have been all over his house and cars. They've even taken tyre impressions and trace evidence from the Jane Walford memorial in Doddington to see if they can link the sheep's head to Hamilton.'

'That's a bit of a stretch.'

'Maybe, but Hamilton has made a fool of a lot of people. They're not gonna rest until he's pinned for everything . . . anything he's ever done.'

'Let's hope they can,' Lockyer said. 'For Andrea's sake.'

'They will,' she said. 'Besides, Hamilton was a collector. There'll be something in the house . . . something linking back to Andrea, I'm sure of it.'

'That's if it's still there,' Lockyer said, holding his beer against his cheek. 'Hamilton's been in and out of that place a dozen times. He could easily have cherry-picked his memorabilia for incriminating evidence.'

'Abbott said there was another officer there, for the most part,' Jane said.

'For the most part,' Lockyer repeated in a monotone. He took a swig of his beer. 'Anyway, it is what it is . . . Tell me, how did Hamilton take it when he was charged?'

'As you'd expect,' she said. 'He's lawyered up and gone no comment so far. Mind you, I'm not sure that'll last. The guy's a classic narcissist. He'll be aching to tell us just how clever he is.'

'Clever or crazy?'

Jane chuckled. 'Both,' she said, 'though I'm leaning towards crazy. Abbott made the mistake of telling Hamilton that we'd spoken to a genealogist who confirmed he was a direct descendant of one of Walford's kids . . . one of his bastard kids. Honestly, Mike,' she said with a soft chuckle. 'Abbott's lucky to be alive. Hamilton was so close to losing it, but lucky for him his solicitor stepped in and got him out of there before he blew.'

'What about Townsend?'

'They're going for "killed in the line of duty", with a post-humous commendation.'

'I guess Atkinson has to salvage something from this mess.' Lockyer cracked his neck. 'Anyway, enough of that. How's it with you? I bet you wish you were home right now.'

'Actually,' Jane said, 'believe it or not, we're having a pretty good time.'

'Is your mother *there*?'

'Yes,' she said, stretching out the word. 'She's preparing the veg for tomorrow. She's currently on the potatoes.'

'Ha, snap,' he said, returning to his potatoes. 'You can tell her I'm doing the same thing.'

'Mum,' Jane shouted. Lockyer was glad she had taken the phone away from her mouth, otherwise she would have deaf-ened him. 'Mike says he's doing the potatoes . . . same as you.'

'Has he salted the water?' he heard Celia Bennett shout back.

'Mum said have you salted the water?' Jane asked.

'Yes, I heard her,' he said, 'and yes, I have.'

'Yes, he has,' Jane yelled. Lockyer pulled his ear away from the phone. She had some lungs on her.

'Remind him to dry them out thoroughly before he puts them in the duck fat and tell him the fat *has* to be smoking.'

'Did you hear that?' Jane asked, coming back on the phone.

'I did,' he said, 'and I will.'

'You know she's going to make me call you tomorrow to check you've done it right?'

'Tell her she's welcome to call me herself,' he said, surpris-ing himself.

'Ahh,' Jane said. 'I knew it. She's reeled you in. It always happens. People start out thinking she's nuts but she wheedles her way in somehow and once she's got you, I'm afraid that's it.'

Lockyer huffed out a laugh. 'That's fine with me,' he said. He didn't know if it was the Christmas spirit, being home or his third beer, but he was in an amazing mood.

'So what's the plan for tomorrow?' she asked.

'I'm picking up Bobby at eleven,' he said, glancing over at the kitchen table. He had gone a bit overboard. There were half a dozen books on birds, and three sets of playing cards with different pictures on the back.

'And Megan?'

'She and Aaron are heading up in time for lunch.'

'Wow,' she said. 'I never thought I'd see the day.'

'Neither did I,' he said, throwing another finished potato into the water.

'It'll be a difficult day for him,' she said. 'Cassie flew to New York this morning.'

'Yeah, Megan told me,' he said. 'I'm just not going to mention it and concentrate on the food. And if all else fails . . . charades.'

'Desperate measures, eh?'

'I might need them,' he said. 'So when are you planning on coming back?' She didn't answer. 'I'm heading into the office Boxing Day, but you don't need to be back that early. Atkinson pretty much told me he's planning on taking you hostage.' He scratched his eyebrow with the back of his hand. 'I've checked the rest of your caseload and there's not much needed 'til after the New Year, so there's no rush – but,' he said, 'that doesn't mean you can swan in halfway through January.'

'I've got some leave due,' she said.

'Jane,' he said. 'You are my protégée. We don't take leave . . . and besides, how do you expect me to cope without you?' The oven timer pinged. 'Right. I have *got* to go because I now have to do something with giblets and I'll admit I'm terrified.'

'You'll be fine,' she said.

Jane ended the call, leaned forward and put her mobile on the coffee table in the conservatory. She took a big gulp of wine.

'Are you planning on helping with dinner, or just drinking it?' her mother said, coming in with a dishcloth and dusting around her.

'I can help,' she said, pushing herself up off the uncomfortable wicker sofa. 'You know, Mum, you should get new furniture for out here. This wicker stuff is dreadful.'

'I know, dear,' her mother said. 'Why do you think it's in here?'

Jane shrugged. 'I don't know.'

'Your father already spends as much time hiding in the shed as he can, and it's the middle of winter. If I put comfortable chairs in here, that will give him two places to hide, and I'll never see him.'

'You could sit out here with him?'

'He wouldn't want that,' she said. 'He likes his quiet time to read the paper, and you know me, I like to chat.'

'Yes, Mum, I know,' Jane said with a smile.

'Don't be a smart alec, Jane,' her mother said. 'Now come in the kitchen and you can help me with the pigs in blankets. You know I hate the feel of bacon.'

Jane followed behind, dragging her feet. The wine felt good as it warmed her from the inside out. She suspected more would be needed to maintain the glow. 'Where's Dad and Peter?'

'Where do you think?' Celia Bennett said in a high-pitched voice. 'They're in that bloody shed of his. My grandson will probably get hypothermia and we'll spend Christmas in accident and emergency, but you know your father, he won't listen to me.'

'Has Peter got a coat on?' Jane asked, taking up residence at the small kitchen table.

'Of course,' her mother said. 'Now here.' She approached with an enormous tray of sausages and two packets of bacon. 'Get wrapping.'

Jane picked up the first packet and opened it. Her mother started singing Christmas carols. She hummed along, realizing as she reached for her first little piggy and its blanket that she didn't like the feel of bacon either. She held the sausage in one hand and stared at it. She should have told him. She wasn't as arrogant as to think she would spoil his Christmas or anything, but if there was one thing Lockyer wasn't keen on, it was change. So she could only imagine what he would think when she told him that Atkinson had offered her a DI role in Bridgwater CID – all she had to do was take the promotion exam and relocate to Somerset. A promotion and a move. Who wouldn't want that? She suspected Lockyer would be one.

'Those pigs won't wrap themselves,' her mother said, giving her arm a nudge.

Jane had never considered leaving London. Never. Peter loved his school and his teachers. She knew he wouldn't miss his classmates; he wasn't much bothered about his peers. She thought about Andy. He had been a welcome absence in the past two weeks. Jane hadn't really thought about him and, for the most part, she hadn't heard from him. If she wasn't in London, if he couldn't get to her with his petty jibes, would he get bored and give up? Part of her thought he just might. Andy didn't want a relationship with Peter – or her, for that matter. He just didn't like being told no.

'Just think,' her mother said, floating around the kitchen. 'In a few months it'll be spring . . . oh, and you know how much Peter loves the sunshine. I'll be able to take him to the beach every day. He can play in the water. He is going to *love* it.'

In hindsight, Jane shouldn't have told her mother anything until she had made up her own mind, but it was such a big decision – she needed help. As soon as the words 'leaving London' had left her lips last night, her mother had moved at a million miles an hour. She had crept into Jane's room this morning with a cup of tea and a list of properties that were, in her mother's opinion, in her price range. *Your father and I will help where we can,* she had said. As well as doing her Phil and Kirsty bit, she had also given Jane a list of schools for Peter. *These three are rated excellent with Ofsted. They are set up for helping someone like Peter. He would have a minimum of two teaching assistants and his own private room where he could study and go for quiet time. It's better than anything he could ever hope to get in London.* Jane knew that part wasn't true, but she didn't want to argue the point. *You can stay with us for as long as you need. I haven't told your father yet because once I do that's it,* her mother had said. *Once he knows you're coming home there's no backing out or changing your mind again. It'd kill him.* Jane picked up another sausage, looked at her mother and smiled. A mixture of railroading and emotional blackmail was her mother's killer combination.

She had sat in the office this morning trying to focus on the case, but had failed. In the end she had written out a list, weighing up the pros and cons. The pro list was longer. In actual fact, there was nothing on the con list bar one name: Lockyer. Not one part of her wanted to leave him, and yet in her heart she knew she had to. It was the best thing for her, her career, for Peter and her parents. The only problem was, she didn't have the first clue how she was going to break it to him that she wasn't going back.

The phone started to ring.

'I'll get it,' her mother said in a sing-song voice. She picked up the phone with a flourish. 'Clevedon 452, 397.' Jane laughed. She loved her mother's phone voice. 'Hello, Michael.' Jane's smile dropped from her face. 'Of course, dear, of course,' her mother was saying. 'Now you'll need to have oven mitts on when you do this, OK? . . . Good. So you'll put the pan directly onto the hob and turn on the back two burners . . . no, Michael, the back two. If you use the front two and accidentally tip boiling goose fat on yourself, you shan't have a merry anything.' Her mother looked at her and rolled her eyes in an exaggerated gesture. 'So you put the pan on and let it get hot, add the fat and leave it until it's smoking, then you put your spuds in, taking care not to burn yourself. You'll need a towel as fat is a devil to get out . . .' Jane tuned out the rest of the instructions. She should just tell him. Get it over and done with. There was no way she would be able to enjoy Christmas with this hanging over her head, and who was she kidding? Lockyer wasn't going to be losing any sleep over her. All he had to do was promote someone like Penny and bang, he would have his next protégée. 'Yes, she's here. Hang on.' Her mother passed her the phone.

Jane stood up and left the kitchen, her mother mouthing, 'Tell him,' as she went. She waved her away and retreated to the conservatory. 'Hi,' she said. 'I can't believe you just called my mother for cooking tips.'

'I know,' he said. 'I'm a changed man, it seems, and I want you to know I hold you responsible. You and my daughter. The two of you are forever jabbering on at me about *feelings* and *letting people in*, and now here I am cooking up a storm for my brother, my daughter, her *boyfriend* . . . who she's moving in with, by the way. Don't even ask. But the real cherry on my shit-sundae . . . do you want to know?'

'Go on,' she said, taking a gulp of her wine, her warm feelings returning with the hit of alcohol.

'Megan called,' he said. 'Her mother . . . my ex-wife, and Brian, her new husband, were meant to be going on a romantic cruise for the festive season. But sadly it's been cancelled due to bad weather.'

'And?' she asked, sensing more from his tone. He sounded amused if a little manic.

'And she didn't like to think of them at home with no

decorations or fucking festive cheer, given they expected to be away. Soooo . . ' There was a pregnant pause. 'They're coming here for lunch.'

Jane spat her wine back into the glass as she started coughing. 'You have got to be kidding me.'

'No,' he said in a sulky voice. 'Megs asked, and I was all ready to say no, but then I heard *you* in my head, chirruping about how important it must be for her – how I should do it for her.' She heard the hiss of a beer bottle being uncapped. 'So she has you to thank for what will no doubt be a freak-show afternoon.'

'I'm flattered,' she said, trying to find the words in her head to tell him.

'You should be,' he said. 'I don't listen to many people, Jane, either in person or inter-cranium, but you're my voice of reason.'

'Thank you.'

'Don't thank me,' he said. 'Just hurry up and get back here. You're the only one who can keep me sane. I rely on you, you know?' His voice was soft. She could hear a slight slur. He had been drinking, but he didn't sound drunk. He sounded sincere – and open. The place she had been trying to get to for seven years, and he had decided *now* was the time to let her in. Jane couldn't speak. 'Now put your mother back on. I have a serious question about Brussels sprouts.'

CHAPTER THIRTY-NINE

Christmas Day

Jane perched on the edge of the rocking chair by the fire, a mug resting on her knees. It wasn't the start to Christmas Day that she had planned, but she wouldn't have felt right making the family wait. 'As I say, I'm sorry to intrude, but I thought you'd want to know that the coroner has released Pippa's body. I've told him to expect your call.' No one was looking at her.

Aaron was sitting at one end of the sofa, Megan tucked in to the side of him. Reverend Jones stood at the mantelpiece, to the side of Jane's chair. His hands were clasped behind his back and he was rocking back and forth on his heels. And then there was Maureen Jones. She was, much like the first time Jane had met her, walking in a slow circle around the lounge offering tea and cake.

'Thank you, detective,' she said without expression. 'It means a great deal to us to be able to bury Pip and we are so grateful to you for coming here, especially today. You must have plans with your own family?'

'Honestly, it's the least I can do,' Jane said. 'As it happens,

I'd promised my son a walk up on the hills anyway, so . . .' In fact, her mother, father and Peter were next door in the pub waiting for her. To make up for her broken promise to go carolling the other night she had told Peter to think of something, anything, he wanted to do with her and, providing it didn't involve space travel, she *would* fulfil his wish, no questions asked. Peter had chosen the Dragon Quest. 'He wants to go in search of Gurt Wurm.'

'Rather you than me,' Claudette said, limping into the lounge from the kitchen on a pair of NHS-issue crutches. 'It's bloody freezing out there.'

'Sit down, dear,' Maureen said, delighted, it seemed, to have someone to fuss over. Claudette looked frail, her skin almost translucent apart from the bruising.

'How are you feeling?' Jane asked, knowing it was an inane question.

'Sore but good,' Claudette said with a slow blink. 'It'll take time to heal, I'm sure, but the main thing is I can . . . I will.' Jane wondered whether she meant medical healing or something more profound, given her recent brushes with death – or more to the point, her ex-husband and a squad car driven by Lockyer.

'I hope you don't think us rude,' Maureen said, pulling her husband away from the fire and manhandling him into a Barbour and a multi-coloured scarf, 'but we promised some old friends of ours in the village that we'd pop over to say a Christmas prayer with them, and—'

'Have a glass of mulled wine, I hope,' Anthony Jones said, giving Jane a wink. People's resilience to tragedy never failed to amaze her.

'Now, Claud, we won't be long,' Maureen said, 'and you have the number. If it weren't so slippy out there, I'd say to come along. Gilly Henderson was only saying to me yesterday that it's been an age since they've seen you.'

'I'm happy here,' Claudette said. 'Aaron can bank the fire up before he and Megan set off. You go. I'll be fine.'

Jane stood to make her own excuses as well. She hadn't drunk her tea, but the scalding hot china had warmed her hands up. 'Oh no, no,' Maureen said, coming over to her and all but pushing her back into the rocking chair. 'Now, I didn't want that. See, Tony, I told you, she'd feel obliged to go if we went.'

'It's fine,' Jane said, making a move to stand again but finding herself blocked.

'Please, please,' Maureen said. 'At least finish your tea and visit with Claudette and the others.' She threw an absent hand in Aaron and Megan's direction. Aaron flashed Jane a wry smile.

'OK,' she said, resigned to drink her tea. Her parents would be fine in the pub. Her dad would be delighted. Celia Bennett didn't agree with public drinking as a rule. Maureen Jones continued to coo and chatter as she bundled her husband out of the room, closing the lounge door behind them.

'Sorry about Mum,' Aaron said. 'She's a stickler for being a good host.'

'If only it were *her* house,' Claudette said, making a face that was a combination of a sneer and a smirk.

'My head is banging,' Megan said, dropping her forehead onto Aaron's shoulder.

He stroked her hair as he stood up, settling her back on

the sofa. 'Someone had a heavy night last night,' he whispered to Jane.

'It was *someone's* turn,' Megan said, turning her face in to a cushion.

'Touché.' Aaron went to the door. 'I'll just get you some painkillers. Are you all right for a sec, boss?'

Jane realized he was talking to her. She was still waiting for her tea to cool down from nuclear to something palatable. 'Sure, sure,' she said. 'I'm fine.' She held up her mug and gestured to the fire as if to demonstrate her point. Aaron shut the door, and she heard his footsteps as he climbed the stairs. She racked her brains for something to say, but drew a blank. What could she say to two people who were not only on opposite sides of the room, but in polar opposite situations? Megan was at the start of a new relationship, full of excitement, love and plans for the future. On the flip side, Claudette had just discovered that her relationship, though in the past, had been a lie. That the man she had been married to, that she had still trusted, was a killer. She had been left broken in every sense of the word. What could Jane say to her apart from empty platitudes? With a sigh she looked up, hoping something interesting yet sensitive would come to her.

She needn't have worried. Both women were asleep; or at least it appeared that way. Megan's face was still buried in the pillow, her chest moving slowly up and down as she breathed. Claudette's head rested on the back of the chair, her eyes closed, her mouth hanging open just enough for Jane to think she had dozed off. She blew on her tea and took a tentative sip.

As the hot liquid touched her lips she remembered something Lockyer had said to her about the day Steph was attacked in her hospital room. *It couldn't have worked out better if he had planned it.* They now knew the 'he' was Hamilton. Jane took a slow breath in through her nose and closed her eyes. If you can't beat 'em, join 'em, she thought. She let herself relax so the tangled thoughts in her mind could unwind themselves. The first was of Cassie. When Aaron's sister had heard someone behind her on the road she had, being so close to home, called her brother for help. Aaron had Megan with him, so it followed she would call her father. So instead of an anonymous response officer tearing up to Nether Stowey to rescue Cassie, it had been Lockyer. And in his absence, Hamilton had walked into Musgrove Park Hospital unchallenged to finish what he had started in Shervage Wood with Steph.

Before Jane could go further another memory dropped into the mix, drawing her focus. Hamilton's obsession with Walford. Jane could feel the heat of the fire warming the leg of her trousers. If her mind wasn't racing, she might be inclined to doze off, too. They had reams of paperwork at Express Park showing Hamilton's life's work. Every detail had been researched and documented. But to have Walford on paper hadn't been enough. The women Hamilton had targeted and killed, Pippa aside, all had similarities to Jane Walford – problems with drink, promiscuity and the like. As DCC and an upstanding member of the local community, Hamilton would have had the inside track. He would have had access to, and been able to identify and single out, women who fitted his purpose – who shared lifestyle traits with Walford's dead wife. The woman he, and now Hamilton, despised.

So now the question. If it was Jane that Walford hated – if it was Jane that he killed – why was Hamilton calling *his* victims 'Annie'? According to Stephanie Lacey, he had shouted the name over and over. It hadn't made sense to Jane before and now, still, it didn't sit right in her gut. She could hear Aaron moving around upstairs, the floorboards creaking above her head.

'The keys,' she said aloud without thinking. She covered her mouth, but neither of the slumbering women flinched. She took another sip of her tea, using its warmth as grease to the wheels in her brain.

Outside the flat in Holford they had found a set of keys that opened the flat and the garage. Jane and the rest of the response officers had assumed they belonged to Townsend; that they had fallen out of his coat pocket when Lockyer had slammed into him. But now Jane knew better. The keys must have belonged to Hamilton. And so another question: why did he have them on him?

She remembered a game Peter had played when he was younger. It was like dot to dot, but rather than the traditional drawing game – where the child would make a line from one dot to the next, following a sequence of numbers until a picture was revealed – Jane's father would knock tacks into a piece of plywood and give Peter one of his grandmother's balls of wool. Peter would then wind the piece of coloured yarn round one tack before moving on to the next and the next. The result was a three-dimensional image. Jane's thoughts felt like those tacks. Apart they meant nothing, but when bound together by a common factor, she would be able to see the image as a whole. If only she could find her common factor, her wool, then she could finish the picture.

Aaron pulled the box right out from under the bed. He didn't know what had made him look here, but something – a memory from childhood, a game he and Pip had played – had sparked an idea in his head. He hadn't been able to think about anything else. The floorboards were loose and noisy. He didn't want them to hear him. He didn't want them to know he was in here. The paracetamol he was supposed to be getting for Megan was in the bathroom. He dropped to his knees and opened the lid a fraction, and then all of the way, holding his breath as the hinges creaked. He remembered the treasure hunts Cassie used to set up for him and Pip. The prize would be sweets, a toy, or sometimes even money. At Christmas she went the extra mile and each clue had its own small gift or treat. But it had been the puzzle that he and Pip loved – the challenge.

He held the letter he had found stuffed down the side of Pip's mattress. The paper was crumpled and torn. Aaron flattened it on his palm as he read and re-read the note; or would you call it a love letter? He looked in the box and pushed aside a knitted scarf, and what smelled like a packet of joss sticks. Pippa's bedroom had reeked of jasmine for about two years during her grunge phase. His fingers touched on and then pulled out a bundle of letters bound together with a fat elastic band. He could see even at a quick glance that the handwriting was the same on each: a loopy, exaggerated scrawl. He would recognize it anywhere. A sound made him stop. He held his breath, straining to locate the origin of the noise. There was a dull thud, followed by a juddering. He let out his breath and relaxed. It was only the heating kicking in. The boiler was ancient.

Aaron repositioned himself as his legs went to sleep and slid out one, then two of the letters from the bunch. He took them out of their respective envelopes and held a page in each hand. looking from one to the other and back again as he read. He frowned. Again, the handwriting he knew, but the names meant nothing to him. He couldn't work out if the letters had been sent and returned, or received and kept. Neither scenario made much sense. He turned over the letter in his right hand and saw a poem, maybe six or seven lines, written small in black ink.

> *We make our bed where her body was found*
> *We lay our heads on the blood-soaked ground*
> *You are the wind in the trees that gave me breath*
> *I am the roots in the ground, the hands of death*
> *Together we smite them, forever we're bound*
> *I am at peace now, she makes no sound*
> *She makes no sound*

Cassie had always said that Pippa was the quickest. She was born first, she walked first, she spoke first – she even died first. And now Aaron knew why. He felt his breath catch in his throat. Part of him wanted to close the lid and push the box back under the bed, leave the room, retrieve the paracetamol for Megan and forget what he knew – go on with his life in ignorant bliss – but he couldn't. He felt a hand on his shoulder, but he didn't turn. There was no one there. It was Pippa. She was here. A tear ran down Aaron's cheek. She was telling him to finish what she had started.

Jane bent forward and put her mug down on the hearth. She took out her mobile and tapped out a message to Abbott, and then, as backup, to Barney. The answer to all of her questions was simple. She just had to change her point of view.

She had assumed that, like Townsend, Hamilton had parked his car some way away and trudged across snow-covered fields in order to get to and escape from Hunter's Moon without being detected. Townsend had parked at the back of the house to expedite his arrival for non-nefarious reasons; but what about Hamilton? And why would Hamilton call his victims Annie and not Jane?

Steph and Claudette both said they had been called Annie when they were attacked. But Hamilton didn't attack Claudette – Townsend did. But Townsend wasn't obsessed with Walford, with his legacy. Townsend was Hamilton's fall guy. So why attack Claudette, why call her Annie?

The simple answer was – he hadn't. And if he hadn't, then why would Claudette say he had? How would she even know to use that name? Again, the answer was simple. Because Hamilton had told her. And where was the car? There wasn't one. Hamilton had been there all the time.

She heard Maureen Jones's words: *Gilly Henderson was only saying to me yesterday that it's been an age since they've seen you.* Jane had thought it strange at the time, given she knew Claudette was meant to have been to the Hendersons' Christmas drinks *with* her sister and husband last week, the same afternoon Cassie was chased through the back lanes of Nether Stowey, the same afternoon Steph was attacked, for the second time. But Claudette hadn't been at the Hendersons' sipping mulled wine. She had volunteered Cassie to walk the neighbour's dog, and then Claudette had followed her, stalked her and made sure she was scared, scared enough to call in the cavalry – to lure Lockyer away from the real victim. Stephanie Lacey.

And the keys to the flat out in Holford – Hamilton hadn't dropped them. He wasn't the one wrestling with Townsend when Lockyer turned up and knocked them both flying. The keys had come from Claudette's pocket, not Townsend's. And the reason Claudette was at the flat? Not for Barbara and Allison. No. They were no doubt a lie, a quick fix to an awkward problem when, as luck would have it, Jane and Barney had turned up and disturbed Claudette and Hamilton doing – whatever their twisted minds desired.

Hamilton had been right. Lockyer had done them both a huge favour when he had turned up and killed Townsend. Hamilton had spoken to Claudette in hospital, and no doubt between them they had come up with an iron-clad story, one that would prove beyond doubt that Townsend was the Hill Killer. Using the name 'Annie' was the clincher – but, as it happened, also their undoing. Jane opened her eyes, unsure how long she had been sitting there. Claudette was looking at her, her head tipped to one side. 'Are you all right, detective?'

Before Jane could answer, Aaron came into the room. He was holding a bundle of letters in his hand. They appeared numerous and well worn, colourful drawings of hearts and flowers on the envelopes that held them. 'Who's Annie?' he said, looking at his aunt, the papers trembling in his shaking hand.

'She is,' Jane said, getting to her feet. 'Hamilton wasn't calling Stephanie Lacey "Annie" that night, was he?' Claudette seemed to shrink in her seat as Jane approached her. 'He was calling *out* for Annie . . . he was calling out for *you*. You were there.' A vein in Claudette's temple began to pulse as Jane spoke.

'You . . . you killed Pip, didn't you?' Aaron said, the colour all but drained from his face.

Claudette was shaking her head, her cheeks flushed. 'It wasn't supposed to . . . I never meant for it to happen like that. She just . . . he said we had to, that we had no choice. I couldn't stop him.' Her voice was thick with emotion. Her eyes were dry and cold.

'You were there when she . . . when they all . . . ?' Aaron's legs seemed to buckle and he collapsed onto the sofa. Megan's head slid off the cushion as she was jolted out of sleep.

'Aaron, what's the . . . ?' But she didn't finish, her words silenced, it seemed, by the icy chill that had changed a cosy cottage lounge into a soulless shell.

Jane shook her head and sighed. 'You're a country girl,' she said to Claudette, 'so I guess you know better than most that it's always better to hunt in pairs. That way there's always someone to watch your back. Isn't that right, Claudette . . . or do you prefer Annie?'

WALFORD

You are pathetic, she had said, pushing past him. *I can't look at you. You make me sick. You are not a man. You are not a man. And I need a man.*

John Walford lay down on the cot in the jailhouse and closed his eyes. Her final words had lost their venom. He had stilled her poisonous tongue forever.

He knew he would hang the moment he picked up that fence post, but the knowledge hadn't stayed his hand. Perhaps he had known before they left the house that night and took the walk over the Quantocks, the night heavy and close. His mind kept taking him back there. He kept seeing her face as her life drained away. Seeing her die had been life enough for him. Jane was right when she said he wasn't a man. He hadn't been a man until the day he killed her – she had paid his passage to manhood with her life. He folded his arms behind his head.

After he was hanged they planned to display his body in a gibbet at the edge of Quantock Common, but he wasn't afraid. He would never fear the hills. Shervage Wood belonged to him. He had been making charcoal there his whole life, and his father before him, and his father before that. The Walford men and the woods were one, and it felt good and right that soon his ashes would feed the very trees that had sheltered him as a boy. He only hoped his body would nourish the saplings and give them the strength to grow. He smiled. If his bones, blood and flesh fed the trees, then surely he would live on in them? Perhaps in another time, another boy would come to make himself a man at the edge of Dead Woman's Ditch. He laughed aloud, spit flying out of his mouth and landing on his cheeks. He hadn't realized the irony of the name until now. 'They'll remember me,' he said to the empty cell. The Dead Woman of the ditch would become *his* dead woman. Her death would be a tale whispered at night by fathers to their daughters and husbands to their wives.

Keep your petticoats close, my dear. For if you let another man lift them, then Walford will come for you. The woods will come alive with him: the trunks his legs, the boughs his body and the branches his arms reaching out for you. And if he catches you . . . he'll slit your throat from ear to ear, and no more bastards will you be able to bear.

Cursed or blessed, the land would forever be his.

Let his name keep them frightened in their beds.

Let his name live on.

HISTORICAL NOTE

John Walford, 1765–89

John Walford was a collier by trade, collecting and burning wood in a turf-covered pit until the process resulted in charcoal, which he would then sell. The pit could be alight for almost a week and couldn't be left unattended, so it's said that he would be alone for days on end with only a makeshift shelter and rations of bread and cheese to sustain him.

When he was still a young man he met and fell in love with Ann Rice, the daughter of a local miller. They were soon engaged to be married, although there are accounts that suggest Walford's mother was against the match.

While he was betrothed to Ann, John began an affair with Jane Shorney. She was the daughter of another collier. Jane fell pregnant and gave birth to a baby boy, John, in 1785. John was duly arrested because they were unwed. He had two choices: marry Jane, or pay for the child. Reports suggest that his mother stepped in at this point and agreed to pay for the upbringing of her grandson. John's relationship with Ann Rice subsequently failed – some say because of pressure from his mother to break off the engagement.

In the meantime, Jane had given birth to another child, a daughter allegedly fathered by John's brother William. In spite of this, John and Jane resumed their relationship and when she fell pregnant again in June 1789 they married.

Less than three weeks later, after a night out at the Castle of Comfort Inn in July 1789, John is said to have beaten Jane to death and cut her throat, dumping her body in Dead Woman's Ditch before going home.

Jane's body was discovered by children, and John was arrested the next day. He was found guilty and sentenced to hang.

His last request was to speak to Ann. They said their farewells, but as they moved closer to embrace and kiss, the executioner separated them and John was hanged. His body was displayed in a gibbet – in view of his parents' house – for a full year as a deterrent to others contemplating violence.

Some say that despite their break-up, Ann had continued to see John in secret, and that in November 1789 she gave birth to John's daughter, Sarah. Ann died just months later.

The 'version' of events retold in *The Night Stalker* is my interpretation of the story, gleaned through research and speaking to locals. However, I do know that some of the facts have been questioned over the years. For example, some say that Dead Woman's Ditch wouldn't have been on John and Jane's route home from the Castle of Comfort Inn and so her body wouldn't have been found there, but would in fact have been found much closer to the village on the side of a road.

However, I have done my best to represent the story as I understand it, so any and all mistakes are my own.

ACKNOWLEDGEMENTS

My list of thank yous grows ever longer, but that in no way dilutes them. I am enormously grateful to the team I have behind me, to people old and new who have helped me with this book, the ones before and the ones to come.

A huge thank you to the Pan Macmillan team, in particular Kate Green, Stuart Dwyer, Susan Opie, Phoebe Taylor, Kate Tolley and Camilla Rockwood. To Justine Anweiler and James Annal for a fantastic cover – I love it. To Kate Bullows for being a one-woman sales machine for the South West. You continue to astound me. And last but by no means least, to Trisha. Thank you for your faith in me and your tireless efforts on my behalf. I'm very lucky to have you.

Thank you, as always, to Janklow & Nesbit and my agent, Hellie Ogden. You have gone above and beyond for me this year and I'm enormously grateful.

Thanks to Iain Porter for sharing your wealth of knowledge about the Quantock Hills and to Debs for lending me your husband for the day.

Thank you to Nicola and Ben for a fantastic day out in Bridgwater. I was lucky enough to go on a ride-along and pick their brains – all whilst trying to look cool as I desperately plugged in my seatbelt as we tore out of Express Park with the sirens blaring. I will be back for more ☺

An ongoing thank you to Mark, Sue and Leanne. Since 2016 was manic with books and baby I didn't get to pillage your memory warehouses as much as I'd have liked. Never fear, you'll be hearing from me soon!

To Grace for being good while Mummy works. To Mother for taking my books out of the library repeatedly and for all your support with the books and taking Grace out for very long walks! Thank you to my family and friends for your continuing love and support. This journey wouldn't be the same without you all. The launch is the focal point of my year (thank you, Sam – this year's cake for *Trust No One* was a masterpiece and tasted delicious, as always). There are too many of you to thank individually, but I hope you know how special you are and how grateful I am.

Thank you to Roger Stacey from the Friends of Nether Stowey for a really good gossip on the history of a village I never knew.

Thank you to Audible and Imogen Church for doing a wonderful job on the series. I love listening to my books almost as much as I love writing them, and that's because of you.

And finally a big thank you to Chris Ewan, fellow crime writer and friend. How did I ever manage without you?! Whether we're doing an event together, teaching or just chatting over coffee with your beautiful family, I'm learning. You have inspired me to think more, to be better and to always, always remember the hook – every good crime novel should have one. And every crime writer should have you, thank you.

That was the short version. If you want the longer version

of why there are acknowledgements at the ends of books, read on . . .

They say it takes a village to raise a child. Well, I think the same applies to a book. *The Night Stalker* started out as a germ of an idea about a car crash at night. Over the past year with the help of research, feedback and input from my publisher, friends (old and new) and family, that initial idea has morphed into a story I hadn't intended to tell.

When my editor Trisha Jackson suggested I base the next book in the Lockyer and Bennett series in Somerset I was delighted. I left London a few years ago and was worried I was losing my feel for the place because, let's face it, a market town in Somerset and south-east London don't have much in common. But the great thing about writing crime . . . you can kill someone anywhere. Murder is mobile!

I know the South West, having grown up here, and the Quantock Hills felt like the perfect place to set an eerie moonlit car chase. I've driven over the hills many times, and the barren and isolated feel at the 'top' never fails to give me the heebie-jeebies. As luck would have it, one of my NCT mums told me her husband worked for the AONB. And so, after a Sunday afternoon chat, I found myself in a 4x4 going up hill and down dale with Iain. I took pictures and asked a million questions until Iain said the magic words – Dead Woman's Ditch. When he told me about the legend of John Walford it was music to my crime-writer ears. Legends, folklore and murder, oh my! I immediately phoned my editor and said, 'Change of plan . . .'

And so the story began to shift, with more emphasis on myths and superstitions, but the changes weren't done – not by a long way. By the time I had finished the first draft I had a niggling doubt. I loved the Dead Woman's Ditch angle but I didn't like the end of the book – the 'why' that's so important to me when I write. So I made another call to my editor. 'Change of plan . . .'

I spent an hour on the phone to Hellie and Trisha, and we talked through what had to come out of the book and what could, potentially, go in its place. You see, I'd decided to change the ending – I just didn't know what I was changing it to. Fortunately, my brother Chris, who *The Night Stalker* is dedicated to, is a wonder. I basically phoned him and said, 'Right. This, this, this, this and this is coming out of the story. This, this and this has to stay in. How on earth do I get from this to this and explain why this happened without changing this and this?' The resulting two-hour conversation put me on track for the new ending and a book that I am thrilled with.

So, in short, without Trisha's suggestion, Iain's knowledge, my penchant for changing my mind, Trisha and Hellie's patience and ideas, my brother's ability to see a story from a whole different viewpoint, not to mention a ride-along and countless other conversations along the way, *The Night Stalker* wouldn't be half the book it is today. So thank you to you all.

You are my village and I'm very thankful.

As *The Night Stalker* was going to print I discovered that one of the locations in the book, the Farmer's Arms in Combe Florey, had been badly damaged by fire. I want to wish the owners the best and hope they are able to reopen very soon.

NEVER LOOK BACK

By Clare Donoghue

He's watching. He's waiting. He knows.

A chilling and compelling debut crime thriller set in south-east London. For all those who enjoy Peter James, Mark Billingham and Peter Robinson.

Three women have been found brutally murdered in south London, the victims only feet away from help during each sadistic attack. And the killer is getting braver . . .

Sarah Grainger is rapidly becoming too afraid to leave her house. Once an outgoing photographer, she knows that someone is watching her. A cryptic note brings everything into terrifying focus, but it's the chilling phone calls that take the case to another level.

DI Mike Lockyer heads up the regional murder squad. With three bodies on his watch and a killer growing in confidence, he frantically tries to find the link between these seemingly isolated incidents. What he discovers will not only test him professionally but will throw his personal life into turmoil too.

NO PLACE TO DIE

By Clare Donoghue

Guilt for the past. Fear for the future.

The body of a female university student is found buried in Elmstead Woods, south London. The circumstances of her death are as unprecedented as they are frightening.

Two men admit to having had relationships
with the girl just before she died.

Both deny murder.

Lewisham's murder squad detectives Jane Bennett and Mike Lockyer must untangle a web of deceit if they are to stop this monster before more innocent lives are lost.

TRUST NO ONE

By Clare Donoghue

He never saw it coming. She always knew it would.

Marriage is complicated. It doesn't always work out.
Sometimes there are things you discover about yourself
and each other which mean the marriage has to end.
Sad, particularly when kids are involved – but all
pretty normal.

Normal, that is, until there's a murder.

DS Jane Bennett and DI Mike Lockyer are called in
to investigate one of south London's most difficult and
distressing cases yet – where family and friends come
under scrutiny in the hardest of circumstances.